SUFFER IN SILENCE

JACK CARTWRIGHT

SUFFER IN SILENCE

JACK CARTWRIGHT

EMILY TREVERNE'S LAUGH CARRIED THROUGH THE TREES, carefree with youth and unquestionable innocence.

"Ready or not, we're coming to find you," she called.

Marie pressed her back up against a tall elm and crouched down so that she could just turn her head to peer over the line of nettles beside her. It was a good spot. The best spot. They would never find her. She had run for more than a minute and taken the path of most resistance to throw them off the scent. She had even doubled back on herself to confuse Digby.

Now, she watched with a glee she could barely contain as Digby came into view, accompanied by his snorts and gruffs as he followed Marie's scent the wrong way. Wearing her bright yellow rain mac, Emily tip-toed behind Digby with her hands over her mouth trying to mask her squeaks and giggles.

But Digby stopped in his tracks. He sniffed at the ground, searching for the scent. The smart pup hadn't fallen for Marie's trap. He doubled back, followed closely by Emily, and he pounded along the forest track until her scent stopped and disappeared into the stinging nettles.

"Wait for me, Digby," Emily called out, and she joined him a few moments later, peering into the space, while Digby found a path through the thick undergrowth.

"Ah, you found me," Marie called out, as Digby pounced on her, and Emily squealed with delight. "What a clever little dog he is."

"I helped him," Emily said defensively. "We both found you."

"Okay, then," Marie said, as she stepped over the nettles and onto the track. "You guys win. You're the best at hide and sniff."

"Better than you?" Emily asked, searching for some kind of accolade.

"Far better than me," Marie conceded. "How about we go home and get some soup? My feet are so cold they're frozen."

"Like ice?"

"Like ice," Marie said, as she gave the working cocker a treat. "I could even ice skate home, they're so cold."

Emily laughed. "No, you couldn't."

"I could. All I would have to do is whip my shoes and socks off and I'd slip and slide all over the place. I should really get them to the fire at home, so they can thaw out. What do you say?"

"One more game," Emily said, and she looked longingly up at Marie, who peered up through the trees to the sky above.

"I don't know. It's getting quite late—"

"Oh, please, can we? We'll be super quick. Digby and I will find you really quickly." She looked up at Marie, pleading with those big eyes. "Come on. You've been so sad recently. I haven't heard you laugh like this for ages."

"Really quickly?" Marie asked.

"Really quickly. The quickest ever."

"Well, okay then," Marie said. "But if you don't find me in two minutes, I'm coming out. It's getting dark and we need to get you home to Dad. Okay?"

She nodded, thrilled to have one more game.

"Okay, you'd better hold onto Digby's collar. I'll call you when I've hidden, okay?"

"Okay, Marie," the young girl said, and she held the dog's collar tightly.

Marie slipped into the trees, zig-zagging through the brush, off the beaten path. She ducked beneath a fallen tree and then crouched in the hollow of its roots. But she was too exposed. She moved on, deeper and further, searching for the ideal spot.

And there it was, beyond the stream. A drain or something. She splashed into the stream, running through the water to throw the dog off her scent, and then climbed up the bank on the far side. She hadn't seen the drain before. She hadn't ventured this deep into the woods before, and from the undergrowth, it looked like nobody else had. The drain was circular, and she could see that at one stage, a metal grill had covered the top. But it had long since been removed and discarded. The small brickwork structure was about two meters across, and on the inside, metal rungs had been installed, presumably for men to go down and clean or unblock it, or something. She wasn't really sure. But the rungs would hold her weight.

She slipped one leg over, searching blindly for the rung, and then the other. She clung to the topmost rung and took a deep breath. "I'm ready," she called, then climbed down two rungs, so that she could just peer over the top of the bricks.

While she waited, Marie glanced down at the old drain twenty feet below. It clearly wasn't used anymore. Even Marie could see that, and she thought that perhaps it had serviced the old, abandoned water tower that stood derelict in the old hospital grounds. But after so many years of neglect, the bottom of the drain was filled with rubbish. Plastic bottles mainly, plus a few old beer cans, and she shuddered to think what else. Rats maybe?

There was no sign of Emily, even after two minutes had passed. Her feet began to ache on the iron rungs, and Marie was about to slowly poke her head up above the bricks to see if she could spy them. Then a nearby branch cracked.

She smiled to herself as footsteps grew closer. But then they stopped, and a sinking feeling grabbed Marie's gut like a strong hand was crushing her stomach. Something wasn't right.

Slowly, she craned her neck to peer up.

And then she saw him. Two feet away. Dressed in black.

Her grip on the iron rung failed.

Above her, a circle of light framed by darkness grew smaller as she fell.

And then pain. Pain like nothing else. Her vision blurred, and the figure of a man leaning over the drain peering down at her from above faded to black.

Then nothing.

CHAPTER ONE

A framed advertisement for Bovril stared down at Detective Inspector Freya Bloom from the back of her bathroom door. It raised a wry smile on her tired face, despite the horrific chill of the toilet seat.

Her little cottage in Lincolnshire was slowly becoming a home, but there would need to be serious changes to her accommodation if she was to stay for a second winter. Still, there was a fine memory attached to the Bovril ad, and she carried the sentiment back up the stairs to her bedroom where she dressed. The central heating took so long to heat up that she rarely bothered to get it going in the mornings. But today was particularly cold, and so she had turned it on at least half an hour ago. She made coffee in her pyjamas and dressing gown, then moved fast. The hot water was fine, and she was sure it was the same boiler that heated both, yet the heating was just another of those cruel mysteries she would never solve. It could be a vindictive bastard, and she had spent more than a few nights huddled beneath a blanket before her colleague, Ben, had taught her how to use the wood burner. He had even brought a truckload of wood from his father's store as a moving-in gift.

The cottage belonged to Ben's father, who provided it to Freya on a temporary basis for next to no rent at all. The idea of moving out into a nice three or four bed, detached house was appealing. However, the move would cut ties with Ben, and despite his arrogance and sickening charm, she rather liked having him around. It was what her ex-husband, Greg, used to call friends-with-benefits, but without the hassle of introducing sex into the mix.

Although, the more she thought about it, the harder it was for her to see what Ben gained from the relationship. They were like an old married couple, except they were not married, and they were not even a couple. She just enjoyed his company, his wit, and his presence.

He, on the other hand, just wanted an easy life, and as far as she could tell, she made his life harder.

It had been six months now since her arrival in Lincolnshire. An initial secondment to the county from London's Metropolitan Police had been deemed fruitful and she now enjoyed a permanent status as Detective Inspector. Ben Savage, an experienced and solid Detective Sergeant, had been in the process of promotion to DI when she had arrived, and thus Freya had thwarted his elevation.

A lesser man might have kicked off, caused a stink, made life hard, or even exposed her weaknesses in an attempt to get her fired. But Ben hadn't. After a rocky start, the man had been by Freya's side since day one. Or day two, if you factored in the time she accused him of touching her backside and then peering through her motorhome window to watch her get changed.

The Bovril ad, as innocent as it appeared, sparked all those memories. To some it might seem like an old, worthless piece of junk; in fact, to Freya, it almost certainly was. But the memories it held now made it invaluable.

She had survived her first Lincolnshire Christmas and January was becoming a memory, although so little had happened that she had barely even noticed that February had arrived and was already in full swing. December and January had been as cold as she had ever known, but when she glanced out of the window down at her little rental car, the weather outside was as bleak as bleak can be.

A howling wind carried sleet horizontally across the fields. Ben's house, which was less than a kilometre away on the far side of the field, was usually in full view, yet from her window, she could barely make out the roofs of the Savage family farm. When she looked closely at her car, she could have sworn she saw it rocking with the wind.

Suddenly, the thought of a cold toilet seat seemed fairly insignificant.

Since her move to Lincolnshire, it wasn't just her resolve that had altered. In place of the three-hundred-pound heels and designer dresses she had once worn, bought from the places where she would rub shoulders with the rich, famous, and privileged, she now wore fur-lined leggings, warm sweaters, and – God forbid she should ever let any of her old friends know – but she even owned an authentic Aran cardigan.

Secretly, she loved them. It wasn't just the feeling of wrapping up warm in the cold weather, it was the feeling that nobody cared. Gucci and Jimmy Choo meant nothing out here, where a good fleece top, a sturdy pair of boots, and a decent hat were vital to survival.

In the kitchen, she filled her thermos cup. It was pink and could keep her coffee hot for more than two hours. That was impressive. Regardless of her acquired taste, of warmth and comfort, and regardless of if she left behind a perfect family life to live alone in an old, rundown cottage in the middle of a field, one thing she would never ever do without was good coffee.

She poured the milk, stirred it into her coffee, and replaced the milk in the fridge, taking a moment to say good morning to the photo of the little boy on the door.

"Morning, Billy," she said, aloud, and touched his nose the way she used to do in real life. He didn't answer back, of course, but one day he might call her. One day he might need her, and she'd be there.

She popped the lid on her thermos cup, aptly named *The Beast*, and loaded her bag with her phone and purse. Collecting her laptop bag from the dining table, which doubled as her home working desk, she opened the front door and braved the outside world.

It's not so bad, she thought, as she pulled the door closed behind her and gave it a shove. But as she did, her foot slid a little on the hard ground. The sleet was turning to snow and the ground was cold enough that it would settle. Ben had said it would, in that confident way that an outdoors man seemed to know everything – when the rain will come, when the sun will come out, when it'll go down. Freya had a hard enough job predicting when the boiler would come on; forecasting mother nature seemed far out of her league.

She trod carefully along the garden path, taking care not to slip on the icy slabs. The little LED on the key fob lit up when she hit the button, but the locks didn't pop. So she had to open the door manually, which, despite having to do this with every car she had ever owned before she had found success, felt like she was stepping back into Victorian times. She had to jiggle the key, but the door opened alright, and she was soon inside, out of the weather, as the wind buffeted across the car.

She had her doubts, but the little engine fired up first time. You had to give it to the Koreans, she thought, they know how to put a car together. It was with some level of smugness that Freya turned onto the little farm track that served as the longest driveway she had ever seen. It was at least eight hundred meters to Ben and his family's houses, and then another five to six hundred metres to the main road.

Conditions were as bad as she had seen. Yet despite the weather, some people seemed oblivious to the danger, driving at the maximum speed limit down the main road, which was essentially a two-way road with a twelve-foot dyke on either side. Freya turned her headlights on, indicated, then pulled out onto the main road. Had the dykes not been there, she might have driven faster. But the threat of the deep ditches made coming off the road all the more perilous. She stuck to forty miles per hour. That was fast enough. Nobody needed to drive any faster than that in this weather.

She kept the radio off, preferring to concentrate on the road ahead. A career in the force had provided her with ample opportunity to witness the horrors of road traffic accidents. Yet clearly, some people needed a little more guidance. A white van pulled up behind her, closing the distance, as if the driver was trying to intimidate her into going faster.

But she wouldn't. She hated bully drivers with a passion. Had it been a liveried car she was driving, they would be keeping well back. But she wasn't, and they were right up her backside, flashing for her to speed up or get out of the way.

Anger set in. She saw herself in the mirror and banished the fear with techniques she had learnt in countless courses. She was Freya Bloom, a Detective Inspector who had locked away more violent individuals than the rest of her team combined. A white van man wasn't going to intimidate her.

The van was so close now that she could read the number plate. Slowly, she reached across to her bag and felt for a pen. They passed a field where a gust of wind caught the car side on, and it veered little, forcing her to pull her hand back and get the car under control. The driver of the van must have seen the mistake, and he dropped back a little. But it wasn't long before he was back, gaining speed, closing the gap.

He's going for the overtake. He's a lunatic.

She held her own, defending her spot of tarmac for all it was worth, and he drew alongside her; the passenger glanced down, completely oblivious to the emotions Freya was experiencing and the danger she was in.

Bright car lights appeared ahead, and Freya held onto her space, while the white van sought that tiny extra bit of speed to get past.

The lights ahead flashed, an early warning from an alert driver. But still, the van driver tried to overtake, trying to intimidate Freya into backing off so he could have his way.

No chance.

He crept over toward her, thinking that she might get scared and back off, but she didn't. The passenger, a large lady with baggy arms, was now looking between her and the car in front. Her eyes were wider now, as the danger became so much more real. A car horn sounded, although she couldn't tell whose it was.

Lights, brighter than the sun. An old diesel engine roared. And Freya winced at the sensory overload with adrenaline pumping through her veins.

She braked, harder than required, but enough that the van driver might move across and live to learn a valuable lesson. He slipped in front of her just in time, as the oncoming car sped past, horn blazing. She watched it in her mirror and wondered what the driver must have been thinking. She watched it so hard, in fact, that she didn't see the van in front come to a full stop in the middle of the road. Not until it was too late anyway, and she had to steer into the dyke to avoid hitting him.

CHAPTER TWO

"WHAT THE BLOODY HELL WAS THAT?" FREYA SCREAMED AT THE man, who scratched at his groin and peered down at her from the roadside. "Are you trying to bloody kill us all?"

It had been a fairly slow-moving accident, but even so, the drop into the dyke had all but consumed the front end of Freya's little rental. It lay half in and half out of the ditch with the left-hand front wheel stuck fast in the thick mud at the bottom. She held the door open, hoping that gravity wouldn't close it as she tried to escape, and the man's passenger soon saw what she was trying to do and miraculously came to help. The woman held the door open with one hand and took Freya's proffered bags with the other, casting them to the roadside with a less-than-elegant fling.

"Don't throw..." Freya began, but it was too late. Her laptop bag landed with a thud, while her tote bag did a kind of flip, then regurgitated her belongings across the road. "Thank you for that."

The passenger, a large lady wearing a thick, woolly hat like Freya's, held a strong hand out for Freya to grab onto. So she made use of her, finding a foothold in the bank, and then heaving herself up. There was nothing of significance in the car. Recovery would have to collect it.

"Now then," the driver said. "You want to be more careful."

Now that Freya was on the roadside, she managed to give him a full appraisal. He was unshaven, unwashed, and was somehow braving the howling wind and sleet in just a baggy t-shirt and tracksuit bottoms.

"Excuse me? Be more careful? You damn near ran me off the road, you lunatic," she said, as she crouched and started throwing her possessions back into her bag. "What do you call that? Trying to overtake me on a single-lane road?"

"It's called the speed limit, love," the driver said, and he made a show of dropping to one knee to help her with her things, starting with the spare underwear she carried, which had originally been balled but had managed to unfurl itself when dopey had tossed the bag.

"Give me those," Freya snapped, and snatched them from his hand and stuffed them into the bag.

"If you're going to drive like an old woman, you should expect to be overtaken. You know? Let others past. We don't all have time to poodle along at thirty-five miles per hour."

"I was doing forty."

"It's a sixty-mile-an-hour road," he argued, as he stood up and enjoyed another scratch of his groin, his loose-fitting tracksuit bottoms providing a clear outline of the itchy culprits.

"It's a sixty-mile-per-hour road in good conditions, you moron," she said. "As competent and responsible drivers, we're expected to use our judgement when conditions are poor, and in case you haven't noticed, this is not exactly ideal conditions."

"Ah, it's a bit of sleet. It's February. What do you expect?"

"I expect to be able to drive to work and get there in one piece. Not to be forced off the road by a white bloody van man. And what about the driver of the other car?" Freya said, as another vehicle slowed and edged around the van, the driver of which lowered his passenger window.

"Everyone alright?" he asked, leaning across to get a better view.

"Yeah, mate. Everything apart from a dented ego I think."

The passer-by smiled and gave a laugh, clearly forming some kind of bond. He drove off, leaving them to it. The white van man beckoned for the woman, who Freya presumed to be his wife, to get back in the van.

"Come on then," he said. "No harm, no foul."

"No harm, no foul?" Freya said, incensed at the remark. "My bloody car is in the ditch."

"Recovery van will be along soon," he said, turning his back on her. "I imagine he'll be busy this morning."

"Wait, where do you think you're going?"

"To work, sweetheart. I can't stand around here all day–"

"I need your details. For the insurance. You can't leave the scene of an accident."

"What accident?" he said, and he glanced down at Freya's sorry-looking rental. "Careless driving. That's no accident."

"Careless bloody driving? I'll give you careless driving."

"You weren't looking where you were going. Too busy looking in the mirror," he said. "That's right. I saw you–"

"You stopped in the middle of the road."

"I put my hazards on. I was going to make sure you were okay."

"I would have been just fine if I hadn't come across you this morning. I'd be at work. I'd be warm. Instead of standing here in the middle of a blizzard, without a car, and talking to a man who... Can you just leave yourself alone, please?" she finished, as he rummaged around his groin seeking the source of the itch. "Now show me some identification. My insurance company will deal with it."

He thrust a hand into his pocket and pulled out a handful of items, including a bank card which was cracked and split, a small wad of notes, and a driving license.

Freya took a photo of the license, then added him and his phone number as a contact in her phone, under the name *Ball Scratcher*. She gave him a missed call so he too had her phone number, and once she had taken a photo of his van and its number plate, she pocketed her phone.

"That's it. Your insurance will be hearing from mine," she said. "You can go back to whatever it was you were doing."

It was times like this that Freya was tempted to produce her ID. But, from experience, the warrant card was a joker up her sleeve that she should only reveal if situations got out of hand.

"You want a ride somewhere?" he asked, and he flicked his keys around his finger as a cowboy might twirl his gun.

She almost laughed at the proposition.

"I would rather hop blindfolded than get in that van with you. You shouldn't be on the road—"

"Okay, okay," he said, and he gestured again for his wife to get in the van. "Have a nice day," he called to Freya.

"Have a nice day," she muttered under her breath, and she watched the van pull away, leaving her stranded in the middle of nowhere. "Nice one, Freya."

The van was still in sight when Freya's phone began to vibrate in her pocket. She pulled it out, glanced at the screen, and tentatively hit the green button to answer the call.

"Ben?" she said, turning out of the wind.

"Morning, boss," he said, sounding more cheerful than Freya had the patience to deal with. "How are you this morning?"

"I've been better," she replied.

"Well, your day is about to get dramatically worse. I've just had a call from Gillespie. Missing person. Nineteen-year-old girl from Dunston. Granger wants us to take a look."

"Oh joy," Freya said. "That'll be a pleasant distraction."

"Yep, thought that would please you. Shall I meet you there? I'll text you the address."

"Erm, it might be best if we travel together."

"No can do, I'm afraid. I'm coming in from the city."

Freya said nothing. She stared down at the ruined rental and sighed.

"Freya?"

"Yep," she said, sounding as positive as she could.

"You okay? Where are you? Sounds like you're in a wind tunnel."

"I've, erm… I've had a bit of an accident."

CHAPTER THREE

"Just don't," Freya said, as she climbed into Ben's Ford and removed her woolly hat. She began tidying her hair in the sun visor mirror. "Don't say a bloody word."

Rubbing her hands together, she savoured the heat on her feet as she pulled on her seat belt. Ben was wide-eyed and staring at her from the driver's seat, incredulous.

Outside, the recovery vehicle was winching the car from the dyke. The entire front left-hand side was coated in thick mud and sleet had collected on the right-hand side of the car. Another hour or so and it would have been covered.

Ben indicated and pulled onto the road, leaving the tow truck behind, and Freya loosened her jacket, warming up from the brutal winds that had chilled her through.

"So, what do we have?" she asked eventually, deeming the ten-minute silence long enough to establish that she was in a bad mood.

"Other than a dead Korean in a dyke?"

"Ben, I'm warning you. My patience is paper-thin this morning."

"Okay, okay," he said. "Missing persons report. Abigail McGowan. Nineteen years old. Last seen jogging in Nocton."

"When?"

"Yesterday. Morning time. Takes the dog at the same time every day. Part of her workout, from what I understand. The dog came home, but she didn't."

"Who took the call?" Freya asked.

"Gillespie was on call. He hasn't been to the parents' house yet. He wanted to wait to see what you think."

"We'll need a route from the parents. Presuming she takes a similar route every day. Do you know the area at all?" Freya asked.

"Sadly, yes," Ben said quietly, then turned away.

"Ben?"

"I haven't been over there for years."

"You said she was jogging in Nocton? That sounds familiar."

"The church," Ben said quietly. "It's where DI Foster was buried."

"Right, yes. Sorry. I should have known that," Freya said guiltily, knowing full well that she had been David Foster's replacement and his death was a sore spot for Ben. "How easy would it be for someone to get lost out there?" she asked, as she checked the names of the houses they were passing. "Here. Blue door."

Ben pulled the car to the side of the road and opened the palm of his hand in lieu of a map.

"Dunston is here. Nocton is here. And on the far side of the woods is Wasps Nest."

"Wasps Nest?"

"The Blanch case last year," Ben reminded her, before continuing. He pointed at the imaginary area between the two villages. "This is all forest and fields. Plus, there's Nocton Hall, which is damn near falling down. There's the old RAF hospital as well, a bunch of old, disused buildings that go right back to the first world war, and then there's the disused water tower–"

"Sounds like a lot of disused buildings in a small space."

"Like I said, it's not a large area, but if Abigail McGowan is missing, we will need dogs, and if we can get an eye in the sky it'll be helpful, if anything just to search the surrounding fields. We're talking miles of open space, and I doubt very much if the farmer will be too happy about a search team trampling his winter crops."

"We're talking about a missing person here—"

"We're also talking about the livelihoods of our locals, Freya," he said. "We need them on our side. It'll be faster anyway."

"That's assuming Abigail is actually missing, and not just lying injured."

He smiled at her and glanced out through the windscreen.

"She's been gone twenty-something hours, Freya. You just waited out there for how long?"

"An hour."

"And how cold are you?"

"Okay, point taken."

"And she was jogging. It's unlikely she'll even have a jacket with her."

"You seem very concerned, Ben."

He shrugged. "It's a missing person. I want to find her."

"I get that. But you seem quite animated."

He sighed and turned to look out of his window.

"Let's just say I know what it's like to be out there. I just hope she's at a friend's house and just hasn't called."

"This is your turf," Freya said. "You lead."

He nodded, and they climbed from the car.

"One thing though," she said, talking to him over the roof of the car, as was their habit. "Do we have any statistics on survival rates for missing people in these parts?"

The snowfall was getting heavier. Large snowflakes as big as ten-pence pieces filled the sky.

"Nothing I'd share with the parents of a missing child, Freya," he replied. "That's for sure."

CHAPTER FOUR

"Mr McGowan?" Freya asked when the man opened the front door. "I'm DI Bloom, this is DS Savage. You reported a missing person. Is that right?"

He nodded, leaned out of the front door, and glanced in both directions, and then the hope faded from his face.

"You'd better come in," he said, and he stepped to one side.

The house was very well proportioned with a wide hallway and had been decorated to an extremely high standard, from the oak flooring to the modest and contemporary light fittings. Freya led, with Ben following close behind, and they moved through into the kitchen – a wide, open space with views out into the large rear garden. A black Labrador sat in its basket by the back doors. It looked up, as if inspecting the newcomers, then laid its head down again and peered through the glass into the garden.

"My daughter," McGowan explained. "Something's wrong. I know it is."

"Well, let's get to the bottom of it, shall we?" Freya said, eyeing the kettle on the worktop.

"Tea?" Mr McGowan said, seeing where her eyes had settled.

Freya appraised the man before her. His shoulders were

hunched like he carried the weight of the world, and his eyes were dark and lined as if he hadn't slept for days.

"I'll make it," she said, and she stepped behind the kitchen island, taking ownership of the space. The distraction would be useful and might prevent Mr McGowan from slipping into his own mind, as was often the case. She filled the kettle and waited. It was one of those types where the water had to filter through before the switch was turned on. "I hope you don't mind me asking. Is there a Mrs McGowan?"

"She died," he replied, seeming to search for something to busy his hands with. "Six years now. It's just Abi and me."

Ben made a discreet note, while Freya searched for cups.

"Top right," he said. "Tea and coffee is below."

"Right. Thanks," Freya said, and while the kettle boiled, she placed her hands palms-down on the kitchen counter. "Now then. Let's start from the beginning, shall we?"

"There's not much to say really," he replied, and he looked between them, from Freya to Ben, and back again. "She went for her run and didn't come home."

"What time was this?" Ben asked.

"Six-ish, yesterday morning. She runs every day."

"And always the same route?"

"Always. I'm pretty strict on that. She would have got home around seven. Listen, I know you probably get this a lot. It's not like her. I'm genuinely concerned."

"That's okay, sir. We just need to understand everything that has happened since seven a.m. yesterday morning," Freya said, as she poured the hot water into the three cups. "What did you do next?"

Again, he looked between them.

"Nothing."

"You didn't go and look for her?"

"Well, no... I mean, not until later."

"But you said you started to worry–"

"Yes, I started to worry, but nothing like that. I'm her dad. It's natural to worry. When your child doesn't come home, all kinds of things go through your head. But I always respect her space. I would never interfere–"

"Right, so you thought she might have gone somewhere afterwards?"

"Well, Stan came home around ten. I saw him in the garden and figured Abi must be home as well. My office is upstairs overlooking the garden. I didn't think too much of it, you know? Figured Abi must have bumped into someone and got chatting."

"Stan?" Freya said, and she followed his gaze to the dog, who was still staring out into the back garden. "The dog?"

McGowan nodded. "He would never leave her."

"I see. So you thought she was home. Is that right?" Freya asked.

Again, he nodded. "I had no reason to think otherwise. I did some work up until lunchtime. Just some personal admin on the computer. I made lunch and called up to her. It's funny. I thought Stan was behaving a bit odd. I honestly didn't think anything of it. But when she didn't come down, I went up to see if she'd heard me calling."

"And?" Ben said, pen poised to continue his notes.

"Well, she wasn't there. I searched high and low. Thought I was going mad. Then I saw it."

"Saw what, exactly?" Freya asked.

"The back gate," McGowan said, and he nodded toward the back garden. "It was open."

"And presumably Abigail always closes it when she returns?"

"Yes. Every time. She worries Stan will get out, see. Then I noticed other things. Her trainers weren't by the back door. Her dirty clothes weren't in the laundry basket, and her phone was nowhere to be found."

"Could she have come home and gone straight out?"

"Where?" he said. "Her car is on the drive, her keys are on the hook, and in this weather? No. She's not silly, my Abi. She hasn't come home. I'm sure of it."

"And that's when you made the initial call, is it?"

"Well, no," he said. "I went across the road to her friend's house first."

"And what's her friend's name?"

"Jess," McGowan said. "Jess Henry. Been friends since they were dots, they have. But she hadn't seen her. I didn't expect her to have, if I'm honest. But you know, you try these things. I can't sit still."

"Here," Freya said, sliding a tea across to him, and then nodding for Ben to collect his. "Mr McGowan, I'm sorry you're going through this. We'll do everything we can to find her. The chances are she's fallen and twisted her ankle. But we need to be prepared in case that isn't the case."

"What do you mean?"

"Well, is there any reason she might not have come home? Did you argue, maybe?"

"Argue? No. Never. She's a good girl, my Abi. I never had reason to argue with her."

"What about boyfriends?" Freya asked, keen to move the subject on.

"Not as far as I know. Not anymore anyway. Listen, is this going to take long? We should be out there."

"Have you been and looked for her?" Ben asked.

"Of course I have. Right after I got back from the Henrys' place, I got home, called you lot. Fat lot of good that did, I might add. Told me to wait twenty-four bleeding hours before I reported her missing. I know my daughter. I don't need some jumped-up–"

"Okay, okay, Mr McGowan," Freya said. "You're right. Nobody knows her like you do. Can you show us the path she takes? DS Savage and I will take a look."

"I can come with you if you like?"

"It's probably better if you stay–"

"Listen," he said, a pained expression forming on his face, "I can't sit here doing nothing. I've already been out there this morning."

"And what did you find?"

"Nothing. I searched high and low, I have..." His voice trailed off, and he began rocking to and fro, biting down on his lower lip. "I'll show you where she runs."

"What if she comes back?" Ben said. "We need somebody here."

"There's a key," McGowan said. "By the back door."

"Even still. Get DC Gold and DS Gillespie here," Freya said, catching Ben's stare. "I think Mr McGowan's knowledge will be useful. That is, if you're sure you're up to it?"

McGowan nodded. "Anything. Can't we get a helicopter to fly over or something? She'll be frozen to death."

"All in good time, Mr McGowan."

"But–"

"If I find that Abigail is in danger, I'll call in every resource available to us. You have my word."

CHAPTER FIVE

"I NEED YOU TWO TO WAIT HERE. DS SAVAGE AND I WILL WALK the route with Mr McGowan," Freya said, as DS Gillespie and DC Gold entered the house. Fresh sleet fell from Gillespie's jacket as he moved out of Freya's way, and with his tactless manner and thick Glaswegian accent, he appraised the situation.

"You sure you don't want me and Ben to go, boss?" he said. "It's a blizzard out here. You'll bloody freeze to death without a decent jacket."

From behind the kitchen counter, Mr McGowan's expression dropped.

"I'm sure I'll be fine," Freya said, and she eyeballed him, until he realised the victim's father was standing within earshot.

"Aye, right," he said. "I'm sure it's not too bad."

"What I want is for you two to arrange search teams. Given the circumstances, time is crucial." She turned to Mr McGowan. "I saw a village hall. Is there a parish councillor?"

"Not as such. But we have a warden," he said. "Mrs Finch. She'll have phone numbers. She could rally people together if you asked."

"Does she live in the village?"

"Yes, she does. Just up the lane. I have her number somewhere."

"Gold, take the number. I want you to prepare a search. Talk to Mrs Finch and get a feel for volunteers. The more people we have out there searching, the more chance we have of finding her. Have them ready to assemble at the village hall on my word and not before. If this weather gets any worse, we won't be sending anyone out there who isn't trained. I'll need approval from DCI Granger before I send the public out there. In the meantime, they can be spreading the word. You can lead the effort. Also, get hold of Anna Nillson and Cruz. We need bodies. The more the merrier. I imagine there's some kind of waiver form for volunteers to sign as well. Talk to Chapman, ask her to print a hundred copies and have them sent down with Cruz and Anna. Again, that's something we can do in the background to save time."

"Ma'am," Jackie replied.

"Now, Gillespie?"

"Aye, boss?"

"Uniforms. As many as Sergeant Priest can find. Call in the wider teams if you need to. As I understand it, there are numerous places off-limits to locals. Nocton Hall and the old hospital, and what else?"

"The water tower," Ben said.

"Is all this necessary?" Mr McGowan said. "Shouldn't we–"

"Nothing is moving until I say so, Mr McGowan, but I can assure you, when I do give the go-ahead, I want people moving fast. This is all in preparation. We may not need a search team. I want to be clear on that point. She's been out there for twenty-five hours now, and this weather is getting worse."

He nodded, biting his lip, and his eyes had reddened at just hearing the possibilities.

"Are you sure you're up for this?" she asked him, and he nodded, resolute in his decision to find his daughter.

"Gillespie, line up the dog team from Lincoln HQ and talk to

DCI Granger about getting a team in the air to search the fields. We might find the helicopter is grounded due to the weather, but it's worth asking the question and having them on standby. Are we clear on everything?"

"Aye, boss," he said again, whipping his jacket off and taking a place at the dining table to start work.

"Gold?"

"Yes, ma'am," she said, noting down the phone number that Mr McGowan was showing her on his phone.

"Then let's go," Freya said, pulling her jacket tight. "I'll call if we find anything."

Stan led, bolting to the back gate the moment Mr McGowan opened the back door. He sat and waited, never once taking his eye off the lock until his owner had opened that too. Then he was off.

"I guess we just follow the dog?" Ben called, raising his voice above the wind. He raised the hood of his parka, so that only from the side his big, square jaw jutted out. He walked beside Mr McGowan, towering over the man like father and child.

It pleased Freya to see Ben wearing the gloves she had bought him for Christmas, but it annoyed her that she hadn't bought herself any. She thrust her hands into her pockets and did her best to keep up with Ben's long strides.

"I always tell her to keep to the same route. Made her promise me she would," McGowan said, turning to call out to Freya.

"She sounds like a lovely girl," Freya said from behind, bracing against what felt like an arctic wind.

"What?"

"I said, she sounds like a lovely girl. Very trustworthy."

"She is. This is so out of character. The type of thing her mum would have done, if you get my meaning?"

"Her mother? No, sorry," Freya called out, as a particularly harsh gust of wind carried a particularly cold flurry of snow into her face. "Perhaps you could explain?"

He stopped, so she stopped, and a few steps further on, Ben stopped.

"Always did the opposite of what you wanted her to do. You know? Just to prove a point."

"And what was her point?" Ben asked.

"I never worked that one out," he said. "But Abigail's a good girl, as I said. Couldn't ask for a better daughter."

"Can I ask about her mother?" Freya said, as they entered a spot where the wind was blocked by a house.

"She died," McGowan said, stopping and turning to face her. He seemed to be enjoying the lull in the wind as much as she was. "Cancer. Six years ago."

"I can't begin to imagine—"

"No. No, you can't. Unless you've been through it, how could you?"

"How did Abigail cope? She would have been what? Thirteen?"

"It destroyed us. Not the death, mind. We knew it was coming. It was the lead-up. The suffering. The not knowing when. That was when I started winding down my work. I'd had enough by the end."

"And what was it you did?" Ben asked.

"Engineering. Always outside. Always cold," he mused. "Abigail soldiered on through school. Did well too, she did. My wife's parents suffered most, I think. Abigail's grandparents, that is. Her brother went off the rails. The family just fell apart. Something like that is supposed to make you stronger. But it doesn't always work out like that."

"Must have been hard for them."

"I think it destroyed them as a family. They're separated now, Abigail's grandparents. Keith, that's my wife's dad, he moved away. Her mum is still kicking about somewhere."

"And the brother?"

"Prison," he said, like just saying the word had left a bitter taste in his mouth.

"Has Abi ever displayed signs of protest before?" Freya asked, sensing Mr McGowan was drifting into his own head space.

"Never," he replied. "She's an angel. Not a pushover. She'll fight for what she wants, but she knows where to draw the line, if you get my meaning?"

"Mr McGowan," Freya said, "I know it's hard, but keep talking. You never know what information might be useful."

He nodded, then gestured at a small kissing gate.

"It's through here. We'll cut through the paddock and into the fields. It's open from there all the way up to the forest. If she's anywhere, she'll be in there out of the elements. She's smart, my Abi. Very smart."

They cut through a small paddock, as McGowan had suggested, and through another gate into a wide, open field. A footpath hugged the extremity of one side, and running alongside that was a dyke, barely visible due to the overgrown grasses and brambles.

With his long legs, Ben stepped over the brambles to the edge of the dyke and peered along as far as he could see.

"Do you happen to know what she was wearing?" he asked.

"Black leggings probably," McGowan replied. "She always ran in them. That and her waterproof shell."

"So she has some protection? What colour?"

"As I said, it's a waterproof shell. Not warm. It's red. Bright red. Can't miss it. Got her it for her birthday a few years ago, so she could be seen if..." His voice trailed away. "You know what I mean."

"Let's keep moving. I want to cover the full route so I can give the search teams clear instructions. This weather is worsening. I don't think we can afford to ask the public to help, but we'll raise a large team of uniformed officers."

"Will that be enough?" he asked.

"They're very good at what they do," Freya reassured him, and she offered him a comforting smile.

They crossed the fields using the footpaths, with Ben checking the dyke every hundred yards or so. But deep down, Freya knew she wouldn't be in there. She wasn't sure how. It was just a feeling. The trees on the far side of the forest were far more interesting. Far more secluded.

A farm track ran from left to right, dividing the fields and the forest, and the moment they crossed the road and entered the treeline, the wind ceased. Looking back the way they had come, Freya marvelled at the snow-covered fields. It was only a light covering for now, but if the snowfall continued as it was, it would be a few inches deep in no time. The road through the forest was tarmac and well-maintained. In fact, the whole area had been well-maintained. Clean, with trimmed bushes. It was the type of place where a red outer shell would stand out. But the forest was a different story.

It was at this point that McGowan stopped. She had to give him credit. He was holding himself together extremely well. Too well, perhaps. He pointed out the route they had taken so far.

"See those roofs? That's Dunston. That's where we've come from. We've walked up beside that dyke and across that field. From here, we'll stay on this road for a bit, then we'll cut into the forest. There's only one path through, and it's well-trod."

"Hopefully the snow isn't settling beneath the trees," Ben said. "We should stand a better chance of seeing her, if she's there."

McGowan nodded. "Agreed. The forest path takes us behind the old water tower. Behind that is the old RAF hospital, and then Nocton Hall. We'll come full circle and come back down the bridleway over there. See that line of hedges?"

"So that's our search area," Freya said. "It's contained. We can get a team in the fields if necessary."

"Farmer won't like that," McGowan said, sounding deflated. He caught Freya's questioning expression and explained. "He reckons someone has been stealing his winter crop. Vegetables mostly. He's been on to the village warden about it a few times. He's even put signs up warning people off his land."

"Okay, well, we can talk to him if need be. But hopefully it won't come to that," Freya said, gauging the search area. "I'd like to do a full loop and get back. With this snowfall and the short days, we need every advantage we can get."

McGowan's positive spirit seemed to be waning. Ben took a phone call before they set off into the forest and stepped away for a moment, so Freya moved closer to the girl's father.

"We'll do everything we can, sir," she said.

"I know. I just keep thinking—"

"Don't," she said. "Stay positive. She needs you right now. She needs you to be strong. We'll find her. If she's out here, then we'll find her."

"I don't doubt that," McGowan said. "My worry is that we're too late."

She glanced across at Ben, who was finishing his call and pocketing his phone. Behind McGowan's back, he offered her a solemn expression and shook his head with regret.

CHAPTER SIX

THEY FOLLOWED THE ROAD INTO THE FOREST, WHERE THE snowfall was far lighter and the wind was mostly blocked by the treeline. Stan ran ahead and stopped at a bend in the road.

An ill-feeling gripped Ben's stomach. It had been years since he had walked through this forest, and it was only now he was actually there that he felt it. He felt the connection to it. It was a terrible place, where dark memories were born. He wanted to voice his opinion, but not now. Not while there was hope.

"Ben?" Freya said, leaving Mr McGowan to walk alone. "Are you okay? You're pale."

"That was Granger," Ben said, keeping an eye on McGowan to keep out of earshot. He cleared his throat and composed himself. "He's vetoed any kind of public assistance. Says it's too much of a risk in weather like this. It's forecast to get worse. Much worse."

"The world has gone mad," Freya hissed, keeping her voice to a minimum. "It's a bloody girl's life we're talking about. What happened to community spirit?"

"Just passing on the message, boss," Ben said, as they crossed a small bridge over another dyke.

McGowan stopped ahead of them and pointed through the

trees on their right. Stan was another fifty metres ahead, as if he was coaxing them forward.

"That's the old water tower. We'll come off the road in a minute. The forest runs behind it. If she's fallen and hurt, that's where she'll be."

"You said you came searching for her earlier? Did you search in there?"

He nodded. "I've been up all night. Out here with a torch for most of it."

"Looks like Stan knows the way," Ben said.

"I followed him this morning," McGowan said. "He took me into the forest. For a while, I thought he'd lead me right to her. But there was nothing there."

Freya glanced at Ben, her expression serious.

They moved fast, and Stan seemed to grow excited at the pace. He turned off the road through a gap in the trees, then waited for them to catch up, then ran ahead, stopping at every turn in the winding path until they caught up. McGowan's description had been accurate. The path led behind the water tower, but access to the tower and the old hospital grounds was blocked by a tall chain link fence.

Ben gave it a shake, searching for any weaknesses, and Stan lay on the ground, resting his head on his paws.

"There's no way through," Ben announced, then turned to McGowan. "Are there any holes in the fence?"

"Not that I know of. They keep it sealed off as best they can. Had some trouble with vandals and all sorts."

"But there's no way for anyone to get in there."

"Not without cutting a hole in the fence, no."

Stan gave a whine. Stepping over to him, Ben dropped to a crouch and placed his hand on the dog's head.

"Where is she, boy?" he asked, and whether through intelligence or excitement, the dog gave a bark that merged into a whine, and he set his head back down on his paws.

Ben grabbed a stick and used it to move the foliage that covered the untrodden parts of the forest floor.

"What are you doing?" Freya asked, clearly trying to prevent him from entering into a full-scale search at this point.

"She was here."

"What? Because the dog barked?"

"I know dogs, Freya," Ben said. "She was here. Something happened–"

"What?" McGowan said, his voice rising. "What happened?"

"That's what I'm trying to find out. You said you called her. Is that right?"

"Of course I called her. It's the first thing I did."

"And it rang?" Ben said. "You heard the call go through, but she didn't answer. Is that right?"

"Yes. Well, yesterday at least. I tried calling all day and all morning."

"And what happens if you try her now?" Ben asked, spying an area of vegetation that appeared to have been flattened a little compared to the surrounding greenery.

"I get a message saying my call can't be connected."

"That's because the battery is flat," Ben said, just as the stick connected with something harder than the weeds. He bent down and, using his gloved hand, reached through the stinging nettles. A few moments later, he produced a mobile phone. It was a new iPhone with a pink case. "Is this hers, Mr McGowan?"

Wide-eyed, McGowan let his mouth fall open. Every fear he had, every terrible possibility he had imagined over the past twenty-four hours, became a shocking reality.

"Yes," he whispered. "Yes, it's hers."

Crouching beside the dog, Ben waved it beneath his nose, and it produced the effect he intended. The dog stood, wagged his tail, and sat beside Ben.

"She was here," Ben said, directing his message to Freya. But McGowan had to hear it. As a parent, he had to know the truth.

They had come out on a whim that they might find his daughter, but now the situation was more serious. "Something has happened to her."

"Abi?" McGowan called out, more frantic than before. "Abi, it's me."

Freya glanced across at Ben, who pocketed the phone as carefully as he could.

"We're going to need more bodies," she said. "Call Gillespie. Tell him to go ahead with his plan. Tell Gold to hold fire on the community search."

Ben was already withdrawing his own phone. He found Gillespie's number and hit dial.

"Abi?" McGowan called, and he began to run ahead, thrashing through the brush.

"Mr McGowan," Freya called, as she chased after him. "We need to preserve the scene."

"Ben?" Gillespie said, when he answered the call. "How's those wee balls of yours? Frozen yet?"

He sounded easy-going, like he and Gold were relaxing in front of the fire.

"No time, Jim. Did you call Priest?"

"Aye, just like you asked me to."

"Well, it's time to hit go. I want to assemble a team." Ben surveyed the area, deeming the McGowan house too far away for a uniform search to assemble. "At Nocton Church."

"Nocton Church? That's where–"

"David is buried, yes," Ben said, finishing the sentence for him. "The thought did occur to me. It's the closest we can get to the crime scene. There's space there to set up a temporary shelter too."

There was a rustling of clothing as Gillespie sat forward in his seat.

"Crime scene? Bloody hell, Ben. Is she...?"

"More than likely. We found her phone. It looks like there was some kind of struggle. There's a flattened area of vegetation. Her phone was on the ground nearby."

"Jesus."

"How soon can Priest's men mobilise?"

"I can have them at the church in under an hour. I'll meet them there and coordinate."

"Good. Thanks, Jim. Can you leave Jackie at the house? Granger vetoed the community search."

"Aye, I thought he might. He won't be a fan of sending the public out in this weather, good Samaritans or not."

"No, so we'll have to make do with uniforms and dogs. And if we can get the chopper off the ground–"

"That's a no-go too, Ben. Sorry, pal. Poor visibility, bad winds. It's a recipe for disaster."

"It already is a bloody disaster," Ben said. "Alright. It's a five-minute walk to the church from here. Call me when you're on the way, I'll meet you. Can you put Jackie on the line?"

He moved back to the footpath, watching for existing boot prints, but there were none. The ground was too hard and debris-covered. He was making his way in the direction that Freya and McGowan had gone when Jackie came on the line.

"Ben, hi, it's me."

"Jackie, I need you to hold fire on the community search. At least until Freya can talk some sense into DCI Granger."

"Understood, Ben. I asked Mrs Finch to wait for my call anyway."

"Gillespie is going to lead the uniformed search. I want you to wait there in case Abigail turns up."

"Do you think she will?"

He waited, pondering a suitable response. But there was no way he could sugarcoat it.

"No. No, I don't."

"Oh, Ben," she said, in that way that only Jackie could. "How's Mr McGowan? He seemed so lost."

"He's holding it together. Keep the place warm and the kettle filled. I'll send him back with DI Bloom."

"Will do, Ben."

She ended the call and Ben searched the forest ahead for Freya and McGowan. They were perhaps two hundred yards away, Freya trying to calm him down as he swiped at foliage wildly in an effort to see if his baby girl was lying beneath.

Ben approached slowly, being mindful of where he stepped, and in the corner of his eye, he spied a small, brick-built structure. It looked like a well or a drain, or something. He pushed his way through the brush, leaped over a small stream, and climbed up the bank. It was a drain, probably something to do with the old water tower when that had been in operation. The steel-mesh grid that had once covered it had long since been discarded. It wasn't a high structure, with just four courses of brickwork above ground, and as Ben approached, he saw the iron rungs that workers had once used to descend into the man-made hole, probably to perform some kind of maintenance.

He edged closer, praying that his intuition was wrong.

But when he looked down into the hole, perhaps fifteen feet or more below him, amidst the sea of bottles and beer cans below, the lifeless gaze of a young girl stared up at him.

He dropped to his knees and collapsed onto the brickwork, smothering his face with his gloves. He couldn't look. He couldn't bear to see the disappointment in McGowan's eyes. The hurt. The pain. The inability to find reason in it all. He'd seen those expressions before and knew that once they had taken root in a father's eyes, they became a permanent fixture. He knew it all too well.

A branch cracked behind him, and Ben turned to find McGowan standing there, reading the unspoken message in Ben's bloodshot eyes.

He didn't utter a word; it was more of a breath. His legs seemed to buckle, and he lunged forward toward the drain. But

Ben caught him and tried to pull him away, each man desperate to overpower the other.

"Don't look," Ben said, and McGowan collapsed at his feet. "Just don't look."

"I have to," McGowan said, and he crawled to the low brick wall, slipping from Ben's grip.

From a few feet away, Freya stood aghast, clearly able to read the situation at hand. She nodded at Ben to let him go.

"Ah," McGowan called, as if he'd taken a blow to his gut, and a sickening feeling grabbed Ben's stomach like the hands of something wild and evil. But McGowan turned and looked between them, with wonder and hope in his eyes. He stammered, unable to put his thoughts into words.

"She's..." he began, and peered down again as if to confirm what he'd seen.

"Mr McGowan," Ben said softly.

But the man tore himself away and slumped against the low brickwork.

"It's not her," he said. "That's not my Abigail."

CHAPTER SEVEN

"Where is she?" McGowan demanded, as Ben coaxed the sobbing wretch from the edge of the hole. Freya watched as Ben gripped his arm and pulled him away. "If that's not her, then where is she?"

"Let's go. Come on, Mr McGowan," Ben said, getting more forceful with his efforts.

With her phone to her ear, Freya peered down into the hole herself.

"She must be here somewhere. She has to be. Who is that? Where's Abigail?" McGowan called out.

"If she's here, we'll find her," Ben said, as he led him away.

"I can't go. I have to find her."

"Leave it to us, Mr McGowan," Freya said, rather more forcefully than she might have preferred. But it got his attention. "We need to get you back home. We need you strong for Abigail."

"My little girl," McGowan whined. His legs buckled and Ben caught him, holding him as if he was a sleeping cat. "She needs me."

"She does need you. She needs you at home," Ben said. "Come on. Let's get you back in the warm."

Freya's call connected, and she turned from the grieving man to focus on the grim contents of the hole.

"Gillespie?"

"Aye, boss. I heard the news. Not good, eh? Poor fella must be worried sick."

"It's worse than we thought," she said quietly.

"Oh no. You found her?"

"We found someone. Female. But it's not her."

"Eh? Another girl?"

"A woman. We found her lying in an old drain. Looks to be part of the old water tower. Hard to say. She's about fifteen feet down."

"So if it's not her, who the bloody hell is it?"

"I don't know, Gillespie. Maybe I should ask her?"

"Alright, alright. I'm just shocked is all."

"Well, you're not the only one. I wasn't exactly expecting to find someone else. I wasn't even expecting to find Abigail McGowan."

"Could she have fallen down there?"

"It's a possibility, but given the circumstances, and the fact that we found Abigail McGowan's phone, I think we need to assume this wasn't an accident. We need to act accordingly."

"I've got uniform en route to the church. From there, it's a few minutes away on foot. They can shut the place down, set up a perimeter."

"We'll need CSI and some kind of lifting gear to get our mystery woman out, and ask Chapman for a list of all missing persons in the area. Tell her to go wider if she needs to. Somebody must be missing her."

"Aye, leave that with me."

"Check with Ben first. He may have a plan for CSI."

"Oh aye, boss. He's a plan for CSI alright. He's been eyeing up that wee blonde one for months now."

"Michaela?" Freya said, and she stared after Ben, surprised

that this was the first she had heard of him taking a fancy to anyone. "Is that right?"

"Aye, but don't tell him I told you so."

"I have far more pressing matters, Gillespie."

"I'm sure," he said. "I'm leaving now. I'll give him a wee tinkle on my way and ask Jackie to stay here."

"Thanks, Gillespie. The fact remains that Abigail McGowan is still missing. We need the area searched, including the old hospital and the water tower. As I understand it, the gates are kept locked."

"I've managed to find the key holder. Local fella. Manages the maintenance of the place."

"Good, let's get those gates open and split the team. CSI aren't going to want two dozen uniforms trampling over the area, so we'll start the search wide and work our way in. Give them a chance to process the immediate area. Talk to the key holder. See if he has any plans of the place."

"Right, got it," Gillespie said, as a rasping sound came across the call, like a strong wind. But it wasn't just wind Freya could hear. It was the sound of voices. Lots of voices. "It's getting worse out here. If this carries on, there's gonna be a few inches of snow by tonight."

"Which is why we need to move fast," Freya said. She peered down into the hole at the girl below, grateful for the canopy of trees that blocked most of the snowfall.

"Holy mother of..." Gillespie said, then let his voice trail away. It was obvious what he was going to say.

"What is it?" Freya asked casually, surveying the area and identifying only one real plausible way into the little copse where the drain was – across the stream and up the bank. Ben, McGowan, and she had been treading all over the scene.

A car door slammed on Gillespie's end and the noise of the wind dropped from the call. Only the rustling of Gillespie's clothes could be heard, and then the sound of his engine starting.

"Gillespie? Talk to me."

"I'm looking at the village hall, boss. I think we might have a problem on our hands."

CHAPTER EIGHT

By the time Freya had followed Ben to the church and a uniform had driven both her and Mr McGowan the two-minute drive back to Dunston, Mr McGowan had fallen into an uneasy silence. Instead of trying to commiserate the man, Freya elected to demonstrate control over the situation by using the radio to talk to Ben and Gillespie, who were coordinating the uniformed search.

But when the car turned the corner into Dunston and drove past the village hall, the driver had to slow to a stop. Two couples were crossing the road, each of them dressed in warm weather gear – hats, gloves, big jackets, and big boots. They entered the village hall car park, which to Freya's surprise was bustling with bodies.

"Stop here," Freya instructed the driver, as she took in the scene. "Gillespie was right. We do have a problem."

"Is this...?" Mr McGowan started, but the sight of more than fifty people all huddled in groups, all dressed to venture out into the weather, had overwhelmed him.

He broke. His voice trailed off into an unintelligible whine and he tried to get out to talk to them. But the rear seat usually carried individuals under arrest, and the handle flapped back loudly. "Let me out. Let me talk to them," he gasped.

"Up here," Freya said, pointing the way to McGowan's house, and then told him to stop. "Help me get him inside."

The uniform nodded and did as Freya had requested, eventually coaxing McGowan up his garden path, where Jackie, who must have been peering through the window, opened the front door.

She eyed Jackie with a less than favourable glare, and then helped McGowan inside.

"There's a tea on the side for you, Mr McGowan. DS Savage called to say you were coming back, so it's nice and fresh for you, okay?"

"Thank you," he replied, almost robotic in tone, and he left them in the hallway.

"What the bloody hell is that?" Freya hissed, then turned to the uniform. "Thank you. I'd appreciate it if you could go and keep order in the village hall. Don't let anybody leave."

"I did tell them, ma'am," Gold said, her voice high and defensive in tone. "I told her to wait for me to give the go-ahead. But she must have made the calls anyway. You know what people are like in these little villages. There's a strong community spirit."

"No, I don't know, DC Gold. Sadly, where I'm from, nobody seems to bother with anything outside their own front door. We can't let these people loose. Granger will have a fit if we send the general public out here in this weather without some kind of disclaimer, and I'm not about to ask for one given the circumstances. These people should be staying at home where it's safe."

"You won't stop them, ma'am."

"What do you mean, I won't stop them? Are you suggesting we let them trample over the crime scene in the name of community spirit, potentially ruining every chance we have of finding the killer?"

"The killer?"

"Oh, hasn't Gillespie told you?"

"Told me what?"

Freya sighed, seeing the break in communications, and she understood Jackie's seemingly lackadaisical attitude to her command.

"We didn't find Abigail McGowan," Freya said, keeping her voice low so that her father wouldn't hear. "We did find her phone beneath a bunch of weeds or something."

"Oh," Jackie said, clearly not following but pretending that she did.

"We also found a body," Freya said.

"A what?"

"Shh. Another female. Late twenties, early thirties. We don't know for sure, but I suspect foul play. Gillespie has redirected uniform to Nocton Church to start a full-scale search for Abigail and to lock the whole area down while CSI do their stuff. She'll need to be lifted out of the drain."

"The drain?"

"Don't ask. I'm sure you'll find out the grim details in due course."

"Do you think it's related?" Jackie asked, and jammed her thumb back towards the kitchen. "You know? Abigail McGowan and this other girl?"

"Hard to say. Abigail is nineteen years old. This girl is much older. Twice her age maybe."

"So do you think whoever dumped the body has taken Abigail?" Jackie whispered. She was so close Freya could smell the faint perfume the young Edinburgh-born detective wore. Her eyes were wide with shock, and her mind was clearly running wild.

"Very intuitive, Gold," Freya said. "Yes. It's a possibility. We'll know more when the search teams have finished. The problem is, we only have about four hours of daylight left."

"So what do you want me to do about all that lot out there? As far as they know, Abigail has gone missing. We can't tell them a body has been found. All hell will break loose. We'll have a riot on our hands."

"I'll tell them," McGowan said, and Freya looked up to find him in the kitchen doorway. "I'll ask them to leave the search to the police. I'd like the opportunity to thank them. You have no idea how it feels to see all those people..."

He broke again, and Freya nodded for Jackie to go to him. Of all her team, DC Jackie Gold was the gentlest. Perhaps it was because she was a mother. She had a way with people under stress, a way that Freya neither had the time nor the inclination to explore.

"If I need your help, Mr McGowan, I'll ask for it. All I ask is that you stay inside and be ready."

"Be ready?" he said, looking to Jackie for an answer, then back at Freya.

"Be ready for when I find your daughter," Freya said. "I can't make any promises. But I can tell you this. Whatever the outcome, I won't rest until I find her."

CHAPTER NINE

"Listen up," Freya called out above the wind. Normally, her voice would carry far and wide, but the blanket of snow seemed to mute her words. "I said, listen up," she called again, and a few heads turned to face her. One person nudged another, who nudged another, and before long, the chain of nudges, nods, and pointing had spread through the crowd like a dose of salts. Standing on the step of the village hall offered Freya a few inches of extra height; it was all she could get and she would take what she could.

"Hush now, everybody," a woman in her late fifties said, with a voice like that of Freya's old school mistress, high and sharp enough to cut through the snow like a blade through soft skin.

"Thank you," Freya said, and she lowered her voice so that people had to concentrate to listen. "First of all, on behalf of Mr McGowan, I'd like to thank you all for coming, for giving up your time, for braving this appalling weather, and for showing him that his neighbours are by his side. Your actions are commendable. I only wish more communities demonstrated such spirit."

A murmur spread through the crowd, which grew to a hum, and then a din.

"But..." Freya began, again her voice lost in the wind.

"Quiet," the lady announced once more, who Freya had by now presumed to be Mrs Finch, the warden. A lady of assumed authority. She wore a heavy coat, a hat, and muddy wellies, and when she raised her hands, Freya saw that they too were covered in mud, as if she had been digging with her hands.

Freya gave her a nod of thanks.

"I cannot let you go."

"Oh, come on–" a man said, voicing his disappointment.

"I cannot allow you all to go out there in this weather. If anything should happen, not only would you be endangering the lives of others, but I could never live with myself. I must ask you all to return to your homes, please."

"You can't stop us," the man said.

"What's your name, sir?" she asked.

"My name?"

"It's a simple enough question."

"Derek," he replied, glancing around him, clearly not appreciating the attention.

Freya waited for the last name.

"Derek Stone," he said finally. "I live up the road."

"Thank you," Freya said. "Listen to me. I have asked for the forest to be locked down. By now, there will be police officers at every entrance and exit. I have asked a member of my team to coordinate a house-to-house investigation, so you can expect to see him shortly."

"You can't expect us to sit indoors while Abi's out there somewhere. She's been gone a day–"

"I can, and I must. Like I said, your spirit–"

"Don't give us that. Why don't you want help? Surely with more people, we can cover more ground?"

"That's all I can say."

"You found her, haven't you?" a voice said, young and male, approximately Abigail's age. "Haven't you?"

"And who are you?"

"Peter Jones," he replied, and nodded up the road. "Live up there. Went to school with Abi."

"Well then, I want you, especially, Peter, to go home and wait for my colleague to come. What you have to say might be useful."

"You didn't answer his question. You're hiding something."

"I can assure you–"

"If something happened, then we ought to know," somebody else shouted out, a female, mid-forties, dressed in what looked to be a ski outfit.

"Yeah, come on," another said.

"This ain't right," said another.

"Silence," Mrs Finch said, and she glanced at them all reproachfully. "Let Detective..."

She waited for Freya to fill in the blanks.

"My name is Detective Inspector Freya Bloom," Freya said, although she was hoping not to give her details away to such a large crowd. "I'll be running this investigation. I can tell you this, so listen up, because I do not have time to distribute updates to anybody and everybody. I'm needed out there in the search. Abigail McGowan has been missing for more than twenty-four hours. We believe we have identified the spot where she was last seen, and we have shut the area down. We have a team of officers conducting a search of the local fields, but it will take time. We have a team of individuals working with our crime scene investigators to search the forest."

"Well then, let us help," the man who had first voiced his opinion said. He was mid-fifties with an old but kind face, with dark rings around his eyes. "Why don't you let us help?"

"Because if anything should happen, then neither I nor the force can be held responsible."

"Yeah, but you can't stop us," Peter Jones called out.

"Yeah," another said, and the sentiment rippled through the crowd.

She studied them. One by one. Nearly all wore a hat or had a hood pulled up. There was an even split of males and females, and not one of them stood out from the crowd.

"You're right," Freya called, then lowered her voice when she had regained their attention. "I can't stop you from going out and searching. I can't stop you from looking in dykes, fields, and wherever you can find. But if you do decide you want to go for a walk, I would advise you to take precautions against the weather, to travel in pairs, or even better, threes. And I would advise you stay well clear of the areas controlled by my colleagues."

"So, we can go?" Peter asked. "We can start searching for her?"

"No. You cannot join the official search, but I can't stop you from walking the area. Mrs Finch, do we have a map?"

"I've printed them off already," a man replied, stepping out from behind Mrs Finch. As if it was some kind of uniform, he too wore muddy wellies, and even had mud on his face from where he'd scratched his chin with muddy fingers.

"And you are?"

"Daryl," he said. "Daryl Finch. I've marked the area on the map, split out five search areas, and given everyone a copy."

"So each team has an area to search?" Freya said, surprised at the organisation. "Well, that settles my conscience a little. See to it that nobody interferes with the official search, and if anybody happens to find anything—"

"Like what?" Peter Jones asked. It was a valid question, but one to which a detailed answer would raise eyebrows and set tongues wagging.

"Anything at all," Freya said, side-stepping what really needed to be said. "Then do not touch it. Alert me or one of my team. And we'll deal with it. But remember. You do *not* have my consent to go out there. The weather is getting worse."

The rumble of agitated voices grew to a din once more, and Freya turned to Mrs Finch.

"Thank you, Detective," Mrs Finch said, her chin held up and chest swollen with pride.

"Don't thank me," Freya said as she approached her, speaking quietly so that only she and her husband could hear. She held her hands up in defence. "I'm not allowing anybody to go out. In fact, I have advised them otherwise. We asked you to hold off yet I find half the village here, which suggests you did exactly what we asked you *not* to do. I've warned them all of the dangers. I've warned them of the weather. I can't do any more than that. This is on you, Mrs Finch. They're your responsibility. I suggest you keep them safe. I suggest you keep some kind of register of anybody who goes out there. I don't want my team to have another body to search for. I hope I've made my position on this matter very clear."

CHAPTER TEN

A TRIPOD HAD BEEN ERECTED OVER THE DRAIN, ALONG WITH A winch and a bosun's chair – a type of plastic seat that connected to the winch, to allow CSI safe access into the hole. Avoiding the few little numbered markers CSI had placed on the ground beside the footprints in the mud, Ben placed his foot on the brick wall and peered down at the two white-suited individuals examining the woman. He must have cast a shadow, as a familiar face peered up at him and raised her goggles onto her forehead.

"Morning, Ben," she said. "You know how to keep a girl busy, don't you?"

"Hi, Michaela. Thought that was you. How's it going down there?"

"As well as can be expected. Are you coming down?"

"No," Ben said, and he backed away a little at the thought of it.

"Not scared, are you?" Michaela asked.

"No," he lied. "There's not much room down there."

"We can squeeze up."

"No," he said, with an abrupt finality. "What have you found?"

"Well, not a great deal. The pathologist will be able to tell us more, but I think it's safe to say she was dropped in here and not carried down, and it was post-mortem, judging by the lack of blood. There is a head injury, but that was probably from the fall."

"Cause of death?"

"At this stage, I can't say. There's no ID either. We'll be lifting her out soon enough. There's nothing down here, and judging by the loose corrosion on the ladder, I'd say whoever dropped her didn't even touch the iron rungs. He carried her here and dumped her like garbage."

"Like a coward, more like," Ben said.

"I couldn't agree more," she said. "But I do try not to let my heart rule my head."

"I see you've processed up here already," Ben said, and looked down at the little markers on the ground. There were also three wooden frames pegged into the ground, each filled with plaster to extract the details of the shoes. "Three different prints?"

"That's yours, DI Bloom's, and, as I understand it from DS Gillespie, a Mr McGowan, whoever he is."

"The father of the missing girl."

"Ah," she replied. "But not this particular missing girl?"

"No. She was what you might call a bonus."

"And the daughter?"

"Abigail McGowan," Ben said, shaking his head. "We're still looking for her."

"Christ. I stand by my earlier statement then. You really do know how to keep a girl busy."

"We haven't found her yet," Ben said. "With any luck, we won't need to involve you."

"Any other girl might take that as a let-down, Ben Savage," she said, looking up at him with a broad smile. She stood and snapped her latex gloves off.

"Ah, come on," Ben said. "How about I make up for it?"

"Is that an invitation to dinner, after all these years?" Michaela said, and her assistant peered up from what he was doing.

"It was an invitation for me to winch you up," Ben replied, and he gave the winch handle a cursory spin as if to support his statement.

"Oh, I see."

She pulled her goggles back down over her face and fished a fresh pair of gloves from her pocket.

"But dinner sounds good," he said. "If you fancy it. I just didn't really..." He stopped, cursing himself for being so awkward when it came to the dating game.

Her assistant didn't look up this time, but he did shake his head, as if unable to believe what he was hearing. Michaela grabbed hold of the iron rung, and in a few moments, she emerged at the top of the drain, reaching out a hand to Ben.

He took it and heaved her out with a little more gusto than was needed, and she stumbled into him. He grabbed her to stop her from falling onto the little markers.

She paused, glanced at his hand on her waist, then turned her head to stare him in the eye through her goggles.

"One step at a time, Ben," she said.

"Oh, sorry. I didn't..." Ben said, and jerked his hand free.

She laughed his embarrassment off, seeming to enjoy the flushed complexion that washed across his face.

"You're going to have to lighten up, Ben," she said, then leaned over the wall to call down to her colleague. "I'll send the rescue team down with a stretcher. You okay down there?"

"Rather be down here than have to listen to you two bleating on," he replied, and Ben smiled sheepishly.

It was a strange thing that when Michaela was working on a crime scene, she seemed to own the place. Her confidence, her abilities, and her control were admirable. But when she stood beside Ben, she seemed to be tiny. He gauged her to be five foot five perhaps, give or take an inch, which made her a good eight or nine inches shorter than him. Enough that when she peered up at him, removing her goggles and pulling off the white hood, her eyes were big and wide.

"I'm sorry. I'm not great at—"

"You'll do just fine," she said, then picked a safe route back to the stream. She stopped at the top of the bank, where a break in the tree canopy allowed a flurry of snow to fall around her and settle in her blonde hair. "I need to make some arrangements before I can release the crime scene, and I need to oversee her removal."

"Right," Ben said, lost in his own thoughts of what she might look like in a dress from across a dinner table. The fact was, though, that Ben knew nothing about dating, and even less about what restaurant he might take her to, given the chance.

"So would you help me?" she said.

"Help you?" Ben said, rousing himself from his wandering mind.

"To cross the stream, Ben. I don't want to get wet now, do I?"

"Right, yeah, of course," he said, and followed her down the slippery bank.

"Of course, you might ask yourself one question," Michaela said, when she was halfway across the stream, balancing on a rock with the support of Ben's hand. "You might ask yourself why whoever dropped her down there didn't leave any footprints when it's clear that the three of you did."

"The thought had crossed my mind," Ben said honestly. "It's a few degrees warmer here than it is outside the forest. The canopy must retain some heat from the daylight. But at night time, the temperate in here will drop. It was close to freezing last night. The ground would have been rock hard."

"And the day before?"

"The day before," Ben said, trying to recall the weather, "it rained all day. But it wasn't as cold."

"Which suggests whoever did this did it last night," Michaela said, and she made the leap to the far side of the stream. "Anyway, that's just my opinion based on what I've seen. However, with the level of rigor mortis, I'd say she's been dead for at least two days."

"Two days?"

"At a guess. Maybe more. No less though. You're the detective, I'll let you figure that one out."

"Your opinion counts," he said, a little too fast. "I mean... it's valued."

"Ah, right. Well, I'm glad my professional opinion is valued."

"Did you want to?" he asked, leaving the question vague and open to interpretation. It was a good way for him to deny he was referring to dinner. He tried to step across the stream in one stride but misjudged it, and his left foot plunged into the icy water. He leaped across, feeling the wetness soak his sock.

"Wet sock?" she asked.

"It's nothing," he lied.

"Smooth, Ben," she said, as she turned and walked in the direction of the church. "I'll give you a call when we've got her out and have handed her over to the pathologist."

"Is that a yes?" he called after her, still none the wiser as to if they were going for dinner.

"Don't let your heart rule your head, Ben," she replied, her voice echoing through the trees.

He watched her disappear around the bend in the footpath and was pondering what she had said, her actions, and the way she had stared at him. He tried to decipher it all, but if he was honest with himself, he needed his brother to tell him if she was just flirting or if she was seriously interested. Jeff was better at all that stuff, despite being younger.

"I was wondering..." a familiar voice said from behind him. It was a voice that held little else but jest, ridicule, and petulance.

Ben turned to find Gillespie standing beside the stream pulling the expression of a damsel in distress. He held his hand out, as if he was reaching for Ben's.

"What exactly is it you're wondering, Jim?"

"If you might help me cross the stream?" Gillespie said, raising his voice to a feminine pitch.

"Piss off. How much of that did you hear?"

"Enough for me to apply my superior detective skills, Benjamin," the Glaswegian replied, as he deftly hopped to the rock and across the stream, "and come to a spell-binding conclusion."

"Don't tell me you've solved the crime and we can all go home?"

"No, don't be ridiculous. I haven't a clue what happened here. I'm as confused as you are. But I do know that wee lass managed to get across the stream without any help, yet she asked you to help her get back."

"Right," Ben said, scratching the growth on his chin, wondering if he should have shaved this morning, or if she liked a man with a beard.

"Want my advice?"

"Do I have a choice?" Ben said. "Or are you going to lecture me anyway?"

"Aye, well. Not lecture exactly. Just some friendly advice from Glasgow's finest."

"Go on then," Ben said, bracing himself for what was more than likely going to be the worst piece of advice he could ever hope to hear.

"Get in there, Ben. She likes you. What do you have to lose?" He strode up the bank, using tufts of grass as footholds. "Besides, you're not exactly getting any younger now, are you?"

"Right," Ben said. "Do you want some advice from me?"

"Aye, this'll be a laugh. There's not much you can teach me in the art of wooing, Benjamin," Gillespie said with a smile.

"This has nothing to do with wooing, or women in any way, shape, or form. Unless, that is..." Ben said, leaving him hanging.

"Unless what?" Gillespie called.

"Unless you can include having Freya kick you into the middle of next week, and then Michaela having to identify you by your dental records?"

"Eh?"

"Crime scene, Jim. You're standing in it."

"Ah, Christ," Gillespie said, as he hopped to a patch of hard ground that didn't have any little markers.

"Nice one. You're now a suspect," Ben joked, as he turned and headed toward the church. "Surrender your boots to the good doctor, you big oaf. One day, I'll let you tell me all about those superior detective skills of yours."

CHAPTER ELEVEN

"LISTEN UP," BEN SAID, CLAPPING HIS HANDS THREE TIMES TO gain the attention of the dozen or so uniforms who were yet to be assigned a duty. Eight others had been sent off in pairs to lock down the forest road at either end, while the other two pairs closed off the entrances to the forest. DC Cruz and DS Gillespie were standing nearby, leaning on the front wing of a police Astra. The snowfall had grown so heavy that it crunched beneath Ben's feet as he paced up and down outside the church. "We're looking for nineteen-year-old Abigail McGowan. According to her father, she was last seen yesterday morning running with her dog. The dog returned, but she didn't. We found her mobile phone in the forest, so we can be fairly sure she was there."

A uniform raised his hand, peering along the ranks of his colleagues as if he had missed something vital.

"You," Ben said.

"Grosvenor," the man said. "PCSO Grosvenor."

"What is it, Grosvenor?"

"We were told CSI were on the scene. We've just seen them cart a stretcher in," he said, and he nodded at the black van parked closest to the forest entrance. "Are we missing something?"

"You're not missing anything, but you're right to ask. While searching for Abigail McGowan, we discovered the body of another woman."

A murmur began, which if Ben had been less experienced, might have grown out of control.

"Enough," he said. "Yes, we have found a body. Are you involved? No. I want us to focus on finding Abigail McGowan. That's our sole purpose. We've got approximately two and a bit hours before we lose daylight, so we'll be splitting into teams. You'll need torches, you'll need cold weather gear, and you'll need radios. You know the drill. You'll each have a buddy. Stay close to them. Stay within your search areas. Gillespie, have we distributed the maps?"

"Aye, Ben. I've marked the route she would have taken, and we've had the gates to the water tower and hospital unlocked. The fella is down there now waiting for one of us to take over. Didn't seem too happy about being out in the cold, if you ask me."

"Grosvenor. Who are you buddying with?"

"Jameson," he replied, and jammed his thumb at the individual beside him.

"Do either of you know this area?"

"Walked my dog here a few times," Jameson said. "I'm pretty familiar with it."

"Do you know the entrance to the hospital and the water tower?"

He nodded. "It's at the end of the lane. Big steel gates, if I remember."

"Good, that's you two taken care of. Go and relieve the key holder of his keys. I'll be sending in a search team shortly. Nobody else in or out. Is that clear?"

They nodded in unison.

"Gillespie, follow them up there and take the bloke's details, will you? We'll need to question him to understand who else has access and if anybody has been in or out of there in the past few days."

"Aye, Ben. No bother."

"I need one more volunteer," Ben said, but nobody raised a hand. "Today please, before I start losing the feeling in my feet."

A young female PCSO raised her hand tentatively.

"Your name?" Ben asked.

"Larson, sir," she said.

"Don't call me sir. I'm a sergeant."

She nodded, and froze like a deer in headlights.

"The good news is you have more balls than the rest of your colleagues. You're with Detective Constable Cruz."

"Eh?" Cruz said. "Me?"

"You're going door to door in Nocton. It won't take long. There's only about two hundred houses."

"Two hundred houses?"

"And of those two hundred houses, I'd say at least fifty have dogs. Correct?"

"Give or take, yeah," Cruz said.

"Right, so where are they walking their dogs?"

"Ah, right."

"They might have seen something. Maybe they saw a car. Maybe they saw someone alone. Maybe they saw someone alone without a dog."

Cruz nodded but was clearly displeased at having to go door to door for the third time in a row. However, the sight of PCSO Larson, as she stepped forward and came to stand by his side, soon cheered him up. Although the same could not be said for Larson's enthusiasm to work with him.

"Take notes," Ben said, then turned to the rest of the uniforms. "Keep your radios on, torches on, and stay close to your buddy. I'll see you in two hours, by which time I hope to have some good news."

He pulled his phone from his pocket and dialled Freya's number, leaning on the Astra as the teams dispersed.

"Ben?"

"Not looking good, I'm afraid," he said. "Michaela reckons she's been dead for more than two days and was dumped a day ago. No visible sign of the murder and no footprints."

"What about Abigail?"

"I just released the first wave of search teams. This snow is getting worse, Freya. If we don't find her tonight–"

"I know. Believe me, I know. You won't believe what I just had to deal with. Half of Dunston want to go out searching."

"Granger won't like that."

"I tried to stop them. But they were organised and they were adamant."

"How hard did you try?" Ben said, smiling at Freya's game plan.

"Hard enough that we have another fifty warm bodies searching for her on this side of the forest."

"Plus the dozen or so on this side. We're losing light. Even with all those people, we won't be able to cover the entire area. It'll take days."

"Yeah, well, we don't have days. Not if our friend in the drain is anything to go by."

"We're getting her to Doctor Bell as fast as we can."

"Oh God. Her?"

"She's the best we have."

"I know, but..." Freya sighed. "I always feel so useless after seeing her."

Ben laughed, but it wasn't really a laugh. More of a loud exhale. But it served its purpose, covering his own worst fears.

"Do you want to tell me something, Ben?" she asked.

"Like what?"

"Like what's troubling you? You haven't been yourself all day."

"No," he said, hearing the tension in his own voice. "I'm just cold, tired, and..."

"And?"

"She's alive, Freya. There's a chance we can save a life this time, instead of searching for a murderer. I just want her found."

"We all want her found, Ben."

"I know," he said heavily. "What are you up to?"

"I've identified an old school friend. One of the volunteers. I'd like to talk to him when he's back. I'd also like to talk to Mr McGowan to get a picture of what Abigail's social life looks like. But first, I'll go and see the friend over the road."

"Jess Henry?" Ben said, as the rescue team emerged from the forest carrying the woman's body on a stretcher. Ben was standing approximately fifty feet away, and he watched with more than a hint of sadness as they opened the van and gently lowered her inside.

"That's her. Hopefully she can tell me what Abigail's social life really looks like. The unfiltered version."

"Want to meet up in a bit? Compare notes? They're just loading the unknown woman into the van. We won't know anything until tomorrow."

"How long do you need?"

"Two hours? I want to get the second wave of search teams out and see what the first wave found."

"Two hours is good. You can buy me dinner. It's going to be a long night."

"As long as you like fish and chips. There's an excellent chippy in Branston."

"You have appalling taste, Ben Savage. If the day comes when you actually find a woman you can tolerate for longer than ten minutes, please do me a favour. Do not take her to dinner, and if you do, let her choose."

"I'll make a note of that," Ben said, and he smiled at how true her statement was, however light-hearted the sentiment. "Do you want to pick me up from Nocton?"

"Is that supposed to be funny?"

He laughed again, this time far more sincerely than before.

"Do you know what they say about people who laugh at their own jokes?" Freya asked.

"I'll collect you from Dunston in a couple of hours."

"And do cheer up, Ben," Freya said, and then ended the call. It was typical of her to always get the last word in, a trait Ben had grown to adore in her. Footsteps crunched in the snow nearby and he looked up to find Michaela minus her white suit and goggles. She wore thick leggings that hugged her surprisingly muscled legs and a heavy parka that, in contrast to her lower half, gave her a cute girl-next-door look.

She glanced at Ben's phone then studied his face.

"You look like the cat that got the cream," she said. "Then choked on it."

"The cream is still out there, I'm afraid," he said, and then he fell in, realising that she was referring to the phone call. "Oh, that. No, that was just Freya."

"Freya?"

"DI Bloom. You remember her?"

"Ah, yes. The pretty one."

"Well, no. It's not like that—"

"It's okay, Ben. Was teasing."

"It's not. Really. We're just friends."

"Right. Good for you."

"Honestly," he said. "We were just discussing the case."

"Which one?"

"Well, both really. We've well and truly opened a can of worms here, and this lot isn't helping," he said, holding his hands out to catch some snow.

"Yes."

"Yes, what?"

"Dinner. You asked me to dinner and I'd like to accept."

"Great," Ben said, and he shoved himself off the car. "That's really great."

"It's just dinner. I'm hoping it'll be great," she said, as if to quell his enthusiasm.

"Yeah, well. Where do you want to go?"

"You choose," she said. "A man should always choose. Pick me up at eight? I can text you my address. I'm not a million miles from here."

"Ah, erm... tonight might be an issue."

"Ah, I see. The search."

"Yeah. Well, I said I'd go over some notes with Freya."

"Right. Of course."

"It's not like–"

"It's okay, Ben," she said, sounding dejected despite her efforts not to.

"I'm serious," Ben said, and he strode over to her as she turned away. "I'd love to. Just not tonight. We've got a missing girl on our hands. How about tomorrow?"

"What if she's still missing?"

"Then I'll make my excuses. I'll work something out."

"I tell you what, Ben, give me a call when you find her, or when it's over, one way or another. You go do what you have to do."

"Don't be like that–"

"It's fine, Ben. You're making it worse."

"Yeah, but..." He sighed. "What are you doing now?"

"Now?"

"Yeah. Let's grab something to eat quickly. We can go over what you found."

"Not really my idea of a fun night out, if I'm honest, Ben," she said, offering him a consoling smile. "I'll call you. In a week or so."

"You don't want me to–"

"No," she said, shaking her head. "I'll call you. Take care, Ben."

CHAPTER TWELVE

THE HENRYS' HOME WAS VERY WELL-KEPT. THE LAWN WAS CUT short and the surrounding borders were neat and tidy. All of which meant that the snow had settled in a neat and orderly manner, almost as flat as the road. The driveway was block-paved and Freya was surprised to see that there were no weeds growing from the cracks. They had been the bane of her life when she had once owned her own house, back in her married days. Her husband Greg would never get out there, and he certainly wouldn't have given the front lawn such care and attention.

She rang the doorbell and stepped back, listening for movement inside. There was a car on the drive, a nearly new Volvo, and there was a light on upstairs. She rang again, in case they hadn't heard her the first time.

The door opened mid-ring and a girl with a towel wrapped around her head peered through the gap.

"Jess Henry?" Freya said.

The girl's face adopted a concerned expression, and she opened the door further.

"That's me."

"Detective Inspector Freya Bloom, I wondered if I might ask you a few questions."

"What about? I'm going out."

"It's about your friend," Freya said, and she pointed toward the McGowan house. "Abigail. Her father told you she was missing, is that right?"

She nodded but shrugged. "I don't know anything. I haven't spoken to her in ages."

"Oh. Mr McGowan said you were close. Is he mistaken?"

"We used to be," she replied, and a particularly strong gust of wind blasted through the doorway, slamming the hallway door behind her.

"Do you mind if I come in?" Freya said.

Jess nodded, albeit with reluctance. She stepped to one side, waited for Freya to enter, then closed the door, leaning on it with her hands behind her back like she was waiting for Freya to say something.

"This is a beautiful home," Freya said, admiring the finish of the house and trying to put the girl at ease. The hallway floor was oak, the doors were oak, and the staircase matched both. The walls were adorned with tasteful pieces of colourful art, interspliced with the odd family photo, professionally taken, posed, and well-lit.

"It's my mum and dad's place. I'm studying still."

"Oh, what are you studying?"

"I'm a hair technician."

"Ah, how lovely," Freya said, thinking her career choice quite suitable for a girl who clearly took care of herself. Although, on reflection, Freya would prefer to deal with the dead than a dozen gossiping women every day. "That must be hard work. Are you home for long?"

"It's just in Lincoln. Kind of like a work experience college thing. Means I can stay here. Top place. Loads of customers. And they tip well, so..."

"Wow. That sounds like you're on the right track. Do you happen to know what Abigail plans to do?"

Jess met Freya's stare, trying to read something in what she said. She shook her head.

"Something in finance, I think," said Jess. "It's been a while since we spoke about that."

"What happened between you two?" Freya asked. "Did you grow apart?"

"I guess," Jess said, then sighed, and pushed herself off the door. "I'm sorry. Where are my manners? I should offer you tea."

She slipped past Freya and opened the door that had slammed, calling out as she walked.

"Do you take sugar?"

"No," Freya replied, stealing a final glance around the hallway, up the stairs, and into the lounge. The cleanliness was consistent throughout. She moved through into the kitchen and found Jess Henry filling the kettle.

"I'm worried about Abigail, Jess," she said, as if they were old friends. "I need your help."

"I don't know how I can help. I really don't know her anymore."

"But you used to. You live across the road. Surely you know who she sees, who her friends are, and what she gets up to."

"Can't Terry tell you all that?"

Freya smiled at her and leaned on the kitchen counter. "How much of your personal life do you share with your parents?"

Jess shrugged, but couldn't meet her stare.

"That's what I thought," Freya said. "There are things that girls know about each other that are simply too complex to discuss with parents. Was she in a relationship?"

Jess turned her back and held onto the kettle as if it would boil imminently, although even Freya could see it still had a while to go.

"Did she have a boyfriend, Jess?"

"I don't know. Why don't you look in her diary or something? I don't even see her anymore."

"Jess, please. She could be in trouble."

The girl sighed, though she kept her back to Freya.

"You do know, don't you?" Freya asked gently. "Is that why you don't talk anymore?"

Jess turned, glaring at her accusingly. But her glare faded to some kind of acceptance.

"Peter Jones," she said. "He lives–"

"In the village, yes. I've met him."

"You've met him?"

"He's out there now searching for Abigail."

"He's what?" Jess said, her eyes narrowing and a look of disgust spreading across her face. She reached into her back pocket and pulled out her phone, tapping furiously.

"As are half the village," Freya said, and she moved across to the window which overlooked the rear garden. There was a large patio area with a table and chairs, plus, in the corner, there was an L-shaped sofa, all of which were covered in neat, canvass covers, which in turn were slowly being covered in snow. In the opposite corner, a pergola covered a hot tub, and between all of this, a snow-covered lawn stretched to the end of the garden. "Abigail has been missing for more than a day now. The last we know, she was out running. She could still be out there, Jess."

"But it's freezing–"

"Whatever differences you have," Freya said, turning to meet the girl's gaze, to solidify her point, "it's time to put them to one side. We need your help in finding her. Did you fall out over Peter Jones?"

She nodded. Slowly, she unwrapped the towel from her hair and set it down. Then she pulled her hair back over one shoulder. She was a brunette with dark features, but her wet hair shone almost black in the dim light.

"Her and Peter used to be an item. They were together for years. Since school, you know?"

Freya nodded, seeing exactly where it was heading.

"But you know how it is. Abi went off to uni. Peter started work–"

"What does he do?"

"Works with his dad. They own a roofing firm or something."

"So they went in different directions?"

"Not entirely," she replied, adopting a sheepish and guilty expression. "When she went away, Peter and I still hung out. Like we always did. You know? We'd go to the match, hang out on a Friday night, go to the pub. Except, there weren't three of us anymore."

"There were two," Freya added, nodding to make it easier.

"Peter told her. He called her up when we first... you know?"

"Right," Freya said.

"Abi sent me nasty messages. Wouldn't speak to me. I tried. She came back last summer and I knocked at her house, but..."

"But?"

"That's it. She wouldn't talk to me. Couldn't even look at me. Said I betrayed her, which I did. But I didn't do it on purpose. We never meant to hurt her."

"And what about Peter?"

"What about him?"

"Do you still see him?"

"Well, yeah."

"And that's why you're getting ready to go out, is it?" Freya asked. "You're meeting him?"

She nodded. "It's not a crime, you know."

"Jess, I'm going to ask you something and I need you to be honest with me," Freya said. She reached out for one of the teas and clamped her hands around it, savouring the warmth. "When did Peter last see Abigail?"

She shrugged again, the way she had done at least three times already. But it was half-hearted. It was more an act of denial than a genuine demonstration of ignorance.

"Has he seen her recently?" Freya asked.

"He says he hasn't," Jess said.

"And do you believe him?"

She stared at Freya from across the kitchen worktop, a look of resilience and defiance in her eyes.

"Yes," she said, nodding. "He wouldn't cheat on me. He knows it would hurt me."

"Do you know what I think?"

That shrug again, followed by a stare out of the window.

"I think Peter saw Abigail behind your back. As old friends, perhaps. He's out there looking for her. He's worried for her. If you were her friend, you'd be out there too. But you're not. Instead, you're in here, in the warm, green with jealousy."

Jess looked away, unable to meet Freya's stare.

Placing her cup on the worktop, Freya moved toward the door.

"Don't go anywhere, Jess," she said. "We may need to ask you further questions."

CHAPTER THIRTEEN

"ALRIGHT, LOVER BOY?" GILLESPIE CALLED OUT, AS HE EMERGED from the little forest road that led to the hospital gates. "I thought I'd find you drooling over that white suit, instead of standing in the middle of the road with your thumb up your—"

Ben glared at Gillespie, just catching him in time before he proclaimed some kind of profanity out loud. From the private ambulance, Michaela looked up as Gillespie came into view, then with a quick, irritated glance at Ben, she spoke to the driver and climbed into her own car.

"Nice work," Ben said. "Next time you have something to say, perhaps you can run it by me before you announce it to half of Lincolnshire."

"How was I to know she was there?"

"How did you get on up there?"

"Ah, come on. Don't change the subject. When are you taking her out then?"

"I'm not," Ben said, and they both watched as Michaela pulled out from the parking spot and drove away without saying goodbye.

"I thought you were going to ask her?"

"I did."

"And she said no?" Gillespie said, sounding surprised. "She was pretty much begging you to when I saw you in the forest. The whole helping her cross the stream thing. I told you to ask her out."

"I did ask her," Ben said, realising that he wasn't going to hear anything else until he had given Gillespie all the details. "I asked her to dinner."

"Then she said no?"

"Yes, well... no. Not exactly."

"Christ, Ben, look at you. You're six foot something, as wide as two men, and most people live in your shadow. Yet you're talking like a bloody schoolboy. Where's your confidence, man?"

"I asked her," Ben said, holding his hands up. "I asked her and she said yes. At first."

"What? She changed her mind?" Gillespie said, sounding utterly incredulous. "You managed to turn her off before you even took her out? That has to be some kind of record, Ben. You didn't try to kiss her, did you?"

"She wanted to go tonight," Ben said. "At eight o'clock."

"Right?" Gillespie said, not following. "So what the bloody hell happened between her saying yes, and even giving you a time, and her driving off frostier than... well, this?" He pointed to Michaela's retreating car.

"I'm meeting Freya tonight to go over the investigation," Ben said. "It's what we do."

"You show Freya yours and she shows you hers?"

"Findings, Gillespie. We exchange knowledge. It's called collaboration."

"It's called royally cocking it up is what it's called, Ben. You didn't tell her you were seeing Freya, did you?"

"She's my colleague."

"Oh, Christ, Ben. You're hopeless, man. From now on, I'm in charge of your love life."

"You're in charge of naff all. It's because of you this happened."

"How do you work that out?"

"Well, if you hadn't provoked me, I wouldn't have asked her."

"And then where would you be? Going home alone again, wondering why nobody wants to share your wee bed."

"I've got this far on my own, Gillespie," Ben said. "It's not like being single is holding me back, is it?"

"How did you leave it?"

"Leave what?"

"The white-suited wonder, Ben. You know? Did you at least try to salvage something?"

"She said she'd call me."

"Oh no, Ben," Gillespie said, and he turned on the spot to walk away. Then after three paces, he turned again, his animated hands gesturing at Ben's incompetence. "What the bloody hell is wrong with you?"

"What? It's better than nothing."

"No, Ben. It's not better than nothing. It *is* nothing. Don't you get it? When a girl tells you, I'll call you," Gillespie said, putting on a mock girl's voice, "it means she won't be calling you and you might as well go home and forget about her."

"Why would she say that then?"

"Because it's easier than telling you to piss off to your face. That's what they do. Everyone knows that."

"You don't know that. I think she'll call me. She seemed genuine."

"She seemed genuine because she's well-versed in telling men she'll call them. How many do you think she's ever actually called?"

Ben shrugged.

"She's single, aye?"

"Well, yeah."

"Right. She probably gets hit on every time she goes out. You know what women do. They'll go into town, hit the bars and maybe a club, and some guys will latch onto them, have a wee dance, buy them drinks all night, hoping for a nightcap. If you know what I mean?"

"I don't think she's like that."

"Aye, that's what you think, sunshine. And yes, sometimes the bloke will get lucky. If he finds the right girl and if she's in the right mood. But more often than not, she'll give him a wee peck on the cheek, take his number, and then guess what?"

"She'll tell him she'll call him?"

"Hallelujah," Gillespie exclaimed, raising his hands in the air. Two dog walkers were walking toward the forest, glancing at Gillespie, wearing rather disturbed looking expressions. The sight of a large man standing before a church in the dying light, raising his hands and calling out *hallelujah* was very likely not how the local villagers practised their religion.

"She's not like that. She's decent."

"Aye, Ben. They're all decent. I'm not saying any of them aren't decent. But it's the language of love. Or, in your case, the language of lust and rejection. You blew it."

The words stung a little. More than Ben would have cared to admit, anyway. He could really see himself with Michaela. She was smart, successful, and grounded. He liked that. It wasn't as if he dreamed of her day and night like a schoolboy. But when they met, which was usually at a crime scene, they had a connection. It was similar to what he felt when he and Freya were close, only without barriers.

How long has it been? he asked himself.

Too long, some inner part of him replied without hesitation.

"You alright there, Ben?" Gillespie asked. "You look like you're gonna have a wee cry."

A layer of snow had lodged in Gillespie's hair and on his shoulders. They had been standing for too long. Ben checked his watch. Another hour and forty-five minutes before he had to collect Freya. He'd need to share some kind of result, or she'd think he'd wasted his entire time chatting up the CSI crew.

"I'm fine," he said. "How did you get on anyway?"

"Get on with what?" Gillespie said.

"You were going to see the key holder."

"Aye, right. He's coming. He's just giving uniform a rundown of the place. The place is locked up like Fort Knox though. Nobody's getting in there without a key."

"Do you think we'll find her, Jim?" Ben asked, putting the whole Michaela debacle behind him, as best he could anyway. "Do you think she's out there somewhere?"

"You're dead set on finding this lassie, aren't you?"

"Aren't you?" Ben asked. "That's why we're here, isn't it?"

"Aye, but there's something about this one for you. You've got a look in your eye I've not seen before."

Ben nodded. He'd done his best to keep his emotions at bay, but clearly his efforts hadn't been good enough.

"I know this place. I know it well," he said, and Gillespie led him to the car, where they perched on the wing, side by side.

Ben exhaled a cloud of breath and was lost in it for a moment.

"Something you want to say, Ben?" Gillespie asked.

Ben considered it for a moment. He stared into the forest, lost in thought.

"Ben?"

"No," Ben replied. "No, there's nothing to say."

CHAPTER FOURTEEN

AN OLD DIESEL ENGINE INTERRUPTED THEIR CONVERSATION and Ben pushed himself off the car, feeling cold and stiff.

"This must be him," Gillespie said. "The key holder. Listen, are you sure you're okay to…"

He paused.

"To what?" Ben asked.

Nodding towards Ben's head, Gillespie frowned at him. "There's clearly something up. Do you want me to talk to him?"

"I'm fine," Ben said. He held his hand up for the van to stop then approached the driver's side, holding his warrant card up. "DS Ben Savage."

"Now then," the driver said. "I want that place locked up. No leaving the gates open. We'll have bloody travellers camping up there in a heartbeat."

"You'll find we're quite responsible people, sir. Sorry, what was your name?"

"Neil Gutteridge," the man explained. His breathing was loud and his large belly rested against the steering wheel of the old transit van. The hem of his t-shirt was just a few inches shy of being long enough.

"Thank you, Mr Gutteridge," Ben said. "Did my colleague question you about any recent movements?"

"Yeah, he asked earlier. I've got a maintenance schedule."

"And how often do you come here?"

"Ah, you know? Once a week. Sometimes more, sometimes less. I just keep an eye on the place really. When it gets overgrown, I get the contractors in. But that won't be until spring. There's some pipework being taken out here and there. Nothing major."

"How much do you know about the drains?"

"Drains?"

"In the forest. You know, the brick things. They're filled with rubbish, but you can still get down into them."

"They're not drains," the man said, eyeing Ben as if he was some kind of idiot. "They're manholes. For the water supply to the old RAF hospital."

"Right," said Ben, encouraging the man to embellish the explanation.

"They had to get their water from somewhere, didn't they?" he said with a hearty laugh. "Damn near eight hundred beds in the hospital and they didn't have Evian back then. That's what the water tower is for."

"I see," Ben said. He knew the holes, the tower, and the hospital were all interconnected, and if he had to suffer the man thinking he was an imbecile to gain the explanation he was looking for, then so be it. "So who looks after them?"

"Nobody. Decommissioned years ago. Supposed to be covered with grates. But you know what kids are like."

"I imagine a task like that would fall on you, would it?" Ben said, and the man's smile faded to suspicion. "If we needed someone who knew about them, I suppose you'd be the man to ask."

"Well, I dare say there's others that know more."

"Fantastic," Ben said. "Did my colleague ask you about plans for the site? I'd like to get a feel for the site. You know, make sure we don't miss anything."

"Like what?"

"Like any more manholes."

"I've got plans. They're at home though. I don't carry them. Too expensive to get printed."

"I can arrange for them to be collected."

"Oh, you don't need to worry about that. I'll bring them to the station."

"No. It's fine," Ben said, imagining the plans being passed from reception into the melee of activity behind the scenes. "I'll collect them."

"Do I have a choice?"

"You'll be helping our investigations, sir."

"What investigations? Listen, that fella there told me you were looking for a missing person. Said I could have my keys back when you were done."

"It's a little more complex than that," Ben said, handing him one of his cards. "Write your address on the back for me, will you?"

Gutteridge did as Ben had asked, although with more than a little silent protest, then handed the card back to Ben and tossed the biro onto the mess on the dashboard.

"I'll see you at nine a.m. And if we could get a copy of the maintenance schedule, please." Then Ben gave the side of the van a slap with the palm of his hand, the universal gesture to indicate the driver was free to move on.

"You learn something every day," Gillespie said. "Here's me thinking we'd found a body in a drain. When all along, it was a bloody manhole."

Ben didn't see the funny side. In fact, he was struggling to find anything remotely humorous about the situation. "A bloody drain or a bloody manhole, who cares what it is? The fact remains that some poor woman was tossed down there like an empty can of

Stella bloody Artois, and Abigail McGowan has been missing..." He checked his watch. "For more than thirty hours. Thirty hours, Jim. I'm wearing a heavy jacket and gloves, and I'm freezing my arse off. She's out in running gear. If we don't find her soon, she'll freeze to death."

"If she isn't dead already," Gillespie said, and he offered Ben a grave expression. "We need to face facts, mate. If we don't come up trumps tonight and she's still out there, then we've lost. But there's another alternative."

Ben knew the alternative. He'd been considering it since he had first leaned over the edge of the manhole and seen the dead woman below.

"If she's not out there, Ben, we could have an even bigger problem on our hands."

Ben's pocket began to vibrate, and he was glad for the inter-ruption for once. He pulled out his phone and read the name of the caller. Gabriel Cruz.

"DC Cruz, don't tell me you've knocked on two hundred doors already."

"No, boss. We've done about fifteen so far."

"Fifteen? You've been gone hours."

"It's been like two hours, tops," Cruz said, his voice rising to a defensive pitch.

"Well, it feels like hours," Ben said, then refrained from complaining about how cold he was. "What have you got?"

"Headlights, boss."

"Headlights?"

"A couple in Nocton. They walk their dog every day. Lovely couple. Invited us in for tea."

"To which I imagine you declined," Ben said.

"Erm, yeah, course. Anyway, the fella said he does a full loop of the forest all the way up to the fields in Dunston every night. It's about a two-mile round trip. Says if he doesn't do it, his dog goes stir crazy."

"Well, that's great, Cruz. Maybe you can add him to your Christmas list. You seem to have made a friend."

"Eh?"

"What else did he have to say?" Ben snapped, seeing a smile spread across Gillespie's face as he overheard the call.

"Oh, right. Said he was on the forest road, over by the cricket pitch, and he saw some headlights, well, taillights to be precise. Red ones. Well, red one, to be even more precise. He said one was broken."

"A broken rear light?"

"Yeah," Cruz said. "He was quite specific. The right-hand light wasn't working. Said they were ahead of him, but he thought it was weird because no vehicles had passed him."

"Maybe it was someone parked up to walk their dog."

"Maybe," Cruz said. "I was just calling so we can maybe look at tyre tracks over by the cricket field."

"Tyre tracks," Ben said. It was the first useful thing Cruz had said all day. He was almost pleased that Freya had inherited Cruz onto her team, which, by proxy, meant that it was Ben's responsibility to manage him. "Good. Good, see if anybody else saw them. Or maybe they saw the car parked up earlier. There can't be too many cars that use that road. I've never seen a single car on it."

"You want us to keep on?" Cruz asked.

"Did you think I'd let you off the hook just because your new best mate gave you and your girlfriend tea and led you down the garden path with a story about headlights?"

"Taillights, boss."

"Whatever. Every house, Cruz," Ben said. "And I need to ask you something."

"Yeah?" Cruz said, like a stroppy teenager.

"When you said, some fella saw head..." He stopped himself, unsure if he could stop himself from melting down if Cruz corrected him one more time. "I mean, taillights, please tell me you got his details."

"Yeah, course," Cruz said, and there was a rustling as he checked his notebook. "Trevor. Number fifty-one."

"Trevor at fifty-one?" Ben said, squeezing the bridge of his nose to quell the beginnings of a stress headache.

"That's right. Fifty-one Main Street. Just near the new social club."

Ben let his head fall back and the snow cooled his blazing forehead.

"Boss?" Cruz said.

"Yes," he said.

"Shall I get on then?"

"Yes," Ben said with a sigh, and he thought of the young detective out there with the even younger uniform. He ended the call and stared at Gillespie in despair. "What bloody chance does she stand, Jim? What bloody chance does she stand?"

CHAPTER FIFTEEN

DC Jackie Gold opened the door to Mr McGowan's house, seeming rather pleased to see Freya.

"How's it going?" she asked, with her soft Edinburgh twang. "Did you find her?"

Freya stopped with one foot inside the house, the other still on the doorstep. The answer to the question was obvious, Freya had thought. It should have been obvious. But clearly she needed to work on her tired and weary expressions in order to convey to DC Jackie Gold that she had, in fact, not found Abigail McGowan.

"Where's Mr McGowan?" she asked, instead choosing not to venture down a route that would only end up in her mild irritation growing in ferocity.

"He's inside," Jackie said, as she closed the door behind Freya. "I lit the fire for him. Been feeding him tea and keeping him company."

"Sounds lovely," Freya said. She didn't have to look in the mirror in the hallway to know that she resembled one of Shackleton's crew – windswept and ice-covered, and with fingers that felt like they would snap off if she tried to unbutton her coat too fast.

"Shall I get you a tea?" Jackie asked.

Freya looked her up and down, expecting to find her in a pair of Abigail's slippers and dressing gown, all cosied up to the victim's father.

"I'm not staying. And neither are you."

"Who's going to stay with Mr McGowan?"

"Nobody. We'll send someone in the morning," Freya said. "Get your things. I'll talk to him now."

She gave a gentle knock on the living room door and felt the blast of heat on her face the moment she stepped inside.

"Mr McGowan?" she said, and he looked up from the armchair, his eyes bright red with fatigue and worry. He looked like he could sleep for a thousand years, but there was no way a parent could sleep. Not until they knew for sure where their child was. For better or for worse. "Is there anything I can get you before we go?"

He opened his mouth, a bitter expression forming on his lips, as if he was about to say, 'you can bring my daughter home.' But he softened, and simply shook his head.

"I can ask a Family Liaison Officer to come, if you'd like. They'll keep you company. Answer any questions you might have."

"I only have one question, Detective," he said, his voice a low growl. "And I doubt very much if a family whatever-you-called-it could answer it if you can't."

"We're working around the clock. We're expecting the first of the search teams back soon, and if there's anything to report, you'll be the first to know. Okay?"

He didn't nod or shake his head. He simply raised his chin, tightened his lips, then stared at the fire.

"I'll be back to see you a bit later. We'll see ourselves out."

Again, he didn't react, choosing instead to stare at the flames as they danced inside the log burner.

"He's been like that all day," Jackie whispered, as she pulled on her jacket. "I felt so useless."

Freya opened the door; the freezing wind found her aching legs and tore through her already dishevelled hair.

"Let's go," she told Jackie. "Before all the heat gets out."

"It's pitch black out here," Jackie stated, as she waited for Freya to join her on the footpath. "How are we supposed to find her in this if we can't find her in the daylight?"

"The trouble is, we can't stop looking. Statistically, Abigail McGowan is already dead," Freya muttered under her breath. "Let's hope she doesn't become another statistic."

"Where's your car, ma'am?" Jackie asked, peering further along the road. "Do you have a new one?"

It was another painful reminder of just how bad her day had been. She hadn't even thought about the car situation for the past couple of hours, not since Ben had reminded her anyway.

"It's in the garage. Ben is coming to pick us up."

"Are you carrying on?" Jackie asked.

"Of course. We can't go home. Not now," Freya said, and Jackie's face dropped a little with disappointment. "Could you honestly walk away and sleep while that man's daughter is still missing?"

"Well, no—"

"So, we push on. Because that's what we do. Until we know for sure if Abigail McGowan is in that forest, lying in a field, or if she's vanished like a fart in the wind."

Jackie stared at her apologetically, and for a split second, Freya saw the bigger picture, and how unreasonable she sounded.

"I'm sorry, Jackie. It's been a long day. I forget you have a child of your own." She sighed and waited for the cloud of her breath to disperse. "It's easier for me. I get it. If you need to go, I'll ask a uniform to take you back. Maybe I should give Gillespie and Cruz a break too."

"It's okay. I'll sort it, ma'am. I'd stay if it wasn't for Charlie. It's just that I've been leaning on my mum quite a lot recently. It's not really fair on her. She sees more of Charlie than I do sometimes. But if…"

She paused, staring up the road.

"If what, Jackie?"

"If we don't find her, Abigail, that is. If we don't find her, then we could be looking at an abduction or worse. I want to be there. I want to be involved. That's where I'm needed. Not babysitting the victim's father."

"Do you feel left out?"

She nodded. "A little, yeah. It's like he's grieving. But not really. Does that make sense?"

"There's no closure for him. One way or another," Freya said. "Come on. Let's get to the village hall. I heard Mrs Finch has opened it up for us to use, and the community search will be getting back soon. You can go from there, and I promise I'll keep you updated."

"Thanks, ma'am," Jackie said sincerely. "Hang on. Community search?"

"Don't ask," Freya said, and she shot her a sideways glance as they crossed the road outside the village hall. She hadn't seen it before, but there was an old, red phone box that had been converted into a book exchange for the locals. A few ducks crossed the road, a mother and her ducklings, all walking in a neat, little row.

"Such a terrible thing to happen in such a beautiful place," Jackie said, as if she was just speaking her thoughts.

Freya eyed Jackie as she admired the little ducklings. She was so soft and gentle; it amazed Freya how she had come so far in her career. She was a good mother, of that Freya was certain.

They entered the car park, where a liveried car was parked with the engine running. A uniform was leaning on it, doing something on his mobile phone.

"I'll see if I can catch a lift. I'll call you later, okay?" Jackie said, handing her a folded piece of paper. "My notes. Not sure if they'll be any use, but–"

"Thanks. Good work. Do what you need to do," Freya said. Then she called after her, "Jackie?"

"Ma'am?"

"You might not realise it, but what you did today was vital. Thank you for persevering."

Jackie nodded her thanks and began talking to the uniform, and as Freya entered the village hall, she turned to find the car reversing, then it pulled out of the car park.

It was right, what she had said to Jackie. Her part of keeping Mr McGowan occupied had been vital. Without someone like her staying close to the man, who knows what he might have done. If, for example, she had left Gillespie with him, the situation might have been totally different.

It was Gillespie's voice she heard from inside the hall.

"I say we get kebabs in. There's a place up the road in Metheringham. I haven't eaten a bloody thing all day."

"Some people haven't eaten, slept, drank, or stopped crying all day, DS Gillespie," Freya said, as she entered the hall and found him sitting with his feet up on a foldaway table alongside Ben, DC Denise Chapman, and DC Anna Nillson. "So I suggest we demonstrate a little compassion, empathy, and understanding. We're here to help, not bitch about the consequences of our jobs."

"Aye, boss. I was just saying–"

"You were just announcing your thoughts to the rest of the village is what you were doing, Gillespie. You can be heard from across the street," Freya snapped, shutting the loudmouthed DS up for good. "Chapman, Nillson, what are you doing here?"

"Finding Abigail McGowan, ma'am," Chapman said. "It was the end of the shift and we thought, well, instead of going home, we'd come and help."

"Especially as there are two cases now," Nillson added. "It's all hands on deck as far as we can see."

"Good," Freya said, after a moment of consideration. "Very commendable. We'll need coffee–"

"Mrs Finch has given us access to the kettle and she even left us some wee sachets of coffee," Gillespie added. He shook one of the sachets at her, hoping to entice her and win some favour. "She's alright, she is. Even left us some biscuits. Bourbons. Not as good as custard creams but better than digestives."

"That's not coffee as I understand it, Gillespie. You know me. I want a flat white, and I want it piping hot. Who's hungry?"

"Aye, well, now you're talking." Gillespie rubbed his hands together and a broad smile crinkled his weathered face.

"Consider yourself in charge of food and beverages," Freya said. "Find out what everyone wants then go and get it. Personally, I don't care what I eat, as long as it's not fried and as long as I have coffee to wash it down with. We're in for a long night."

CHAPTER SIXTEEN

A FEW MORE COLLAPSIBLE TABLES WERE CARRIED IN BY CRUZ from the little storeroom in the village hall, and both Chapman and Nillson claimed one between them. They set up their laptops and connected to the internet via hot spots from their phones.

Meanwhile, Ben had taken some of the paper from the photocopier tray, and in lieu of the white board they would have used back in the incident room, he began drawing out what they knew. It wasn't much. On the first piece of paper, he'd written the name *Abigail McGowan* in the centre with a line connecting it to *Terry McGowan*. In brackets, he added *widowed*. Another line connected Abigail McGowan to Jess Henry, and along the line itself, he wrote *friend*.

"Ex-friend," Freya added from over his shoulder. He made the change, adding an *ex* as a prefix. "Good. Now add Peter Jones and connect him to Abigail and Jess."

As instructed, Ben wrote the name, and then connected them to form a triangle. He craned his neck to look up at her.

"Is that right?"

She nodded. "Peter and Abigail used to date, but when Abigail went to uni, Jess..."

"Dirty cow," Ben said, shaking his head. He even heard himself tutting, as his father often did. "Who else do we have?"

"Is this Abigail McGowan we're talking about?" Chapman asked from behind her makeshift desk.

"Yes, I'm just trying to map out her network."

"She has an uncle somewhere. On her mother's side." She flicked through a few sheets of paper. "Jason. Jason King."

"Mr McGowan mentioned him," Freya said. "You'll find he's currently under Her Majesty's pleasure. Find out what for."

"Is that all we've got?" Ben asked.

"She's quite a private person, and not very sociable by the sounds of things. She liked to keep healthy, and when she came home from uni, she would spend time with her dad," Freya said, slipping DC Gold's notes onto the table. "Sounds like the perfect daughter, doesn't it?"

"We've all seen what the perfect daughter is capable of," Ben said, referring to a previous case in which a young girl seemed to lead two lives.

"Where is Jackie anyway?" Chapman asked. "Is she still with Mr McGowan?"

"I sent her home," Freya said. "Charlie needs her. She made a good point earlier, and I think we retain any favours where we can."

"What do you mean?" Ben asked. "What did she say?"

"If we don't find Abigail out here tonight, or tomorrow, we'll be looking at an abduction case. If that happens, we'll be busier than ever."

Nodding, Ben drew a line beneath Abigail McGowan's name.

"Anything else for the McGowan case?" Freya asked.

"Headlights," Ben said, adding the word *Headlights* to the sheet, aligned with the name Trevor.

"Trevor?" Freya said, as if questioning his writing. "Is that it? No last name?"

Ben shook his head. He'd clearly had words with the young DC.

"No wonder he's still out there," Freya said. "I wonder if we should bring him in. How long has he been at it?"

Checking his watch, Ben did a rough calculation in his head. "Three hours. Give or take."

"Let's get him back here to warm up and debrief us," Freya said. "Anna, would you give Cruz a call please? Uniform can fetch him."

"Ma'am," Nillson said, reaching for her phone.

"Right then," Ben said, grabbing a fresh piece of paper and setting Abigail's sheet to one side. "Unknown." He wrote the word in the centre of the sheet, and with nothing else to add, he added a full stop. "Anything at all?"

"Not until pathology get to see her," Freya said.

"I'm hoping they work an overnight shift. If the two are linked, which, I mean, it's highly likely..."

Nodding her agreement, Freya chewed on her bottom lip, something Ben had seen her do only when she was on the cusp of an idea.

"We need every second we can get," she said, lowering her voice in case one of the community search teams returned. "I think we all know Abigail isn't out there anymore."

Both Chapman and Nillson stopped working and looked up at her.

"Agreed," Ben said, though it pained him to say it. "If we don't presume the worst, we'll be hit with some sort of negligence claim. The media will have a field day."

"Talking of the media, I'm surprised we haven't seen anybody yet."

"They're too busy writing stories about which school built the biggest snowman and how the snow has stopped the trains. It won't be long though. The minute we upset one of the villagers, they'll be on to the papers about it. Then we'll have to go public. As soon as we do that, if Abigail *has* been abducted, the culprit will go to ground."

Freya pulled a grave expression. She locked stares with Ben and chewed her lower lip again.

"What have you done, Freya?"

"I might have accidentally rubbed Mrs Finch up the wrong way."

"What? How?"

"It's her fault that half the village are out there. She went against my direct advice."

"So what? You had a go at her?"

"Well, not exactly. But I did put the responsibility on her. She may have taken offence to it."

Ben sighed and leaned back in his chair, tossing his pen onto the table, where it rolled and came to stop beside the only word on the sheet of paper. *Unknown.*

"Now I know why she was keen to give us this place," Ben said. "She wants to be seen to be doing all she can to help the effort, while we're doing whatever we can to hinder it. You're going to have to give a statement. If she goes to the papers, we'll have Lincolnshire Today on the doorstep, and we're not really in a position to get them off the property. We're sitting ducks here."

"I'll deal with it," Freya said. "I'll go and see her. What else do we have?"

"Neil Gutteridge. He's the key holder for the hospital. We're going to his house in the morning to collect the plans. He also has a maintenance schedule. Some contractors have been in recently. Might be worth following up on."

"Anything else?"

"No. I'm hoping that by the time we're done with him, pathology will be in a position to give us a preliminary report on our unknown. Ideally, we need an ID. Once we have an ID, we can inform the next of kin, and Chapman and Nillson can see if there's a link to Abigail McGowan. It's a bit hit and miss, but we are where we are. This is day one of a murder investigation and day two of a missing persons investigation. Someone out there knows something. It's just a matter of time before we get a break."

"Can you talk to forensics to see if they found anything of use?" Freya asked.

"Erm, yeah," Ben said, feeling his face redden. "Anna? Do you want to give Michaela a call?"

"Oh really?" Freya said. "I thought you'd be all over that?"

"Ah, you know. Anna knows her well enough."

"Right," Freya said suspiciously, but she was professional enough not to push for answers in front of the team. "Meanwhile, the snow is showing no signs of stopping."

"Forecast says it'll be heavy snow all day tomorrow," Chapman said. "Heaviest February snowfall since nineteen fifty-four, apparently."

"Oh joy," Freya said. "What else could possibly go wrong?"

"He's back," came a loud and obnoxious voice from the doorway.

"Oh God," Freya muttered, and rubbed at her temple.

Gillespie stepped into the hall carrying what looked like enough food for the entire community search team. He kicked the door closed with the heel of his foot.

"Had to drive bloody miles for this lot," he said, dumping the bags onto Chapman's table, who, as the entire team knew, valued space and tidiness more than anybody. She nudged it all away, defending her area with a look of utter disgust. "Did you know, the nearest Maccy Dees is all the way up by Sleaford?"

"There's two in Lincoln. Why didn't you go there?" Anna said.

"Oh yeah right, and fight my way through the evening traffic. It always amazes me how people drive in this weather. It's a wonder I didn't see half a dozen cars upside down in the dykes."

Freya blushed and glanced at Ben. He gave her a quick shake of his head to indicate he hadn't said a word.

"Anyway," Gillespie continued, "Ben, you've got a triple McWhatsitcalled. With cheese, I might add. Anna, Denise, you're down for the McChicken sandwiches. And, boss, I got you a salad. Get stuck in, guys."

"What did you get?" Chapman asked.

"Me?" he said, as if he had been waiting for somebody to ask. "What did I get?"

Chapman smiled and nodded, refraining from encouraging him by laughing.

"I got myself the best thing ever to come out of the golden arches, Denise."

It was typical of Gillespie to leave people hanging. He waited for somebody to ask.

"Go on," Chapman prompted him. "What did you get?"

He grinned, delighted with himself, and reached into a little bag separate from the rest. "A McFlurry."

"A what?" Freya said.

"It's ice cream," Ben explained, shaking his head in disbelief.

"I know what a bloody McFlurry is," Freya said. "The question is, why on earth would anybody in their right mind want an ice cream when it's minus two degrees outside and there's more snow, according to Chapman, than any February since nineteen fifty-two."

"Fifty-four, ma'am," Chapman corrected her, then blushed and sank back in her seat following Freya's glare.

"It's amazing is why," Gillespie said, in a voice that could have been ripped right from the trailer of a Hollywood blockbuster. "Sweet and creamy ice cream, delicate flakes of chocolate, all covered in a sticky, sweet sauce." He took a spoonful and smacked his lips. "Mmm, mmm. Got myself a double quarter pounder meal for dessert too."

Freya stared at him and Ben watched her, waiting for the

explosion. It would be a gentle rumble at first, and depending on how Gillespie responded, the aftermath would either be fast and furious, like a scatter bomb, or it would be a single, catastrophic, devastating blow.

"What?" Gillespie said, when he saw Freya's incredulous glare. She said nothing.

"It's just ice cream," he said, shrugging the attention off.

She leaned toward him, her fingers splayed on the desk supporting her weight, knuckles white with rage and her unwavering stare penetrating him.

He held the little cup out. "Do you want some, boss?"

She shook her head, slowly, almost imperceptible. It would be the latter of the two explosions. A single catastrophic and devastating blow.

"A salad?" she said, so quietly that Ben barely heard her.

"Aye," Gillespie said, and he fished it from the brown paper bag for her. "There's a fork in here somewhere too."

Suddenly Ben felt guilty holding his burger, and he set it down on the open wrapper. He glanced across at Anna and Chapman who each did the same.

"A salad, Gillespie?" she said, a little more forcefully, just as the whine of an approaching missile might grow louder as it grew nearer.

"Aye," Gillespie said. "You said you'd eat anything as long as it wasn't fried. It's not fried, boss."

"I've been on my feet, freezing my bloody arse off all day, and we very likely have an all-nighter in front of us, and you expect me to live off a bloody salad?" She scooped it, opened the lid, and tipped the contents onto the desk. There were a few loosely cut tomatoes which were far floppier than Ben knew tomatoes to be, and a handful of soggy lettuce leaves. It wasn't even a nice herb lettuce like Romanian. It was the boring iceberg stuff that Ben's dad grew on his farm and sold by the truckload to supermarkets.

"It's not fried," Gillespie said again. Then his eyes lit up as if he'd just remembered something. He reached for another bag and produced a takeaway cup with a familiar green lid. "Ah! I did get you a flat white though. Stopped at Starbucks especially." He slid the cup across the table, clearly not willing to reach out, which would have been akin to putting his hand into a woodchipper.

Freya gazed down at the cup. With one hand, she flicked the lid off, peered at the contents inquisitively, then took a sip.

"What do you think?" Gillespie said, and that infectious smile of his returned.

"What do I think?" she asked.

"Aye," he squeaked, and glanced at Ben for support.

"It's a latte."

"A what?"

"A latte, Gillespie."

"No," he said in disbelief. "No, that's not right."

"Are you calling me a liar now?"

"No, but..." He searched the bag, perhaps expecting to find an answer inside. He withdrew the receipt, stared at it, and then at Freya.

"Well?" she said.

"Aye, it's a latte," he said, defeated.

Reaching across the table, Freya scooped up the soggy lettuce, and tomato, and dumped it all unceremoniously back into the plastic container. Then she placed it neatly on the desk before her. Reaching across to the remaining paper bags, from inside one, she pulled out what Gillespie had referred to as dessert – a double quarter pounder with fries – and she placed them on the desk beside the soggy salad. She then took the McFlurry from Gillespie's hand, to which he offered no resistance. She wiped the spoon with one of the tissues from the bags, and then put the salad container into Gillespie's hand, which he accepted in complete silence.

She took a spoonful of the ice cream and watched as Gillespie peered down at the salad and then back at Freya in horror.

"There's a fork in there somewhere," she said, licking the ice cream from the plastic spoon, then winked at him and put on, what Ben considered to be, quite a good take on Gillespie's thick Glaswegian accent. "Get stuck in."

CHAPTER SEVENTEEN

F REYA HAD FINISHED HER DOUBLE QUARTER POUNDER AND WAS
leaning back in her chair, picking at Gillespie's fries, when the
first of the community search team arrived back. It was the man
who had first spoken when Freya had addressed them all in the
car park, and he stumbled across to the wall-mounted heater,
laying his hands out flat to warm them through. His hood and
shoulders were covered in snow, and he left large, wet footprints
on the floor. In just a few seconds, a pool of water was gathering
by his feet as the ice on his clothes melted in the warmth.

He glared at the bags of takeaway, then at Freya and the team.

"Gillespie, get that kettle on," Freya said. Then she addressed
the man, "We're just grabbing a bite. Do you want to join us?"

Slowly, he peeled off his hood, then his gloves, and finally he
pulled the beanie hat from his head. The parts of his face that had
been exposed were bright red, and he took a moment to savour
the heat.

"Tea or coffee, fella?" Gillespie called from the far side of the
room.

The look of disappointment on the man's face was so severe
that Chapman waited for the man to look away, then deposited

the remains of her fries in one of the brown paper bags, wiped her hands on a tissue, then got her head back down into her laptop.

"Coffee," the man replied eventually.

"Sugar?"

He shook his head.

"Milk?" Gillespie asked, oblivious to how bad they all looked by eating takeaway while half the village were out in the cold searching for Abigail.

He nodded, but clearly wasn't happy.

Car headlights swung into the car park, washing light across the windows. The engine stopped and Freya heard car doors closing and voices, one of which was shrill and authoritarian.

In a flash, Freya pulled at the empty bags, scrunched them all together, and dropped them into a wastepaper bin that Ben held up. He dropped the bin to the floor and kicked it to one side just as Mrs Finch entered, holding the door open so that a cold breeze blew through the room, and all the heat the team had been enjoying was replaced with icy, damp air. Mr Finch followed, carrying what Freya thought to be the largest pot she had ever seen. It was the stainless steel type that caterers use at events.

He carried it to the table that Chapman was using and, with an almighty sigh, set it down. An irritated expression appeared on Chapman's face, and she shifted up a little closer to Anna.

The door slammed closed and Mrs Finch inhaled the air, the way a schoolteacher might catch a whiff of a student's lunchtime cigarette. She glared at each of the team, then at the wastepaper bin.

"Been having a party, I see," she said.

"Just a quick snack before we head out again," Ben said, thinking fast.

"How did you get on?" she asked.

Ben shook his head dejectedly.

"I'm just making teas and coffees," Gillespie announced, and

Freya realised he hadn't been around when they had discussed Mrs Finch. "Can I get you anything?"

Offering him no response at all, Mrs Finch began barking orders at her husband.

"Let's have two more tables, and can you get the plastic bowls and spoons from the car? We'll set it all up here, so that when everybody returns, we can offer them something nice and warm to eat. God knows, they deserve it."

At any other time, Freya might have interjected. She might have reminded the lady that the team were using the space to investigate a crime. She might have also reminded her that some of their discussions and paperwork would be confidential. She glanced down at the two sheets of paper that Ben had written on, and deduced that, to the untrained eye, their efforts appeared to be akin to that of a schoolchild's history homework who had found a video game far more engaging.

One by one, the community search team returned. Ben took a call on his phone and walked to the far end of the hall, holding his finger in his free ear to focus on what was being said.

As much as Mrs Finch had irritated the hell out of Freya, she had to admit that whatever was in the huge pot smelled delicious, and if she had known it was coming, she would have refrained from stealing Gillespie's burger and chips, and ice cream.

"I see you've all eaten already," Mrs Finch said. "So we'll keep this for the workers, if that's okay with you?"

"Actually, I haven't eaten," Gillespie said, as he handed the man his coffee. "And boy does that smell good."

"You haven't eaten?" Mrs Finch asked, looking confused.

"Aye, well, I went and got everyone burger and chips, but I gave mine to the boss. You know? Been on her feet all day, out there in the cold and all that. We've got a long night ahead of us. Need to keep the boss in good shape, eh?"

Freya shook her head in disbelief. Not only was he the only one who wasn't bloated from the McDonald's, but because he had been and got them, he was the only one of the team still wearing his jacket. Freya could even see the dark patches on his shoulders from where the snow had collected.

"Well then, I guess we'll make an exception for you," Mrs Finch said, and she deftly scooped up one of the plastic bowls from the pile and ladled some of the hotpot into it. She handed it to him with the same care and attention as she had shown the villagers.

Smug and content, Gillespie settled into Ben's empty chair.

"Aye, this is more like it," he said, his broad smile seeming to stretch his entire face like it was made from plasticine. "Did you make this, Mrs Finch?"

"Yes. As soon as I had opened up the hall for you lot to work from." She glanced at the two sheets of paper. "If that's what you've been doing."

"It's proper," Gillespie said. "Just like my grandma would have made. If I had one, that is."

"You didn't have a grandma?" Mrs Finch asked, as she handed one of the new arrivals a bowl with a curt smile.

"Well, maybe. I didn't meet her though. My parents weren't really ready for kids. Sent me off to a home when I was a wee nipper."

"Oh, that's awful."

"Not really," Gillespie said, shrugging the hardship off. "I like to call it character building. Made me who I am today."

"For better or worse," Freya uttered under her breath, a little louder than she had been aiming for.

"Well, if it counts, we're grateful to have you here. The more people we have actually out there looking for poor Abigail, the faster we'll find her."

It was at that moment that Ben whistled from the far end of the room and waved for Freya to join him.

"Do excuse me," she said. "I'll leave you humanitarians to fix the world while DS Savage and I do some police work. That okay with you, Gillespie?"

"Aye, boss," he replied, then burned his mouth on a spoonful of the hotpot. He searched for a drink to cool his mouth down and reached for Freya's latte. But she whisked it from the desk just before he could grab it, and she left him behind, waving air into his mouth and panting like a dog on a summer's day.

With the phone to his ear, Ben shook his head as she approached. He put his hand over the microphone and nodded for her to come closer. It was only when they were just inches apart that with one eye on the feasting searchers, he delivered the bad news.

"Forensics strategy is complete. They've been through the entire area. They've got lights, generators, and three dogs. Haven't found a bloody thing."

"Is that Michaela?" Freya asked, gesturing at the phone.

"No, it's her colleague. Michaela has gone home, wasn't feeling great or something."

Freya rolled her eyes.

"So if she's not in the immediate area, and the community search haven't found anything," she surmised, "then we're left with only one real option."

Ben nodded, and she left him to finish his call, turning to face the growing team.

"Are we all back?" Freya asked Mr Finch, who had been so dili-gent earlier with providing maps and a register. She approached him, and he glanced nervously at his wife who was spooning hotpots.

"All but three. But I've spoken to them. They've stopped at the pub for a bite."

"Has anybody found anything?"

"Not a sausage," he replied.

"What's this?" Mrs Finch asked, seeing Freya talking to her husband. She handed the last of the hotpots to a young woman whose hands were somewhere inside the arms of her winter coat and ventured over to Freya and her husband like some kind of jealous wife. "What's going on?"

"I was just asking if anybody had found anything."

"Well, if they had, they would have said, surely?"

"I was just checking before we make any assumptions."

"And what assumptions might they be?" Mrs Finch asked.

Freya inhaled a lungful of air. In her mind, her response was bitter and delivered a few homes truths about her real opinion on Mrs Finch and where she could put her bloody ladle. But the reality was she needed her onside, and Freya had already done enough damage.

"We have to consider that she might not be out there," Freya said, loud enough for her team to hear. Chapman, Anna, and Gillespie all looked up, Gillespie with a dribble of hotpot on his chin. "Mr Finch, I'm going to need the names of everyone on your register."

"Why?" Mrs Finch asked, her tone indignant.

"Because, statistically, crimes are committed by someone the victim knows," said Freya, putting her back in her box. "I'll start with Peter Jones. Where is he?"

CHAPTER EIGHTEEN

"Is every pub in Lincolnshire called the Red Lion?" Freya asked, when Ben pulled into the village pub. "Can't they come up with something a little more creative?"

"It's four hundred years old," Ben replied. "What do you expect them to do? Change the name just because there's another pub with the same name half an hour away?"

"It was just an observation, Ben. No need for petulance."

"It's also the most common pub name in Britain," Cruz said from the backseat. Ben watched as he glanced across at Larson in the hope that he might have impressed her with his general knowledge. But clearly spending the day with Cruz had been enough for her, and she gazed out of the window, politely ignoring him. "What are we doing here anyway?"

"Word has it that Peter Jones, Abigail McGowan's ex-boyfriend, has stopped off here for a bite," Freya said. "I'd like to have a word with him. See if he can tell us a bit about Abigail's last week. Plus, seeing as you two missed out on dinner, if you can call it that, I figured you might want to get some food."

"Food?" Cruz said. "Here?"

"Is there something wrong with the establishment?" Freya

asked.

"Well, no. But normally we'd get a sandwich or something and have to make do. I'm not complaining."

"Good. Because it's either this or a homemade hotpot."

"Homemade hotpot?" Cruz blurted out.

"Are you going to repeat everything I say, DC Cruz? Or can I have some time to actually do some thinking? Seeing as I spend half my life thinking for you as well."

Cruz silenced, and the mood in the car was as frosty as the ice that had yet to melt on Ben's car bonnet.

"If you want pub grub," Ben added, hoping to lighten the mood, "you're in the right place. I recommend the homemade pie. The gravy is the best you'll get anywhere. I promise you that."

Again, Ben watched Cruz turn to the uniform he had taken under his wing.

"What do you fancy? Hotpot or pub grub?"

The poor girl looked mortified. She stared at Ben in the rear-view mirror. "Are you two eating with us?"

"No, we'll be talking to Peter Jones. We'll leave you guys here to eat in peace. They should have the fire on too so you can warm up a bit, then take a walk down to the village hall."

"Village hall? What's in there?" Cruz asked.

"DC Chapman, DC Nillson, and DS Gillespie," Freya replied. "Any more questions? Or perhaps you'd like us to drop you off at an Italian or something?"

Cruz continued to gaze at Larson, his eyebrows raised in question. "Fancy it?"

If she had meant to hide the sigh that she emitted, then she did a very poor job of it. "Okay, okay," she said, and pushed open the rear door.

Cruz could barely contain himself as he climbed out of the car and led his colleague into the pub. Ben sat watching with more than mild amusement.

"That should make up for spending a day in the cold," Ben

said.

"That poor girl," Freya remarked. "First of all she has to follow him around, listening to him spout random facts about God knows what, then she's forced to eat dinner with him."

"Ah, he's not that bad. He just gets excited, that's all. We were young once."

"When I was his age, I wasn't still living with Mum, Ben. In fact, when I was his age, I'm pretty sure I had my life all mapped out."

"Oh yeah?" Ben replied, opening his door and bracing himself for the cold. He climbed out and waited for her to do the same so he could insult her across the roof of the car, as had become the standard practice. "How did that work out for you?"

"I may have deviated," she said, closing her door. "But I'd say I've done pretty well."

"Tell me about this plan. What was it you had mapped out?" Ben asked. "Kids? House? Mortgage-free? Independence?"

"I am mortgage-free," she said.

"Don't take this the wrong way, Freya. You've just signed your divorce papers, only two months ago you said goodbye to the child that wasn't actually yours, and you rent my dad's old farm-worker's cottage."

"I'm independent," she argued, seeing through Ben's harsh truth to find some kind of positive note.

"This morning, you crashed your car into a stationary dyke on a road so straight the Romans could have built it. In fact, I think they actually did build it. How are you getting home?"

She stared at him, either angry or upset, but clearly running out of valid arguments.

"I'm the senior ranking police officer in a murder investigation," she said. "I'll get a driver if I have to."

"Murder investigation?" a voice said, and they both turned to find a young lad, maybe twenty years old, standing outside the pub about to light a cigarette.

"Peter?" Freya said, peering at him in the darkness. "Peter Jones? Is that you?"

He hadn't lit his cigarette yet. He was dumbstruck by what he'd overheard and was glued to the spot.

"You said it was a murder investigation. Have you found her?"

"Oh, don't take any notice of what I said," Freya explained. "How did you get on today?"

He shrugged and shook his head, which Freya was fast learning to be the local standard for a negative response.

"You didn't find anything on your search?" Freya asked, hoping to get him to actually say the words.

He shook his head, but stared at her with what Ben could only describe as a hatred in his eyes.

"What area were you assigned?" Ben asked. "Am I right that Mr Finch assigned each team an area?"

"Top of the forest," Peter said. "Where it meets the farm road."

"That's on Abigail's route, isn't it?"

He nodded. Even in the dim light, with snow settling on his neatly groomed side parting, Ben could see that he was what a young girl might deem as a good-looking bloke. He was clearly fit and trim, and his cold-weather jacket was North Face. He took care of himself and cared for his appearance.

"You used to date her, didn't you?" Freya asked, and he stiffened at the question. "It's okay. I was just wondering if you might be able to help us a little."

"How? We're not together anymore."

"But you used to be. I was wondering if maybe she ever deviated from the route her father showed us. Maybe she had another route she liked to run occasionally?"

"No. She wouldn't. Not without his say so."

"Is he strict then? He seems like a nice man, but being police officers, people aren't always as they seem. Do you know what I mean, Peter? People don't always show their true colours."

"He's okay. But yeah, he's strict. She has to be home early, and I was never allowed…"

He stopped, as if he might have said too much.

"Peter?" Freya said, hoping to coax him into finishing his sentence.

He puffed out his cheeks and checked behind him to make sure nobody could hear. "I was never allowed to stay over. You know? When we were together. Made things a bit awkward."

"Right," Ben said, seeing where he was going. "So you had to get creative?"

"Kind of. She'd sneak out sometimes. Not often. But sometimes. It all got a bit much in the end. She wanted to go serious."

The words resonated with Ben. It was like he was staring at himself ten years earlier. The only difference was that Ben had never given a hoot for branded clothing. At that age, he had worn the same few shirts and the same few pairs of jeans. He rarely wore trainers, as the land around his dad's farmhouse back then had been mud, mud, and more mud. To finish off the look, not a single comb ever touched Ben's head until every second month, when he would be dragged to the kitchen along with his brothers for his father to take a few wild snips at his hair with the kitchen scissors.

"And you didn't want that?" Ben asked.

"I loved her," he said, defending his morals. "We got on well, and all that. But I don't know… When she went away to uni, it gave me time to think about what I really want."

"And it wasn't to settle down and have kids?" Ben said.

He nodded. "Not yet, right. I mean, maybe one day."

"It's okay," Ben said. "I hear you."

"And you don't think Abigail would have deviated from the route?"

He shook his head. "Not a chance. Since her mum died, they got really close. He's a bit overprotective, I think. But what do I know? I'd probably be the same."

"Do they argue, Peter?" Freya asked. "Abigail and her father? You said they were close, but is that just to appease her overbearing father?"

He smiled, as if he was remembering a time, and then nodded. "They only argue if Abigail doesn't do as she's told. If she toes the line, then he's probably the best dad you could ask for."

"Pete?" a voice called from inside the pub. A young girl in her early twenties emerged from the pub, wrapping her arms around herself to keep warm, despite wearing a tiny, little dress that showed more of her chest than it suggested and left very little to the imagination. "You said you're buying me a drink? I told you not to leave me on my own."

"I'm coming," he said, and he backed away, pocketing the cigarette in his breast pocket. "You haven't found her yet, have you?" he asked before he turned. It was a question that required no reply. He blinked once, adopting a sad expression, and took a deep breath.

"Peter?" the girl hissed. She had stepped back inside and was glaring at Freya, pulling her dress down to cover herself.

The young couple slipped back inside, and Freya, too, puffed out her cheeks, exhaling a cloud of breath that seemed endless. She let her head fall back and watched the vapour disperse.

"She's a handful," Ben said, watching the young woman prance beside Peter back into the saloon bar, her hand smoothing her dress over her backside. She looked back and caught him staring, then smiled slyly before disappearing out of sight.

"That's Jess Henry," Freya said. "She was Abigail's best friend once."

"Oh, I see," Ben said, and a few pieces of a very blurred jigsaw fell into place. "And he's Abigail's ex-boyfriend."

"Formidable couple, don't you think?" Freya said, and her expression told Ben they had earned themselves a very warm spot on Freya's very short hitlist.

CHAPTER NINETEEN

THEY HAD BEEN BACK AT THE VILLAGE HALL FOR NEARLY AN hour when Gillespie gave a snore and woke himself up.

Chapman stopped typing. Anna stopped flicking through her files. Ben lowered his phone. And Freya, who had been staring at those two absolutely pointless sheets of paper, opened her mouth, speechless.

"Sorry," Gillespie said, clearing his throat and sitting up in his seat. He exhaled loudly and rubbed at his eyes. "Drifted off there."

Something deep inside Freya wanted to bark at him, to vent all her frustrations in wild fury, to belittle him, to verbally pull his pants down and spank him like a small child in a supermarket.

But she couldn't do it. She gazed around at the team and saw that same gaunt, exhausted expression on all their faces.

"Ben, who's on the gates at the hospital?"

"I spoke to Sergeant Priest. He's got some shifts worked out, but he can't hold it for much longer. I reckon midday tomorrow, he'll want to pull them off."

"Shall we call it a night then?" Freya proposed. "Tomorrow's going to be even harder."

The community search team had all dispersed, and to Freya's surprise, Mrs Finch had entrusted the keys to the hall to Chapman. It might have been a different story had Freya still been in the hall when the locals had left.

"I won't lie," Ben said, "I feel like I'm flogging a dead horse here. Until we hear from pathology, we've got nothing to go on."

"We do have the register of people who joined the community search," Freya said.

"So? They're all villagers. They're all helping."

"Believe me," Freya said, "it wouldn't be the first time an abductor or, dare I say it, a killer joined the hunt knowing full well the missing person isn't there."

"I second that," Gillespie said. "Saw it on a documentary. That fella that killed that little girl–"

"That narrows it down," Ben said.

"You know who I mean. Was all over the papers. He was the caretaker at the girl's school or something."

"Are you referring to the Soham murders, Gillespie?" Freya asked. "Ian Huntley."

"Aye, boss. That's it. Shocking, it was. The fella even joined in on a press conference, spurting some bull about how he just wants to help get her home safe."

"It was two girls, as I recall," Freya added. "But you're right, surprisingly. And that's exactly why I want everyone on the search register cross-referenced with the database. Chapman, this looks like something for you. Check the sex offenders register and check for criminal records. Flag anything. We're short on leads here."

"Ma'am," Chapman replied, never one to question Freya's requests, and always one to be pleased with a research project.

Just then, there was laughter from outside, female, loud, and... No. It couldn't be.

The door burst open and there was a flash of a bright green police jacket as Larson stepped into the room, followed closely by

Cruz. Their smiles faded as they saw the whole team staring at them.

"Did you have a good time, kids?" Gillespie said, seizing the opportunity to belittle Cruz in front of the way-out-of-his-league PCSO Larson. "I thought I told you to be home before it got dark. You wait until your father hears about this."

"Leave off, Jim," Cruz said, and Larson gave him an appreciative look. Moving to the wall heater, Cruz laid his hands flat against it. "It's bloody freezing out there."

There was something different about Larson that only became clear when she removed the black, woolly hat she was wearing and returned it to Cruz with a nod of thanks.

"We're going to call it a night," Freya said. "Larson, thanks for your help today. I'll make sure Sergeant Priest hears about it."

"Thank you, ma'am," she replied. Then she flapped her arms against her sides, as if to say, 'Well, so long.'

"Do you need a ride home?" Ben asked. "I can drop you at the station."

"We're going to need a ride too," Chapman said. "My car's at the station."

"Yeah, mine too," Nillson added.

"Cruz?" Ben asked.

"I don't have one," he said, and his face reddened with embarrassment.

"Eh?" Gillespie said, seizing another opportunity to ridicule the poor boy. "You do have a driving license though, right?"

"Yeah, course. I just, erm... well, I haven't got around to buying one."

"How do you get about then?" Freya asked. "Especially here. I mean, Lincolnshire isn't exactly densely populated, is it?"

"No, it's one of the least densely populated counties in the United Kingdom," Cruz remarked, spurting off another random fact before he had actually considered the consequences.

"Right," Gillespie said. "What do you have? A pushbike or something?"

"No," Cruz said, pulling a face.

"Skateboard?"

"I use my mum's car," he explained, then turned to Larson, who, to her credit, didn't seem in the least bit fazed by the prospect. "When she's not using it. Saves me money."

"I see," Gillespie said. "I suppose she makes you a packed lunch as well, aye?"

"Come on, it's been a long day," Freya said. "So what do we have, two cars?"

"Where's *your* car, boss?" Gillespie asked, and Ben lowered his face to conceal the smile that was spreading across his face like a wildfire.

"I told you, it's in the garage."

"Aye, but it's a rental, right?"

"Yes. It still has to be maintained. It's not a magic car."

"Right. But don't they give you a replacement?"

"Why are you so interested in my car all of a sudden?" she asked, glaring at Ben.

"I'm not. I was just wondering is all. Just looking out for you, boss. These roads can be treacherous in this weather. Especially for you London folk. You're not used to the country lanes."

"I can drive perfectly fine, thank you, Gillespie," Freya said. "I'll ride with Ben. We'll take Cruz and Larson, if you'd take Nillson and Chapman?"

"Aye, not a problem for me. I'm going home to my cold and empty house with my cold and empty fridge."

"With your cold and empty heart?" Cruz offered, and Larson laughed out loud, snorting accidentally.

"Aye," Gillespie replied. "Something like that."

"Well, at least you don't have a cold and empty stomach," Freya said, and she peered into the pot, then looked up at Ben. "Are you thinking what I'm thinking?"

"What? We take that home and demolish it?" Ben asked, nodding. "I'm game."

"I meant, we put the rest into bowls and take it up to the gates. Might help keep uniform awake. They're probably cursing us right now."

"I guess that's the decent thing to do," Ben said, and he stood to help her spoon it into the plastic bowls.

Gillespie looked on, watching their every move.

Freya didn't have to say anything. She looked at him questioningly.

"I was just wondering," he began, and glanced at the bowls. "You know?"

"Oh, you mean you were wondering if there will be enough for you to take home to your cold and empty house?" Freya asked.

"Well, aye, if there's any left, like."

"Let's see. Do we take the food from our cold and hungry colleagues standing out there in the dark on their own? Or do we feed the lazy Detective Sergeant who honestly thought that I would be happy with a few soggy pieces of lettuce and half a bloody tomato for dinner?"

"Ah, well, you don't have to be like that—"

"Ben? Thoughts?"

"I'm pretty sure they'll be hungry up there. And after all, it is the right thing to do," Ben said, spooning another ladle into a bowl.

"Right, let's count them," Freya said. "There's two bowls each for the uniforms, which leaves four bowls left over."

Gillespie was almost salivating at the sight of the hotpot, even with the skin that had formed since it had cooled.

"I might take one for myself," Freya said.

Nodding, Ben agreed. "Yeah, I'll take one. Chapman? Nillson?"

"It would save me cooking," Chapman said, seizing the chance for efficiency.

"I'll eat it in the car, so I can flop into bed," Anna said. "Keiran will have to make his own dinner tonight. I am bagged."

"Did you want to take some?" Freya asked Cruz and Larson.

"I couldn't eat a thing, boss," Cruz said. "I had the homemade pie in the pub. I'm stuffed."

"And you had half of mine," Larson added, at which Cruz grinned like a schoolboy.

"So that just leaves..." Freya began, and looked into the pot. "Ah, it's all gone."

"All of it?" Gillespie said dejectedly.

She banged the ladle against the empty pot to get the remains of the hotpot off it, and then tipped it up for him to see.

"Want to lick the bowl?" she asked, but Gillespie shook his head, trying his best not to look annoyed. "Seeing as you have the keys, Chapman, we'll leave you lot to lock up. Thank you all for today, and thank you for working late. I'm sorry to say that I might be asking for more of the same tomorrow."

"Aye, well, maybe tomorrow I'll bring in something delicious," Gillespie said. "And maybe I won't share it. See how you like it."

"You mean from your cold and empty fridge?" Ben asked.

"Not from my cold and empty fridge, Ben. Oh no. From the bottom of my very cold and very empty heart."

CHAPTER TWENTY

THE LANE THAT LED FROM NOCTON TO THE HOSPITAL WAS A pitch dark, single-lane track. The headlights of Ben's Ford cast shadows into the forest that seemed to stretch on and on. They passed the old Nocton Hall, according to Cruz anyway. The combination of a moonless sky and severe snowfall meant Freya could barely see a few feet out of the passenger window.

"So what else did you learn today, Cruz?" Freya asked. "I heard about the headlights. Anything else? Did anybody else see the vehicle? Am I to expect a detailed report?"

She had meant to ask him the question earlier, but with the day being as gruelling as it had been, she'd decided on reading his report rather than listening to him explain every detail.

"Report, boss?" he said, as a schoolboy might question his homework. "There's not really much to write."

"So it shouldn't take long then, should it? But it would be good to know which doors you knocked on, who you spoke to, what you asked them, and what their responses were. You never know when you might find a little nugget of information. It all counts."

"Nobody else saw headlights. Only the one bloke. But I think there's something in it. He said that he rounded a bend on the forest road and saw the taillights ahead. But nothing had passed him."

"What does that tell you?" she asked.

"He was parked up," Larson said, then glanced across at Cruz apologetically.

"Go on," Freya said, encouraging her to elaborate a little.

"Maybe he or she had parked there, walked their dog in the forest, and then gone home?"

"They might have been picking berries?" Cruz added.

Freya turned to look at Ben, who was focusing on the road and slowing to a stop.

"Do people pick berries in a blizzard usually? Not being a country girl, I'm not familiar."

Ben applied the handbrake, peered out of the windscreen, then checked his mirrors.

"The only berries to pick in these parts would be sloes or blackberries," Ben said. "They won't be ready until August or September. I imagine there's a few more species. But I doubt anyone would come out and get them in this. Mushrooms, however, now that's a different story."

"You can pick mushrooms here?" Freya asked. "Isn't that dangerous?"

"If you don't know what you're doing, then yeah, of course."

"Is it likely that somebody would come out in the snow to pick them?"

"Depends on how much they want them," Ben replied. "I wouldn't, personally."

She turned to look into the back of the car.

"So it's more than likely a dog walker."

"Or a bird watcher," Cruz said, determined to get a right answer. "They come out in all weather."

Ben nodded his agreement.

"Right," Freya said. "Your job tomorrow is to find out what car it was, who owns it, and what they were doing. That'll keep you both busy."

"Both?" Larson said, sounding surprised. "Am I with you again tomorrow?"

"I'm sure I can swing it with Sergeant Priest if you'd like to work on something a little more interesting."

"Thanks, ma'am," she said.

"Does that mean we're knocking on doors tomorrow?" Cruz asked, his face a picture of despair.

"It means you'll do whatever it takes to find out who owns that vehicle. Personally, I'd talk to CSI to see if they found tyre tracks during their search earlier today."

"Right," Cruz said hopefully.

"And, of course, I'd also go door to door to make sure I've covered all possible angles. See if anybody was out bird spotting or walking their dog."

"Right," Cruz said, a little more dejectedly.

"Is this it?" Freya asked, squinting to see through the snow, which was falling so heavily now that it was settling on the car bonnet before it had time to melt. The old hospital gates were ahead of them, wide open, and the headlights partially lit the dark and empty space beyond.

"There's the car," Ben said, unfastening his seat belt. "If they've got any sense, they'll be sitting inside it. I'll go." He held out his hand to take the McDonald's bag which Freya had used to carry the bowls of hotpot, and then climbed from the car.

Freya, Cruz, and Larson watched him walk up to the police car, tap on the window, and then bend down, wiping the snow from the glass to peer through. He tried the door, which opened, and the light came on inside. He placed the bag in the footwell, then looked around.

"Grub's up," he called. But there was no reply.

Sensing something was amiss, Freya unfastened her seat belt and joined him, pulling her jacket around her.

"Have you lost them?" she asked, treading carefully on the icy road.

"The keys are in the ignition," Ben said, and he felt the bonnet. "Still warm."

"Do you know their names?"

"Priest didn't say. He just told me he'd have it covered. If we left the gates open and the place was vandalised, we'd be opening ourselves up to all sorts."

"Maybe they're walking a patrol."

"It's a big site," Ben said. "And as far as I know, this is the only way in or out."

Just then, there was a shout from somewhere far off. Somewhere beyond the gates. The sound was muffled by the snow, but it was definitely male.

"Did you hear that?" Freya asked.

Ben nodded, closing his eyes to focus.

There it was again.

Ben turned back to the car.

"Cruz? Get out here, mate."

It took a few moments for the young DC to emerge from the car, and he appeared less than happy about it.

"What do you want to do?" Ben asked him. "Stand here and make sure nobody comes through? Or go and look for them?"

"Eh?" he said, liking the sound of neither option. He huffed, and glanced back at the car. But whether that was because he was missing the car heater or if he wanted to stay close to Larson, Ben couldn't tell. "I'll stand guard, if you want."

"Thought you might choose that option," Freya said, as Ben moved back to the car and opened the boot. He produced a couple of torches, checked the batteries, then slammed the lid. "Stay here. If anybody comes, call out."

Intrigued, Larson also climbed from the car to join him.

Freya studied them both for a moment. They were young,

inexperienced, and tired. She was asking a lot of them, but it was times like this that made all the difference.

"Keep the engine running and the headlights on," Ben advised. "We'll be as quick as we can."

"Right," Cruz said, with a little less confidence than he probably hoped.

"Ready?" Ben said, handing Freya a torch. He didn't wait for her; instead, he ploughed on into the old hospital grounds. He didn't look back until they were moving out of the range of the car headlights behind them, when he began to call out. "Hello? Anyone here?"

There was no response, and he turned to find Freya just as she caught up with him. The snow covered her boots and settled in her hair, and the ice had already begun to form on Ben's unshaved face.

"Want to split up?" he asked. It was the one question she knew he was going to ask, and the one question she had been dreading.

"Not really. The last time I was alone in a forest, things didn't work out so well," she said. "I'd prefer not to have a repeat of that incident."

He nodded, and then stepped out of the light, flicking on his torch.

"Hello?" he called, his voice muted by the snow. "Anyone here?"

A branch broke somewhere ahead of them, and before Freya could say anything, Ben was running. His torch light flailed in the dark, stopping only occasionally when he searched the grounds around him.

"Damn you, Ben," she hissed, then ran after him. But after about twenty yards, she was scanning the ground to see where she was treading when there were footsteps in the snow to her left. They were fast, like somebody was running. She shone the beam of light across the trees in front of her, just as a dark shape plunged from the darkness, knocked her to the ground, then ran at full pelt toward the gates.

"You okay?" Ben said, pulling her off the ground.

"Just get after him," she hissed, snatching her arm from his grasp, and then calling out for Cruz and Larson. "Cruz? Coming your way."

The assailant avoided the car headlights, keeping to the shadows as much as he could. Ben's torch light found him twice, but was then lost as he sank back into the trees.

"You okay, ma'am?" a voice said, breathless from running. Freya turned to find a young PCSO coming to a stop beside her. "I saw him run from the trees. I was going to call out but I found Griffiths. It all happened so fast."

"Griffiths?" she said, recognising the name from a case only two months before. "Where is he?"

The officer shook his head. "He's down. Looks like he's been whacked with a branch or something. Bleeding from his head."

"Is he conscious?"

"Yes. But he needs attention."

"Have you radioed for help?"

"I have. They're on their way now. He's over there," the officer said, shining his torch light at a small heap about a hundred metres away. Freya just saw the flash of the fluorescent strip on his jacket. "Shall I go after him?"

"Yes, go," Freya said, making a decision on the spot. "I'll see to Griffiths."

"Righto," he said, and with a final glance back at his colleague, the officer ran towards the light, leaving Freya alone in the darkness.

CHAPTER TWENTY-ONE

IT WAS IMPOSSIBLE TO RUN WHILE KEEPING THE TORCH LIGHT on its target. Twice Ben had found the man, gauging him to be about six foot tall and carrying bulk. Either that or he was wearing thick layers, which was more than probable. He was at the treeline, positive that the man had slipped into the shadows, when there was a scuffle at the gates and both Cruz and Larson called out. One of them then cried out in pain.

Ben darted for the gates, only to find Larson helping Cruz up from the ground. He was rubbing his backside and pulling a face to show he was hurt.

"Which way?" Ben called. Ahead of him, the lane was in pitch darkness. To his left, the forest would take him back toward the manhole where the body was found.

"That way," Larson called, pointing into the forest.

"Bloody would be, wouldn't it?"

He ran on but was forced to slow as low-hanging branches whipped at his face. He shone the light in a full three-hundred-and-sixty-degree circle, slowly, studying anything that even looked remotely like it was moving or man-shaped. There was nothing.

Onward he walked, calming his breathing so he could focus on the noises around him. An owl hooted somewhere to his right, and ahead of him, a few birds fluttered from their roosts, flapping wildly. Pigeons, Ben thought, judging by the racket they were making.

It wasn't long before he came to the stream. Shining his light into the trees ahead of him, he searched for boot prints. But the ground was frozen solid, and no snowfall had broken through the canopy above.

Everything was against them.

He crossed the stream, climbed over a fallen tree, and misjudged his footing. He fell to the ground, cursing, and when he stood, his ankle gave way.

Fighting the urge to curse out loud, he hobbled on, navigating by memory, which, in the dark forest, wasn't as accurate as he'd hoped. But by luck or pure chance, he found what he was looking for – the circular, brick structure buried deep beneath the trees beside the hospital fence.

A few thoughts came to mind when he considered what he might find. Another body. The man he had been chasing. But no. He shone his light onto the rungs, working his way down into the chasm, and all he found was a carpet of old beer cans and plastic bottles.

"Damn it," he hissed to himself.

Dropping down, he sat on the edge of the manhole and rubbed his sore ankle. He could walk it off, but he knew it would one of those injuries that proved to be a pain in the backside until the next day, and even then it might make its presence known should he lose his footing again. The cold was bitter but he pulled a glove off with his teeth, then the other, so he could slip his fingers into his boot to feel for any lumps or bumps. The ankle was swollen already, and he cursed inwardly at the misery the injury would cause him in the near future, not to mention how it would make stumbling back to the car more difficult.

It was there, in the darkness, that Ben was able to channel his energy into Abigail McGowan. The girl was lost. She had been out there somewhere. Maybe she had met somebody. He'd have to see if the tech guys could unlock her phone tomorrow. Maybe there was a message or something. Maybe she had arranged to meet someone? Freya seemed keen on pursuing the Jones lad – Peter, the ex-boyfriend. It would make sense. It had been with a pretty convincing confidence that he had confirmed McGowan's statement, that Abigail wouldn't have ventured off-course. That she would have stayed on the path dictated to her by her dad.

And then there was the father, who until Freya and Ben had spoken to the Jones boy, had seemed quite amenable. But clearly, there was a darker side to him. Or maybe he just had to be strict, given that he'd raised her partly on his own. Under the circumstances, Ben could understand the need to keep his daughter in line. Losing her would mean losing the only memory he had left of his wife.

But still, Ben thought, it takes all sorts.

Somewhere in the forest ahead of him, a twig snapped. It was only slight, but enough to set Ben's senses alight. He killed the torch and pocketed it, then quietly fumbled for his gloves. It seemed as if every breath he took was loud, regardless of how hard he tried to quieten it. In through his nose, out through his mouth, and even then the cloud of breath gave him away.

Another snap of a twig, and this time, a rustle of a jacket. He was close, whoever it was. If he was to leap the stream, Ben would surely hear him. He could wait for the man to climb the bank, and then pounce. He wished he'd taken a radio from the car. It was a bloody stupid idea to go out looking. He should have called for backup. Freya would be going ballistic by now.

She would have to wait.

He watched the stream for a dark shape to move against the black and still forest. But other than the sound of his breathing and the thumping of his heart, there was nothing. He was sure he could hear his pulse. Was that even possible? It had to be, because what was playing in his head sounded like the beat of dance music. The type teenagers played in their cars, so loud they could hardly hear.

Nothing. No dark shapes. No more snapping twigs. If it was indeed the man they were looking for, he had to cross the stream to get to the manhole.

Unless... Ben thought. Unless he doubled back and followed the fence line. It was a route Ben hadn't taken. It had been overgrown when they were there earlier. He swore it had been. He'd looked, hadn't he?

Doubt crept in like a winter fog, and it was all Ben could do to sit there, freezing his extremities off, nursing a sore ankle, and waiting for a man who, for all intents and purposes, was probably a killer, and if not a killer then an abductor. Close enough.

And that was when he heard it.

The rustle of a branch against a winter jacket. It was unmistakable. It was close. Closer than...

Wide-eyed, Ben slowly began to turn, to search along the pitch-black fence line. Beyond were the old hospital grounds. But the fence had been intact. Now that, he was sure of. He had seen the razor wire on top. Whoever was out there wasn't planning on climbing the fence. They were coming to the manhole.

The question was, were they coming to make a deposit, or were they coming for Ben?

As still as can be, Ben watched, and sure enough, from the murky shadows, the figure of a man appeared. Charcoal against the night. A vague shape. Black. There were no colours, no textures, no dimensions. Just black and blacker, with only the manhole between them.

Had he seen Ben?

Surely not?

Ben's breathing had been loud enough. But somehow, there was an uncertainty about the man in the way he moved. He was close enough now that he could overpower Ben and push him down the hole, what with Ben's ankle the way it was.

Ben prepared to launch himself over the manhole at the dark shape, now just a few metres away. It was going to hurt. Ben knew it. He would cry out in agony; it was the only way he would be able to power through it. So he had to make it count. He adjusted his footing on the brickwork, wincing at the pain from just that tiny movement. The man was at the far side of the hole now. Surely he had seen Ben.

But Ben had the advantage of being lower. He wasn't framed against the sky as his assailant was.

It was now or never.

Biting down on his lower lip, Ben dug the sole of his boot into the ground then stood. Taking his entire weight on his injured ankle, and using the low brick wall as a launchpad, he threw himself across the hole, arms outstretched to grab at anything he could – hair, a jacket, a face, if that was what his fingers found.

He cried out, the searing agony sending bright lights across his eyes, and even mid-jump, he knew his damaged ankle had let him down.

His fingers found something and he tensed his hand. But his leap had fallen short. His shins found the low brick wall, and the cold air found fresh blood almost immediately.

But he had him. He had the man's jacket and he wouldn't let go. The man writhed beneath him; he called out, but Ben couldn't fathom his words. His ankle screamed louder and his shins felt like they were on fire. His fingers found the soft skin of a man who didn't shave.

He paused, and the person beneath him exhaled in sharp, frightened bursts.

While Ben's torso and weight pinned his assailant down, and his left hand restrained the flailing arms, the fingers of Ben's right hand explored their face, the way a blind man's might. He'd seen it in one of Lionel Richie's videos once. He was sure. But this wasn't a blind girl searching the features of the man she loved. It was eighteen stone of Benjamin Savage the third, trying to fathom who he had captured.

"Cruz?"

"Boss?" came the reply, his voice as high as Larson's, if not higher.

"What the bloody hell are you doing?"

"I-I..."

And then Ben felt it. A warmth on his thigh. Moist. The sensation was sudden and unexpected.

Cruz exhaled in sharp jolts as if he might cry.

"Have you..." Ben said. "Oh Christ, you have, haven't you?"

"Please, boss," Cruz whimpered. "Please don't say anything."

CHAPTER TWENTY-TWO

THREE TIMES DC CRUZ HAD ASKED IF HE COULD HELP BEN walk, offering the use of his shoulder. But not only would Ben's weight cripple the much smaller man, if Cruz's groping hand even touched Ben again, he would have to handcuff himself and confess to a murder so obscene that they'd have to rewrite the rule books, coming up with a new addition to the way the courts categorised murder.

Ben's shins were on fire, his ankle felt at least ten inches in diameter, and to top it off, he'd lost a bloody glove. He'd find it tomorrow, of that he was sure. In fact, thinking about it, he'd make a point of sending Cruz back to the hole to find it for him. There was a good chance Ben would be office-bound, and the thought of that only fuelled his anger.

But that anger dispersed when Ben saw the approaching blue lights flashing through the forest.

"What's that?" Ben asked.

"Ambulance, boss," Cruz said from behind him.

"I can see it's a bloody ambulance, Cruz. I mean, who's hurt? Did you find him? Was I out there looking for nothing?"

"No, it's Griffiths. Whoever it was gave him a whack or something. I'm not entirely sure. DI Bloom sent me off to find you. She told me to look for your torch light."

"Why didn't you call out?"

"Eh?" Cruz said, which Ben had learnt was the young man's way of buying time while he thought of a more appropriate response.

"Why didn't you call out? If I had known it was you–"

"You should have had your torch on."

"I thought you were the bloody killer–"

"I thought *you* were the killer," Cruz said, his voice rising to almost record-breaking levels of pitch. "Pissed my bloody pants, didn't I?"

Ben gave a laugh. A low and thunderous grumble of a laugh. Like all the fear and anxiety he had experienced in those past twenty minutes or so had all combined in a slow release.

"It's not funny, boss. I mean it. Don't say a bloody word. Especially not to Larson."

But Ben was unstoppable. He couldn't even string a sentence together. He felt his chest heaving in and out, and he had to control his breathing, but it was too late. He let his head fall back, and the climax of his outburst poured from him like his laughter was alive. Like it needed to get out. Birds flapped from where they were resting, causing snow to fall down into the forest, and Ben's laughter, trapped beneath that canopy of leaves and snow, seemed to echo on and on.

"Ah," he said, his face hurting from the effort of smiling more than he had for as long as he could remember. "Oh my God, you kill me, Cruz."

Unsure whether or not to join in, Cruz just stood there. He gave a snort, but it was obligatory more than anything.

"Please, boss," he said softly.

Ben sighed, his laughter spent. He inhaled a chestful of freezing air and suddenly felt the chill reach the layer of sweat on his back, the layer of sweat caused by DC Cruz's inability to call out and identify himself.

"Run ahead," Ben said. "Go and make sure Griffiths is okay."

But Cruz didn't move.

"Did you hear what I said, DC Cruz?"

"Please, Ben," he replied. "I mean it. Don't say anything."

"Okay, okay. I won't tell Larson."

"Anybody. You won't tell anybody. Promise me."

"I just gave you an order, Cruz. And do I have to remind you about the bloody injuries you just caused me?"

"I don't know if I could face it," Cruz said, ignoring what Ben was asking him to do.

"Face what, son?"

"Gillespie. And..."

"And?"

"I think I'm in with a chance. You know?" he said, and he shone the torch to his face and nodded his head toward the gates, which by now were only fifty feet away.

"You think you're in with a chance with Larson?" Ben asked.

"Shh. Keep it down. I think she likes me."

"What makes you think that?"

"Well," Cruz began, "she hasn't rolled her eyes or laughed at me since dinner. I think I've made a good impression."

"You think you made a good impression?"

"Yes," Cruz, said, hissing his responses at Ben, who was making very little effort to speak quietly. "Don't let me cock it up. I feel bad enough as it is."

"For letting me slice my legs open, you mean?"

"No, for pissing my pants."

"Okay, okay," Ben said. "Tell you what. You run ahead and tell Freya I'm okay before she sends somebody looking for me... somebody *else* looking for me," Ben corrected himself. "And I won't say anything about you getting scared and–"

"Promise," Cruz said.

"Alright, alright. Just go."

Using a tree to support himself, Ben watched the young DC head toward the lights. Ben's car headlights were still on and he guessed his engine was still ruining, and Cruz's silhouette reminded him of a cowboy, the way he kept his legs apart when he walked, presumably due to the discomfort of the wetness. The bloke must be freezing, Ben thought. He gave another laugh, but this time it was just the single stab of laughter that emerges during times of incredulity.

"What a bloody night," he said to himself. "What a bloody night."

"Ben?" Freya said, as he reached the safety of his own car and turned to lean on the front wing. He gave a groan of relief at making it unaided and found Freya standing before him. "What the hell happened to you?"

"Long story," he said. "How's Griffiths? What happened?"

"He took a blow to the head. I'm guessing you're empty-handed? Or have you found the culprit and tied him to a tree?"

"I couldn't find a suitable tree," he joked.

"Shame. I'd like to throttle the bastard."

"What? It's not serious, is it?"

"It wasn't. But he's taken a turn for the worse. Lying in the snow probably didn't help."

"He's okay though, right?" Ben said, suddenly very aware that his own minor injuries were completely insignificant.

Freya looked to her right, just as the ambulance headlights began to bounce across the grass.

"We'll have to wait and see. He was conscious, and I tried to keep him awake, but..."

Ben let his head drop forward. He sighed loudly.

"Whoever it was knew we were here."

"I thought that," Freya said.

"They came back to remove something. Something they left behind maybe?"

Freya nodded her agreement. "And we let him get away."

"No," Ben said. "No, we'll get him. He's close. He knows we're onto him, and he still has Abigail."

"That's my worry."

"If he has Abigail, he has the power. He won't do anything to her. We have to find her."

"Right, I wondered where we were going wrong," Freya said, then her face softened. "Sorry. I'm tired and being flippant."

"Has anyone called Sergeant Priest?"

"He's sending in replacements. Two units this time, and boy is he letting me know about it."

"He's okay. He's short on labour. But at the rate this is escalating, we'll be calling in support from Lincoln HQ before you know it."

"I won't let that happen," Freya said.

"No. I'll work all night if I have to. I'm going to find Abigail McGowan. I owe it to her."

Freya studied him quizzically. She opened her mouth as if she was about to say something, but thought better of it.

"Come on. Let's get those legs of yours sorted out. There's not much we can do here in the dark, especially in this bloody weather," she said, coaxing him toward the passenger door of his car. "Is the weather always this bloody bad here?"

"It's winter," Ben said, as he lowered himself into the passenger seat. "What did you expect? Wait until summer. You'll be moaning about how hot it is."

The ambulance pulled up beside them and the rear door opened.

A friendly face peered around the door.

"I'm going with him to the hospital, ma'am," the man said. It was the PCSO who had been with Griffiths. "I owe him that much."

"Okay, I'll tell Sergeant Priest," Freya said. "Sorry, I didn't catch your name."

"Gavin, ma'am. Gavin Wright."

"Well, good work tonight, Wright. I'll be sure to let Sergeant Priest know."

He nodded his thanks and the ambulance door closed as the driver pulled away. It disappeared around the corner leaving Ben and Freya in silence.

"Where's Cruz?" Ben asked.

"And Larson?"

Freya shone her torch light into the grassy field the ambulance had just driven across.

"Cruz?" she called out. "Larson?"

"Ma'am," came Cruz's feeble voice. They emerged from the darkness and strolled through the gates side by side. "We were... erm, just checking the place out," Cruz said. "Bloody awesome buildings, eh?"

"Find anything interesting?" Ben asked. "Anything to whet your appetite?"

Cruz glared at Ben, then allowed himself to force a smile.

But it was Freya who, sharp as ever, eyed Ben with a stare that she wouldn't let go.

He winked at her and whispered, "Boys stuff."

CHAPTER TWENTY-THREE

"By rights, I should have made a comment about how grateful I am we didn't end up in a dyke," Ben said, as they came to the crossroads on his father's land. Ben's house was down the track to the left, nestled in a U-shape with his brothers' house and his dad's. Freya's, one of the old farm cottages, was down to the track to the right.

"By rights, I should have made you drive and watched you suffer," she said. "I'll drop you and take your car. Then I can pick you up in the morning."

She turned left, driving slowly to be sure to stay on the snow-covered track. To come off now at this stage would only cause total ridicule, and Freya was far too tired to deal with that politely.

Completing a full circle of the little roundabout outside the three modest houses, she came to a stop so that the passenger door was closest to the house.

"Thanks for a turbulent and tiring day," Ben said, shoving the door open and lifting his leg out. "I'll be ready early. Come and get me when you're ready."

He heaved himself out of the car, using the door for stability.

Then, fishing his keys from his pocket, he prepared to limp to the front door.

"Sleep well," he called, as he closed the door.

Freya gave a long sigh. She couldn't just watch her friend suffer. Killing the engine, she unfastened her own belt, opened the door, walked around the car, and shoved her shoulder beneath his arm.

"Come on, hop-a-long, as much I'd love to, I don't have the energy to laugh at you anymore."

They made it to the front door, and taking the keys from him, Freya unlocked it and shoved it open. There were two steps for him to navigate, and it felt like his full weight was bearing down on her as he climbed them. With her arms around his waist, she gripped onto her wrist to provide greater support. Then, as they passed through the doorway, they had to turn side-on, facing each other. With his injured ankle still on the top step, Ben stopped and peered down at her.

"This is awkward," he joked.

"I can make it even more awkward, if you like?" Freya replied.

"Oh yeah?" he said, smiling down at her.

"I can let go and leave you here. I'd say that would be pretty awkward for you."

"Well, you might just find me here in the morning," he said, clearly in a substantial amount of pain. "If you chip away at the ice, I might even be alive."

"Come on. Lean on me. I don't have that kind of time in the mornings."

Of all the times they had shared over the past six months, this was the closest they had been. Was he feeling what she was feeling? Or was he more concerned with the pain his legs were causing him? Either way, she savoured his smell for a while. Ben was not the type of man to wear expensive aftershave. A simple deodorant was about the extent of his effort. But still, there was something about that smell that was alluring.

She heaved him through into the hallway, and then through the door to the living room.

"Three more steps," she told him, as she coaxed him toward one of the armchairs. Turning him so that he could simply fall into the seat if needed, she faced him, held his hands, and lowered him down. There was no drama about the move, and in her mind, he pulled her onto him in a calamitous yet fortuitous act that resulted in her straddling him. Fully dressed, of course. But that would be okay.

"Thanks," he said, pulling himself up into a comfortable position and leaning forward so Freya could stuff a cushion down between his back and the chair.

"How's that?" she asked.

"Could be better."

"Oh, how so?"

"I could be in bed."

"If you think I'm helping you up those stairs–"

"I think we'd make it, Freya, but I wouldn't want to come down in the morning."

"Right." She looked away, unsure if he was referring to her staying up there with him, or...?

She set to work untying his boots, busying her mind with other matters. His left boot came off with ease, and she placed it on the hearth. The right boot however, caused him quite a bit of discomfort. But it was only as she grabbed his leg to give it a final tug that he winced and snatched his foot from her grasp.

"What's that?" she asked.

"Just a scratch. It's okay."

Cautiously, she lifted the leg of his trouser and was horrified to see a deep cut, at least the size of a fifty pence coin. A trail of blood had meandered down to his sock and dried.

"Bloody hell, Ben. How did that happen?"

"Let's just say Cruz would be knocking on every door in the county if I had my way."

"Right," she said, getting to her feet. "You need sorting out."

She strode to that kitchen, filled the kettle, and put it on to boil, then returned to the living room and, using a handful of kindling from the little basket Ben kept, she started a fire in the log burner, exactly how he had shown her.

"You're a master fire lighter already," he remarked, as the flames took hold and she placed a log inside, closing the door to watch the flames through the little window. Secretly pleased with herself, she savoured the heat. The truth was that he had shown her how to build a fire many times, but even so, she didn't always get it right.

The heat was sudden, welcome, and needed. The old house was not quite as cold as outside, but almost. Freya's old cottage, however, would be just as cold as the outside, if not colder. She didn't have the luxury of double glazing, and the gaps around the doors were large enough that she half-expected snow in the hallway when she returned.

The kettle raged then clicked, and within a few moments, she had filled a bowl with water, adding a little cold to the mix; she was after all, not a total monster. She found some clean cloths in the cupboard and carried them through to the living room, setting them down beside the fire. Using the large footstool as a seat, she pulled at his trouser leg.

"Up," Freya instructed, just as she might have done to the boy she had raised as her own when he had fallen down and grazed a knee.

But the material wasn't budging and, if anything, was pulling at the wound. She gave a sigh and looked up at him apologetically.

"Get them off."

"Eh?"

"Off, Ben. I can't clean it like this."

"Can't you just—"

She stared at him with that stare she had also used on little

Billy. Few people could circumnavigate that stare, and Ben wasn't one of them.

Reluctantly, he unfastened the button, unzipped his fly, and began to raise his hips from the chair. He paused and looked at her suspiciously.

"Is this some kind of joke?" he asked. "Do you have a camera or something?"

She raised the cloth from the bowl and gave it a squeeze so the hot water ran through her hands and back into the bowl. "I've never been more serious. Off."

He pulled them down to his knees; from then, she took over. Grabbing hold of a leg in each hand, she stood before him and pulled gently to avoid the material rubbing over his wound. She folded them neatly and lay them over a nearby dining chair, and he lay before her, as vulnerable as he'd ever been.

It was then that she saw the wound, almost identical in size, shape, and depth on his other leg.

"Ben, what the...?"

He pulled a face as if he'd been caught out. "Yeah, that happened too."

"How the bloody hell did you walk back to the car?"

"With difficulty, Freya," he replied.

His socks came off with ease and she tossed them to one side. Then, putting another log on the now raging fire, she set to work cleaning his wounds. He was a briefs man, something she hadn't really considered before, but if for some crazy reason, somebody had asked her, she would have guessed he was a boxers man. She preferred briefs, at least on men who had the means to fill them and who were trim enough that excess skin didn't hang over the band. And Ben fit that criteria with ease.

"You're enjoying this, aren't you?" he said, as she dabbed at the second leg, carefully wiping away the dry blood.

"There's a fine line between seeing you squirm and looking after you, Ben," she replied softly, concentrating on what she was doing. "Besides, if I don't get you fixed up, I'll have to deal with Gillespie and Cruz on my own. Not a thought I relish, if I'm honest."

She found a first aid kit in the kitchen then dressed and wrapped his wounds before applying the hot cloth to his ankle and wrapping it tightly in bandages. She pulled the footstool closer, rested his leg on hers, and gently felt for anything worse than a sprain. His legs were tight, and as she massaged her way further along his leg, she admired the shape of his thigh. It was thick yet toned, which was unsurprising given the sheer size of the man.

She left him with his feet on the footstool and emptied the bowl in the kitchen sink. The kitchen was so neat and tidy that she spent the next few minutes tidying away the mess she had made. When she returned to the living room, she stopped in the doorway. There he was, lying with his feet up, his toned legs shining in the firelight. He gave a soft snore, not the violent torrent Greg used to keep her awake with, but the gentle sound of restful sleep. A sleeping bear.

Perhaps on any other occasion, she might have sidled up beside him. The fireplace was as good a place as any to destroy her career, after all.

But she didn't.

Instead, she found a pair of blankets on a shelf and laid one over him. Perhaps it was the thought of returning to her freezing cold house and having to get warm all over, or perhaps it was the idea of just being near him. She couldn't be entirely sure. But the second armchair was free, and after sliding it closer to him as quietly as she could, she pulled her boots off.

Then a thought struck her.

It felt wrong, but she knew he wouldn't mind. Creeping up the stairs, she found his bedroom, which was showroom neat. Scary neat. To the extent that he would have a fit if he ever saw Freya's. She found a t-shirt of his and some jogging bottoms, then stripped and put them on. She had to fold the waistband of the jogging bottoms over a few times, but they would be fine. They were soft and stretchy, but most of all, they were Ben's.

After adding three big logs to the burner, she settled down in the chair beside him and pulled the blanket over her, then stretched out to share the footstool with him, just as they had done at Christmas. It seemed a lifetime ago now. And just like she had done at Christmas, she stared at the fire, letting her mind run in all directions.

But unlike that wonderfully quiet Christmas, she did not fall asleep thinking of what Ben might be like. She did not slip away with her wild and sordid imagination. In fact, the last people she gave thought to before her mind closed down for the day were Abigail McGowan, the unknown lady, and the man who had knocked her to the ground. In that order.

CHAPTER TWENTY-FOUR

Freya opened her eyes. The fire had burned out and a cold chill ran through the old house. It took a few seconds for her to remember where she was, and a few more for a pang of guilt to sweep over her. Had she overstepped the mark by staying? If not, then she had definitely crossed some kind of boundary by wearing his clothes. His chair was empty. The blanket she had covered him with had been folded neatly and now lay over the back of the chair.

The cold air she inhaled was perfumed with the enticing fragrance of coffee. Had she been in her own house, where she often fell asleep in her armchair, she might have slipped into her slippers and shuffled into the kitchen. The floor was cold when she stood, but she couldn't bear to be the messy one, so she switched from foot to foot while she folded her blanket and laid it over the back of her chair to mirror his.

A hiss of water from upstairs indicated he was in the shower. Perhaps venturing upstairs to get dressed into yesterday's clothes would be pushing that line to a yet undiscovered realm. So she poured a coffee from the pot, pleased to see she had at least convinced him of the benefits of proper coffee and not the cheap stuff he used to buy.

She would wait, she decided, until he was dressed, and then if he needed help to descend the stairs, she would be on hand. The only item that was out of place in his kitchen was a piece of paper. Clearly, Ben had been scribbling some notes while he waited for the coffee. The scrawling was reminiscent of the two pieces of paper he had started in the village hall the previous day. Only this version showed the unknown lady and Abigail side by side. Abigail's father, Jess Henry, and Peter Jones were all present, connected in much the same way as they had been yesterday, but there was a dotted line between the two victims. A connection. That was his angle. How were the two victims connected?

She had to agree. It was a good angle to start with, as was the meeting with the key holder for the old hospital. They needed an understanding of who had come and gone, perhaps on a contractual basis, in order to eliminate subjects, or indeed open doors to new possibilities they had yet to consider. There were so many moving parts to the investigation yet so few tangible results. Granger would give her grief the moment she stepped through the door. Of that she was certain. It was not a thought she relished. Taking the pen, she began to add some of her own thoughts.

CSI, she wrote in the top corner. Then added, *revisit hospital*. Whoever had been at the hospital last night hadn't taken that risk lightly. They had been there for a reason. To remove something. To hide something. Or to cover up any evidence. But perhaps in doing so, they had left boot prints. Or maybe someone had seen them. They would have had to park nearby too, unless they were local. In which case, Cruz may have already spoken to them. Maybe in the very act of Cruz going from door to door, he had alerted the culprit.

Check Cruz list, she added, wincing a little as the neat sheet of paper on which Ben had started illustrating the victims' networks now included a to-do list. That would bug him. His OCD would flag the addition and he'd likely start over on a fresh sheet of paper. She smiled at the thought. Of how neat he was. Of how he lived his life. So basic, yet so orderly.

But she had started, so she continued.

Pathology, she added, then added some sub-headings. *Identification. Cause of death. Time of death. Toxicology.* That element alone would kick-start a whole raft of tasks that would need distributing throughout the team.

Search register, was the next heading she wrote, remembering she had assigned Chapman the task of searching through the register to see if there had been a person of interest among the community searchers. She considered the faces of those who had spoken up, and tried to recall the faces of those who hadn't. Of those who had stood in the sidelines savouring every moment of heartfelt sorrow for the missing girl. He would have felt powerful. The act of standing among them would have thrilled him. Like Ian Huntley. He might even have gained some kind of sexual gratification from the experience. If there was someone worth investigating, what was the link to Abigail? If indeed there was a link. Or had the opportunity arisen? A chance too fine to let go? Was Abigail in the village? Maybe she was being held in an outbuilding in a garden?

Headlights was the final item she added to the list, and then added Cruz's name, as she remembered Ben assigning him the task of exploring that particular avenue.

The hissing shower stopped and Freya swallowed her coffee. He would need a moment to dry and get dressed, so she waited a while longer, taking the time to look out of the kitchen window. Although it was still dark, light from the house lit the garden, and the sky looked as bleak as the previous day. Ben's father's fields surrounded the plot and, as she understood it, stretched as far as she could see. Everything would be white, cold, and as unappealing as the thought of putting on yesterday's clothes to go home to a freezing cold house to get showered and dressed.

Five minutes is enough, right? He is a bloke after all. It's not like he does anything to his hair. A quick towel off, a spray of deodorant, and he'll pull on a clean set of clothes.

She rinsed her cup and set it down on the draining board. Then, after a moment's deliberation, she decided that it looked messy, so she dried it with the tea towel and put it back in the cupboard. Freya ambled through to the hallway, listening for a clue as to what stage he was at and if he was having any trouble with his wounds. It was while she was listening that a dark shape appeared through the little window in the front door. It grew larger and darker, and took the form of a person. Somebody reached out to knock, and without thinking, Freya opened the door.

"Oh," she said, seeing a familiar yet disappointed looking face standing in the snow. "It's you."

"I'm sorry, I was just passing, and I thought..."

Michaela stopped talking, defeated. She looked Freya up and down, appraising her outfit, and drew a conclusion.

"It's okay," she said, turning to walk away.

"Shall I tell him you're here?" Freya called out.

"Who is it?" Ben said from the top of the stairs, and he dropped down to sit on the top step to get a better view, just as Michaela turned back. She took one look at him, glanced down at his towel, then glared at Freya as if to say, 'You bloody keep him.' She turned to walk away, shaking her head all the way to her car. "What was that about?"

Michaela slammed her car door.

"Haven't a clue for sure," Freya said, not revealing what she suspected, and what, if Ben was any good with women, he would have concluded for himself. "Were you expecting her?"

"No. I'm not even sure how she knows where I live."

"I thought you two were getting along?"

"We were until I cocked it up yesterday," Ben said, studying his wounds, giving Freya a view of far more than she had bargained for. "You don't think these need stitches, do you?"

She turned away, unsure of where to go or look, or what to say. The ceiling seemed like a good option; the light fitting was interesting. Ancient, but interesting.

"Freya?" Ben said. "They're still weeping."

"You'll need to dress them," she said, finding a sudden interest in the wall, where an old photo of the Savage farm had been framed and hung. It was black and white, and a man who Freya surmised to be one of Ben's ancestors was leading a shire horse, which in turn was pulling a plough.

"You couldn't grab the first aid kit for me, could you?"

He was smoking a pipe too, Freya noticed. And he wore a thick shirt, open at the front. Must have been during one of those hot summers Ben had mentioned.

"Freya?" Ben said, a little louder. "Sorry, could you grab the first aid kit for me?"

She closed her eyes, not daring to face him.

"Sure," she said after a moment's deliberation. "Why don't you get dressed and I'll throw it upstairs for you?"

"Can't you help? What you did last night seemed to–"

"You're hanging out, Ben," she said, louder and sharper than she had intended.

"Eh?"

"Put the mouse back in the house."

"What are you talking about?"

But Freya refused to look up at him. As much as she would have loved to, now was not the time for her filthy and sex-starved mind to be tempted with all Ben had to offer.

"Oh, bloody hell. Why didn't you say something?" he said, as he struggled to pull himself up, holding his towel together and limping off the stairs while keeping himself covered.

"What was I supposed to say?" she said, doing a poor job of

concealing her amusement. "Morning, Ben. How are your legs today? Nice penis by the way."

"You don't think *she* saw, do you?" he asked, and there was a panic in his voice. "Michaela, I mean."

The words stung a little. Like it mattered more that he could have somehow offended Michaela. Like what Freya thought didn't matter. Two words sprang to mind with bitter disappointment.

Friend zone.

"I honestly don't know," Freya called out, as she grabbed the first aid kit from the kitchen. She came to the bottom of the stairs, where she found him looking down holding his towel tight around him. She readied herself to toss it up to him. "Here, catch."

She threw. He caught. All without drama. And Freya retrieved her boots from the living room. Slipping into the cold leather without socks was an awful experience at that time of the morning, but needs must. She found Ben's car keys and re-entered the hallway. "I'll pick you up in thirty minutes," she said.

"I thought you were going to help–"

"I think I've seen enough for one day, Ben," she replied. "You're a big boy. I'm sure you'll work it out."

"Really?" he replied, with that boyish smile spreading across his freshly shaved face. "Nice *and* big? Haven't had compliments like that for a while."

She slammed the front door behind her, instantly remembering that she'd left her clothes in a pile on his bed, including her bra and underwear. She climbed into the driver's seat of the car, already shivering from the cold. Her house was a forty-five-second drive away so there was little point in getting the heater going. But she paused for a moment, resting her head on the steering wheel in dismay. He was a nice guy. He wouldn't touch her clothes, would he? No. He's far too well-mannered. Far too clean.

Oh my god, he's going to fold them, isn't he? Friend zoned or not, the thought of Ben handling her underwear sent a shiver down her spine that, for once, the weather was not responsible for.

If this was a clue to how her day was going to be, it would be a long and eventful one, she thought, biting her lip with a secret glee at the events that had unfolded. Michaela was well and truly off the scene, and the lewd imaginings that had occupied her mind during those cold and lonely nights now had substance.

CHAPTER TWENTY-FIVE

THE INCIDENT ROOM DOOR WAS NOTORIOUS FOR SQUEALING like a wounded beast when it opened, squealing when it closed, then slamming with a boom that was reminiscent of a shotgun being fired.

It was a sound that, during those office-bound days, Freya grew accustomed to as each day progressed. But in the mornings, it irritated the hell out of her. Not just because of the racket it made, and apparently had done for years, but because it announced her arrival to those whose office was a little further along the corridor. In particular, DCI Will Granger, who had a knack for not only registering that somebody had arrived for work but could somehow tell who it was.

"Bloom?" he called out from his office, and she shuddered, not for the first time that day.

"Want some help?" Ben asked, holding onto the door for support.

"I'm a big girl," she replied, instantly regretting her choice of words.

"Nice," Ben replied, reminding Freya of what she had said

earlier. A statement she just knew she wouldn't be living down for a while. "I'll be in here."

The door squealed and banged, and Freya winced at the sound. Staring at the corridor ahead of her, she thought of all the other stations she had worked from. From small towns in Essex and Kent, and into London, where the number of Detective Inspectors was greater than the number of Detective Constables where she had ended up. They had been fun times. The fight to the top was often dirty. Opportunities came with far more regular occurrence than out here in Lincolnshire, where the only real move was into Lincoln HQ. But the thought of moving there was not attractive. In fact, the more she considered the idea, the more she liked this place.

There had been two DIs when she had arrived – herself, and an arrogant moron named Detective Standing. It had been two months since Standing had transferred to Lincoln HQ seeking greater opportunities. Two of his team had transferred with him, while Granger had seen fit to merge the remainder of his team into Freya's. Hence she now managed Gillespie, Cruz, and Nillson.

She wondered if a transfer to Lincoln HQ would be a smarter move than staying.

"Bloom?" Granger called out once more. "Don't leave me waiting."

If one grumpy, old DCI and a few halfwits on her team were all she had to put up with, she could handle it.

She pushed open his door and entered without him even looking up. Freya was not one to tolerate authority being shoved in her face, and over the past six months, she and Granger had come to an understanding. He had stopped telling her to sit, as she so often refused, preferring to stand than be positioned in the lower seat with little opportunity to defend her actions.

"Guv?" she said, as innocently as she could manage. She closed the door behind her, placed her bag on the floor, and stood at his desk.

He leaned back in his chair, made a point of closing a window on his computer, clearly something confidential, then folded his hands behind his head. Had he been wearing a pair of shorts and a Hawaiian shirt, Freya might have asked him if he wanted a pina colada.

But he wasn't.

In fact, it was then she noticed he was in full dress uniform. She spotted the jacket hanging on the old hat and coat stand he kept. The buttons were gleaming. The revelation did not bode well.

"Press conference. Today at one o'clock. What do we have?"

"Who told them?" Freya asked, knowing full well that it must have been the interfering old schoolmistress, Mrs Finch.

"Kind of irrelevant, don't you think?" he asked, and for some reason, he was keeping his voice low. He wasn't frothing at the mouth as he often did and his complexion had yet to reach the alarming tone of a ripe tomato, as it usually had by now.

"Abigail McGowan is missing. We've conducted a search of the local area. Scene of Crime have been through with a fine-tooth comb and half of Dunston volunteered to perform a community search, despite my efforts to stop them." She added the last bit in to make it clear the search had not gone ahead under her authority.

"Anything at all?" he growled.

"Ben and I paid a visit to the old hospital last night. Sergeant Priest's men were assigned to guard duty. Apparently the place is a hot spot for vandalism and all sorts. When we arrived, the officers were nowhere to be found. We then identified an intruder. Ben gave chase—"

"Ben?" he said, his eyebrows raised.

"DS Savage, guv. DS Savage gave chase, as did one of the uniforms and DC Cruz who was with us. The other uniform was hit and injured quite badly. PCSO Larson and myself arranged medical assistance for him."

"Is he okay?"

"I came straight in here, guv. It's first on my agenda."

"Anything else?"

"For the press conference?" she asked.

"Anything at all. I'll filter the results as I see fit."

"I presume we're not mentioning the unknown just yet?" she checked.

"No. Unless, of course, during yesterday's fiasco, you managed to let that particular mess become public knowledge."

"I believe that particular crime has been contained," she said, adding emphasis on the word *crime*.

"You believe?"

"I'm sure it's contained."

"And? Have we got anywhere with that?"

"Ben and..." she began, then backtracked. "DS Savage and myself will be visiting the pathologist later this morning. We're looking for an identity, cause, and time of death. That'll be enough for us to make a start. Chapman has checked regional stations. No missing persons fit her description. So she must be from outside, or her disappearance has yet to be noticed."

He nodded, seeming to be suitably impressed with the news, or lack of. But given that it had been one day, Freya felt confident her summary demonstrated control and competence. That was as much as he could hope for at this stage.

"I'm taking a different angle on this," he said, leaving little room for Freya to argue if she felt the need. "I'm going to ask the public for help."

He left the statement open, allowing Freya to draw her own questions from it.

"A vehicle was seen on the forest road around five thirty a.m. on the morning Abigail was first reported missing. I'd like to know if anybody else saw it. If so, do they remember any detail? Make, model, colour."

"Driver?"

"If we can, guv. That was the morning the weather turned. We might get lucky though."

Again, he nodded. It was going too well. By now, he would normally have been tearing into her, doing his best to belittle her and to remind her that if it hadn't been for him, her secondment to Lincolnshire would have ended the day she walked in.

But he wasn't. Something wasn't quite right.

"Anything else?" he asked, making a note on his pad.

"Just a general call to dog walkers to see if they saw Abigail. If so, what time was it? If they saw anybody unfamiliar. Abigail ran the same route every day. Dog walkers tend to do the same. Somebody might have seen something."

"Got it," he said, and placed his pencil neatly beside his pad. He leaned forward again, interlocking his fingers across his stomach. Granger was a lean man in his late fifties. He was experienced, as far as Lincolnshire was concerned, but Freya always wondered how he would fare with a busier command, where competition was high and not for the fainthearted.

"Will that be all, guv?" she asked, again calling upon the innocence she had found in her repertoire a few minutes earlier.

"Only that you have one day," he said.

"One day, guv?"

"One day," he repeated, nodding as if to support his statement. "If, and I mean if, you have nothing substantial to give after that, I'll be calling in Lincoln HQ."

"What?"

"I have to, Freya," he said, and to his credit, he didn't seem happy with the prospect. "This could easily be a double murder case."

"We handled a serial killer what? Two months ago?"

"By the skin of your teeth, DI Bloom, and not without serious consequences."

He was referring to DC Gold being dragged into the back of the killer's van and very nearly being his final victim. Granger was right, but damn him anyway.

"If we cannot demonstrate progress, then we'll be seen to be holding up an investigation for what can only be deemed bragging rights and pride."

"That's unfair–"

"The media would have a field day. We'd be shut down before you even collected your things and went back to London, and I for one am not going to let that happen under my command. Better to bring in help when we need it. God knows we help them enough. If I have to ask for a returning favour, then I will."

"Yes, guv," she said, not even convincing herself.

"One day, DI Bloom. That's all you have. I need something substantial. Something that proves you and your team are capable."

"Like what?"

"Like a living breathing Abigail McGowan, damn it," he snapped, slamming his hand down on his desk. "Well? The clock is ticking, DI Bloom. Do not be the reason this department is swallowed by Lincoln HQ."

____

CHAPTER TWENTY-SIX

____

FREYA OPENED THE INCIDENT ROOM DOOR SLOWLY, prolonging the squeal. The hum of chatter and fingers on keyboards stopped for a second, and the team all looked up at her. A balled-up piece of paper hit Cruz on the side of his head, and he, very admirably, Freya thought, refrained from reacting. Gillespie, however, who had been in mid-throw when Freya had entered, reddened and gave her an apologetic look.

"Briefing, two minutes," she said quietly, and moved over to the white board.

She was joined by Ben, as she knew she would be. His limp was still apparent, but he was far more agile than Freya thought he might have been when she had seen the wounds and the swollen ankle the previous evening. But she said nothing, still pondering the words of the older and wiser DCI Will Granger.

"I can do that if you like?" he said.

"What I need is for you to gather the facts. We need a plan, Ben, and we need one fast."

"What did he say?" Ben asked. "I mean, clearly we need a plan. I want to find Abigail more than anybody, but–"

She moved closer to him, stepping into a spot where very few people would be able to see her face, and therefore would be unable to read her lips.

"We need something substantial. Something concrete. A lead," she said. Then she added the word that had cut her through to the bone, "Today."

"Or what?"

"Or HQ will be invited to share their resources and therefore opinions, and therefore take over, therefore taking all the glory, therefore making us look incompetent."

"Therefore we won't be on the investigation," Ben finished.

"Therefore, therefore," Freya said, hearing the bitterness in her own words.

"Can they do that?"

"What? Make us look incompetent?" she said, and took an exaggerated glance around him at the team, predominantly at Gillespie. "I wonder?"

"I need to be on this, Freya," he said, and it was with such certainty that he said it that Freya's ear pricked. There was something in the way he had said the word *need*. She stared him in the eyes and watched as they moistened, then reddened, and he looked away, finding solace at the far end of the incident room.

"What's wrong with you? It's not like you to get worked up over an investigation. You don't normally get yourself hurt. You're trying too hard. There's something you're not telling me."

"I just..." He inhaled, long and deep. "I need to do this. I need to find her. She's out there, isn't she? She's still alive. You know it as well as I do."

"I'm hopeful, although with every passing minute..."

"Exactly. With every passing minute, the chances of us finding her diminish. And if HQ are brought in, how long is it going to take them to get up to speed?"

Freya shook her head.

"Right," he said. "We can't let it happen. If we don't find her, nobody will. Let's make it bloody happen. In fact, no. It's happening. Today. We find her or I don't know..." Ben had worked himself up so much that he faltered and stumbled on his words.

"Get something substantial?" Freya suggested. "Find out who our mystery woman is? Make the connection to Abagail?"

"That'll put us on the right path," Ben muttered, then shook his head. "Sorry. I, erm..."

"It's okay. Talk to me."

But he shook his head again. "I just need to do this, alright. It needs to happen."

"Okay. Well, then let's make it happen," said Freya, and she looked him in the eye to make sure that whatever emotion it was that had raised its ugly head had gone. "Bring everyone close."

"Let's go," Ben said, raising his voice to be heard above the hum of noise that had grown. He clapped his hands three times and began moving chairs into a semi-circle.

Chairs scraped, bags were zipped, and laptops slammed closed. In a few moments, the team was gathered around the white board. Ben took a seat and they waited for Freya to speak. She left them waiting a few moments longer, just to ensure she had their undivided attention.

Looking around the room, she found Ben, DC Gold, DC Chapman, DC Nillson, DC Cruz, and DS Gillespie. An unlikely team, each of them with their own unique skills. None of them were dead weight, even Gillespie who, when push came to shove, was as competent as Ben. And even Cruz, although not the brightest spark, was actually capable of a lot more than he gave himself credit for.

"Day two," Freya began, "and as it stands, all we have is a plan. I'm now looking to you, my team, for answers. We don't have long, so when I talk, I want concise responses. Bullet points. Okay?"

"Ma'am," Gold replied.

"Aye, boss," Gillespie announced, louder than the others who all mumbled some kind of confirmation.

"Right. Firstly, what do we know about Griffiths? Does anybody have any news?"

"It's not good, ma'am," Anna said, checking around the room to make sure she wasn't speaking out of place.

"It's okay, Nillson," Freya said, encouraging the young Detective Constable to speak up. She had shown promise in the past few months, perhaps as a result of being kept on a tight leash while she worked under DI Standing. All she lacked was a bit of confidence, which was easier to get than it was to reign it in, Gillespie being a prime example.

"Some kind of haemorrhage, I think. I spoke to Sergeant Priest earlier. I caught him in the car park. Poor bloke. I think he spent all night there."

The room was silent. Griffiths was a solid uniform to have on side. Both Freya and Ben had called upon him on more than a few occasions.

"Please do me a favour," Freya said. "Get me his address. Do a whip-round for his family and send him some flowers."

"Flowers?" Gillespie scoffed, then cursed himself for the outburst.

"Well volunteered, Gillespie. Anna, when you've done the whip, give Gillespie enough to get a nice bunch. Thirty pounds ought to do it."

"Thirty quid?" Gillespie said. He seemed to be on a roll.

"Are you volunteering to raise that amount?" Freya asked him.

He shook his head.

"I presume you can be trusted to buy a nice bunch of flowers? Griffiths is one of our own, after all."

"I guess."

"You should try down the high street," Jackie said. "My mum goes there. He always does her a nice bunch."

"On the high street? There isn't a flower shop on the high street."

"There is. Right at the other end. He's been there years."

"Oh, you mean the old fella? The one with the dodgy hip? Walks like C3-PO?"

Freya winced at Gillespie's uncanny ability to find some kind of visual fault in everybody he described.

"That's him. Tom, his name is. Tell him my mum sent you. He might even give us a discount."

"Have we finished?" Freya asked.

"Aye, sorry, boss. Just getting the lowdown on where to buy flowers."

"Anna, send the rest of the money to the family with a card. I'll start it off. One hundred pound. I'll get it out of the ATM later."

"A hundred quid?" Gillespie exclaimed.

"For Christ's sake, Gillespie. Must you repeat everything I say?"

"Aye, I can't help it, boss. You keep surprising me. A bloody hundred quid is... is... Well, it's..."

"A hundred quid?" Ben said, unimpressed.

"Aye, Ben. That's like a month's food shopping."

"Well, hopefully that money goes towards the family getting to and from the hospital and any other costs they may incur. He was, after all, helping us with the investigation and if you've ever been off work through injury, you'll understand how hard it can be. Now, Chapman, where are we with the community register?"

"You'd be surprised at who lives in that village, I can tell you," she began, and was about to venture into a detailed report of her findings when Freya had to cut her short.

"Bullet points, Chapman. Please."

"Sorry, ma'am. Aside from minor driving offences, possession of class-C drugs, theft, and disturbing the peace, it's a dead end."

"That's a pity. I was hopeful we'd uncover something there."

"I did find something, though, ma'am," Chapman said.

"Go on."

"I read your notes on the dad. Terry McGowan. He mentioned that when his wife died, the family fell apart."

"That's right. I imagine it had a significant impact."

"He also mentioned the wife's brother..." She flicked through her notes searching for a name. "A Jason King."

"Yes, I believe Mr McGowan said he went off the rails. Ended up in prison."

"He was being held at HMP Askham Grange. It's an open prison in York."

"Right?" Freya said, fearing the next words that would come from Chapman's mouth.

"He escaped two weeks ago. It's been kept under wraps as the prison is already under scrutiny from locals."

"Abigail's uncle. Have we done a deeper dive on him?"

"I'm all set, all I need is your go-ahead, ma'am," Chapman explained.

"Do it. Find out anything you can, okay? See if he has a record and get in touch with Askham Grange to see if he's been found or seen. I'm sure there will be an effort underway to bring him into custody."

"Okay, ma'am."

"I can help her if you want?" Gold said. "It might be quicker with two."

Freya looked between the pair of them, then nodded.

"Whatever it takes," she said. "Cruz? What are you doing? How far have you got with the mystery vehicle? How many doors have you knocked at?"

"Dead end, boss," he replied. "We've got half of Nocton to do, and we haven't even hit Dunston yet."

"Do you have a plan?"

To her surprise, Cruz nodded. He unfolded a printed map and handed it to her. It showed both villages, Dunston and Nocton, each with a highlighted area showing the houses closest to the search area, with a secondary ring around each showing those houses out of the immediate area.

"I've split each village in half. Those more likely to walk their dogs near the crime scene, and those that are more likely to walk in the other direction, away from the crime scene."

"That's very good, Cruz."

"Thanks, boss," Cruz said, chuffed with himself.

"What about the vehicle?"

"The vehicle? I'm still looking into that."

"Good, before you go back to door knocking, I want you to meet SOC at the old hospital. Have them go down the forest road once more."

"And while you're there," Ben added, "go to the manhole where the woman's body was found and pick up my glove that you lost last night."

"That *I* lost?" Cruz blurted. "How did I lose it?"

"I'm pretty sure it was you who lost it, DC Cruz," Ben said, and he cast the young DC a knowing glare.

"Ah, yeah. Well, maybe it was me. No worries."

"Gillespie, where are you at?"

"I was going to head down to the old hospital again. You know? Stay close to CSI."

"That might not be a bad shout," Ben said. "It's reasonable to assume that whoever attacked Griffiths last night is our man. Which means there's a chance he was removing something, or covering up evidence. We think the uniforms spooked him. That's why he ran. In which case, he might not have finished the job."

"Aye, right. I'll take them round again. It's a big site though, Ben, and this weather's not getting much better. Damn near five inches of snow out there in places."

"So take boots," Freya said. "Are we all clear on what we need to do?"

"Erm," Cruz said, his face a picture of confusion. "Not that it's any of my business, but if we need to get hold of you?"

"We have a meeting with Neil Gutteridge, the key holder,

in..." Freya checked her watch, prolonging her last words. "Twenty minutes. After that, we'll be heading to the pathologist to pick up an initial report. Anyone office-based, be ready. As soon as we get a positive ID on the body, I'll be handing out tasks. So whatever you have to do now, do it fast. It's going to be a long day."

"Ma'am," Jackie called out by way of a confirmation.

"Aye, boss," Gillespie said. "It'll be a long one alright."

"A long, cold, and miserable day," Cruz added, airing his thoughts. His expression stiffened when he caught Freya's glare.

"Cheer up, Cruz," Gillespie said, as people started to collect their belongings and disperse. "You could be out walking the streets."

CHAPTER TWENTY-SEVEN

THE KEY HOLDER'S PROPERTY WAS LOCATED ALONG A NARROW lane in nearby Branston Booths, which was mostly farmland, with just a few private residences. After the long driveway, which was perhaps fifty metres, the property opened into a well-presented area with space for around ten vehicles. Beside the driveway was the main house. It was a new-build with solar panels on the roof, and was of sympathetic design to the outbuildings to the left. Each was marked with a little sign. The first was named *The Tool Hut*, and the second, *The Dairy*. To the right of the house was an old, decrepit tractor shed, distinguishable by its high roof and tall doors. That, along with a small, brick building about the size of two phone boxes, seemed to be the only buildings that were yet to be either knocked down and rebuilt, or rescued and refurbished.

The property had clearly been a small farm with an orchard behind it poking up over the outbuilding roofs.

A blanket of snow lay over the scene, bringing a peacefulness to the place.

Ben parked beside an old Transit van, then climbed from the

car and pulled his jacket tight around him, raising his collar to protect his neck from the harsh wind.

"How serene," Freya remarked over the roof of the car. "A little pocket of paradise."

"Looks like he's going self-sufficient," Ben replied. "My guess is those two buildings are bed and breakfasts, and it wouldn't surprise me to find a substantial allotment out the back somewhere."

"Can that be done here?"

"Self-sufficiency? Yeah, I'd say so. He's got solar panels, the orchard. All he'd need is a well or a borehole. He'd have rabbits, pheasants, and who knows what."

"Incredible," Freya said, and for once she appeared truly surprised.

Casting an eye across the scene, Ben spotted that one of the tractor shed doors was ajar. He limped toward it and made their presence known.

"Mr Gutteridge?" he called. "It's DS Savage. We spoke yesterday."

A figure emerged from the open door, waved a hand, then closed and locked the door.

"Now then," he said, pocketing the keys in the front pocket of his well-worn overalls. He wore a woolly deerstalker hat and his scarf was pulled up over his mouth. "Been in the wars, have you?"

"Ah, it's nothing much," Ben replied. "You remember I said we'd pay you a visit?"

"I do. I might not have much, but I do have my facilities," Gutteridge replied, tapping his head with a fat forefinger. "Haven't found her then?"

"Sadly not," Ben replied.

Gutteridge shook his head. "Terrible shame. Let's get inside, shall we? See what we can do about that."

He led Ben toward the front door and Freya followed. Inside, the hallway was large, with a staircase leading up to the first floor. There was a door straight ahead and another to the left.

"Gloria?" he called out. "We've got some company."

Freya closed the door behind her, and the place silenced.

"Nice place," Ben said. "Are you self-sufficient?"

"Damn near," Gutteridge replied. "Built this from the ground up. Knocked the old house down and put this in its place. Keeps us warm at any rate."

Just as he said that the door ahead of them opened, and a small boy poked his head through as if he was scared to venture out of the living space.

"Hello," Ben said, and the boy shied.

"Go on, Daniel. Back inside. Tell your ma to get the kettle on now." Gutteridge coaxed the boy into the living room. Then he turned back to Ben and Freya. "Go through to the office," he said, extending his arm towards a door off the hallway "I'll be with you shortly."

The door closed behind him, and they entered through the doorway on their left. The office was nice. It was an old, classic design that suited the place. There was a log burner against one wall, a large desk beneath the window, and the largest of the walls was covered by a huge bookcase. Every inch was filled with books and magazines, including topics from farming, to sustainability, and even a section on health care. Freya selected a book called *Don't Give Up*, which according to the jacket had been written by a Doctor Ahmed Al Yousef. The tagline read, *If you want to be a parent, you can be*. Ben rolled his eyes at Freya's choice and selected a book on crop selection for the self-sufficient home.

"I used to have a bookshelf like this," Freya said, and she seemed at ease surrounded by a wealth of knowledge. "Except I didn't have an entire section on health care."

"I'm a nurse," a voice said from the doorway, and with an instant sense of guilt, Ben replaced the book he had been perusing. She was a pretty lady, rotund with rosy cheeks and curly, dark hair. She wore a simple apron over a floral dress that accentuated her ample arms. "I'm Gloria. It's nice to meet you."

Holding the book up, Freya made an educated guess. "Midwifery?"

But Gloria shook her head. "Anaesthetist," she said, then nodded at the book. "We've been trying for our second."

"Oh," Freya said, and hurriedly put the book back. "I'm sorry I didn't mean to–"

"It's fine," she said with a smile, then nodded at the wall above the log burner where a simple wooden cross had been fixed to the brickwork. "If God wills it, it'll happen."

"Indeed," Freya muttered.

"Anyway. Tea? Coffee?"

"Not for me, thank you," Ben said. "We're actually short on time."

"Alright, alright," a voice said from the hallway. Neil Gutteridge appeared behind his wife, minus his overalls and hat. His hair couldn't decide which direction to point, so elected for them all, and now his scarf had been removed, Ben saw the little tell-tale sign of egg yolk on his unshaven chin. "Was just getting out of my overalls."

"I'll leave you to it," Gloria said, then tutted, licked her finger, and rubbed her husband's chin. She shook her head playfully. "It was a pleasure to meet you both."

"Likewise," Ben said, as she disappeared through the doorway into the lounge.

"Now then," Neil Gutteridge said, moving toward an old filing cabinet that had been positioned in the corner of the office. "You wanted plans, right?"

"And the list of contractors," Ben replied, and looked to Freya in case she wanted to add something.

But Freya's complexion had turned a deathly pale. She wore what Ben could only describe as the deadliest expression he had ever seen on her face.

"Freya?" Ben said, hoping to rouse her from her trance-like state.

"You?" she said.

"Me?" Gutteridge replied, nodding.

"You're the key holder for the old RAF hospital at Nocton?"

Again, he nodded. For a moment Ben thought he might encounter a similar accident as Cruz had the previous night. But he held it together. "I am."

"Bloody white van man," she spat. "You nearly bloody killed me."

Gutteridge's face morphed into a look of recognition and regret.

"You're her," he said, pointing his finger at her and edging back. "You're the mad woman–"

"Mad woman?" Freya said. "You tried to overtake me and you forced me off the road."

"You were driving so slow I had to overtake."

"It was bloody snowing."

"It's Britain. It snows. The country doesn't come to a stand-still just because it snows, does it?"

Ben fought the urge to respond to that one himself, considering his answer to be irrelevant to the argument.

"There was a twelve-foot drop on either side of the very icy road."

"Oh, you mean the perfectly straight road? The road the bloody Romans built?"

He had a point.

"I don't care who built it," Freya said. "I was using it, and as a road user, I expect other drivers to show a little patience and respect. Not force me into a ditch."

"I had places to be, and I'd spent a good ten minutes watching you check your hair in your mirror. You people make me sick. You think the world owes you a favour. Let me tell you something," he said, shaking his head. "It doesn't. If you can't drive in a straight line, you shouldn't be on the bloody road."

"You just stopped there. What was I supposed to do?"

"If you hadn't been looking in the mirror, you might have seen me in time, or maybe swerved around. There was a twelve-foot drop on one side of my van and a clear road on the other. And it's a bloody dyke not a ditch. It's full of run-off water."

"I know. I put my car in it, you—"

"Okay, okay," Ben said, raising his voice to be heard above them both. "Enough." He limped to stand between them, holding his arms out to keep them both at bay.

Gutteridge turned to Ben. "If I'd have known she worked for you, I wouldn't have bleeding bothered offering to help—"

"He works *for* me," Freya shouted, just as the boy appeared at the doorway, again poking his head around. He looked up at his dad with big, brown eyes.

"Let's just calm down," Ben said, raising his voice. "Right, we're not here to discuss an accident that involved you two. We're here on police business."

Gloria stepped into view, coaxing the boy from the doorway. She eyed her husband, giving him a glare that, in Ben's opinion, Freya would have been proud of.

"Get him out of here," Gutteridge shouted at his wife. Then he turned back to Ben and slapped a pile of folded A0 plans on the old, wooden desk.

"And the maintenance schedule?" Ben said, lowering his voice to try and ease the tension.

"It's in there," he mumbled.

Ben fingered the plans, taking a peek inside but not wanting to step from between the still-seething Freya and the volatile key holder.

"Can I draw on these?"

"Draw on them?" Gutteridge said, and it was clear any further help from him was well and truly out of the window. "Why do you want to draw on them?"

"We have search teams. It would be useful if we can mark them. Are they the only copies?"

"No, but I have to get them printed. Place in town does them, but they charge a fortune. Seven or eight quid a pop."

"Wow, seven or eight quid?" Ben said, unsure if the man was genuine, or if he was being difficult as a result of Freya's outburst.

"Leave it, Ben," Freya said. "Clearly Mr Gutteridge is not willing to help us in our enquiry. Because he knows he's wrong–"

"I've heard enough," Gutteridge said. "I invited you here to help you with your enquiry, or whatever it was."

"It's a missing person," Ben said. "A young girl."

"Aye, well. I said I'd help, didn't I? Didn't realise I'd get bombarded with insults from a jumped-up princess who won her driving license on a scratch card." He snatched up the printed plans. "If this is the thanks I get, I'd like you to leave."

Ben slammed his hand down on the sheet.

"Look, Mr Gutteridge, perhaps we got off on the wrong–"

"Don't Mr Gutteridge me. You're not staying a minute longer."

"At least let us have the plans. I'll return them when we're done."

"Return them? Here?" he said, as if the very idea was preposterous. "I don't think so."

"I'll buy them then. What did you say? Seven quid?" Ben asked, and he fished a ten-pound note from his wallet and placed it on the desk. "Here, keep the change."

Gutteridge stared at the money, cocking his head to one side.

"I'll have to have new ones printed."

"Well, that should cover it."

"And parking. Bloody expensive, it is, in town."

Shaking his head, Ben produced a five, and placed it on top of the ten on the desk.

"Fuel," he added. "Long way from Branston Booths to Lincoln."

Ben added another five and snapped his wallet closed. "That's all you're getting."

Snatching the notes up, Gutteridge stuffed them into his pocket.

Freya moved to the door, giving Gutteridge a filthy look as Ben collected the plans.

"Write your number down. We may wish to contact you," she said.

"Will it be you who calls?"

"Not if I can help it, Mr Gutteridge. I'll have somebody far lower down the food chain call you if we need to. Somebody who shares some common ground. The toilet cleaner perhaps, although I dare say even that's a stretch of the imagination."

Ben held out his pen, shaking his head at the pair of them and their childish behaviour.

Embittered, Gutteridge wrote his number on the schedule, then slipped the pen into his breast pocket.

"Can I just ask, Mr Gutteridge, why you were on the road so early in the morning?"

He shrugged, then looked from Freya and back to Ben. "Check the maintenance schedule. Had to open the gates, didn't I?" he said, then swiftly left the room and opened the front door for them.

"Wait," Ben called, and Gutteridge slowly closed the door. "Are you saying that there was maintenance work happening that morning?"

"Not in the morning. Night time. Have to do it then, see. Had to turn the water off."

"And do you have the names of the engineers?"

He nodded, as if he had already provided Ben with all the information he was happy to give up. He nodded at the plans and reopened the door. "In the schedule. Will that be all?"

"For now," Freya said, and she brushed past him before he had a chance to reply.

"That was a bit uncalled for," Ben said, when the front door had closed behind them. He limped to the car and waited for Freya to join him.

"So was running me off the road, Ben," she said. "But am I crying about it?"

"I meant the twenty quid I just paid him for some old plans."

"Well, it looks like he's had us both over then, doesn't it?" Freya said, finding humour in the events that had just played out. She unlocked the car and spoke to him over the roof. "I shall not hear another word about my accident, or the entire team will learn of how Mr Gutteridge swindled you out of your hard-earned cash."

CHAPTER TWENTY-EIGHT

"Are you sure you're okay to drive?" Freya asked, as she hit dial on Ben's phone and dropped it into the centre console. She studied the maintenance schedule for the second time to make sure she was reading it correctly. "I'm quite capable, you know?"

"I'm fine. My ankle is easing off a bit now. My shins are bloody killing me though."

"Shane Dooley," Freya called out, as soon as Anna Nillson answered her call. "Pipe fitter. Works for Derwent and co. Some kind of engineering firm."

"Ma'am," Anna said, typing her notes as Freya spoke. "Dooley was at the hospital the night before Abigail went missing. Find out everything you can about him. If you need help, ask DC Gold."

"Will do," Anna replied.

"And call the company's number. They must have a website or something. Find out if he had anybody with him. I want to know exactly what he did during his visit and whereabouts on the site it was. If he's touched anything, CSI might have his prints."

"I'll call if I get any problems, ma'am," Anna replied.

"Please don't, Anna," Freya replied quietly.

"Don't call you?" The confusion and slight panic was evident in the young DC's voice.

"Don't hit any problems. We need this lead. I'm giving you an opportunity. Run with it for me. If he's willing to show us what he did and where, then have him meet Gillespie. I want you in that office driving leads. Is that understood?"

"Ma'am," Anna replied, with a little more punch to her voice.

Freya ended the call. "She'll go far, that one."

"Couldn't agree more," Ben said, slightly distracted.

"Got the hots for you, too."

"Who? Anna?" Ben said, and whatever he was thinking about was no longer taking priority. "Behave."

"It's true. I've seen the way she looks at you. Girls know these things."

"She's twenty-something."

"And you're the older man. We all go through it. Some of us even go the other way."

"The other way? You mean, like–"

"No, Ben. I mean we turn our attention to younger men," Freya said, shaking her head at his immaturity. "Most of us get over it, though," she added, as she sifted through the papers Gutteridge had sold Ben. Most of them were barely readable, torn and tattered, and the ink was so faint that she would need some kind of scientific equipment to see the detail. But it was what they had, and Ben had folded them so that the area with the manhole was front and centre of the top fold.

"Did you get over it enough that you couldn't help but admire this younger man's–"

"How did I know you were going to go there?" Freya said.

"I'm still reeling from the compliment?"

"I did not compliment your–"

"You said it was a nice penis."

"I said I... it..." Freya said, stumbling on her words. "I was making a joke. It was contextual."

"You also said I was a big boy."

"Don't get carried away with yourself. I meant you're not a young boy anymore, and before you turn that into some lewd discussion point, I was referring to you applying your own dressings."

A moment of silence passed, during which neither of them looked at each other, but from the corner of her eye, she could see him grinning.

"You scared Michaela off with it anyway," Freya said at last, and then laughed at Ben's misfortune. Ben didn't see the funny side, which stung a little. He was clearly cut up about the events of the morning and Michaela walking off in a huff. "And yes, if it makes you feel any better, I thought it was perfectly acceptable."

He opened his mouth to speak, but Freya had foreseen that.

"And I shall hear no more about the mouse being out of his house. We're supposed to be investigating a kidnapping and a bloody murder."

The Bluetooth system beeped with every number she pressed. She hit dial and nothing happened.

"Bloody wrong number."

"You can't be reading it right," Ben said, as they entered Lincoln Hospital grounds.

"There's a number missing. Look."

"I'm driving."

"There's supposed to be eleven digits. There's only ten."

Freya caught a glimpse of Ben's childish grin.

"Don't say a bloody word," she said.

"Now I do believe he's had you over twice."

He pulled the car into an empty space, applied the handbrake, and sat admiring her as she fought to contain her frustration at the man.

"Oh yeah?" she said. "Had me over twice, did he? Are you sure there are eleven numbers in a phone number?"

Ben made a show of counting his own number in his head.

"Yeah, I'm pretty sure."

She handed him the pile of papers. "Why don't you write your number down and count them?"

He reached inside his jacket for his pen as Freya opened her door. She bent to watch him search his other pockets.

"Had *me* over twice, did he?" she said, and closed the door as Ben tossed the papers across the dashboard and let fly a torrent of questionable obscenities and perverse profanities, each one aimed directly at his new best friend, Mr Neil Gutteridge.

CHAPTER TWENTY-NINE

It was gone ten a.m. by the time Freya and Ben walked the long corridor to the pathologist, taking it slow for Ben who, to his credit, was soldiering on despite his obvious discomfort.

Freya hit the button, and from inside they heard a muted buzzer, like a swatted wasp in its death throes.

"I hate coming here," Freya said, to Ben's amusement.

"I thought you'd be used to it by now."

"Used to what? Bodies?" she said. "Oh, I can deal with those. Sometimes it's the living I struggle with."

"You've made that much obvious already," Ben replied as an internal door opened and closed and then, with a loud click as the electro-magnet disengaged, the outer door opened.

"My two favourite detectives," the pathologist said with a beaming smile, far beyond what Freya was capable of that day. "Come on then, won't you? You'll let the heat in."

The Welsh-born pathologist wore her hair in what Freya could only describe as a helmet shape, with a fringe and a sharp cut around the sides. Her face was round and was adorned with more piercings than Freya had ever seen on one individual. She dreaded to think where else was pierced. But to top the look off, she seemed to change the colour of her hair with the seasons. Today it was green. A bright, unmistakable, and quite shocking green.

"Good morning, Doctor Bell," Freya began, hoping to get off on good ground with the slightly eccentric pathologist. "How have you been?"

Doctor Bell stepped to one side and nodded for them to come in with an expression like they had been standing for hours and she was tired of holding the door.

"Oh, you know me, Freya. Spend my days in body cavities, and my evenings, well..." she said, shaking her head. "I probably shouldn't talk about those in front of the likes of you, if you know what I mean?"

"No. No, I don't know what you mean," Freya said.

But Bell moved the subject on quickly, pointing at various cupboards in the little waiting room. "Hats in there, masks in there, and if you want to protect your clothing, I'd suggest one of our snazzy aprons. Bottom cupboard."

"Aprons?" Ben said. "We don't normally have to wear aprons."

"No, but to be fair, you don't normally come when we're so busy. The fridge is packed, it is. Haven't the space for another, even if it fell from the skies. Besides, him upstairs keeps telling me that guests should really be covering up."

"God?" Ben said, a quizzical look on his face.

"God? Now why the bloody hell would he be telling me to tell you to wear aprons? No, if he ever spoke to me, he'd be telling me to stop getting out of my box on cheap wine and find myself a good man."

"Right," Ben said slowly. The conversation with Doctor Bell had begun as they usually did – cryptically and on a tangent.

"I'd tell him cheap wine was easier to find and didn't fart in bed. What's a girl to do? No," she said, jamming her thumb upwards to the ceiling, "him upstairs. The boss. The almighty himself. Well, the other almighty as he'd have you believe, anyway.

Probably couldn't even open a cardboard box, let alone a rectal cavity."

Freya grimaced at the thought, and the doctor caught her expression.

"It's okay. We won't be doing that today," she said, and clapped her hands. "Right then, let's go take a look-see and I'll show you what I found."

She pushed through into the main room, a large space, clinically clean, with a number of stainless steel benches in a row that resembled an operating theatre on a large scale. Huge ring lights on booms hung above each bench and, as was her practice, Doctor Bell had ensured that only one body was out while guests were present.

The woman on the bench had been covered with a blue sheet, and Bell led the way. She stopped at the end of the bench, turned, and waited impatiently. Then she spied Ben hobbling along.

"Well, what the devil's happened to you, now?" she asked.

"Long story," Ben replied.

"Go on, then," she said.

"What?" Ben said. "Go on, what?"

"Go on then and tell me. It's not like she's going anywhere anytime soon, is it now?"

"I'd rather—"

"Is it your knee?" the doctor said, studying the way he was limping, then changed her mind. "No. It's both legs. You've injured yourself. Ankles? No. Shins." She held her index finger up like she had just had an *ah-ha'* moment. "Shins it is. You've been running. Shin splints?"

"Yes, that, pretty close."

"Ah, you want to be careful, Benjamin. I'll have you up on my bench one of these days."

"I'd prefer if that wasn't going to happen for some time," Ben said, slightly unnerved at the prospect.

"I did a therapy course a while back. You'll be surprised what a massage can do for you," she said, flexing her fingers with a series of cracks. "And a pair of strong hands."

"I'm not sure a massage will fix me, if I'm honest," Ben said.

"First and foremost," Freya cut in, "we're looking for some sort of identification, cause and time of death. Anything else will be of benefit, of course, but we do need those details to pursue the investigation."

"Straight to the point. You're in a hurry. Gotcha," Doctor Bell replied. "Well, you'll be pleased to know, we have the cause of death and we have the approximate time of death. Well, the day, at least."

"ID?" Ben said.

"It's a mystery," she replied. "We've run her through all the known databases, but we've had no matches. It's almost like she just turned up."

"Is that nationwide?" Ben asked.

"Of course. All the major services are linked now. There's a few that haven't digitised their old records, but for the most part, if it's out there, we can get it."

"And you can't find her at all? Not even dental records?"

She shook her head. "If her dentist was a poky wee hole in a tiny little village, then there's a chance her records haven't been uploaded yet. That's if she even had a dentist, and if they kept her records. I had a transient in here a few months back who we identified from their dental records."

"That must have been pleasant," Ben said, without thinking.

"Yeah, right. Alcoholism, drug use, smoker. You name it, this fella was on it. Anyways, we got a match. Turns out he was from some tiny little village in the arse-end of nowhere up north, and we got a match. Even with *his* gnashers. But then, on the same note, we've had unknowns come in with perfect teeth and we've struggled to find them anywhere. You never can tell."

"Damn it," Freya said. "Right. Let's get on with it. Time is in extremely short supply today, Doctor Bell. So if we could be brief?"

The doctor placed her hands on the woman's arm, as if she had some kind of connection to her, or was a friend of sorts. She stared at Freya, holding her gaze as she spoke.

"This woman has been through hell, Freya. I can tell you that much. I've had to do some pretty serious cleaning up. I'm not certain of what conditions she was living in, but from what I can see, it was far from optimal."

"What are you saying? She was homeless?" Freya asked.

"Not homeless. I don't think so anyway. She's too well fed. Toxicology came back clean. She's no deficiencies. She's not short of anything."

"She's healthy?"

"But awful dirty," Doctor Bell finished. "Dog dirty. Living in a hovel kind of dirty. I'll spare you the details."

"Thanks. Cause of death?"

"Suicide," the doctor replied in an instant. "Indirectly, a heart attack."

"A heart attack?" Freya said. "She's too young, surely?"

"Induced heart attack," Doctor Bell added. "We found traces of organic material in her teeth. Deposits of the same material in her throat, probably from regurgitation, and the remains of at least forty grams of undigested organic material in her stomach."

"She swallowed something?"

"I'd say about two days before she was brought here, which makes it three days ago, give or take. By swallowing the organic material, she would have experienced severe nausea, vomiting, dizziness, and diarrhoea."

"What was it?" Ben asked, shifting his weight between feet.

"Do you want a chair there, Benjamin?"

"No," he said, doing the typical man thing of powering through.

"If that wasn't bad enough," the doctor explained, returning her attention to Freya, "the convulsions would have been debilitating."

"Convulsions?"

"Then her heartbeat would have become irregular. Skipping beats. Slowing down. Speeding up," she said. Then she added with finality, "Stopping."

"That sounds horrific."

"That all depends on your circumstance, now, doesn't it? If, say, she was deeply unhappy, suicide might have been a better alternative."

"Yeah, but without going into detail, there are far..." Ben struggled to find the words.

"Better ways?" the doctor asked.

"Yes," said Ben, not wishing to elaborate anymore.

"I agree. But then, that's not my job to work it out, is it now?"

"What was the organic material exactly?" Freya asked.

"Ah. Did you ever see Miss Marple?" Doctor Bell asked, to which Freya nodded.

"Of course. As a kid."

"I used to love those shows. All of them. Colombo, Bergerac, Morse, and of course, Hercule Poirot," she said, in a very bad French accent.

"Right?" Ben said, urging her to explain.

"Organic material? Suicide?" she said, seeming to be absolutely dumbfounded that neither Ben nor Freya had even made a guess. "Foxglove, for Christ's sake."

"Foxglove?"

"Yeah. All those shows had at least one episode where the killer used foxglove to poison their victim. You've seen it. Little purple flowers."

"I'm not too good with fauna," Freya admitted. "Ben's the farmer."

"I know foxglove, yes. It's everywhere. It grows like a weed here."

"There you go."

"So what makes you think it's suicide?"

"Ah, that's easy. See, it only takes a few grams, maybe a leaf or two, to do some serious damage to someone. A little more to do a proper job, if you know what I mean?"

"Go on," Freya said, intrigued as to where the doctor was going with her analysis.

"In all those shows, oh, you should have seen them, they seemed so innocent."

"Doctor Bell," Freya said, hurrying her up.

"Right. Gotcha. Anyway, in all those shows, the killer used to crush a leaf up and put it in the victim's drink or food or something. Maybe poison them over time." She leaned on the bench and lowered her voice. "Madam here damn near swallowed a pint of the stuff. There's tons of it inside her. You can't tell me that's not suicide. Unless the killer forced it down her throat, in which case you'd expect some kind of bruising to correlate to that."

"But there's none?"

"No physical damage at all, except for the damage to her skull, that is, which occurred post-mortem. Michaela was telling me about how she was found. It's a right old conundrum, this one."

"Anything else?"

"Yes, as a matter of fact. Something which might help you understand what she was going through." She stared at Freya again, as if it was a woman to woman thing. Her eyebrows cocked unevenly.

"She was pregnant?" Freya guessed, thinking that could be the only reason for her to single out Freya, the only other female.

"Six weeks, by my estimate," the doctor said. She wrinkled her nose. "Give or take a week on either side."

"So she worked out that she was pregnant, and–"

"Wasn't too happy about it."

"So why not have an abortion, or something?" Ben said innocently, and doing his best not to upset the females in the room who may or may not have a strong opinion on the matter.

"Maybe she was Catholic?" Doctor Bell said. "Maybe she was just plain old scared? Wouldn't be the first one I've seen."

"Is there any sign of..." Ben began, clearly hoping the doctor would pick up on where he was going, thus avoiding the need for him to finish the sentence.

But she didn't. She waited.

He sighed. "Sexual interference?"

"None. Not recently anyway. She's no virgin, I can tell you that. But nothing recent."

"Can we get DNA from the foetus?"

"Do you have a month?" the doctor said. "Even then, this baby has his or her own DNA. A direct match is out of the question. Similarities, yes, but if you need a solid angle, that isn't it."

"How sad," Freya said, feeling the woman's arm beneath the sheet. "You said you cleaned her up."

Doctor Bell nodded, showing a certain kindness that her otherwise brash exterior often concealed.

"Top to bottom," she said. "If you'll pardon the pun."

And then she ruined it.

"I didn't get a chance to see her before. She was in a hole in the ground and her face was..." Freya's voice trailed off. She was unsure if she really needed to see.

"Would you like to see her?" Doctor Bell said. "I think she deserves to be seen and not hidden away. She's quite beautiful."

Freya nodded and glanced at Ben, who stepped back from the bench out of some weird sense of etiquette.

Carefully, Doctor Bell raised the corner of the sheet then peeled it back to rest on the woman's shoulders.

"See what I mean?" she said. "Beautiful."

"She was," Freya said, admiring her skin and her cheekbones, imagining her when she was alive. She could picture her in a summer dress, with her long, blonde hair and fields of tall crops behind her. "She's a picture of beauty. She could have been a Hollywood actress, a model, a singer, any idol a girl could have. And yet, something, or someone, had driven her to this? It doesn't make sense."

Looking across at Doctor Bell, Freya found her to be quiet, as if she was reflecting on her own thoughts. She turned to Ben, hoping he might add something. He usually knew what to say.

"Ben?"

He was lost in his own world. His eyes had teared and reddened again. His mouth fell open and even his lower lip trembled, before he controlled himself and began to speak.

"She wasn't a Hollywood actress," he began, shaking his head. "She wasn't a model or a singer. She was a daughter. She was somebody's friend. She was somebody's lover."

"Ben?" Freya said, sensing he was losing his trail of thought. He looked up at her, fighting the urge to let his emotions go; she could see it in his eyes. Something far more human than she had ever seen in them before. "What is it?"

"Her name was Marie Treverne," he said. He licked his lips, and even Doctor Bell gazed at him, confused yet too polite to interrupt. Shifting his gaze to the pretty woman on the bench, he stroked her hair once, then retracted his hand as if that was enough. That one touch was all he needed. "And I loved her."

CHAPTER THIRTY

"Ben?" Freya whispered. "Ben, talk to me."

"Give him a moment," Doctor Bell suggested, and she moved around to stand beside him. "Come on, Ben. Let's get you sitting down, eh? That's what you need. A nice chair to–"

"I don't need to sit down," Ben said, and he pulled his arm away firmly, but without risking offence. That was Ben's way. A gentle giant. And it pained Freya to see him like this. "I just want to be with her."

"You knew her well, didn't you, Ben?" Freya said, and then waited. She turned to Doctor Bell. "Perhaps some tea?"

"Oh, tea. Now there's a thought. I'll just be a jiffy or two." She paused mid-step and turned as if to ask how he liked his tea. But then she thought better of it and disappeared through to the room where they had been given gowns.

"I'm sorry," Ben said, and it took a few moments for Freya to gauge whether the apology was for her, or for Marie.

"Ben, please. If you knew her, you have to talk to me."

"I knew it was. I knew it, Freya," he said, fighting the tears. "Her hair. In the hole, it covered her face. I couldn't see."

There had been times in the past six months that Freya had

wanted to give it all up and tell him how she felt. But that had
been a girlish dream. It had been borne of girlish fantasies that
craved physical connection. Something sexual. There had been
times, in the same period, that she had looked upon him as one of
the best friends she had ever had, then disregarded the notion
due to the short amount of time they had known each other.
There had been times, just as the previous night, she had just
wanted to curl up beside him. All fantasies aside. Just be with
him. Just touch him. But she had refrained, with too much to lose.
His friendship, for a start. But now was different. Now was a time
when he actually needed her. Now was a time that she could hold
him, like a sister, or a friend, or a partner. Now it didn't matter.
And she held him. Pulling him tight, she knew she couldn't take
away whatever pain he was feeling, but they could share it. She
could absorb some of the blow for him. Whatever he was thinking, whatever memories were playing out in his mind, as she knew
they would be, he would know she was there. Standing beside
him. Holding him. Helping him through.

A warm tear landed in her hair, and his limp arms found her.

They stayed that way for longer than Freya cared to remember. It was something she had longed to do for months. To hold
him. To be there. But now she was there, she wished there had
been no need to be. She would have quite easily walked out of the
door with him hobbling beside her, both of them none the wiser
as to the woman's identity.

Marie Treverne, she said in her mind's voice. Not a local name.
But one that suited her beauty regardless. Because she was beautiful. Of that, there could be no doubt.

"Did I ever tell you the reason I joined the force?" asked
Freya, but Ben didn't answer, just as she knew he wouldn't. She lay
her head against his chest and spoke to him more to calm him
than for any other reason. "It was because I was bullied. Bullied
for who I was. Bullied because my father was a rich man and my
mother was a gypsy's daughter. I had my hair pulled, my skirt

pulled up in front of the entire school. I had my bra snapped as soon as I began wearing one, and the older I got, the worse it got. Kicks, punches, you name it. Girls can be so spiteful. By the time I finished school, I was done. I swore to myself that I'd never go through that again. That I'd do something to make me stronger." She gave a snort. "The truth was that, just through sheer endurance, I didn't realise how strong I'd become. How resilient. I think that's why I did well in the force. Because I didn't give up."

"You did tell me," Ben said, his voice cracked and wet.

"I know," she told him. "I know. We were in my cottage. You were sitting by the fire. I had made dinner."

"Risotto," he said.

"Risotto. Yes. I remember asking you why you joined. Do you remember?"

He didn't answer, just gave a gentle squeeze.

"You looked at me today. Earlier. In the incident room. Your eyes. I remember now when I saw that look before."

He prolonged the squeeze. But she had to continue. She had to get it out of him, if not for the investigation, for his own sanity.

"Was Marie the reason, Ben?"

"Yes," he said, and swallowed hard.

His chest heaved against her, but she didn't mind.

"Were you and Marie an item, Ben?"

"No," he said, his voice a little more controlled than before. He inhaled and exhaled, and his breath was sweet. "We were... She finished with me."

"Why?" Freya asked. "Am I allowed to ask?"

"A Savage, Freya. I'm a Savage. I didn't need to be tied down. I was untameable. Wild. At least, that's what I thought. She wanted one thing. I wanted another."

"She wanted more..." Freya held the last word, just to make sure. "She wanted to get married?"

He nodded.

"And you didn't want to?"

"No. Of course not. I was young. I was selfish," he said. "Savage by name, savage by nature, I guess."

"You're not."

"You're biased," he said, cutting her off. "I destroyed her. It's as simple as that."

"No—"

"She would have done anything for me. She was going to tell her father about us."

"He seriously didn't know?"

"Nobody knew about us," he said. "When she left, I played it over and over in my mind. I waited, hoping she'd come back."

"And she didn't?"

"No," he said, and she felt him shake his head slowly. "No. So I went to her house. But she wasn't there. I spoke to her dad who said she'd gone out somewhere with her little sister and the dog."

"To the forest?"

He nodded. It was slight, but she felt it.

"Ben, are you saying that she hasn't been seen since that day?"

"Yes," he said, his voice thick, yet somehow he managed to sound in control. Like he had come to terms with it, but not really. "Nobody ever came looking for me. Nobody ever suspected me. Because nobody ever knew. The weeks passed, and still, she hadn't been found. Months, years, and I swore, Freya. I swore I'd make it all better. I swore I'd find her, I just..."

"Just what, Ben?"

"Got caught up, I guess," he said. "I used to go out all the time. You know? Looking for her. Mistaking other women for her and stopping them, only to find it wasn't Marie. I don't know when, but I guess I just came to terms with her not coming back. But she was here all along. Somewhere. I shouldn't have given up on her. I should have found her, Freya. I could have found her."

"And you did," she said, seeing hope in that one little line. "You did find her."

"I was too late. I was too late for her. But I promise you this. I'll find Abigail. I won't stop until I do."

Freya opened her eyes. She hated to, but she slowly relinquished her grip and felt the warmth of him give way to the cold space. Whether to help him or to help herself, she didn't know, but she stayed close, sliding her arm around him as a friend might. And together they looked upon her, Marie, and her beauty.

And in that moment, Freya saw her once more. She wore that summer dress Freya had imagined before. She ran through those fields like she had done before. And the sun shone through her golden hair just as Freya had seen in her mind's eye.

But this time, she wasn't alone. This time, Ben was with her. A younger, more virile Ben. A picture of strength, and one who was yet to carry the burden of lost love on his shoulders.

Freya held him there, in her mind. Did she wish she had known him then? Did she wonder how he had been? A younger, less cautious Ben, who for some reason wore the tainted badge of the Savages on his heart.

No, she thought. I like him just the way he is now.

"We'll find Abigail, Ben," she said. "We'll find her together."

CHAPTER THIRTY-ONE

THE WALK TO THE CAR HAD BEEN SILENT AND SLOW, WITH BEN doing his best not to let his ankle become a problem. Freya assessed the situation, not for the first time that morning. The man could barely walk and the icy ground made a fall even more likely. Running would be out of the question, for sure.

And then there was Marie Treverne. The right thing to do would be to call it out. Say it how it was. Conflict of interest. There was no other way of putting it. But those three words would destroy Ben.

He stopped at the car. The snow that had been on the bonnet in the morning had melted during the journey to the hospital. But it had now been replaced with a fresh coating. Only half an inch thick. It wouldn't stay there for long. But it was a sign that the weather would not be letting up for a while.

Ben's shoulders sagged with the news, the discovery, the recognition. Whatever it was, it weighed on his mind. But without a doubt, there was a fire in his eyes. A determination. Raising his hand, he let the keys drop from his grip into hers.

He was at least relinquishing that responsibility. They sat, buckled up, and Freya started the car. Something needed to be said. Surely he would be thinking the same thing.

"Granger can't find out about this," he said quietly. He *had* been thinking it. "He'll take me off the investigation. It can't happen, Freya."

"I know," she replied, feeling the battle between cowardice and loyalty rage inside her. "This is just between you and I. She's just another body–"

"She's more than that–"

"She's just another body as far as anybody else is concerned. Nobody needs to know."

He nodded, seemingly satisfied with that response.

"Thanks," he said, and his eyes took on that lost look once more. She hoped it would be the last time she saw him like this. That he would snap out of it. But somehow she recognised the futility in that hope.

"What are friends for, Ben?"

"I know but–"

"We all have our demons. We all have a past. We can't change that, Ben. God knows I wish I could change mine. But then..."

"Then what?"

"Then I wouldn't have come here. I wouldn't have met you." Letting her hands fall to her lap, she relaxed for a moment, hoping that what she had to say made a difference. "I believe that people come into your life for one of three things. A reason, a season, or a lifetime."

"A reason, a season, or a lifetime?" he repeated, more to fill the empty space than anything, she guessed. "Which am I?"

Ignoring him, she continued, "A reason, is James Marley."

"He was a serial killer–"

"And my dealings with him were for one reason. That I should come here," she said, leaving no room for argument. James Marley had been her investigation, her nemesis, and the cause of her own suffering. "A season? DI Standing. Without him, I wouldn't have the team I have. He's gone now. On to new adventures. But he's the reason we now have Cruz, Gillespie, Nillson. It all adds up. As much as I couldn't abide the man, he was in my life short-term for a purpose."

"Lifetime?" Ben said.

"That's you, Ben. In whatever form our friendship takes, I believe that I will know you now for the rest of my days. That's how you have to look at things. That's how you have to understand the people around you. That's how you get to move on. Don't forget those reasons and seasons, of course not. But you must embrace the fact that because of Marie, you're no longer the Savage boy that causes local fathers to lock their doors when you're nearby. You're no longer the carefree, selfish young man you were. You're on your way to becoming a DI, and more probably, you're the most respected man in the station.'

"I doubt that—"

"I don't," Freya said. "I don't at all. And one day, you will make DI. One day, our careers will separate, and when it happens, I want you to know that I'm not going anywhere. I'll be there. Even if I'm in the sidelines working on other cases, I'll be there."

"You won't be," he said, shaking his head.

"Won't be there?"

"In the sidelines. You'll be beside me. I'll make sure of it," he said with confidence. "Now, let's go. I want to go and see her dad."

Pulling from the car parking spot, Freya felt the tyres slide a little on the icy tarmac. She drove slowly while Ben dialled a number, and then he settled back into his seat as the call connected.

"Ben?" It was Jackie's voice. The girl who had at one time been in competition with Freya over Ben's affections. It turned out that Gold was just another good friend to Ben. But she wondered if she had known about Marie. Or if Ben had bottled it up inside alone. "Good news. We've done some digging on Shane Dooley, the pipe fitter. He was at the old hospital grounds the morning

Abigail went missing. Worked all night apparently. And guess what? He drives a van."

"That's a decent start," Ben said. "Anything else?"

"He's got a record. Mostly brawling. You know? ABH, disturbing the peace, and that. Nothing serious, but you never know."

"Can you send me his address? We'll pay him a visit."

"Will do."

"Anything else?"

"I think Anna's just doing some more digging on Peter Jones. He's a bit of a wild one. I can see why they were fighting over him. A lovable rogue, you might say. Anyway, DC Cruz has been to the crime scene. Gillespie took him down there. He has your glove."

"Not the biggest news we've had on this case, but I'll take it," Ben said.

"He also found something else."

"Go on," Ben said, and exchanged a hopeful glance with Freya.

"A hat."

"A hat?"

"He found it in the forest, close to where he picked up your glove. Said it was hanging in a tree, like somebody had left it there, or maybe it snagged on a branch."

"What type of hat is it?"

"A beanie. You know? The woolly type that covers your ears."

"Any indication of whose it might be?"

"Could be anyone local. It's branded with Lincoln City Football Club. My guess is that our man is local and supports the Imps. He might even be a season ticket holder."

"Jackie, it's Freya," Freya called out, as if it wasn't already obvious. She eyed Ben, warning him to prepare himself. "I want you to do three things for me. Firstly, get that hat to the lab. Ask Sergeant Priest to have it hand-delivered. Call ahead so they're expecting it, and ask them politely to get on it immediately."

"I can't see that going down too well," Ben said, giving her a knowing look.

"It's a key piece of evidence, Jackie. I need you to own it. When they have it in the lab, I want you to call them every hour on the hour."

"Eh?"

"Trust me, they'll soon want it off their list."

"Right, I'll have a go, ma'am," Jackie said.

"Then, find what you can on an investigation into a missing person. Marie Treverne."

"Right. Is that recent?" she asked. "We checked all the missing persons reported recently. How far back am I going here?"

"Twelve years," Ben said.

A pause ensued, during which time they could almost hear the cogs in her bright, young mind click into place.

"Twelve years? Is that—"

"A confirmed ID," Freya added, cutting the conversation short. "Thirdly, invite Peter Jones in for a chat. In fact, no, don't worry, I'll have Gillespie do it. I want you in the office."

"Ma'am," she replied. "I can pass the message on to Gillespie if you want?"

"Thanks, Jackie, leave Gillespie with me. We'll be in later to interview Jones. Just hold him in an interview room. Keep him occupied. Find out what you can."

"I can talk to him if you like? I might, you know..."

"No, DC Gold, I do not know," Freya said, insinuating that she did indeed know what Jackie had meant but wanted to make her feel uncomfortable by voicing it.

"Well, I was thinking he might open up to me. Maybe I can appeal to his, erm..."

"Are you saying he might talk to you because you're younger?"

"I saw it on a documentary. Worked well by all accounts."

"Then do it," Freya said reluctantly. "I want to know his exact movements over the past three days. I want every second accounted for."

"Leave it with me, ma'am," she said, clearly happy with the responsibility.

Freya ended the call.

"Peter Jones," she said, not at all surprised. But Ben didn't seem to be happy with the news. His eyes blazed with rage. "What?"

"Peter Jones?" he said, shaking his head. "He would have been about six years old when Marie went missing. If the same man had taken Abigail McGowan, then it's not Peter Jones."

"Then we have to consider that they may not in fact be linked, Ben," she told him flatly. "Jess Henry said something about Peter going to the football game. There's a good chance the hat belongs to him."

Ben said nothing. He stared ahead, lost in his thoughts.

"But that doesn't mean we'll give up on Marie," Freya said. "We'll get to the bottom of it. You have my word."

CHAPTER THIRTY-TWO

THE HOUSE WAS ALMOST EXACTLY AS BEN REMEMBERED IT, ONLY weathered and aged, like Ben's memories. The hedge that ran around the perimeter had at one time been trimmed, squared, and orderly. Now it had the appearance of an old man's beard – wispy, unkempt, and capped with snow.

The gravelled driveway which had once been maintained was now mostly mud. Thick weeds had taken root, sprouting through the blanket of white like flags of an invading army, marking the seizure of the land. The same could be said for the lawn, which Ben remembered being striped, short, and trim, but was now knee-high, browned, and more weed than grass. It was so tall that it seemed almost untouched by the heavy snow that had carpeted the surrounding land.

The house, a two-story, detached building, was brick, but the windows were rotten, the roof sagged, and the front door was almost lost to foliage. Parked down the side of the house was an old Ford Sierra estate. The tyres were flat and rust was working its way through the bodywork, though it was clear it had been a light blue, once upon a time. Through the grime on the number plate, Ben could make out it was an E registration. He did a calculation in his head and determined it was a 1986 or 1987 model.

"I remember this place," he said to Freya, as she parked the car and applied the handbrake. He pointed to the new-build houses that had been developed in the surrounding fields. "It used to stand alone. The nearest house was a few hundred metres down the road. It's fallen to rack and ruin."

"Are her parents still together?"

Ben shrugged. "I never got to meet them, remember?"

"Of course. But didn't she ever speak of them?"

"Maybe. I obviously wasn't listening though. I had more important things to think about."

"Such as?" Freya asked, clearly alluding to his teenage sexual appetite.

"My motorbike," he said. "That's all I ever cared about. At least, until she called it off."

"And you realised you missed her?"

"Yeah, something like that. I realised I'd never find anybody quite like her. If that counts as missing her, then yeah."

"Shall we?" she said. "You don't have to tell him who you are. In fact, it's probably better if you don't. I'll do the talking if you want."

"Let's do it. I need to face him. I need to look him in the eye," Ben said, using the door to support his weight as he climbed from the car. The sprained ankle was on the mend; it was just a little tight. But the deep cuts on his shins burned like fire whenever he walked.

He pushed a clump of ivy to one side and ducked beneath the rest to enter the little porch. But then he hesitated. Of all the things he and Marie had shared, all those times, the only time he had ever stood in that spot was when it was too late. He remembered her father peering up at him, wondering who he was, or perhaps recognising him and disapproving of a Savage boy on his doorstep asking after his daughter.

"You okay?" Freya asked.

He knocked on the door by way of a response, then stepped to one side to allow Freya to shelter under the porch. The few moments that passed became a full minute. Freya knocked the second time, harder than Ben had. A standard three raps on the little window in the front door.

"Mr Treverne?" she called out. "Mr Treverne, it's the police. We just need a few moments of your time."

"Shall we come back?" Ben said, leaning past Freya to try knocking one more time, harder than before and louder.

But there was no movement inside and nobody called out.

"Maybe we should," Freya agreed, and she stepped out into the snow, the wind catching her hair. "Ben?"

He was peering through the little window. Not searching for Marie's dad, but seeing if there were any photographs on a sideboard or hanging on the wall. A sign that Marie's memory still lived on in a place other than own his mind, and his own heart.

"Ben?" Freya said, a little sharper.

He turned and found her gazing at the corner of the house, where the old car was parked. He stepped out of the porch, and there, dressed in an old Barbour jacket, wellies, and trousers that looked to be as old as the car, was Marie's dad. Unmistakable, undeniably Marie's dad. The wide eyes, the high cheekbones, and the rich, full lips. He was an old man now, though his ragged appearance was no doubt due to the loss of his daughter.

"Mr Treverne?" Ben said. "Is that you?"

With his hands stuffed into his pockets and his jacket flapping in the wind, he could have been a black and white photo. He had that accusing look that people wore back when cameras were rare items and having your picture taken just wasn't natural, unless you were Rita Hayworth or Elizabeth Taylor.

"I know you," he called out, staring Ben directly in the eye. "I've seen you before."

Shaking his head, Ben shifted his weight, forcing his left leg to suffer so his right leg could recover for a few minutes.

"I don't think I've had the pleasure, Mr Treverne."

"You're a Savage," he said.

"I'm a policeman now," Ben said, nodding.

He fished his ID from his pocket, and the old man scoffed and dismissed it with a wave of his hand.

"I'd recognise you anywhere."

"Oh," Ben said, suddenly feeling for the first time as if it were him in the dock and Marie's father was judge, jury, and executioner.

"Your dad," he began, "tyrant, he was. Yes. Yes, I remember you. You had brothers."

"That's right. Two of them," Ben said.

"Can we talk inside?" Freya asked, clutching her jacket closed and clearly freezing cold. "We'd like a few moments of your time."

"I heard you the first time, miss."

"It's important," Ben said. "It's about Marie."

The mention of Marie's name caused not an iota of emotion in the man's face. Though there seemed to be so much excess skin that, for all Ben knew, behind it there may have been a raft of expression taking place.

"Whatever you have to say, you can say it out here."

"Mr Treverne, we have some news. There's been a..." Ben paused to swallow.

"A development," Freya finished for him.

"What kind of development?"

"Can we go inside?" Freya asked. "It's freezing out here."

The old man looked back over his shoulder at the road. He sucked at the inside of his lip, causing the entire lower part of his face to shift. Then he nodded, and gestured for them to follow him.

He led them around to the back door, and as soon as they stepped into the covered yard, the noise of the wind died down.

Mr Treverne fished his keys from his pocket then seemed to take an age searching for the correct one. It took at least another minute for him to insert the key, fumble with the lock, then push the door open.

They entered straight into the kitchen, a small room with a terracotta tiled floor and a wooden bench. The heat from an AGA hit Ben almost instantly, and he limped to the bench where he could lean in some kind of comfort. He sneaked a glance through the internal door into the hallway, but still couldn't see any pictures of Marie.

"Now then," the old man said, filling an old kettle from the tap. His hands shook from age rather than the cold. He set it on the AGA then turned to stare at each of them accusingly. "What news?"

"We've found Marie," Ben said. He'd been waiting for the moment when Mr Treverne asked the question. There was no room for fluff or padding. The man had little time for his heart-strings to be tugged. The news had to be delivered just so. Freya, however, clearly thought otherwise, and while Marie's father was reeling from Ben's statement, she glared at him, wide-eyed. "It's definitely her."

"My Marie?" he said, reaching out to grab a chair, or the bench, or something.

Acting faster than Ben had been able to, Freya caught him and eased him toward a chair, where he leaned on the old, pine table, clearly shocked at the news.

"My Marie?" he asked again.

Ben nodded.

"It can't be. She's been gone for…"

There was no attempt to calculate the years. His words trailed off, and all manner of expression made it to the surface of his soft and unshaven face.

"I'm sorry to be the one to tell you," Ben said.

"You're the eldest one, aren't you?" he said, his voice cracking.

"I am, yes. It's Ben. Ben Savage."

"You knew her. You were in her year. Or close, at least. She used to talk about you."

"I did know her, yes. I remember her well." Ben searched Freya's face for help, but he was on his own on this one. "She was lovely. A kind girl."

Mr Treverne nodded, as if he accepted the compliments on her behalf.

"How do you know it's her then?" he asked, his face twisting in disgust. "After all this time. I mean, she'd be–"

"I recognised her."

"You did what? She's been dead gone ten years, and you say you recognised her? You must have the wrong girl."

"Mr Treverne, she wasn't dead."

"Eh?"

"She died recently. Three days ago."

"Three days ago? That's not possible, I–"

"Dad?" a voice called, and a cold wind blasted through the house before the front door slammed.

It was Marie. That voice. So unmistakable.

"Dad, are you here? There's a car on the drive."

She stepped into the doorway, then froze when she saw Ben and Freya. The eyes. The jaw. The cheeks. It was like he had stepped back in time. He felt a cold rush across his skin and the hairs on his nape stood on end.

"Dad?" she said, peering around Ben to see her father. "Dad, what's going on? Who are these people?"

"Police," Freya said, flashing her warrant card. "I'm Detective Inspector Bloom. This is my colleague–"

"They're here about Marie, dear," he said, and then Ben realised. The similarities were uncanny. The way she held herself, the way she pulled her hair back and to one side. "They found her."

"Found her?"

"Emily?" Ben said, uncertain of the reality, but sure as hell in his mind he was right.

"Yes. How do you know my name?"

"Knew her, didn't he?" the old man said. "One of the Savage lot up the road."

"I went to school with Marie. I knew her, but—"

"I know you," she said, and she placed her bag on the table beside her father. "You're the farmer's boy."

"I moved away from the family business," Ben said. "As you can see."

"And you said you found her? Is that right?"

Ben nodded. "I wish it was good news."

"She's dead then," the girl said, placing her hand on her father's shoulder. "For sure, I mean."

"I'm afraid so, yes."

"How?"

Ben glanced at Freya, while he swallowed what would have been catastrophic news if he had even tried to explain in detail.

"We think Marie took her own life," Freya explained.

"Suicide?" Emily scoffed. "Marie? But why would she—"

"She was pregnant," Freya said. "Six weeks."

"Pregnant? But... Stop. None of this is making any sense. She *wasn't* dead?"

Freya shook her head apologetically.

"All this time, my sister was alive? And we were right here?"

"I'm afraid so."

"So where was she? There's no way she would have done that to us. She would have come back."

"I don't think she had much choice in the matter," Ben said, stopping Emily from venturing down a path of denial.

"You what? You mean she was kidnapped and held against her will?"

"I can't see how else it would have happened. You're right,"

Ben said. "Given half an opportunity, she would have come home."

"When did she…"

"Three days ago. The pathologist has reason to believe she poisoned herself. We're investigating, of course."

Emily nodded, seemingly speechless.

"I won't stop, Emily," Ben said. "I won't stop–"

"This is about that other girl, isn't it? The Dunston girl?"

"I'm sorry, I can't really say anything about–"

"It is. I know it is. It has to be."

"We can arrange for you to see her," Freya said. "If you'd like to, that is."

The old man nodded and rested his head on his only remaining daughter's hand.

They stayed like that for long enough that Freya gestured to Ben that it was time for them to leave. She opened the back door and stepped outside, giving Ben a moment with them.

He placed his card on the pine table.

"If you'd like to talk," he said, and Emily nodded dismissively. "I'll ask someone to be in touch. To take you to see her."

He stepped outside, wiped his eyes, and took a breath. But before he closed the door on the people who, in a different life, he might have referred to as family, he watched them and saw her, Marie, in Emily's face, her movements, and in her eyes.

"Come on," Freya said, coaxing him away. She helped him back around the house, allowing him to lean on her. But it wasn't his shins that gave him cause to need support. Not then anyway. He stopped beside the old Ford Sierra estate and accepted a tissue from Freya so he could wipe his eye.

"Sorry," he muttered, slightly ashamed to be so open about his emotions. He knew she would tell him not to be sorry. That was what people said. But still.

"Ben?" she said, and he waited for her to tell him it was okay to show emotion. That he was only human. "Ben?"

He pocketed the tissue and stared at her. But she wasn't looking at him with a concerned face as he thought she would be. She was frowning at the car. Specifically, the window in the rear door.

He shoved himself off the car and stood beside Freya, once more leaning on her, this time because of his shins.

"What do you make of that?" she asked.

CHAPTER THIRTY-THREE

Detective Sergeant Jim Gillespie was cold. The thought ran through his mind that if his gentleman's jewels hadn't retracted so far back into him, they would have frozen off by now, and the CSI team, who were once more scouring the ground, dropping their little numbered markers here and there, would have claimed them as evidence.

"How you getting on, Michaela?" he asked, more as a distraction from the cold than anything else.

"You'll know when we find something, DS Gillespie," she replied, then looked up at him through her goggles. "Because I'll tell you. Now, if you don't mind, I'd like to focus."

"Aye, course. No bother," he said, looking up at the trees then around at the forest. Then finally, he took his fourth or fifth glance into the manhole. Nothing had changed. A white suit was on their hands and knees at the bottom, and he took his fourth or fifth stab at trying to guess if it was a man or a woman beneath the suit.

"You alright down there?" he asked, and they peered up at him, their hood, goggles, and mask covering their face and hair. They nodded, then returned to what they had been doing.

"Erm, Michaela? Who's down there? Do they have a name?"

"Pat," she replied, growing more irritated by the second.

"Pat, right, aye," he said, convinced she had known he was trying to work out if it was a male or female and had provided a false name just to annoy him. "I suppose that's short for something?"

"I suppose it is, yes."

He took another glance down into the hole.

It could be a fella. A slightly small fella, like Cruz, with feminine hands and fingers. Might be a good thing, considering he's sifting through piles of garbage. Slender fingers might be an advantage. But then, it could be a female. A woman. It would have to be a slightly butch woman. He wasn't sure if the white suit added any padding to the shoulders and the backside. Not many women Jim knew would be happy spending their day down the bottom of a hole sifting through piles of rubbish, especially when they had done the same job the day before.

Except maybe Michaela.

"You, erm, you like all this stuff then, do you?" he asked, and Michaela's head bowed in surrender.

"What?"

"All this? You enjoy piecing it together, do you? Finding a hair or a little blood splatter. That your thing, is it?"

"I'm a forensic scientist. I spent seven years in university to be the best at what I do. I have a PhD, two masters degrees, and I was the youngest female in my field to lead a Scene of Crime team. So, yes, DS Gillespie, I enjoy what I do. I enjoy *piecing it together*, as you say. I get a thrill from finding the link that puts the bad guy away. If you have any more questions, then can I please ask that you send me an email? I'll respond when I'm back at my desk."

"You have a desk, do you?" he said. "I always thought you lot spent your time looking through those things... you know, what's it called?"

"A microscope?" she asked tentatively.

"Aye, that's it."

"I'm afraid if that's your understanding of how forensics really works, then I might suggest you begin seeking a career in a different field. I would have expected a Detective Sergeant to have at least a basic understanding of our role and how we go about obtaining objective facts, so that people like you can stand up in court and be certain you have the right man for the crime."

"Aye, well, I don't really do the standing up in court thing. Not my style. That's more DI Bloom's job. And Steve's, when he was around."

"Steve Standing?"

"Aye, yeah."

"He's not around anymore?"

"No. Transferred to Lincoln HQ. More opportunity, he said. Between you and me, I don't think he got on very well with DI Bloom."

"I can't imagine why."

"Aye, I know. She's a bit of a hard one, but she's alright."

"I'm sure she is," Michaela said. "A hard one, that is."

"She's not that bad. You just need some thick skin, is all. She'll never hold a grudge. I mean, I've pissed her off royally and she's been fine the next day. I figure as long as I don't upset her until the afternoon, my mornings are usually alright."

"Are you serious?"

"Eh?"

"Give me strength."

"Ah, you're doing alright. Can I help at all?" he said, and took a step toward her, to which she immediately protested.

"Please, you're already close enough."

"You did this bit already, though, right? I'm alright here?"

"Sadly, yes. Had I known you were going to be looking over my shoulder, I might have saved that area until last."

"Ah, come on. How's it going with Ben anyway?" he said. "I think you pair would be great together."

It was the first time she'd faltered with her words. She normally sounded a bit like Freya, with her public school upbringing and her hoity-toity accent. But she was quiet.

Gillespie leaned over the edge of the hole.

"Hey, Pat? What do you reckon? Michaela and Ben. Cracking couple, eh?"

The white suit peered up, shook his or her head, and then returned to his or her work.

"Aye, that's what I thought," Gillespie said. Then he muttered, "Lively one, that one."

"DS Gillespie, are you here just to annoy me, or are you serving some sort of purpose that I cannot for the life of me fathom?"

"Eh?"

"What are you doing here?"

"Oh aye. Boss said to stay close to you. Said not to let you out my sight. Said the slightest little thing you find, I should report it. Time is of the essence, she said." He tapped his watch to emphasise the statement. "So, will you see him then? He's dead keen on dinner, you know. Although, between you and me, he's not that experienced."

She sighed, and carried on working while Gillespie spoke. He wrapped his coat around him tightly and folded his arms to hold it in position.

"Aye, I gave him some pointers, like. I mean, what's a bloke to do when your mate likes someone as much as he likes you? And if I'm honest, I think he's punching, if you know what I mean. He hasn't a clue. Honestly. He thinks a bag of chips and a stroll along the river is a decent first date. I told him. Listen, Ben, I said. Women love romance. Italian restaurants, a show, and no cheeky grabs of the backside. Keep it clean. Aye, well... Hopefully, he paid attention. The fella hasn't been on a date for all the years I've known him. Must have saved an absolute fortune. Reckon he'll go all out on you though. All he ever bloody talks about."

"Sorry?" Michaela said, interrupting his thoughts.

"Eh?"

"You said, all he ever talks about."

"Aye, yeah."

"Are you referring to me?"

"Aye, yeah," he said, nodding. "Who do you think I'm talking about? It's not old *Personality Pat* down there, is it?"

"Did you know I paid him a visit this morning?" she said, raising her goggles and adjusting herself to a more comfortable kneeling position.

"Oh aye," he said. "Gave him a wake-up call, eh?"

"Well, that wasn't my intention. I believe I caught him in the shower."

"Oh, lucky you," Gillespie said, sensing some more juicy details to follow. "The sly old bugger said nothing to me. You wait until I see him."

"Well, you see, I had no intention of even stepping into his house. I was merely going to offer him one more chance. We had an altercation and I may have overreacted."

"Well, it happens—"

"So I was hoping just to let him know that dinner was, in fact, still on."

"Well, good for you, Michaela. I like a girl that knows what she wants and—"

"But it was your boss who answered the door."

"Eh?"

"She was wearing what I can only imagine were Ben's clothes. You know? T-shirt, joggers. She was clutching a coffee and, judging by her hair, she had only just woken up."

"Eh?" Gillespie said again, unable to believe what he was hearing.

"Do you understand what I'm telling you, DS Gillespie?"

"Erm..."

"She stayed the night."

"No."

"It certainly looked like it."

"No."

"Ben came to the top of the stairs when he heard me," she said, matter of fact.

"Aye, see."

"Semi-naked."

"No."

"So you see, DS Gillespie, you can sing Ben's praises all you like, but I will never be taking a midnight stroll along the River Witham sharing a bag of chips with him. Not on your nelly."

"I don't believe it."

"Well, don't take my word for it. Ask him yourself."

"I know what it was," Jim said, and Michaela looked up, with just a glimmer of hope in her eyes. "Ben was injured last night. I forgot all about it."

"Injured?"

"Aye, yeah. Can barely walk, the poor fella."

"Well, how bad is he?"

"Nigh on broke both his shin bones," he said.

"Is he okay?"

"Hard to say with Ben. You know how he is. Like a dog with a bone when he gets his teeth into a case."

"Well, how did it happen?"

"Erm, right here, as far as I can tell. That's why you lot are back. Cracked his shins on the wall somewhere. Launched himself at the suspect in the dark and misjudged it. You know, because of his ankle."

"His ankle?"

"Yeah, he sprained it chasing the bloke. I would have just given up. But no, not Ben. Carried right on. I'm surprised you didn't find him down there this morning. Freya was probably helping him get fixed up. She lives up the lane next to him. You know? In one of those wee cottages."

Gillespie's pocket began to vibrate, and as much as he hated to, he let go of his jacket, letting the cold air in, and fished his phone from his pocket. "Hold on," he said. "DS Gillespie?"

"Gillespie, it's DI Bloom."

"Ah, how you doing, boss?" he said, pointing at the phone and gesturing to Michaela to wait one minute. She rolled her eyes and carried on working, only with less vigour than before, as if she was pondering what he had said.

"Aye boss," he said, pleased with the little seed he had sown.

"I need you to take a couple of uniforms and bring Peter Jones in."

"The lad?"

"Yes. Do not arrest him. Invite him to come and give a formal statement. Explain it'll help with our enquiries. But do not, under any circumstances, arrest him until we have something concrete."

"Ah, right. The hat?' Gillespie said.

"Exactly. Plus, he had a relationship with Abigail. I think there's more to it than he's letting on, and we need to get him away from his girlfriend."

"Ah, Jess Henry?" Gillespie said, just to confirm he had all the facts.

"That's right. Bring him into the station. I'm going to let DC Gold interview him, but I want you standing by."

"Ah, I see. The whole age thing? Think he might open up to her, do you?"

"Yes, actually," Freya said, sounding surprised. "Can I leave that with you? Ben and I still have a few more people to see. We'll be back in the station this afternoon."

"Aye, boss. You leave it with me."

"Oh, Gillespie?"

"Aye, boss."

"Any news on Griffiths?"

"Sorry. Not yet. I've asked Sergeant Priest to keep us all in the loop."

"Good, thanks. Right. I'll leave you to it. And remember, invite him to come in. Keep him on our side. You're not working for Steve Standing now."

"You leave it with me, boss," he replied, and ended the call. "Well, I'll love you and leave you."

"Are you off?" Michaela said. "That's a shame."

"Aye, well, you know? No rest for the wicked," he said, standing and leaning over the manhole for the last time that day. "Cheers, Pat. See you soon?"

Pat looked up at him, shook his or her head, then returned to his or her work again.

"Doesn't say much, that one, eh?" he said to Michaela.

"That's why Pat is one of the best," Michaela said. "Doesn't fall foul of irritating distractions."

"So, shall I tell Ben to give you a call then?"

"No, I'll call him—"

"Oh no you don't. Come on. Give him a chance. I don't believe for a minute that he and..." He thought about Ben and Freya and shuddered. She had become like their mum, and that was just... "No."

Michaela smiled at him. It was as if she was doing her level best not to but somehow it came through.

"Go on," he encouraged her. "If there's one thing I can tell you about the fella, he's absolutely shocking at talking to women. Hasn't a clue. If you think he and Freya Bloom are at it, you're off your trolley. Honestly."

She was considering it. It was written all over her face.

"Shall I?" he said again. "Get him to call you?"

"Tell him he has one more chance. No more."

"Aye, you're a sweetheart, you are."

"And can I just ask you one thing, Jim?" she said, raising her goggles once more.

"Aye, anything."

"Are you always this irritating?"

He laughed, and some birds in the trees above him took off, scattering the snow that was resting on the canopy.

"That was a ruse, lass. You might have a PhD and some other stuff, but you just fell for the oldest trick in the infamous Gillespie book of tricks."

"Excuse me?"

"Oh, come on. I had to get you to talk to me somehow. How else was I going to convince you to agree to have dinner with Ben? I'd have more luck talking to Pat down there."

He winked as a dumbfounded grin escaped Michaela's mask. She'd been had, and the fact that she didn't care could only be good news for Benjamin. Gillespie turned on his heels military fashion and marched the few steps to the stream, leaving a very bemused forensic scientist kneeling on the ground, probably wondering what she was going to wear on her date, he thought.

He crossed the stream and climbed up the bank, and was just a few steps onto the footpath that led to the church when his phone rang again.

"Gillespie, it's Gold," she said, her voice sounding urgent.

"Aye, Jackie."

"I need your help with something urgently."

"Well, you're in luck. I'm putting out fires all over the show here," he said proudly.

"There's been a report of a disturbance in Dunston. A fight or something. It's the McGowan house."

CHAPTER THIRTY-FOUR

THE SNOWFALL WAS SO THICK THERE WAS NO OBVIOUS SIGN OF where the tarmac ended and the grass verge began. The only clear indication of the change in terrain was the steep drop into the dyke. The last thing Freya needed was to put Ben's car into the dyke, yet somehow, since leaving the Treverne house, she felt less capable, as if she was more vulnerable and her world could change in a heartbeat. The slip of a car tyre, giving chase to a suspect, or going for a jog in the morning; life was somehow more precious after seeing a parent grieve for their child.

"Anna, it's Ben," he called out while Freya drove. "I'm trying to reach Jackie but she's not picking up."

"She's on the line with Gillespie. Sounds like there's been a break-in or some kind of disturbance in Dunston."

Freya and Ben exchanged concerned glances, both coming to the same conclusion.

"Peter Jones?"

"No, it's at the McGowan house. A neighbour reported it. Broken glass, shouting, and God knows what else. I think she's sending Gillespie there to deal with it, plus we've got uniform on the way."

"Good work," Ben said. "Did you hear the news?"

Feeling Freya glance in his direction, Ben pushed on. He had to talk about it. He couldn't keep hiding it away.

"What news? I've been looking into Shane Dooley. He's a character, I can tell you."

"We've got a positive ID on the unknown."

"Oh, yeah. Jackie was looking for the old file." There was a rustling of papers, and then Anna came back on the line. "Marie Treverne?"

"That's her," Ben said. "I need you to go through the investigation. Make sure the protocols were followed. See if they missed something."

"I see David Foster was on the investigation," she said, more in conversation than to make a point.

"David?"

"Yeah. He was a DC back then. Ah, look. You'll never guess who led the investigation."

"Will Granger?" Ben guessed.

"Yeah. What do you know? It's hard to imagine them back then."

"Anna, I want you to do me a favour. I want you to look into the father for me. See how well he was checked out, if there were any observations made at the time. We're looking for inconsistencies."

"You don't think—"

"We're just covering all angles. Nothing of substance. Not yet."

"Right," she said, scribbling her notes loudly. Freya could picture her, with her pad neatly positioned beside her desk phone with a little pot of pens and highlighters.

"We also need a property check. See what he owns. See if there are any outbuildings, basements, or maybe he has another place somewhere close by."

"You think he was keeping his daughter locked up?"

"We don't think anything right now," Freya said. "We're just covering all angles. We believe Abigail is still alive. If that's the case, then we need to understand the lay of the land. When we do make a break, we'll need to act fast. Check satellite imagery if you need to."

"Will do, ma'am," she said.

"Good, well done. Is DC Gold off the phone yet?"

"She is. Shall I pass you across?"

"Please."

The line silenced for a moment, and Ben exalted loudly. "At least we have access to the lead investigator," he said. "I'll set up a meeting with Will Granger. We might find something we don't already know."

"No," Freya said, a little faster than she perhaps should have.

"What do you mean? Why?"

"I'm sorry, Ben. Our focus is Abigail McGowan. Until we know for sure that the two cases are linked–"

"How can they not be?" he said. "You just told Marie's father that we'd do everything we can to find out who was responsible for her death."

"I know, I know. But look at it from DCI Granger's point of view. He's under pressure to find Abigail. We've got leads we need to follow through on. Shane Dooley. Jason King, that's a strong lead. Peter Jones."

"Peter Jones is just a boy."

"He's old enough, strong enough, and more than capable of overpowering Abigail McGowan."

"This is ridiculous."

"Listen to me, Ben. Sure, go ahead and have Nillson do some digging on Mr Treverne. If that makes you happy, then that's fine by me."

"There was a bloody Lincoln City Football Club sticker on his car."

"Guess what? We're living in Lincolnshire. Half the county

will be supporters."

"I don't believe you. All that crap about finding her killer."

"That's just it, Ben. She killed herself. You were there. You heard what Doctor Bell said. For all we know, Marie Treverne might have just had enough and been living alone for the past twelve years."

"That's rubbish and you know it."

"Yeah, well. My point is, to keep Granger happy, we need to follow up on leads. If we don't, guess what? Neither of us will be working this investigation. We'll be handing it over to Lincoln HQ, and you know what that means?"

"DI Standing?" Ben said.

"Exactly. Do you want him coming in halfway through and finishing off what we couldn't do because we were too preoccupied with the past?"

"Preoccupied?"

"You know what I mean," Freya said. "We've got leads. We need to follow up on them. When we're done, we can expand our search. If, and I mean if, we hit brick walls, if Dooley and King turn out to be nothing, and Jones turns out to be completely innocent, then we'll put more energy into Marie's case. But if one of those leads has the slightest chance of finding Abigail alive–"

He nodded. "I get it," he said, and turned to stare out of the window.

"I made you a promise, Ben. I told you we'd find out who's responsible. And we will. But Abigail must come first."

He nodded again. "I know. And you're right. Of course, you're right."

"*You* also said you'd find her, Ben," she said softly. "You told me you owed it to Marie."

He said nothing.

"This is our chance. *Your* chance. We can't bring Marie back, but we have a chance at saving Abigail. That's where we need to focus our energy. For all our sakes."

CHAPTER THIRTY-FIVE

"Anybody home?" Gillespie called out. The McGowans' front door was ajar, so he gave it a nudge with his boot and peered inside. Inside was silent, so he entered cautiously. "Mr McGowan?"

Outside, and further along the street, a car was accelerating hard. He leaned out, saw a Police Astra, and waited for them to come to a stop. Holding up one finger, he indicated for them to wait, then pointed to his eye for them to keep an eye out, and moved back inside. From the hallway, he could see into the kitchen. It looked as if a shelving unit had been pulled over. There were framed photos on the floor and a potted plant had smashed. To prevent the intruder from bolting past him, Gillespie closed the door, but caught his hand on something sharp. A pointed shard of wood was jutting out from where the lock had been forced. The lock itself was hanging by just two screws.

"Anybody home?" he called out. "It's the police. If you're in here, then I'd suggest you make yourself known."

The living room was tidy and the dining room was immaculate, but when he moved through to the kitchen, he began to understand. Not only had a shelving unit been pulled over, most likely from some sort of struggle, but a kitchen knife was missing from the little wooden block. A bag of pasta was strewn across the work surface and the hob had been left on, presumably for the empty saucepan that was sitting beside the sink.

The back door was unlocked and there was blood on the handle. And when Gillespie peered through the glass, he found the gate at the far end of the garden to be open.

He pulled a blue latex glove from his pocket, opened the door, and stepped outside. A strong wind rushed through the house and the front door slammed, then bounced open without the lock to secure it. On the patio, there were three footprints that Gillespie took to be made by a running shoe. Keeping to the edge of the lawn, he traced the prints to the back gate where they trailed off into the fields, the same way Abigail would have run a few mornings before.

But despite the blood on the door handle, there seemed to be none anywhere near any of the prints.

He retraced his steps to the house, re-entered, and called out once more.

"Mr McGowan, it's DS Gillespie. If you're in here, let me know."

Stopping at the front door, he peered outside, nodding at the two uniforms who were now standing beside the car, waiting for further instructions.

"Sit tight, lads," he said, then ventured up the stairs. "I'm coming up. If there's anybody here, make yourself known. Last chance."

The panel on the bathroom door had been kicked in, and on closer inspection, Gillespie found toiletries scattered across the room. He toed the first bedroom open, finding what must have been Abigail's room. The wardrobe had been emptied onto the bed, drawers had been tipped upside down and tossed to one side, and there were bags strewn across the room – handbags, sports bags, and little makeup bags.

But there was no sign of anybody.

A shove of the next bedroom door, however, told an altogether different story.

He stared for a moment and let his head fall forward. He closed his eyes at the sight of Mr McGowan lying half on the bed and half off.

Then he heard it. A sign of life. The faint gurgle of blood in his throat.

"No way," Gillespie said to himself, almost in disbelief. Stepping across the room, being careful not to touch anything, he used his gloved hand to push open the window, then whistled down to the uniforms.

"Ambulance," he called. "Pronto."

He pulled his phone from his pocket, dialled Ben's number, and set the phone to loudspeaker. Then, taking care not to interfere with anything, he reached down and felt Mr McGowan's neck for a pulse.

"Gillespie," Ben said when he answered the call. There was heavy road noise, so Gillespie spoke loud and clear.

"Ben, I've attended the McGowan house. Had a report of a disturbance."

"Yeah, Anna said. What's the news?"

"Ah, it's not looking good for him. House is trashed. Front door has been kicked in. There's clearly been a struggle of some kind. I found him upstairs. Lost a lot of blood, but I have a pulse," Gillespie explained. He placed the hand without a glove in front of McGowan's mouth and felt the faintest breath, warm but weak. "He's breathing. Looks to be a stab wound to his gut. It's hard to see. He's on his front, but the bed's covered in blood. His hands are slashed too. Probably from defending himself. Can't really see if he's wounded anywhere else without moving him."

"You're going to have to move him then," DI Bloom said. "We can't have him bleeding out on us."

"Aye, I bloody knew you were going to say that. Hold tight then."

Gillespie stood over the man, who was half-sprawled on the bed, face down with his legs draping across the floor. He felt beneath him, then retracted his gloved hand. It was covered in blood.

"Ah, Christ," he called out, and heaved McGowan onto his back, then dragged him onto the bed completely. "He's losing a lot of blood. It's definitely a puncture wound of some sort."

"Keep pressure on the wound, Gillespie," Freya advised.

"Aye, what the bloody hell do you think I'm doing?" he called out, stripping a pillowcase from the pillow. He ripped open the man's shirt, grimaced at the slice in his flesh, then pressed down hard.

"Need us to call emergency services?"

"It's done already. Should be on their way."

Keeping pressure on the wound, he leaned over and lay his face over McGowan's mouth, feeling for that faint breath of air.

"You okay, Jim?" Ben asked.

"Aye. He's alive still. I don't know how long for though. It's like a scene from Carrie in here. Hard to say exactly what went on," he called out. "He's got a pretty serious knife wound to his gut. He'll need stitches and more blood for sure, and I wouldn't be surprised if there's some internal bleeding. He's in a bad way, Ben."

"That's if he makes it that far," Ben added.

"Aye. He also has some damn awful bruising to his face. I'd say a broken nose, judging by the swelling."

"Have you had a look about, Gillespie?" Ben asked.

"Aye, blood on the back door, footsteps out through the gate and across the field. Trainers. Male, judging by how big they are. Kitchen is messed up. So I'd say the intruder got in, found McGowan in the kitchen, and—"

Loud footsteps bounded up the stairs and one of the uniforms poked his head into the room.

"Hold on, Ben," he called out, then addressed the uniform. "One of you stay here and wait for the ambulance. The other, go out the back door. Follow the footsteps. See where they end up."

The uniform nodded and slipped away again.

"Sorry about that. Got a couple of uniforms here, thank God."

"Who do you have?" Ben asked, knowing the team well enough to decide how competent they were.

"Ah, forget the fella's name. Looks like the fella from Scooby Doo. Messy hair. Scraggy beard. Built like a rubber broom handle."

"Jefferson," Ben added. "He's good."

"Aye, well. He'll be halfway across the fields by now, so hopefully he's as good as you say he is. Where was I?"

"You said you think the intruder found McGowan in the kitchen," Freya said.

"Oh, aye. I noticed a kitchen knife missing from the block. Shelves pulled down, pasta everywhere, blood on the door. It's like a Friday night in Lincoln down there."

"So somebody broke in and attacked him?" DI Bloom called out. "Or do you think there was some other motive?"

"Hard to say, boss. Abigail's room has been turned over. I mean, I know she was a teenager, but she couldn't have lived in that. Wardrobe's emptied, drawers turned upside down."

"Somebody was looking for something, maybe?" Ben said.

"I'll stay here and deal with the ambulance, and I'll call if what's-his-chops comes back with anything."

"Jefferson," Ben said.

"Aye, that's the fella. Can you give Michaela a call? We're going to need this place going over with fine-tooth comb. I'll go with McGowan. If he comes around, and I manage to get any sense out of him, I'll call you."

"I'll, erm, ask Jackie to get CSI. We're about to see Shane Dooley."

"Ah, don't be a coward, Benjamin. Give her a call. I had a wee chat with her earlier. She's expecting your call."

"You did what? What did you bloody say?"

"Are we really going to discuss your love life while a man is bleeding to death?" Freya asked.

There was a silence, then...

"What the bloody hell did you say?"

"Ah, relax, Ben. She said she came and saw you earlier. Said she saw something she shouldn't have, if you know what I mean?" Gillespie said, trying to speak in code for fear of making things awkward between him and the boss. "But, not to worry. I convinced her to give you one more chance."

There was a silence from the other end of the line, and a flash of blue caught Gillespie's attention.

"Ben?"

"I don't have time for this right now. I'll talk to you later."

"Aye, looks like the ambulance has just turned up anyway," Gillespie called out. "Remember, call her. I won't always be here to help you."

"Gillespie, while you're there, I want you to do something for me," Freya said.

"Aye, boss. Will that be before or after I get the dying man to the hospital?"

"During," she said, ignoring his petulance. "Jess Henry and Terry McGowan both mentioned a diary. Abigail's diary."

"A diary? What is this, nineteen twenty? Do people even keep them anymore?"

"Young girls do, Gillespie. Not everybody has a life they would rather forget. Search her room. Call me when you're done."

CHAPTER THIRTY-SIX

"He's on another planet," Ben said, stabbing his finger at the little dashboard screen. "I swear, if he 'ayes' me one more bloody time…"

Freya laughed, grateful for the opportunity. As small as it was, she felt the need to make the most of it. But the lift in mood was short-lived and Ben returned to his silence.

"What do we think?" Freya asked, as they approached Shane Dooley's house. She pulled the car to the curb and applied the handbrake, keeping the engine running for the heat. She wasn't out of ideas to bring Ben back to life just yet.

"Somebody wanted McGowan out of the way."

The idea floated, then dissipated.

"Or Abigail isn't missing," Freya countered. "She came back maybe to get some things, thinking her father would be at work. They fought. And she ran."

"She wouldn't stab her dad, would she?"

"I've seen stranger things," Freya said.

"He did say the footsteps led out of the back. Exactly the way Abigail usually goes for her run."

"Which makes me wonder what Mr McGowan had done that was so bad Abigail would run away in the first place."

"I was thinking the same. What if..."

He stopped, and stared at the Dooley house.

"Go on," she encouraged him.

"What if Terry McGowan was a possible for Marie?"

"That's a stretch."

"I don't know," Ben said, doing his best to convince her otherwise. "They've got land. He owns that field behind their house. What if he had Marie locked up?"

"For twelve years?"

He stared at her. He wasn't kidding.

"For twelve years, Ben?" she said, shaking her head. "Where's he supposed to have kept her?"

"There could be an outbuilding. Or a barn or something."

"Ben, it's zero degrees out there. Are you honestly suggesting that Terry McGowan could have locked Marie up in a barn and that she could have survived twelve long winters?"

"I don't know what I'm suggesting, Freya," he said. "My mind doesn't seem to be in tune with reality right now."

"No. No, it doesn't."

He turned back to face her as she spoke those words, slightly hurt by agreeing with him.

"Or Terry McGowan could genuinely be the victim of some kind of attack," Freya said. "Five minutes ago, you were accusing Marie's father. Now you think it's Abigail's father?"

"I'm airing my thoughts. I'm not convinced of either."

"We can't go accusing everyone. We need some kind of direction. We'll go in and see Dooley. We'll get a feel for him, find out what he did at the old hospital that night. Who he was with. Then we'll go back to the station. I think we need some perspective here."

"Maybe I'll talk to Will," he said, and gazed out of the window.

"About Treverne?" Freya said. "You know you can't do that."

He gave a mock laugh and glanced back at her with distaste written all over his face.

"About some leave," he said, and shoved the door open.

Freya followed suit, closing her door and leaning on the roof of the car, where one of them would normally have the final word.

But Ben had hobbled off. He was halfway up Dooley's front path, and by the time she had caught up with him, he had already knocked on the door and was searching for his warrant card.

"Ben, come on," she said. "You know it's the right thing to do. Our focus has to be on Abigail."

The front door opened.

"Do you see me complaining, Freya?" Ben asked, then turned to the man at the door. "Shane Dooley?"

"Yeah."

He wore black tracksuit bottoms, old trainers, and a t-shirt stained with some kind of sauce on the front. His forearms were heavily tattooed, and Freya imagined the artwork continued up his thick arms across his body. She caught a glimpse of the wing of a bird beneath his collar.

"Detective Savage. This is Detective Inspector Bloom. Mind if we have a word?"

"Eh? What about?"

"A missing girl. Can we come in?"

"What? No. Don't you need some kind of warrant?"

"A girl is missing, Mr Dooley."

"Yeah, heard about that. Terrible thing."

"She's been for missing three days now. So if you don't want us to come in, I can only assume you're guilty in some way and have something to hide. In which case, I'll have a dozen officers here in under an hour, along with a warrant to search your home, your vehicle, and any other property you might have. So we'll be coming in anyway."

"Can you do that?"

"Do you have anything to hide, Mr Dooley?" Ben asked, clearly demonstrating that his patience had just about expired.

"No. Course not."

Ben raised his eyebrows, questioning what the man was complaining about.

Dooley shoved the door open and stepped to one side, allowing Ben to hold onto the door frame and pull himself up.

"Is he alright?" Dooley asked Freya, who followed.

"Time is of the essence, Mr Dooley, as I'm sure you can imagine," she replied. "Shall we use the kitchen?"

Ben was leaning against the counter, slightly breathless from the pain and effort. He slapped Gutteridge's plans down on the worktop and unfolded them.

"What's this about?" Dooley said. "My wife will be home soon. I don't need her coming in finding you lot here."

"Guilty conscience?" Ben asked.

"Clean conscience," Dooley replied. "Shady past."

He spoke with a heavy Yorkshire accent. Not slow and methodical like Sergeant Priest; he spoke fast, somehow managing to skip syllables here and there.

"We've been speaking to Neil Gutteridge."

"Oh right," Dooley said, rolling his eyes at the emanation of the man's name. "Converted you, has he?"

"Converted us?" Freya said.

"Nothing," he said dismissively.

"He tells us you were working at the old RAF hospital in Nocton three nights ago."

"Right."

"Is that correct?"

"Yeah."

"Can you tell us a little bit about it?" Ben asked.

"What do you want to know? We were stripping out the old pumps. Is this about the scrap? I only did it the once, and I paid my dues."

"Scrap?" Ben asked.

Dooley sighed. "I were caught. A few months back. We've been stripping out pipework, and all sorts, for nearly eighteen months now. Well, you know how it is. Christmas was coming an' all that."

"So you run a load of scrap in for cash?" Ben said.

"Yeah. I was caught. Fair do. Haven't done it since."

"Did you happen to see anyone while you were working the other night?"

"You mean other than Steamboat?"

"Steamboat?"

"Yeah. Fella I worked with. Didn't Gutteridge tell you about him?"

Ben collected up the handwritten maintenance schedule Gutteridge had provided and spotted a name below Dooley's.

"William Stevens?"

"Yeah. Willy. We call him Steamboat."

"Is he into boats, then?" Freya asked, still not getting to grips with the local way of applying nicknames. She had already met two of Ben's friends, Squawk and Snowy, and had yet to fully understand the origins of their names.

"No," Dooley said. "He's just got big ears. You know? Like the Mickey Mouse cartoon." He raised his hands to his head to mimic big ears, but Freya failed to see the humour.

"Did either you or..." She couldn't bring herself to refer to the man's nickname. "William see anybody while you were working at the hospital two nights ago?"

"No. It were just us."

"What time did you start work?" Ben asked.

"Around eleven. Had to do it at night, see? You know? To isolate the system. Had to disconnect it from the village. Big job, it were."

"Was," Freya corrected him.

"Eh?"

She shook her head and sighed.

"And what time did you leave?"

"Oh. Not until early."

"Not until early?" Freya said. "That doesn't make sense."

"Morning time. Early morning. Getting light, it were."

"And you used the main gate, through Nocton, did you?" Ben asked.

"Aye, yeah."

Ben slid the plans around and searched for his pen, then realised he didn't have one anymore. Freya offered hers, which he handed to Dooley.

"Can you identify whereabouts you were working that night, please, Mr Dooley?"

"Is that your van outside?" Freya asked. "The Transit van?"

"Yeah. Well, not mine. It's the firm's. But I just take it home."

"And does your colleague have a van?" Freya asked.

"Steamboat? A van?" He laughed. "He can't even drive."

Freya caught Ben glancing at her, both dismissing the man they called Steamboat.

Dooley pored over the plans, pulling the pages apart, tracing the route through the huge compound. Then he marked an area with a cross.

"Here. Pump house two."

"There are two pump houses?"

"Yeah. First one's over by the water tower. Feeds the water through the filtration system, then sends it up top, so during the night the hospital could turn the power off. Gravity-fed system. Genius really."

"But you worked here?" Ben asked, pointing at the cross.

"Aye, we did, yeah."

"And you didn't venture anywhere else?"

"No point. We're on price work. Get paid the same if it takes one hour or ten."

"Do you know if there's any other maintenance going on right now?"

"Now? Yeah. There's always something going on. Someone is always there doing something. Mainly stopping it falling down, I think. Heritage and all that. It'll be houses soon. Mark my words. Already done the barracks. New estate in Nocton. You know it?"

"I think so," Ben said, seeming irritated by the tangent.

"That were barracks, that were. This lot'll go the same way. All the way up to the field." He pulled the pages apart, searching for the area he was talking about. "Hang on. You've a page missing."

"A page missing?"

"Yeah, look. See here?" He pointed to the most easterly point of the site, where an old road cut through and ran off the page. "You're a page short. There's two buildings out there. You'd miss it if you didn't know where they were. All overgrown and that. Anyway, all that'll be flattened soon, you mark my words."

"Thank you, Mr Dooley," Freya said, and while Ben, who was visibly seething at Gutteridge, folded the plans, she offered Dooley one of her cards. "If you happen to think of something that could help out the investigation."

He accepted the card with suspicion, studied it, then pocketed it. He moved toward the front door, and once more, Freya glanced at his trainers, noticing the grime and mud that had dried on the sides.

"One more question, if you don't mind?"

With his hand on the door handle, he stopped and glanced back at her, his eyes narrowed. But there was no fear in the way he was standing, nor were his hands shaking, as a guilty party's might.

"Where were you last night, Mr Dooley?"

"Last night? Here. With my wife."

"And she'd be able to confirm that, would she?"

"If you asked her nicely."

"Don't go anywhere, Mr Dooley. We may need to ask you some more questions," Freya said, allowing him to open the door.

When the front door had closed behind them, she offered a hand to help Ben, which he shrugged off with an, "I'm alright."

"So what next?" she asked when they reached the car. She leaned on the car roof to see if she could get him to engage. "Your call."

But instead of opening the passenger door and leaning on his side, he approached her and held out his hand. "Key."

Cautious that he appeared to be near breaking point, she slowly placed the car keys in his hand.

"My call?" he said.

She nodded. "Your call. I give in. We go after Marie's abductor and hope it's the same man who has Abigail. Or we go after Abigail. Make your mind up, Ben. I hate seeing you like this. It has to be your choice."

"Abigail is still alive. She has to be," he said.

"You sound so certain."

"I have to be," he replied. "Just like I have to be certain it's the same man. I'm driving."

CHAPTER THIRTY-SEVEN

"Jackie, talk to us," Ben said, as he settled into the driving seat, adjusted, and checked the fuel gauge in one habitual movement. He felt in control. Injured legs or not, he needed to make things happen. "Do we have updates?"

"Ah, Ben. We've gone from having no leads to too many," she said, her voice sounding tired over the phone.

"Can never have too many, Jackie," Freya said. "What do we have?"

"First off, Peter Jones is downstairs in a cell. Jefferson chased after him from the McGowans' house. Had to drag him across a field. You should see the state of them both."

"Well, he ran. That's a guilty sign if ever I saw one," Ben said.

"Yeah, but guilty about what?" Freya added, leaving it open for them both to ponder. "Next?" she said, moving the update along.

"Gillespie escorted Terry McGowan to hospital. He's stable but unconscious. Lost a lot of blood. Doctors reckon it'll be at least a day until he wakes up, and that's if he survives the surgery."

"Jesus, it gets worse," Ben said.

"I know. The good news is that Cruz is on top form. I think it's that uniform he has with him–"

"Larson?" Ben said.

"Yeah. He's like a different bloke. Went back to some guy's house he spoke to yesterday."

"Is that Trevor at number fifty-one?" Ben asked, remembering how the young DC had failed to even get the man's last name.

"Trevor McFarland, yeah, that's it. Fifty-one Main Street."

"What did he say?"

"Cruz showed him images of the backs of vehicles in the dark with the taillights on."

"Right?" Ben said, almost disbelieving what he was hearing. "What vehicles, exactly?"

"All the vehicles he could think of. Transit van for Shane Dooley, Volvo estate for Terry McGowan. He even has a picture of a Mini Cooper. Abigail McGowan's car."

"And what did Trevor at number fifty-one say?" Ben asked.

"None of them," she replied. "Only that it was a big vehicle with a broken taillight."

"That narrows it down," Freya mumbled. "We can strike Dooley off our list. I just saw his van and both lights are well and truly intact and dirty. Not new."

"What else do we have, Jackie?" Ben asked. "These leads are going nowhere."

"Well, you might also like to know that the lab came back with the results of the hat Cruz found."

"Go on," Ben said.

"Jason King," she said. "They found some hairs with the roots in the fabric of the hat and matched it to the DNA record in his prison file."

"The uncle?" Ben remarked. "I thought he was on the run?"

"He is. We spoke to HMP services. They're keeping it on the lowdown. Don't want the press running away with it. But he's out, and do you want to know what else I found?"

She was using that tone of voice she always used when she was proud of what she had found. And to be fair to her, it usually meant good information.

"Go on," Freya said.

"Terry McGowan."

"Sorry, what?" Ben said, his face taut and pulled back in disgust. "Terry McGowan's hair is in the hat?"

"That's what they said. But it gets better," Jackie said, her voice filled with glee. "Terry McGowan and Jason King were originally questioned during the Marie Treverne investigation."

"Questioned?"

"Questioned and released. No evidence. Although there was doubt over King's innocence. I've got the warrant here signed by DI Granger. Shall I go and get him?"

"No," Freya said. "Not yet. But it does sound like we need to bring Jason King in."

"Right, that'll be easy. It's not like nobody's looking for him," Ben quipped, then regretted his tone. "Do we have an image of Jason King, Jackie?"

"Sending it through now," she replied, slightly distracted. "Do you want the final piece of news? Anna's just handed me it."

"Is it a signed confession from someone we haven't thought to question yet?"

"No. It's Terry McGowan's employment history."

"Don't leave me hanging, Jackie," Freya said. "We're running out of time here."

"Fifteen years as an electrical engineer, before he retired when his wife died."

"So?" Ben said. It was like she was enjoying teasing them, and Ben's pulse was already struggling to cope.

"The company he worked for had the contract to manage the old hospital grounds."

"When did his wife die?" Ben asked.

"Fifteen years ago. Breast cancer," Jackie said, clearly demonstrating her knowledge of the investigation. "Guess who his apprentice was?"

"Jason King?" Freya said. "His brother-in-law?"

The wind was well and truly sucked from Jackie's sails. Even over the phone, Ben could hear the disappointment in her voice.

"Four-year apprenticeship," she said. "Then, judging by his record, he started going a bit wild. There's a few minor offences, then things ramp up. Broke into a woman's house and got into bed with her."

"He raped her?" Freya asked.

"No. He didn't touch her. He was just there when she woke up. He said he didn't remember a thing. He was still fully dressed as well. He was arrested for it and received a caution. But he re-offended."

"How often?"

"By the time they caught up with him again, he'd broken into the homes of more than a dozen women. He didn't touch one of them."

"And this was after Abigail's mother died?"

"Yeah. Pretty soon after."

"How old is Jason King exactly?" Ben asked.

"Born in seventy-nine. That makes him early forties."

"So he would have been thirty years old twelve years ago," Freya said, pulling her own phone from her pocket.

"Not only that," Jackie continued. "But Marie Treverne was reported missing two months before he was sentenced."

"I recognise him," Freya said.

She showed Ben the image, but he didn't recognise him at all.

"He was part of the community search," Freya said. "He would have been paired with somebody. Check the register. Chapman has it."

"He's our man?" Ben said, as the sound of rustling papers and distant voices came over the call.

"Hat. Previous record. The hat and the hair. He was part of the search. It all stacks up. We just need to find him."

"He's not on the list," Jackie said, slightly breathless.

"And why would he be?" Ben asked. "He's on the run."

"How many names are on that list?" Freya asked, and she stared at Ben that way she did when an idea was forming.

"Erm, fifty-three," Jackie said with a little hesitation. "Yeah, fifty-three."

"So how is there an odd number when everyone was buddied with one other person?"

"Not sure, ma'am," Jackie said, and she flicked her papers loudly again. "I've got a name on their own. Looks like someone didn't have a buddy."

"Who?" Freya said, then she took the wind from Jackie's sails once more. "Don't tell me, Peter Jones?"

"That's what the register says. Do you still need me to interview him?"

"Considering he's attempted to kill Terry McGowan and there's a strong possibility he was with Jason King during the community search, I think the softly-softly approach is null and void, if I'm honest, Jackie," Freya said. "But you can try by all means. Let's get him to confess to the McGowan attack, then we can apply for extended custody. CPS will back us with a confession. A lot of this will depend on whether or not Terry McGowan wakes up."

"Anything else I can do, ma'am?" she said.

"Get word to Sergeant Priest. Tell uniform to be on the lookout for Jason King. Give him the image and a description, Jackie. Good work. Keep in touch with Cruz and Gillespie. Don't let them feel alone. If they need help, they need to ask. We're just picking up the remaining plans for the hospital. We'll be on-site in under an hour. By close of business today, I want the search complete," Freya said.

"What about Peter Jones? Will you be seeing him when you get back?"

"Let's see how you get on with him. Take Chapman into the interview with you. You'll need all the support you can get."

"Will do, ma'am," Jackie said, and Freya ended the call.

"She's coming on, isn't she?" Freya said, referring to Jackie's confidence levels.

Ben slowed, searching for the gap between the hedges. She didn't need a response to her comment about Jackie. "This is it. Fen View House."

"Ben?" she said, and he sucked in a lungful of air as he pulled the car to a stop. "We'll find her. I do mean to keep my promise."

A gust of wind rocked the car, and the trees that lined the drive leaned with the force of nature. "I know. It's just…"

"Go on?" she said, her voice soft and motherly.

"I made a promise to her. To Marie."

Freya met his stare, and he wiped his eye. "We're close," she said.

"I know."

"Will you be leaving your wallet in the car this time?" she said, clearly hoping to lighten the mood.

"I most certainly will. And I might even ask for my pen back," Ben replied.

Ben and Freya exchanged few words as they walked to the door, and Ben felt his shoulder ache from sagging. The weight on his mind had altered his posture, and even stretching did little to alleviate the pain in his shoulder blade. The open fields around them offered little protection from the wind, and Ben's jacket flapped wildly. Freya, meanwhile, was having a battle with her hair, which slapped against her face with every other gust, then blew off in a different direction.

A little face came to the window in the front door, then turned and ran. Moments later, Mrs Gutteridge opened the door, her apron fastened around her waist.

"Mrs Gutteridge, we're so sorry to bother you again," Freya said loudly over the wind. "We were hoping to have another five minutes with your husband?"

"Oh, I'm afraid he's not home," she replied, as Daniel's little face peered around the doorway.

"Hello," Ben said to him, dropping to a crouch and hoping to entice the boy out from behind the door.

But he turned and ran, screaming, and disappeared into the lounge.

"He's quite the shy one," Mrs Gutteridge explained. "Shall I tell him you called? Neil, that is."

"Well, it's actually quite urgent. Is there a chance we could wait?"

"Wait? Erm. Well, I suppose. I don't know how long he'll be, mind."

"His van is on the drive," Ben said.

"Oh, we've got another. More of a family car. He did say he was going into town. Get some printing done or something. Could be a while."

"Right," Ben said.

"Would you happen to know where he keeps the plans for the old hospital at Nocton?" Ben asked, as a particularly brutal gust of wind nearly knocked him into Freya. "You see, I paid him quite handsomely for a set this morning, and he's left us a page short."

"He never did?"

"I'm afraid so," Freya added. "We've come rather a long way."

"He's a tyke, that husband of mine. You wait there."

"It's quite cold," Freya said.

"I'll be quick, don't you worry. Stay there, mind."

"We will," Ben called, as she closed the front door. Then he immediately stepped back onto the driveway and ducked around the side of the house. He could hear Freya calling after him, presumably asking him what the devil he was playing at in that public schoolgirl voice of hers. But when she joined him and stepped out of the wind, she understood.

"Oh, that's better. It's bloody tiring, this wind," she said. "I feel like I've been dragged through a hedge. I'm not even going to attempt to do anything with my hair tomorrow. There's absolutely no point. Now I can understand why..."

"Why what?" Ben said, assembling his own crop of tangled hair with one hand.

"Well," she said, "now I understand why everyone wears hats around here."

"We don't all wear hats," he said.

"Maybe you should. I think you'd look rather fetching in a little, felt fedora. Maybe a little feather in the band."

She stopped speaking and pulled a face of utter disgust.

"Do you smell that?" she whispered.

"Smell what?"

She began sniffing at the air, edging closer to Ben.

"Smell what, Freya?"

She sniffed for another few seconds and came to a stop near him.

"Urine," she said, and Ben's heart sank. He thought of Cruz the night before, and remembered how he'd felt the dirty little...

"Tell me you can smell that," she said.

"Probably the old privy," Ben said. "Looks like it's about a hundred years old."

"They don't still use that, surely?"

"I don't know. Why don't you ask him next time you crash into him?" Ben said, and it felt good to smile.

"I did not–"

"What you two doing around here, then?" Gloria Gutteridge called out, holding onto her apron but clearly not feeling the cold on her ample, bare arms.

"Just keeping out of the wind, Mrs Gutteridge," Ben said. "We were getting quite windswept out there."

The boy's face appeared below her, reminding Ben of those cartoons where three or four people would peek around a corner, as if they were stacked on top of each other.

"This what you're looking for?" she asked, and she waved a folded piece of paper, which Ben accepted. He peeked inside the folds, not daring to open it fully but seeing the familiar lines and the little information boxes at the bottom right-hand corner.

"Perfect, Mrs Gutteridge. You're a star, thank you."

"Well, best you come away from there. Treading all over Neil's plants, you are."

Freya immediately glanced down at her feet, and then up at Ben, who was glancing at his own feet. The entire property was covered in a six-inch blanket of snow. Any plants that were beneath it wouldn't be having the best of times.

"I do apologise," Freya said, in her most respectable voice. "We didn't realise. Listen, I was wondering. Do you still use that?" She pointed at the privy, trying her best not to appear judgemental.

"The outhouse?" Mrs Gutteridge said, a smile spreading across her face. "No. Not anymore. Though I did have to use it when we first came here. Before Neil put a bathroom in."

"Ah, right. It's just we…" She paused, a little longer than what Ben would have called comfortable.

"I imagine Neil still uses it when he's working out here?" Ben said, trying to rescue Freya.

"Yeah. Probably does. He'll go anywhere, him. One of men's pleasures," she said to Freya specifically, with that shared expression women use when talking of their husbands. She seemed comfortable with the freezing temperatures, despite even Ben, who was used to the cold, starting to lose the feeling in his feet.

"My husband was the same," Freya replied. "I caught him peeing in the wardrobe once."

Mrs Gutteridge's face dropped in a look of utter disgust.

Daniel, however, beamed at the idea.

"That was a long time ago," Freya backtracked. "We're divorced now."

"Divorced?" the woman replied. She covered Daniel's ears by pressing his head into her thigh with one hand on the side of his head. "Alright. We'll have none of that talk around here. You have what you need. I best get on. We've got guests arriving in a bit and I haven't even changed the sheets yet. I'll be blown if I can understand why people want to come out in this, and I'll bet they leave a one-star review."

CHAPTER THIRTY-EIGHT

A SENSE OF EXCITEMENT RAN THROUGH DC JACKIE GOLD. SHE closed the interview room door and sauntered over to the desk, where Denise Chapman, Peter Jones, and a duty solicitor were already waiting.

She nodded for Chapman to hit the record button on the wall-mounted tape machine, then stated the date and time, and introduced herself, before requesting that the other attendees each state their names.

She stared at Peter Jones throughout. He was sullen, staring at the floor, and judging by the red marks around his eyes, had probably been crying in the cell. His clothes had been removed, as had his trainers and socks, and the disposable coverall that Sergeant Priest had provided him was baggy and ill-fitting. One size fits none.

"Hi, Peter," Jackie began.

It was weird, she thought. For months she had been in awe of DI Bloom, who had become a female role model. She was powerful, she stood her ground, and she was able to outsmart any of the men in the team, including DCI Granger and Detective Superintendent Harper. If there was one woman Jackie wanted to emulate, it was her. Yet, here she was, being asked to lead an interview in a murder investigation, and she had to drop all that power play. She had to soften her expression, as if she was talking to Charlie, her boy. She had to show understanding, empathy, and be someone Peter would want to open up to, even if he didn't really know it yet.

"I heard you had a bit of trouble earlier?"

He shrugged but didn't look up.

"It's okay. I've actually just spoken to my colleague. He's at the hospital with Mr McGowan. He says he's going to be fine."

The duty solicitor made a note of that comment, then cleared her throat and waited for Jackie to continue.

"That's good news, eh?" Jackie said, and invited Chapman to join in. "Isn't it? Good news?"

"For both of you," Chapman said, clearly not following the softly-softly approach. She stared at Jones as if he were something she'd trodden in.

"Well, why don't we start at the beginning?" Jackie suggested. "I just need to understand why you did what you did. But first, we need to formally caution you. It's just a process we need to follow, but you need to listen very carefully, okay?"

"Okay," he said, steeling himself to hear the words that would make it all so final.

"Peter Jones, you're under arrest on suspicion of attempted murder following an attack on Terence McGowan earlier today. You do not have to say anything, but it may harm your defence if you do not mention when questioned something which you later rely on in court. Anything you do say may be given in evidence."

"And what is it that you're suggesting Mr Jones has done?" the duty solicitor asked, pen poised.

"Today, somebody kicked Mr McGowan's front door down. They then confronted him with a knife, engaged in an attack on the man, which ended upstairs, whereby Mr McGowan received a severe cut to his abdomen. They then turned Abigail McGowan's bedroom upside down searching for something and escaped out of the back door. If my colleague hadn't arrived when he did, we would be sitting here now discussing a murder enquiry. Luckily for Mr Jones, we are not. He pulled through. Still unconscious, but stable."

"So can you please confirm why you believe Mr Jones is guilty of this crime? I'm assuming you have some kind of evidence?"

"Have you just come out of uni?" Chapman said, her tone and mannerisms mimicking that of DI Bloom's. "Seriously. Have you just collected your certificate, flung your hat in the air, and caught the bus down here? We followed his footsteps in the snow. We found him hiding in the fields behind Mr McGowan's house, and his clothes and hands were covered in blood."

The duty solicitor stared at her, not appreciating being made to look a fool. But Chapman had more to say. However, she too had clearly been watching DI Bloom, and was playing the part extremely well. Too well, in fact. Too well, when the strategy in this particular instance was to go in light. To get Jones talking. If she carried on much more, he was likely to break down in tears and clam up tighter than DI Standing's wallet.

"So unless, Peter, the blood belonged to somebody else, and you just happened to be hiding at the very spot where the footprints finished, I think we can quite competently state the obvious. You did it. All we need is to understand why."

"Thanks, DC Chapman," Jackie cut in, trying to rescue the situation. "It's okay, Peter. You can talk to us. You were close to Abigail. We get it. We know you're upset. But why Mr McGowan? Why attack him?"

"Were?" he said, looking up for the first time and with confusion written in the expression on his face.

"Sorry?" Jackie said, feeling all her plans for a brilliant interview slip away.

"You said, *were* close. What's happened? Have you found her?"

"Just calm down, Mr Jones," the duty solicitor said. "I'll advise you when to speak."

"You bloody calm down. She just said something has happened to Abigail."

"I didn't mean to make it sound like–" Jackie began.

"If you've found her, we deserve to know," Jones said, his voice becoming more aggressive.

"Nothing has happened to her, Peter."

"So where is she?"

"We don't know yet. We have teams looking for her."

"But you said–"

"She's missing, Peter, and that's all we know right now," Chapman said sharply. This new assertive character was so far from the Chapman that Jackie knew that even she was taken by surprise. "We're here to discuss the attack on Mr McGowan. Nothing else."

Slightly taken aback by Chapman's outburst, Peter looked across at Jackie.

"You'd tell me, wouldn't you?" he said quietly.

Jackie nodded. "Yes. I know how close you *are*. I would," she said. "But we really do need to understand why you attacked Mr McGowan, Peter. It could have been so much worse. The more you help us now, the easier it'll be."

"Yeah, right," Jones said.

"It will be. I promise. If you cooperate, that'll be taken into consideration. Come on. Tell us what happened. What made you do it?"

"I think we're just wasting our time, DC Gold," Chapman said. "We might as well just charge him now and be done with it. Let the courts decide what happens to him–"

"It's Terry," Peter cut in. "He's..." He stopped, and glanced between Jackie and Chapman, then settled back on Jackie, his eyes moist.

"Go on," she said, encouraging him to continue.

"He's not who you think he is. I mean, yeah, he's got a nice house and he idolises his daughter. But it's all crap. It's all lies. He's up to something."

"Up to something?"

"Yeah. Although, I don't know what exactly. He's always over there. In the old hospital. He goes there at night. We saw him once. Jess and me. We saw him, and he didn't like it one bit. Changed directions and everything. Pretended he was just out for a stroll. He's a bloody liar is what he is."

"And you think he had something to do with Abigail's disappearance?" Jackie asked.

Peter nodded emphatically. "Yes. That's why he doesn't let her run a different route. She did it once, and he went bananas at her. He has her believe it's so he knows where she is. But look how that turned out. Where is she now, eh?"

"Sorry, slow down, Peter. You think Mr McGowan is strict about the route Abigail runs because...?" She left the question for him to finish.

"Because if she runs any other way, there's a chance she'll see him and find out what he's up to."

"But you have no idea where he goes, and you have no idea what he does, yet you think he's up to no good?" Chapman asked, clearly not falling for a word he was saying.

Jackie, however, was open to ideas about Terry McGowan. There was something to him. She had spent the day in his house with him. In fact, out of the team, she had probably spent the longest with the man. He wasn't exactly shifty. He was just like her friends' dads. But he had been quite careful about what he said. It wasn't something she had noticed at the time. But now she thought about there being more to Mr McGowan than the team had been led to believe, she could see it. The pauses before he spoke, the delay, and careful and considered articulation of his responses.

"Do you believe he's responsible for Abigail's disappearance, Peter?" Jackie asked.

He shook his head, then looked up from where he was staring at his hands and stared directly in her eye. "No. Not directly, anyway."

"Peter, did you try to get Terry McGowan to tell you what he's up to?" Jackie asked. "Is that why you attacked him?"

"I didn't mean to," he said, after a contemplative pause. "But I saw him through the window when I walked up to the house. He was putting something in a bag. A plastic bag. Like from the supermarket, you know? I saw him. And he saw me. He wouldn't open the door to me. He pretended he wasn't there."

"So you kicked it in."

"Yeah. I know I shouldn't have. But Abigail has been gone for so long," he said, and the dam that held back the tears finally gave. His voice rose and grew louder, and his face reddened as his emotions began to pour out. "Three days. Three days? This kind of thing doesn't happen here. Not in Dunston. Not even in Nocton. It's the stuff you see on telly. Not here. We're bloody scared. All of us. We're scared."

"I know. It must be hard. Believe me. And just for the record, Peter, we don't need to go into details, but it was you who attacked Terry McGowan, wasn't it? I just need you to confirm it."

He nodded, remorseful, but sure of his own actions.

"For the tape, Peter. Can you confirm it in words?"

"Yes. Yes, it was me who attacked Mr McGowan. It was all me."

"Thanks, Peter. I promise that'll go a long way. You've really helped us today. I'll make sure it counts for something, okay?"

He nodded again, and finally Chapman passed him the tissues that were sitting on the ledge above the tape recorder. It was like she was holding out on him until he confessed and earned himself a tissue.

"Just one more thing," Chapman said, adopting the bad cop personality once more. Perhaps, Jackie thought, she had come to enjoy the role so much she wanted one last stab at it. It was rare the two DCs got to interview somebody together, so why not stretch it out a bit?

But Chapman had an angle that Jackie hadn't considered.

"What was it you were looking for in Abigail's bedroom?"

"Eh?" Peter said, and he looked to Jackie for support.

"Abigail's bedroom was turned upside down. I presume it wasn't looking like that when you were there yesterday, DC Gold?"

"No. I popped in and had a look round. It was pretty tidy actually."

"So, that means the intruder, who we have clearly identified as yourself, Peter, ransacked the room. What were you looking for?"

"I didn't even go in her room," Peter said.

"Oh, come on. You were the only one in there."

"Honest. Look, I've just confessed to..." He paused, and regained control of himself. "I'm hardly likely to lie about going through her things after what I've just told you, am I?"

"Do you remember the statement that my colleague read to you at the beginning of this conversation?" Chapman said.

"What? About what I say being given in evidence and all that?"

"That's it. I want you to think very carefully, Mr Jones. Did you, or did you not, go through Abigail McGowan's room in her house today, before or after you attacked her father?"

"I haven't got a bloody clue what you're talking about," he said, his face screwing up in disgust at the thought. "I bloody love her. I'd do anything for her. I would never go through her stuff."

CHAPTER THIRTY-NINE

THE LIGHT WAS FADING FAST. ALREADY THE GLOW OF LINCOLN city lit the sky to the north, and the brightest of stars could be seen in the east. When Ben and Freya arrived at the hospital gates, the teams were winding down their search. Tired, cold, and weary, more than a dozen uniforms were packing away lights and pouring hot drinks from flasks.

Ben shared their weariness as he parked the car in the middle of the little lane. A few of them looked up, shielding their tired eyes from the bright lights. He killed the engine, and felt the length of the day in every muscle in his body. "You sure about this?"

"It's our last hope," Freya said. "We cock this up, and we'll be reporting to Lincoln HQ tomorrow."

"Doesn't bear thinking about," Ben said.

They opened the car doors together and did not have a quick discussion over the roof of the car. Ben hobbled forward, driven on now only by his sheer determination to find Jason King and bring Abigail home. If that was all he could offer Marie, then so be it.

"Listen up," Freya shouted, and Ben was grateful for the

surrounding forest that blocked the fierce winds. The snow still fell but it was tame compared to what they had experienced over the past few days. "I know you're all tired. I know you've all been working hard over the past few days. But we have one more area to search–"

A series of groans and complaints ensued.

"I know, I know," Freya said, holding her hands up in defence. "But we think this will make a difference. The man you are looking for is Jason King. We believe he's here somewhere."

A few of the uniformed officers continued to load the transport with their gear. A murmur arose from the others, but nobody took any action at all.

"We believe," Freya said, with a little more gusto than before, "that Jason King is the man who attacked PC Griffiths. We believe he has Abigail. And we need your help to find him."

The murmuring died to a mumble, then stopped, and the first uniform stepped forward. It was the officer who had been with Griffiths during the previous night. He looked tired in the fading light and gaunt, yet he was alert. He looked about him for others to join, and they did. One or two at first, then more.

"The more of you that help, the faster this will be," Ben called. "This is the final push."

In the end, every single one of them put aside their own fatigue to join the effort. They crowded around Ben's car as he laid the missing page from the plans across its bonnet.

"Here. Across this perimeter road. We're told there are two buildings hidden by the trees that our search hasn't covered. That's it. That's all we're asking. We need a detail on the gate. At least four of you. If we flush him out, he'll run. He's not afraid to fight for his freedom, as we know."

Four of the uniforms stepped forward, checked their torches, and stood to one side.

The remaining men and women formed a line, and when joined by Freya and Ben, they marched across the snow-covered ground. The sky to the east was so dark, the treetops merged with the sky seamlessly. When on the open ground, the line spread out to cover as much area as they could. There were eleven of them in total. Eleven torches sweeping the ground, the treeline, and shining on the buildings they had already searched, logged, and documented. Then they came to the road. The area on the far side, as Dooley had suggested, so overgrown that a person might be forgiven for thinking it was impenetrable. But ways in were found, were made, were forced with the cracks of branches.

The two buildings seemed to be devoured by foliage on the outside, as nature reclaimed the space. Silently, Ben split the team in half. He and Freya with three uniforms took one building, and the remainder of the team hit the other. The door had once been heavy duty. But over the years, rot had weakened the wood and newer security had been installed. Modern hasp and staples shone in the light against the old and dulled wood on which they were fixed. There were new padlocks too. But the heavy boot of a uniform took care of the need for a key. The screws that held the fittings in place were ripped from the rotten wood with ease. Ben shone his torch light inside. The corridor was long with rooms on either side, and there seemed to be a space halfway down, perhaps where the administration was carried out.

The floor inside was covered in debris – broken glass, dead leaves, and even smashed crockery. A few of the walls closest to the door had been tagged by local kids with spray paint. Some efforts were more artistic than others, from simple initials and first names to full-on masterpieces that filled entire walls.

Ben peered inside the first room, finding the skeletal remains of two old, iron-framed beds. Nothing else. There had been mattresses at one time, but a dark ash-covered stain on the floor and a few old bed springs were all that remained of them.

They moved on. There were around twenty smaller rooms off the corridors, and once the initial shock of seeing the place had eased, progress was made. Two of the uniforms went ahead to start at the other end and work their way back where, eventually, the five met in the middle outside the last room. The door had been locked with a key, which meant the lock was still functional. Ben sought the man with the heavy boot, and he gladly stepped up to the challenge.

Was this it? Ben thought. Had the stress and emotion of the past few days come down to this? A single room in an old building buried in the woods? Would they find Abigail inside, and if so, would she be alive?

The thud of the uniform's boot echoed around the empty building. Yet the door held fast.

Would they even find Jason King inside, or had he made his escape?

Another boom echoed and dust from the old ceiling fell in the dark space around them.

Had this place been used to hold Marie? Had she been here? Had she screamed inside these very walls where nobody would hear her? But there was no connection. He couldn't feel her here.

The door gave on the third kick. It slammed back against the wall and three uniforms bundled inside, torches waving in a dizzying frenzy. And the word Ben had been dreading echoed.

"Clear."

They were silent for a while, as each of them dealt with their dying hope in their own way. Ben looked at Freya who seemed to be lost in her own little world. Imagining what it was like to be here when it had been operational perhaps?

Ben imagined what it would be like to be kept here. In the darkness. Frightened, cold, and too terrified to move.

Radios began to crackle, the signal hampered by the thickness of the walls. A few of the uniforms began to move toward the exit, dejected.

"It was a good effort," Ben said to Freya, as she fingered the wooden door frame.

She shone her light around the walls of the now vacant room.

She crouched and studied a spent Coke can. It still gleamed as a new can might, perhaps a result of the darkness, where light hadn't tarnished its sheen. But the branding was old. A few years at least. Not the modern type.

"I really thought we'd find her," she said, damning herself for believing.

"We will," he replied, but there was a doubt in his voice that even he recognised.

From the doorway at the end of the corridor, a bright torch light waved along the corridor and settled on Ben.

"Boss?" a voice called. "We've got something."

Without even questioning the information, they moved. Freya waited for Ben, helping him along, but he shrugged her off, telling her to go on. He was the last to leave the first building and the last to enter the next. But when he did, he found a renewed effort. The building was laid out identically to the last, and uniforms, who had perhaps taken a cursory look beforehand, were now searching every room high and low. A glow of torch light emanated from one of the rooms further down the corridor, and two uniforms were standing outside, one of which waved at Ben.

This is it. This was where he'd find Abigail. This was where he'd keep his promise to Marie. Where he'd make everything okay.

"She's not here," Freya said, summing the find up in a few piercing words the moment he entered the room. "But she has been." She held a red, waterproof jacket up for him to see. It was small enough to belong to a teenage girl, and well-worn. Ben pulled on the last of the latex gloves he kept in his jacket and searched the pockets. His hand touched something small and hard, and he closed his eyes as he felt that connection. To Abigail, not Marie, but somehow it was the same. Somehow it mattered just as much.

He withdrew his hand and opened it palm-up.

"A dog biscuit," Freya said.

"Stan," Ben replied.

There were no windows in this particular room. Only a single iron-framed bed stood in the corner. A sleeping bag had been laid out, and when Freya examined the rubbish, she found modern bottles of water, chocolate bar wrappers, and even a sandwich carton that still had a tiny, green piece of lettuce inside. Stacked beside the mess were four empty corned beef cans; every morsel of meat had been removed and the insides gleamed.

"He's gone, isn't he?" Ben said, and Freya nodded.

"Let's leave this to CSI," she instructed, and coaxed everyone from the room.

Freya turned to Ben and stared up at him with tired eyes. Somebody who didn't know her may have said she looked defeated. But Ben knew otherwise. There was a fire in that hollow gaze, and although the flame was waning, as long as it still burned, there was hope.

"We've got her jacket. We know she was here, and we know who took her," she said.

CHAPTER FORTY

"I've got some bad news."

Gillespie's voice came through the car's speakers as clear as day, but Freya wished she hadn't heard him. She wished that the line was cut, or the signal dropped, or anything that could stop him from continuing.

But it didn't, and his voice continued.

Ben was driving, and he somehow managed to restrain himself from encouraging Gillespie to continue. Probably from fatigue and the pain in his legs, Freya thought.

"I didn't find a diary. Searched high and low."

His voice had a distinct lack of sarcasm, flippancy, or humour. The news wasn't great, Freya had to admit, but there was something else.

"Is that all?" she asked.

"No," he said, his voice low and shamed.

"I don't have time for guessing games, Gillespie."

"I might have made things a bit worse."

"I can't possibly imagine how they could be any worse right now."

"I've been kicked out of McGowan's room," Gillespie said,

then hurriedly tried to defend his actions. "I was trying to get the bastard to talk. Nurse took offence to it."

"What do you mean, Gillespie?" Freya asked. "Terry McGowan is the victim. What do you expect him to do, wake up and tell you who attacked him? We know who did it. It was Peter Jones."

"Aye, I know *that*, but... Wait. Haven't you spoken to Jackie yet?"

"No, we've been trying to find Terry McGowan's daughter."

"Any luck there?"

"Yes, Gillespie. She's sitting in the back of the car doing her nails. In fact, she's asked if we can swing by McDonald's on the way home."

"Alright, no need for that. I feel bad enough as it is."

"What happened?" Freya asked, feeling the beginnings of a stress headache take root. "Bring us up to speed."

"Jackie managed to get a full confession from the lad."

"Peter Jones?" Ben asked. "And to be clear, you mean a confession for the attack on McGowan?"

"Aye. But that's not just it. Apparently, he attacked him because he thinks Terry McGowan is part of something. Reckons he's up to no good."

"Up to no good?"

"In the old hospital. Couldn't say what it was, only that he's been cagey and secretive. He's a control freak. Remember how he said Abigail isn't allowed to run a different route?"

"Yes, standard stuff for a concerned parent," Freya said.

"Aye, well, it's also pretty standard for a parent who doesn't want their daughter to see something they shouldn't, if you know what I mean? Something he's been doing in the old hospital."

"But Abigail runs past the old hospital. We walked the route with him. Surely if he was up to something, he would keep her as far away as possible."

"Aye, boss. But you can't see in, can you? You can't see a bloody thing from the forest. It's all overgrown. And if he knows which route she'll take, he can control the situation."

"So he's been visiting the old hospital, where he used to work for fifteen years?" Freya said, glancing across at Ben.

"Aye, that's about the size of it. The question is, why bother?"

"Because he's been helping his brother-in-law," Freya said. "He's been bloody helping the very man who kidnapped his daughter."

"Who? King?" Gillespie said. "The uncle?"

"We found his little hideout in the hospital grounds," Ben added. "Along with Abigail's waterproof jacket. HMP services still list him as missing, but whatever you do, do not mention that to anybody. The last thing we need is them holding us accountable for a media frenzy."

"Ah, Christ. Do you need me to do anything?" Gillespie asked. "I'm done for here. I've got a uniform on the door, just in case, but the nurses are looking at me like I'm bloody Fred West or something."

"No. No, go home, Gillespie. I think we have what we need. We've found where King was staying, and we've got the hat and Abigail's anorak. We'll make a plan to bring him in tomorrow. Get some rest. We'll need your A-game tomorrow."

"Aye, boss. You too."

She ended the call.

"What was he bloody thinking?" she said. "If Granger gets wind of him leaning on Terry McGowan, that'll be it."

"Granger won't hear about it. He was desperate, that's all. We're all bloody desperate."

"Yeah, but we're not all sitting there waiting to interrogate a man whose daughter is missing and who has just narrowly escaped death."

"So why didn't you say something?"

"I was close, Ben," she said, her rage expiring. "But he's been through the same as us. He's just as tired as everyone else, and he's worked bloody hard. Plus, if I know him well enough, he'll be doing a far better job of beating himself up than I would."

"Want a drink?" Ben said.

"Honestly, yes," she replied. "But can I deal with standing in the pub with your mates, Squeaky and Snow? No."

"Snowy and Squawk," Ben corrected her.

"Oh, of course," she laughed, through sheer exhaustion more than humour. "How could I have possibly got their names wrong?"

"And besides, they're not my friends. We've been through this."

"Right, yeah, they just drink in the same hole as you."

"Something like that," Ben said, agreeing for the sake of agreeing, and clearly without the energy to argue that his pub of choice had been standing long enough to have earned its dishevelled appearance; it wasn't some modern take on an old building to create an effect. But he said nothing and drove, his tired eyes glazed and still.

"Have you spoken to Michaela?" Freya asked, seeing if he had taken Gillespie's advice and made contact for that one last chance.

"I sent her a message," Ben said, and glanced out of his window before adjusting his collar, both nervous and involuntary twitches.

"Wow."

"Wow, what?" he asked.

"Nothing," Freya said, doing her best to conceal the smirk that was spreading like some kind of disease across her face. She turned away to peer out of her own window.

"What is it?" he said. "What are you bloody laughing at?"

That was it. She could restrain it no more. The force of her trying to hide her smile forced the air from her mouth with a rasping sound, which then developed into a giggle, and then a full-on laugh that was by no means a mere by-product of fatigue.

"Freya? What the bloody hell?"

But the more her laughter wound him up, the more it made her laugh.

She was still giggling to herself and wiping her eyes when Ben pulled onto the farm track, gunned the engine, and purposefully steered the passenger wheels over the bumps. Bracing herself, Freya held onto the dashboard. "Whoa, careful. Slow down."

"When you tell me what you're laughing at."

"Ben, you're going to–"

"Crash?" he said, staring directly at her and not at the road.

"Ben, look at the road."

"Tell me what you're laughing at."

"The road."

"Tell me."

"Oh, for God's sake. I'm laughing at you sending her a message," Freya said, being his eyes for him. "Now look where we're bloody going."

Turning his attention back to the road, he eased his foot off the accelerator.

"You could have bloody killed us," Freya said, and lowered the window for a moment to let some cold air in.

"I've been tearing up and down this track every day since I was thirteen years old. I know every single bump and every hole. In fact, when I was younger, I used to take my girlfriend down here with my eyes..." He stopped mid-sentence and took a breath, as if his brain had caught up with what his tongue had lined up to say. "Anyway..."

"Marie?" Freya asked.

He nodded.

"Used to use my dad's truck in the winter," he said, then smiled at a memory he didn't need to share. "She hated it."

"The truck? Or the driving with your eyes closed?"

"Both."

"You seem to have wooed Marie just fine. What happened?"

"What do you mean?"

"Well..." Freya said, and began gesticulating, as she fought to find the words that wouldn't damage his pride. But all she could think of saying to support her wild hand gestures was, "Michaela."

"What about her?"

"Oh, come on, Ben. First of all, you want to take her to a chip shop. God knows what she saw this morning. And now, when she finally agrees to give you one last chance, you bloody text her."

"I was busy."

"Make her feel special, Ben. Trust me, listen. Hi Michaela, I'm sorry, I'm flat out here, but I thought I'd just call you, you know, to arrange dinner," Freya said, mimicking a man's voice. She went on to present how she thought Michaela might have reacted. "Oh, that's lovely, Ben. No worries. Pick me up at eight."

"What the hell was that?" Ben asked, as he came to a stop outside Freya's house.

"That was you and her," Freya said, amused at her own impersonations. She followed it up with one more to really drive the point home. "And by the way, Michaela, I'll try not to cock it up this time, alright? See you at eight."

She got out of the car before he had time to react, then leaned back inside, out of the wind.

"How about that drink inside?" she said, and closed the door before he had time to argue. She heard the engine switch off and his car door open, and she smiled to herself at how easy to manipulate he could be. She called out, "Probably best if you clean those wounds as well. You'll end up with gangrene or something."

Watching him hobble up the garden path, dead on his feet and with pain etched into the lines on his face, he was a sight to behold. All six-foot-something of him, walking as if he'd been caught short and needed the washroom as a matter of urgency.

"Now what?" he asked, as he drew near and brushed the snow from his hair.

He stopped before her and she stared up at him, smiling. And she thought she knew why Marie had fallen for him yet Michaela hadn't. Perhaps Freya was just the second girl in his life who truly understood him?

"What are you gaping at?" he asked irritably, wrapping his coat about himself to keep warm.

"Nothing," she said.

CHAPTER FORTY-ONE

AS A CITY GIRL, BORN AND RAISED IN THE HOME COUNTIES, Freya knew the best places to lunch in Chelsea, the best dressmakers, and what the order of events would be at Ascot.

But after more than six months of living in the countryside, she still hadn't a clue what it was for, or what it did. Not only could she not walk anywhere, as everywhere she wanted to go was too far to walk, but there was no tube, no black cabs, and to top it all off, there was water on the inside of her windows in the morning.

She braved the freezing day, having woken early, and wrapped herself in her dressing gown. She had selected her finest trouser suit, which she could wear with a pair of tights underneath, and started the shower. It usually took a few minutes to get hot so she returned to her bedroom to pick out her underwear. She would have loved to be cutting tags off a new pair of panties or adjusting the strap on a new bra. But she had been shopping in Lincoln only once, and all she had come away with was a Saint Christopher for her ex-husband's son Billy, which she'd had engraved with her phone number so he could always call her, a ridiculously oversized stuffed dog, which was an impulse buy in case the pendant hadn't pleased Billy, and a pair of leather gloves for Ben.

So she selected her favourite underwear of what was clean and leaned out of the room, searching for the tell-tale sign of steam emanating from the bathroom.

Nothing yet.

She moved to the window, eyed the droplets of condensation, and stared out at Ben's house across the fields, searching for his lights in the dark morning gloom. It was then she noticed it was no longer snowing. In fact, not only was it not snowing, but the tree at the edge of the field was still.

Today was turning out to be a good day.

She glanced over her shoulder towards the bathroom. No steam yet.

Staring back out of the window, she wondered what Ben was doing. No doubt he was already up and about, showered and dressed, and cleaning, or whatever it was he did. She guessed he must have done his housework early in the morning, as he was always out late working with her and the house was always sickeningly immaculate.

Still no steam.

She marched across the room, ducked inside the bathroom, and felt the cool air. She ran her hand beneath the shower without thinking and snatched it back when the icy water splashed over her.

"You've got to be kidding me. Not today."

Hurriedly, she turned the shower off and ran downstairs. The boiler was on; at least, the light was. She hadn't a clue what any of the buttons did.

It annoyed her when she had to call Ben. She was supposed to be standing on her own two feet. She had at least learnt how to light the log burner and how to stack wood. But boilers were a bit out of her comfort zone. Maybe one day. She might not know what the countryside was for, but she would do her damnedest to work it out.

She resorted to desperation and pity.

"Oh, Ben, the shower's cold," she said, when he answered the phone.

"Check the boiler," he said, sounding irritatingly chirpy, as she knew he would be.

"I am checking the boiler, and guess what? It's still here, fixed to the wall."

"Well, what does it say?"

"What do you mean, what does it say?" she snapped. "How the bloody hell am I supposed to know what any of it means? It was working last night. I had a shower as soon as you left."

"Is your heating on?" he asked.

"Yes. Yes, I felt it earlier. Can't get out of bed without the..."

She ran a hand over the radiator in the kitchen. It was warmish. Not hot. Not like it had been. She was sure it had been on.

"Freya?"

"It's cold," she said, accepting defeat. "But it *was* hot."

"You've run out of oil then," he said. "When did you check it?"

"Oil?" she heard herself say in that hoity-toity voice she was trying to so desperately to lose. "Oil? I put oil in my car. Well, a man does it for me. Why do I need to oil my house? It's not bloody squeaking."

There was a silence, during which time Freya could only assume he was laughing at her, or trying not to, at least.

"Ben?" she said.

"We're in the middle of nowhere. Do you honestly think we have a gas pipe running all the way through the fields?"

"Well, I've never really thought about it."

"Grab a bag. Get in your car. You can use my shower. I'm done. I'm ready to go and get Jason King."

"How long have you been ready?"

"Since about six a.m.," he said. "I even dreamed of it."

"On any other occasion, I'd insult you, Ben," she said, and was pleased to hear the desperation gone from her voice. "I'll be a moment."

"Right," he said, then, figuring what her next request would be, he sighed. "I'll come and get you."

"Ben?" she said.

"Yes?"

"Thanks."

The next five minutes were, in Freya's mind, just like one of those scenes from a Hugh Grant movie. The type the director adds in to illustrate a hurried effort. Clothes in bag. Makeup in bag. Shoes in bag. Lock door. Get in Ben's car. Drive less than a kilometre. Skid to a stop.

The only thing she really noticed during that time was that Ben hadn't had to de-ice the windows, and the wind hadn't tried to give her a Marilyn Monroe moment with her dressing gown when she had walked to and from the car.

"It's not as cold," she said, as Ben unlocked the front door. "And the snow has stopped. Is it over, do you think?"

He glanced out at the fields, at the sky, and then at Freya.

"What do your expert farmer's eyes tell you?" she asked him.

He stared back at her, his expression solemn. "It's not snowing anymore."

She was in the shower within a few minutes, savouring the heat of the water.

"Ben?" she called out. But he didn't respond, so she called louder. "Ben?"

"What? What?" he replied, and she heard him running up the stairs. "You okay?"

"Yes, I'm fine. I was just going over the plan."

"What plan?"

"Exactly. We need one."

"Right," Ben said. "We're going after Jason King, aren't we?"

"We are. So, we'll need uniform. As many as we can get."

"I'll talk to Priest," Ben said.

"Maybe a dog unit too. King is clearly adept at sleeping rough."

"Who's to say he hasn't just upped and legged it? He hasn't got anywhere to go now."

"Anywhere to go?" Freya said, as she switched the shower off and reached for a towel that wasn't there. "Towel?"

"What?"

"Can you pass me a towel please?" she said.

"What, do you want a foot rub as well?"

"Later, maybe," she said, hearing the mock irritation in his voice. Then she added, "McGowan's house."

"What about it?"

"Jason King. It's the one place he'll know he can go."

"He can't take Abigail there."

"No. No, he might be a bit crazy, Ben, but he's not stupid. If she's alive, he'll have kept her somewhere."

The door opened enough for Ben to reach through with a towel, which she accepted, used it to dry herself quickly, then wrapped around her torso, folding a knot on her chest.

She opened the door and Ben made a point of averting his eyes as she hurried through into his bedroom and closed the door, leaving it slightly ajar so they could continue their conversation.

"How sure are we it's him?" Ben asked.

"It's the best lead we've got."

"But why? Why kidnap his own niece?"

"Think about why he was in prison in the first place," Freya said. "He's a desperate man. He misses his sister. It was her death that sent him over the edge. He needs someone. You know? To hold. To love him. He was put in a minimum security hospital. What does that tell you?"

"He's minimal risk."

"But still a risk. We can't have men like him walking the streets. But he doesn't deserve to be locked up based on the crimes he was convicted for. He's messed up, Ben."

"But still, why his niece?"

"He doesn't want to hurt her. Of that I'm sure." She pulled on her underwear, snapped her bra into place, and listened. There was a long pause, and Freya imagined Ben would be reeling from the fact that the more they discovered about Jason King, the more they realised the two crimes were, in fact, not related. "We'll get to her, Ben," she said softly.

Freya placed her hand against the door, biting her lower lip. His pain was evident in his silence. She knew if she pulled the door open she would find him battling tears, being the man, searching for some kind of inner strength.

"This is about Abigail," he said. "We need to find her."

"So we hit the McGowan house. We go to the station, brief the team, brief Granger, and then find King."

She was pulling on her trousers over her tights and had just stood to do the top button up when the door opened slowly. He didn't stare at her. Not in a sexual way, at least. He held her gaze, his eyes fixed on hers. She could have been wearing a clown suit and he wouldn't have flinched. Glad she had chosen the bra that she had, she met his stare.

"And if we don't find him there?" he asked. "Granger will be on the war path."

"He wanted something substantial. This is substantial. Now it's just a matter of time until we find him," she said, pulling a vest over her head. She released her hair from the loose bun she had pulled it into before showering, and let it hang free, shaking her head to add some volume. "The hardest part will be once we actually find King."

Leaning on the door frame, Ben shook his head slowly, appraising her as if they had just met. His admiring gaze rolled from her feet to her eyes, but his expression was empty and somehow dangerous. "He'll tell us where she is," he said. "You mark my words."

CHAPTER FORTY-TWO

THE INCIDENT ROOM DOOR SQUEALED OPEN, SLAMMED AGAINST the wall, then squealed shut like a wounded beast. Freya marched in, dropped her bag on the floor, and sat on the edge of her desk, silent.

Outside, the sun was only just cresting the horizon and only a few of the office lights had been switched on. The room had that end of winter feel. There was hope for brighter, warmer, and longer days.

One by one, the team stopped what they were doing and looked up at her, except for DC Nillson who was on the phone, making notes. Usually, Gillespie would have been the last to sense the change in atmosphere and peer up from his laptop. But this time, it was Cruz, leaning over his phone with a grin from ear to ear.

Freya waited a few more seconds, and eventually it was Chapman who, with a polite kick to his shin, caught Cruz's attention.

"Oy, what the–"

He found Freya staring at him, a look of utter incredulity on her face.

"Oh, erm, morning, boss," he said, rubbing his shin and eyeing Chapman.

"Good morning, everybody," she said, keeping her voice low to ensure they listened hard. "Today is the day we find Abigail McGowan. Today is also the day we find Jason King and lock him up. Hopefully for the rest of his miserable life. But that part isn't down to us. Our part is to bring him in. That's all we need to do."

"Aye, boss," Gillespie began, and Freya sensed a long-winded and slightly aggressive monologue about how they'd make him suffer was imminent. "If I get my hands on the bastard–"

"We'll treat him with the respect he deserves," Freya said, again quietly. "In fact, this might be the most sensitive investigation we've worked on together. We would all like to imagine what Jason King's life will be like following today. Some of you, Gillespie, might even like to give him a few little digs of your own."

"Aye, well, I wasn't saying that–"

"There will be no police brutality. Not now, not ever. We have to channel our emotions," she said, and found Ben staring at her. She spoke directly to him, "We have to forget about the past. Forget about what it is he's done. What crimes he's committed. Who he's hurt. The fact of the matter is that he knows where Abigail is, and we do not. He has the upper hand and he'll know it. It'll be the joker up his sleeve. He'll use it to gain some kind of advantage before his trial. He'll try to negotiate a shorter term, or benefits, or even special visiting rights."

"Shame there'll be no-one to go and see him, then, eh?" Gillespie said.

"Oh, he'll have visitors," Freya said, and the team looked at her in astonishment. "His parents are still alive. Abigail is still alive. And right now, Terry McGowan is still alive."

"Why would they go and see him in prison?" Jackie said. "After what he's done?"

"Because they always do, DC Gold. Because they always do.

They might be seeking some kind of explanation. They might even fall for the lies he'll no doubt tell. But that's not for us to decide. All we can do is bring him in, treat him well, and use our brains, DC Cruz."

At the mention of his name, Cruz looked up from his phone, his face a picture of confusion.

"Eh?" he said.

"We use our brains, DC Cruz. We coerce the information out of him. We kill him with kindness. He's sleeping rough. He broke his parole, and he'll be cold, hungry, and tired. We're not going to find out where Abigail is by dragging him across the forecourt on his knees and tossing him to the floor of the custody office."

Chapman nodded, as did Gold, and after seeing the others agree, so too did Cruz.

Gillespie neither nodded nor confirmed that he understood, but as much of a clown as he could be, Freya was quite confident she could rely on him.

"DS Savage?" she said, her eyebrows raised. "Do I have your assurance that no harm will come to Jason King?"

He held her stare for a moment longer, though his eyes suggested he was elsewhere. Perhaps he was running through a forest. *The* forest, calling Marie's name. His eyes told a story of love and loss and regret where, in the final scene, he was peering down a hole staring at Marie's broken body.

"Ben?"

He roused from his thoughts, blinked, and sensing the team all staring at him, he nodded.

"Good," Freya said. "Now we have that cleared up, here's how it's going to happen."

Anna Nillson put the phone down and looked up, as if she had something to say.

"Nillson, who was that?"

"Sergeant Priest, ma'am," she replied, beaming. "He's had a

uniform parked up the road from the McGowan house all night in an unmarked car. Definitely someone in there. Not sure who though. He advised them to just watch and report if anybody comes or goes."

"Are they covering the back gate?"

"Yes. Whoever it is, they're trapped inside."

"Good work. That confirms it. Gillespie, you'll take the rear entrance to the McGowan house with DC Cruz and uniform support. DS Savage and I will take the front. Speak to Sergeant Priest and make sure we have enough resources. I want transport too. King is a known offender. He might have escaped from a low security prison, but we're taking no chances."

"What if he's not there, boss?" Gillespie asked. "I mean, he's hardly likely to be swanning about in his brother-in-law's dressing gown standing by the coffee machine reading the paper. He'll know we're after him. He'll not wait around."

"That's why we're hitting him early," Freya replied. "It's seven-thirty now. I want him in custody by nine. DCI Granger wanted something substantial. King is our man. It doesn't get much more substantial than that. And as for what we do if he's not there, DC Gold, DC Chapman, that's where you come in. I want you here coordinating. If he's inside McGowan's house, he'll have access to Abigail and her father's cars. Check ANPR. He might lead us to Abigail."

"What about me, ma'am?" DC Nillson asked, seeming a little perturbed that she hadn't been assigned a role.

"I want you to babysit Terry McGowan. If he can talk, then I want you in there. Softly, softly though. Don't pressure him. We're not bullies, remember?"

There was a notable shift in the mood. Jackie Gold averted her eyes. It was only a few months ago that Freya had asked Jackie to do exactly the same thing, and she had been dragged into a van and very nearly became a killer's next victim.

"Take a uniform with you. PCSO Larson if you can get her."

DC Cruz looked up at the mention of the name.

"Ah, welcome to the briefing, Cruz," Freya said. "How's your girlfriend?"

"She's not my..." he started, the way a schoolboy might. He stopped and sighed.

"Do you think you could find out if she's in today?" Freya asked, knowing full well that Sergeant Priest downstairs would be the one to manage her shift.

"She's in," Cruz replied without thinking.

"Okay, well, perhaps after this, when you meet her in the stairwell for a quick snog, you could ask her to come up and see Anna?"

"Yeah sure," he said, then changed his tone. "I mean, I can message her if you like."

His embarrassment raised a few smiles. But the mood was far from jovial. The past few days had taken its toll on everyone. They were focused and ready to find King, and then bring Abigail home.

"Is everyone clear?" Freya called out. "Gillespie, round up the troops. We leave in ten minutes."

"Aye, boss," he said. "We'll be dragging Jason King across the forecourt in under an hour, you mark my words."

Freya glared at him.

"It was a joke," he said, holding his hands up in defence. "But when we do bring him in, we should celebrate with decent coffee. This body is a machine, you know? And it needs oiling."

"One last thing," Freya called out over the hum of chatter and activity. They all stopped and looked up at her. "Thanks for your hard work these past few days. I just need one last push from you. A hard push. Harder than ever. There's a lot riding on this morning. If we get it right, then we bring Abigail home."

Before Gillespie could offer an abrasive, "Aye, boss," or Gold could announce her polite, "Ma'am," there was a new noise, alien to the morning.

From the far end of the incident room, in the dark space that had once been occupied by DI Standing and his team, the sound of clapping came. It was slow, like the obligatory demonstration of appreciation for a poorly performed show at a back street West End theatre. Everybody stilled. From the shadows, a figure emerged, and Freya knew who it was before he stepped into the light.

"Bravo, Freya. Bravo," Detective Inspector Standing said.

He came to a stop a few feet from her, and Ben sat up, ready to defend her. But there would be no physical attack. Standing's offensive would be mental, strategic, and political. And despite Freya having her entire team around her, including Gillespie, Nillson, and Cruz, who had once worked under the man, she knew he would win.

He wore a long, double-breasted jacket over a new but cheap, off-the-shelf suit. His shoes were polished and his hair had even been styled into a neat side-parting.

"Steve," she said, in place of the alternative names she was considering. "It's a bit early for you, isn't it?"

"Oh no, Freya. What you see before you now is a new man. The new me. The early bird catches the worm, and all that."

"It's a shame you didn't catch the worms while you worked here. You might still be welcome if you had."

"I might have, if the worms were big and juicy enough."

"And I suppose the worms they feed you at Lincoln HQ are big and juicy, are they?"

"You could say that," he replied. They spoke as old enemies do. As if it was only them in the room. "But sometimes I have to venture out into the sticks and deal with a particularly big and juicy worm that the local coppers can't handle."

"We've got it under control."

"I can see that," he replied. "Sadly, it's all a bit too late, isn't it?"

"We're bringing Jason King in–"

"Correction. You're helping me bring him in."

He stared at each of the team individually, nodding once at Gillespie, although it wasn't a particularly friendly nod. It was a nod that recognised his betrayal.

"How's it going, Jim? Like your new team?"

"Ah, come on now. We're all friends–"

"Another correction. We used to be friends. See, a leader needs separation from his followers. You know? A line in the sand." He stared at Freya, who had once used that very phrase with him. He had refused the offer of peace, and she had subsequently humiliated him through competence. "I'm SIO on this investigation now."

"No, you are not–" Freya began, but he held up a hand, calmly and confidently.

"If you'd like to take it up with DCI Granger, then be my guest, DI Bloom. It was, after all, him who invited me to come." He shook his head, smiling at her with the smile of a winner. A bad winner. "But when you're done, I suggest you meet me down in the car park, and I'll show you how we deal with men like this Jason King character."

"*We've* done all the hard work, Standing," she said, defending her team.

"Oh, and I'm grateful, Freya. I'm grateful to everyone. We will, however, be using a slightly different tactic. One that my old friend, DS Gillespie, alluded to earlier."

"Don't do this, Standing," Freya warned.

He leaned in close, so that his face was just inches from Freya's. She could smell the coffee on his breath and was repulsed at the cheap aftershave he wore.

"There will be no softly-softly approach. That's not how you win the respect of a criminal like Jason King. A known offender with form. Oh no," he said, "my team are downstairs. You remember them. Vaughan and Moray. We're going to drag him across the forecourt on his face, and by the time I'm finished with him, he'll be begging to help me find Abigail McGowan."

The incident room door squealed open. It didn't slam into the wall or squeal closed as it usually did. DCI Granger stood in the doorway, hands on hips.

"Guv, what's all this about?" Freya asked.

"You're too late–"

"You asked for something substantial. We got you substantial. We've got evidence King was at the scene. We've got links from Abigail's father to Jason King."

"Too little, too late," he replied. "We need arrests, and we need Abigail McGowan found."

Standing smiled at her efforts. It would be a public defeat, and one which would take a long time to recover from.

"This is an outrage, guv, and you know it–"

"You," Granger said, raising his voice to cut her short, "have had three days to find Abigail McGowan. You failed. I'm not here to bend to your pride, DI Bloom. I'm here to make sure we find that poor girl. I'm here to make sure the media know we're doing all we can. That we're not sitting around, drinking coffee, being slung out of hospitals, and rallying members of the public to go walkabout in the worst blizzard we've had for fifty years."

A silence fell on the room as each of Freya's team digested the information.

"DI Standing is SIO as of this point. You'll do as he asks. You'll surrender all, and I mean all, of your evidence, notes, phone calls, and messages. Everything. I expect you and every member of this team to help him in any way you can. Do I make myself clear, DI Bloom?"

She stared at Standing, who was doing his best not to look smug, and failing.

"DI Bloom?" Granger said, the way a Sergeant Major might reprimand a new recruit.

"Crystal clear, guv," she said, then turned to her team, feeling their combined but futile support. Then she turned to face Granger. She searched for some kind of strength, and spoke as a leader should. "If it means we find Abigail McGowan, we'll do whatever we have to do."

CHAPTER FORTY-THREE

"This is absolutely bloody typical," Freya said, slamming the passenger door. She snatched at her seat belt, and the centrifugal lock kicked in, causing her to snatch at it some more, until she finally let it reel itself back in and she started again, slowly and with an accompanying deep breath.

Ben said nothing. He didn't look shocked or concerned about her little display of emotion. He just sat waiting for her to settle.

"Finished?" he asked.

"It looks that way, doesn't it?" she replied, hearing the sharpness in her voice that she reserved only for people like DI Standing. "Sorry."

"It's okay. Better to get it out here than in front of Jason King," he said, then added, "or worse."

"I'm not a barbarian, Ben."

"I know, I know. I'm just saying. You're safe with me. Get it all off your chest now."

"We were so close. If he bloody nails this now—"

"So what if he does? It's about getting Abigail back, isn't it?"

DI Standing and his team, DCs Moray and Vaughan, plus another individual Freya didn't recognise, were in Standing's car.

He stopped at the gates, sounded his horn, and with one arm through his window, he gestured for them all to follow as a king of old might have rallied his men on horseback and led the charge.

"Part of me hopes King isn't there," Freya said. "Is that wrong?"

"Wrong, but understandable," Ben said, as Gillespie knocked on the window.

Ben lowered the window and Freya waited in silence as the convoy began to move off in front of them.

"Mind if we jump in with you guys?" Gillespie asked, and nodded towards Cruz who was busy talking to PCSO Larson on the fire escape steps. "My car's buried behind all that lot. Jason King will be sitting in a prison cell getting the rubber glove treatment before I can get that out."

"Thanks for the image, Jim," Ben said, and then nodded for him to get in. "Be quick, Captain Mainwaring is leading the troops and we wouldn't want to be late on our first day."

"Oy, lover boy?" Gillespie called in front of the entire forecourt, where three uniform-filled cars were all waiting behind Ben. "DI Bloom says to put her down and hurry up."

As riled as Freya was, she saw the humour in the comment. She turned to watch Cruz running across the forecourt, while a blushing Larson waited for DC Gold to meet her.

"Sorry about that, I was just, erm..."

"Asking for your underwear back?" Gillespie asked from the seat behind Ben.

"Shut up," Cruz said defensively, the way a teenager might react to a comment his older brother made. "I was just checking she was okay to go. You know? With Jackie."

"Aye, right," Gillespie said. "It's funny, because I heard DC Gold on the phone to her a wee while ago."

"Can we focus on Jason King, please?" Freya said. "It's bad enough that we're now being led by a complete moron without having two teenagers in the back of the car."

"Ah, listen, boss," Gillespie said as Ben pulled out into the convoy, releasing the vehicles behind him, "he might be leading it now, but we really know who did all the hard work."

"That's right, boss," Cruz added. "Where was he when it really mattered?"

"Well, thanks for your support, guys, but if that is Jason King at the McGowan house, I'm afraid DCI Granger won't see it that way and neither will the media."

"But it's not about Jason King, is it?" Ben said, as a reminder to his previous conversation with Freya.

"Aye, it's about getting Abigail McGowan home and safe. Not that there's much of a home left for her after what Peter Jones did," Gillespie said. "The poor girl's going to walk into a bloodbath. You should see it in there. It's like a scene from Nightmare on Elm Street. Blood up the door, up the walls. Not to mention the man's bed. Soaked it up like a big, soft sponge, it did. Aye, you mark my words. They'll need the fire brigade to hose that place down before she goes back in there."

"You paint a pretty picture, don't you?" Cruz grumbled.

"Peter Jones?" Freya said, and she turned in her seat to find Gillespie. "What did he say to Jackie about Abigail's room? She interviewed him. I read the transcript. He said something about –"

"He didn't go in there," Gillespie said, giving her an agreeable nod. "Aye, I thought the same. Figured he was probably lying."

"He just confessed to nearly killing a man with a knife. I doubt he'd be afraid to tell us about going through Abigail's bedroom."

"Unless he was looking for something in particular," Ben said.

"Or unless somebody else was looking for something in particular. Somebody who knew the place was empty."

"Jason King wouldn't have known the place would be empty," Gillespie said. "Unless he was watching it. And let's face it, he's not likely to sit outside the house of the girl he's just abducted."

"Pull over," Freya said.

"What? We're in a bloody convoy."

"Just stop the car," Freya snapped. Ben indicated, then slowed and pulled into a small layby, signalling for the rest of the cars to go ahead.

"We can't change plans," Ben said. "We've got Standing up there about to go in guns blazing."

Freya stared at him as her thought process took over. The facts were all there, but they were a jumbled mess.

"You're going to change the plans," Gillespie said, as if he could read her face.

"Standing's going to slaughter us," Cruz whined.

"Well, this is kind of important. Besides, he won't know." Freya said, just as Ben's phone began to vibrate and a name appeared on the little dashboard screen. *Steve Standing.*

"You were saying?" he said, as Freya reached forward to hit the red button to ignore the call.

"Right, if we weren't in the firing line before, we are now," Gillespie commented. "He'll have seen us in his mirror."

"The only people that knew the route that Abigail runs are her father, Peter Jones, and...?" Freya said, ignoring their concerns about Standing, and hoping one of the team would fill in the blank.

"Jess Henry," Ben said, and his head jerked up as if an idea had just sparked. "You told me that Jess and her were close friends. They could see into each other's bedrooms."

"So what?" Gillespie said.

"Don't you see?" Freya said, as the theory took form in her head.

"Erm... well no, not really."

"Ben, drive," Freya said.

"Where?"

"The convoy. Follow the convoy. Standing is about to get a nasty surprise."

Ben pulled back out onto the road and put his foot down, just as Standing's printed name flashed up on the screen.

"Oh God," Cruz said from behind Freya.

She looked across at Ben as she reached forward, finger poised. Then she took a breath. She hit the green button.

"DI Standing," she said, and his voice came back at her crackling with the volume of his anger.

"Where the bloody hell do you think you're going? My instructions were for you to follow me."

"Car trouble, Steve," Ben cut in. "Just had to check my tyres. Can't be too careful, not in these conditions."

"Conditions?" he said. "Conditions? I'll show you what conditions you lot need to be careful of if you're not careful. I want you on scene right now."

"We're one minute behind you, DI Standing. No need to get your knickers in a twist," Freya said.

"There's only one thing that'll be twisted if you're not there when we go in, Freya. And that'll be Granger's face when he tears you a new backside."

Granger's wrath had already crossed Freya's mind, but now it was solidified. Only it wouldn't be her on the receiving end.

"Sounds like fun, Steve," she replied. "We'll see you in about three minutes. Bye."

"Bye?" Gillespie said from the back seat. "Bye? He's going to be apocalyptic. What did you have to wind him up for? He'll be a raging pitbull by now. I can see it now with Moray, Vaughan, and the other fella, all in the car with him, witnessing the horns growing out of his head."

"We're going to be fired," Cruz said.

"Nobody is going to be fired, and nobody has horns growing out of their head," Freya said calmly. "Ben, can we go any faster?"

"Thought you weren't worried?"

"Oh, I'm not worried," she said. "I just don't want to miss Standing make a complete idiot of himself."

CHAPTER FORTY-FOUR

THE CONVOY WAS HALTED ON CHAPEL LANE, THE MAIN thoroughfare through Dunston. The McGowan house was down one of the right-hand turns ahead. Ben passed the liveried cars and pulled in behind Standing. Within seconds, Standing's door was flung open and the car's suspension rocked as he seemed to shove himself from the car and stride towards Ben, coattails flapping in the wind.

"What was all that about?" he shouted before Ben could lower his window. "You heard Granger. I need your full support. You don't just pull out of a convoy like that."

With the window open and Standing doing very little to conceal his outrage, Freya took the opportunity to drive her wedge further into his cracks.

"You have six members of CID and close to a dozen uniforms all watching you right now, DI Standing. Perhaps we can discuss the issue of DS Savage's vehicle check another time." She leaned toward him a little and nodded toward the side road ahead of them. "Maybe we should go and arrest somebody? Don't you think?"

"Granger will hear of this," Standing replied, his finger

pointing at her accusingly. "You're up to something. You heard what he said. You are to give me your full support."

"And here we are," she replied. "Ready and waiting. Are we keeping to my plan, or have you devised your own?"

"No," he said, shaking his head. He bit down on his lower lip and stared her up and down with distaste. "No, you lot can stand and watch. I'll show you how this is done."

He turned to the cars behind them and gave another of those gung-ho waves, then stared at Ben. "You lot stay at the back."

Standing strode to his car, climbed inside, and slammed the door, before leading the convoy into the side street. Three liveried cars followed and Ben parked at the back, then switched off the engine.

"If he gets Jason King—" Ben began.

"If he gets Jason King, then he gets Jason King," Freya said, closing off any avenue of conversation. She needed peace to let the elements of her theory come together. But there was a piece missing, and no matter how hard she tried to clear her thoughts, it eluded her.

They watched as DCs Moray and Vaughan, alongside two uniforms, made a run for the rear of the property. DI Standing and who Freya assumed to be his new DS accompanied two more uniforms to the front door of McGowan's house. One of the uniforms carried what Ben referred to as the big, red key – a handheld weighted ram used for forced entries. The remaining uniforms gathered outside, ready to react on demand.

The big, red key did exactly as it was designed to, and the front door, which had been hastily repaired following Peter Jones' forced entry, was torn from its hinges. Standing shouted, his DS shouted, and together they all bundled into the house.

"Ten," said Freya, and Ben eyed her suspiciously. "Nine. Eight."

"What are you doing?" he asked.

"Seven. Six."

Glancing from Freya to the house like he was watching a tennis match, Ben appeared horrified.

"You're just going to let him do this?"

"Five. Four. Three."

"Freya, he's making a mistake."

"Two."

"I can't watch," Cruz whined.

"One."

A figure appeared in the doorway. It was a girl, no more than twenty years old. She wore a branded baseball cap, a sweatshirt with the hood pulled up, and tight jeans that revealed the outline of a body that life had yet to tarnish.

"Bingo," Freya said.

Standing shoved her out of the house, gestured for a uniform to get her out of the way, then turned and headed back inside.

"Let's go," Freya said, climbing from the car, leaving neither Ben nor Gillespie any time to argue.

She marched up the road as Jess Henry was being led toward her own house by a female uniform.

"Stop right there," Freya called out, and the uniform stopped and looked to Standing, clearly a little uncertain if she should be listening to Freya.

"What're you doing?" Standing called out, and a wry smile crept across Freya's face. She didn't turn to face Standing, but she pictured him in her creative mind as he strode from the house and up the road to where Freya, the uniform, and Jess Henry were standing. Freya waited until his footsteps were close enough that he could hear what she was about to say.

"Jess Henry, I'm arresting you on suspicion of attempted murder. You do not have to say anything, but it may harm your defence if you do not mention now anything you later rely on in court. Anything you do say may be used as evidence."

"DI Bloom," Standing roared, and if there had been any neighbours who had yet to hear the commotion in the street, they were sure to be aware now. "Under whose authority–"

"My own authority, DI Standing. You're here to arrest Jason King for the abduction of Abigail McGowan. I'm here to arrest Miss Henry for the attempted murder of Abigail's father, so please don't interfere."

"I didn't–" the girl replied, but her attempts faded with a dismissive wave of Standing's hand.

"You dare to go against DCI Granger's orders?"

"DCI Granger instructed me to hand the Abigail McGowan investigation over to you. He did not instruct me to do anything with the attack on Terry McGowan. What do you want me to do? Let a suspect walk away on your say so?"

"And this is the best friend, is it?" Standing said, turning to Jess Henry. "You're Abigail McGowan's friend, are you?"

She nodded, then shrugged as Freya knew she would.

"I have reason to believe that this girl was Terry McGowan's attacker."

"What? I did no such thing–" Jess began, but Freya was already one step ahead. She turned to face what remained of her team all standing beside Ben's car. "Detective Sergeant Gillespie?"

"Boss?" he called back, clearly not overly keen on the idea of standing between his old DI and his new DI.

"Can I borrow you for a moment?"

He made his way slowly toward them. If Standing would have had hackles like a dog, they would have been on end. By refusing to go to HQ with Standing, Gillespie had clearly been deemed a traitor, outcast by the man who pretty much led him from Detective Constable to Detective Sergeant.

"Aye, boss?" he said, when he got within a few metres.

"Detective Sergeant Gillespie, this is Jess Henry, Abigail McGowan's best friend," Freya said. "Well, she used to be anyway."

"Aye, I've seen her about. There's a photo of her with Abigail

McGowan in Abigail's room."

He managed to hold the conversation somehow without once looking at Standing. The mood was, as Freya's father might have put it, fractious.

"Miss Henry, for your information, Detective Sergeant Gillespie here is the reason you're not under arrest for murder," Freya said, putting the fear of God into the girl. "He found Terry McGowan moments after Peter helped you escape. Saved his life, in fact. Isn't that right, DS Gillespie?"

"Has this got anything to do with Jason King?" Standing asked. But his words fell on deaf ears. Freya had a point to prove, and with or without Granger's orders, she would not fall at this penultimate hurdle.

"Gillespie?" Freya said, encouraging him to have his say.

"Aye, well. I wouldn't put it quite like that."

"Oh, come on. If you hadn't have walked in when you did, if you had run through the back gate and given chase, Terry McGowan would have bled to death. You know he would."

"Well, it was nothing really. I was just checking the house. You know? Like you showed me a hundred times, boss," he said, and stared across at Standing. That was a small win Freya was willing to let DI Standing have. There would be more wins in the next few hours, and the tally would be close.

"Tell us about what you did when you went upstairs in the McGowan house," Freya said.

"Do I have to listen to this?" Jess said, her tone obnoxious and arrogant.

"Yes," Freya snapped. "Yes, you bloody well do. Go on, Gillespie."

"I found Mr McGowan–"

"Before that, Gillespie. You went upstairs, and you checked the bathroom, then you checked Abigail's room. What did you find?"

"Ah, well, not a lot to be fair. It had been turned over."

"Turned over, Miss Henry," Freya explained, to make sure she was absolutely clear on the term, "is what we call, robbed, rifled, gone through. Do you know what I mean? Like a burglar does."

"I get it," she mumbled in reply, and stared at the ground.

"Okay, let's make it easier. What *didn't* you find?"

"Eh, boss?"

"I asked you to find something, didn't I? I asked you to look for something in Abigail's room," Freya said, and she turned to Jess Henry, adopting a manner as patronising as she possibly could. "You see, Miss Henry, do you remember that time I came to your house? When we first started looking for Abigail?"

The girl shrugged and nodded, still staring at the ground.

"You mentioned something to me. It was only in passing, but you see, I remember. That's what I do. Do you remember what it was you told me? A tiny snippet of information?"

She shook her head.

"I'll help you," Freya said. "Gillespie, I believe I asked you to find Abigail McGowan's diary, did I not?"

"Aye, boss. That was it. A diary."

"And did you find it?"

"Nothing. Checked every drawer. Every cupboard. Under the bed. Under the cabinets. All the places people hide stuff. Wasn't there."

"I thought that was odd, Miss Henry. You see, Mr McGowan also mentioned that diary. So I know Abigail keeps one," Freya said, leaving her to ponder that thought for a few moments. Even Standing was buying into the arrest at this point. He may live at the far end of the social spectrum to Freya, but he wasn't a stupid man. "Gillespie, I want you, with DI Standing's permission, to enter the McGowan house. Go straight to Abigail's room and search once more for me."

"For the diary?"

"For the diary," Freya said, nodding.

"Aye, well, if that's what you want me to do," he said, and after a second's thought, Standing gave him the nod, and he made his way.

"You see, Miss Henry, we've been watching this house all night. Front and back. But you knew that, didn't you?"

She shrugged, and at any other time, her silent responses would have been getting boring. But Freya was enjoying herself.

"You saw them, didn't you? When you let yourself back into the house?"

"Eh? No–"

"You went in through the back door and you went straight to Abigail's bedroom to put the diary back to keep yourself in the clear. But you found yourself trapped. Couldn't move, could you? You couldn't make a run for it. You would have been seen. You would have been caught. There would have been a commotion, in the dead of night, in a beautiful village like this. You would have been shamed. Imagine what that would have done to your image. I dread to think," Freya said.

Freya stared around at the neighbouring houses and found the nearby doorways filled with men and women either in their dressing gowns or ready for work. Each of them with a look of utter disgust on their faces. Freya looked down at Jess once more, then, lowering her tone, she delivered the final piece of this particular puzzle.

"You were inside the McGowan house when Terry McGowan came home. He found you rifling through her stuff, didn't he? You let yourself in the back door using the key that only friends know about. You know the one. Under the plant pot. You even let poor old Stan out, knowing full well he'd make a run for it. He's probably out there now looking for Abigail, what you should be doing if you were any kind of decent human being."

She stared up at Freya, one side of her nose raised in a bitter sneer.

"You needed to see her diary because you saw Abigail and Peter getting it on one night," Freya said, and she glanced up at the two bedroom windows that almost faced each other. "But you couldn't prove it. You weren't sure. But when Abigail went missing, you went and had a look for the diary. She must have written that down, surely, you thought. And she did, didn't she? There was an entry. Perhaps it detailed exactly how it felt to be in Peter's arms again? What did Terry McGowan do? Did he drag you down the stairs, Jess? Did he slap you about? Did he threaten to call the police?"

"Shut up," Jess snapped, her face a picture of guilt. "You weren't there. What do you bloody know?"

"You grabbed a knife from the block in the kitchen and you turned on him. Were you upset because your boyfriend prefers Abigail? Is that it? Maybe she does more for him? Maybe he prefers brunettes? Or, maybe, it's just because she's not a spoilt, selfish bitch like you."

"Hey now," Standing said, and although it pained Freya to think it, he was right to stop her saying more.

"Boss?" Gillespie called from the doorway, and the three of them all turned to face him. The fate of that nineteen-year-old girl would be decided in the next few seconds, and Freya reached for her arm, tightening her grip.

"Find it?" Freya called.

And Gillespie raised his hand, in which was what looked to be a pink, leather-bound A5 notebook with a fluffy tassel as a bookmark.

"You know where he is, don't you?" Freya said.

"I don't know what you're talking about—"

"Don't lie to me. You know where Jason is. You saw him, didn't you? You and Peter. You knew what he was doing."

Jess Henry let her head fall forward. Her shoulders slumped in resignation, and that hardened shell she used to protect her fragile, needy mind, cracked as the tears began to fall.

"Make it easy on yourself, Jess," Freya said. "Tell us where Jason King is now, and we'll let it be known that you cooperated."

CHAPTER FORTY-FIVE

THE SUN HAD RISEN BUT WAS MASKED BY THE HEAVY CLOUD cover. The snow that had fallen for nearly three consecutive days was melting, allowing the grass to bask in the light. The old hospital grounds were still, save for a few rabbits that were brave enough to venture out and pick at the freshly uncovered fauna, avoiding the ever-present eyes of the kites and kestrels circling in the sky.

The team assembled at the gates, minus the two uniforms who had escorted Jess Henry to the station where she would wait in a cell for Freya to return.

A very chirpy Neil Gutteridge parked his van at the back of the queue, and wearing the same tracksuit bottoms he had been wearing when Freya had first met him, he strode alongside the cars with a tuneless whistle emanating from his pursed lips.

A sense of dread washed over Freya as she prepared to be humble in the hope that her first altercation with Gutteridge was not announced in front of Standing.

"You lot will make your bleeding minds up soon," he called out when he was just twenty feet away, to which Standing, who had been surveying the old hospital grounds, turned and hissed for him to be quiet. Taking Standing's advice, Gutteridge unlocked the gates, mumbling to himself. Then, finally, as he withdrew the chain, he offered Freya a smile that, had she not already met the man, would have appeared innocent and helpful.

Holding his hand up to keep everybody back, Standing entered the grounds, peering around the trees that ran alongside the fence line for a sight of the water tower.

"You," he said, pointing at Gutteridge, "is there a rear entrance to the water tower?"

"Rear entrance? What for? It's not a bleeding theatre."

"Is that a no?" Standing snapped, already irritated by the man.

"Yes." He added a solemn nod and confirmed his answer, and Freya smiled inwardly at how Standing had very quickly rubbed him up the wrong way. "Would you like me to draw you a picture?"

"No, that won't be necessary," Standing replied. "What I'd like is for you to move out of the way so my team can do what we've come to do."

"Here then, is he?"

"What?"

"The fella you're after. Here, is he? In the grounds?"

Standing glanced at Freya, who held her hands up defensively.

"Don't get me involved. This is your investigation," she said.

"Get him out of here," Standing said, and gestured for two uniforms to escort Gutteridge back to his van.

"I see. You wake me up and get me out of bed, and this is the thanks I get, is it?" Gutteridge called out as the uniforms coaxed him from the area by the gates. "Should make some kind of complaint, I should. Call my mates at the papers, or something."

At the mention of the press, Ben immediately looked up from the plans he had sprawled over the bonnet of his car, and then nodded for Gillespie to instigate some kind of damage repair.

"He can be difficult," Ben explained to Standing. "But Gillespie will get through to him."

"I hope so, for your sake," Standing replied, then approached Ben. "What do we have?"

"Exactly as Gutteridge said. Single entrance. Fenced all the way around, topped with razor wire. I say we cover the perimeter with uniforms then hit the water tower from the front and the sides. He'll have no escape."

Standing may have nodded, but his expression conveyed a far different message. Had there been an alternative plan of attack, he would have implemented it to be sure that it would be his plan they followed, not anybody else's. But the geography and the structure of the water tower provided very few options. "That's pretty much all we can do."

Clapping his hands three times, Standing waved a few key uniforms over, refraining from calling and alerting King to their presence. He pointed at the printed lines that marked the gates on the plans, then announced his plan.

"The plan is simple. We're here. The water tower is there, five hundred yards away. I want you to split into pairs, I don't care who goes with who. I want two behind the fence next to the water tower in case King decides to risk the razor wire. Then I want two here, here, here, and here," he said, indicating the points of greatest coverage along the perimeter. "That leaves two on the gates and two with me. DS Savage, DI Bloom, DC Cruz, and DS Gillespie will be with me as well."

"Do you really need eight of us to hit a building with a single entrance, DI Standing?" Freya asked.

"No. But if you think I'm letting you out of my sight for a single moment, you've got another thing coming," Standing replied, checking his watch. He gestured at his own team, DC Moray, DC Vaughan, and his new DS, a broad yet short man with a shaved head and dark rings around his eyes. "Coordinate your teams and be in position in five minutes. The rest of you, follow me."

He folded the plans and slapped them into Ben's chest. "This better work, Savage," he mumbled beneath his breath. "Or I'll be sure to let Granger know whose plan this was."

The bigger man, both physically and mentally, Ben's expression remained the same, indifferent to Standing's words and unaffected by his tone.

Marching through the gates onto the grass, where the melting snow was causing a faint mist, Standing led. Freya and her team followed, while the two uniforms walked to one side. In the next field, beyond the treeline where Griffiths had been attacked, the top of the water tower stood tall above the trees. Standing stopped there and waited a few seconds for the team to catch up. He checked his watch, clearly waiting for the five minutes to expire so that the uniformed pairs could be in position.

Ben moved forward to peer through the trees, while Standing, despite his sanctimony, appeared agitated.

"At least it's not snowing anymore," Gillespie said, in an effort to lighten the mood. "Might even have a bit of sunshine later, eh?"

"That'd be nice," Cruz said, seemingly pleased for the distraction. The mood between Standing and Freya was clearly having a negative effect on the young Detective Constable's nerves.

"What would be nice would be if you pair focused on what you were doing," Standing spat, and checked his watch again. He nodded at the radio on one of the uniforms' chest. "Is everyone in position yet?"

The PC, who Freya had seen on occasion but had yet to get to know, lowered the volume on his radio, turned away, and spoke into it. A few seconds passed as each of the pairs reported back, then he turned and gave Standing the nod.

"This is it," Standing said. "Spread out. Ten metres apart. If he runs, there's no way he's getting through us."

They broke through the bushes with little care for noise and, as instructed, walked in a single line toward the water tower. A uniform was positioned on either side, with Gillespie and Cruz beside one of them, and Ben and Freya beside the other. The spearhead was Standing, taking centre stage, and not for the first time that day, Freya imagined there truly was a belief in his mind that he was leading the cavalry in a battle, not for land, or for governance, but for promotion, power, and his almighty ego.

They stopped just twenty metres from the old, brick tower, which, with the faint mist at its base and decades of neglect, appeared as miserable as Cruz, who, if it hadn't been for Standing, would have been moaning about his wet shoes.

Leaning forward to gain the attention of the two uniforms at either end of the line, Standing gave a silent order for them to approach the steel-plated door set into the brickwork on the right-hand side of the structure.

They ran across the ground, gave the lock an inspection, then nodded back to the team, confirming it was unlocked.

Leaning forward again, Standing signalled for Ben, Cruz, and Gillespie to join them. That left just Standing and Freya. And she would have had it no other way.

When all five men were standing at the door, Standing gave a cursory glance around the grounds. Then with a gesture like he was striking something with a hammer, he gave his command.

The grassy field from which Freya and Standing were watching was enclosed on all sides by dense trees. So when the uniform stepped back and slammed his heel into the door, the sound echoed all around in those few brief moments before the shouting began. They bundled through the door, their voices echoing from inside in a melee of testosterone and adrenalin.

"No hard feelings, DI Bloom," Standing said, his chin out, ready to accept his reward with delight.

"You really can be a sanctimonious prick sometimes, DI Standing," Freya said. "Have you ever wondered why you haven't made DCI yet?"

"Every day," Standing said, the insult washing off him as if he was made of Teflon. "I can only put it down to opportunity. Do you really think that poky, little station in the sticks is going to take you where you want to go?" He scoffed and raised his collar against the cold, his eyes firmly fixed on the water tower door.

"Well, then I must congratulate you," she said. "I hope that the opportunities for success come thick and fast for you."

"You can't sweet talk me into submission, DI Bloom. I didn't get here on sentiment."

"No," she replied quietly and thoughtfully, enough that from her peripheral she could see him turn his attention to her. "But you did fail to spot one escape route in your plan. I mean, it was *your* plan, after all, wasn't it, DI Standing?"

She turned to him, offering her best winning smile.

"Is that right?" he said, although with much less confidence than before. And it was then that a few paths aligned in his mind. She could almost see the cogs in his head fall into place. Freya struck herself another proverbial dash on her side of the tally. DI Standing realised his folly, and that arrogant sanctimony was replaced by what Freya could only describe as fear of failure. Slowly, his gaze washed over the tower, from the grassy base to its lofty heights.

And on the roof of the old Nocton water tower, Jason King stepped into view.

CHAPTER FORTY-SIX

"He's not here," Cruz said, almost childlike. He was like a boy who had been teased with the promise of chocolate and was disappointed at not finding any.

"He's been here," Ben said, seeing a corned beef can, the same as the ones he'd seen in the hospital building. The space inside the tower was fairly small. There were four large, concrete plinths with steel bolts jutting out, presumably from where heavy machinery, such as the pump sets Shane Dooley had been talking about, had once been positioned. The space was divided by two large walls so that, should you look down at the floor from above, the usable floor might resemble the letter H.

From above? Ben thought, gazing upward at the void.

Gillespie and Cruz both shuffled about on the far side, and it was only when Ben found the steel ladder that ran the entire height of the building to the tank itself and beyond that his idea began to mature.

It was an idea that was solidified when he heard voices from outside.

"Mr King," Standing called out, and the shuffling from the

next room stopped as Gillespie and Cruz both heard it. "Mr King, my name is Detective Inspector Standing. I have a warrant for your arrest."

Both Gillespie and Cruz bolted for the door and burst into the light outside. But Ben knew what they would find. They would find Freya and Standing staring up at Jason King on the roof.

"I suggest you come down. There's no escape for you," Standing continued.

But there was escape. There was almost certain escape, which would leave Abigail McGowan lost forever. Or at least until it was too late.

Holding onto the rungs, feeling the cold bite of the steel, Ben peered up. The ladder came to an abrupt halt halfway up the tower, where a small platform and a door would lead him to the external ladder. From there, he would have to brave the elements another fifty feet to the top. A steel frame had been built around the ladder so that, should a worker fall, their descent would be limited to the confines of that open steel shaft. On reflection, Ben would have preferred to fall onto the concrete, given the choice, where death would be swifter, rather than bouncing off the sides of the steel frame, breaking limbs, or cracking his skull on the iron rungs.

He put the thought to the back of his mind, and another struck him.

What if Abigail was up there with him? Certain death for them both.

His sprained ankle was now a muted throb when he put his weight onto it, but his injured shins still produced sharp, dagger-like pains. With no good leg to start from, he began his climb, searching for a foothold that hurt the least. He found if he used his heel, there was less pressure on his shins, but it made climbing slower, and only twenty feet up the fifty-foot climb, he had to pause to take a breath. Standing's voice came to him loud and clear in the moment of rest. His forearms burned with the exertion, and his legs had already begun to tremble, but something in Standing's voice told him that if he didn't reach the top soon, his climb would be fruitless.

"Don't do it, Jason," Standing said. "All we want is Abigail. You can do what you want when we have her."

Of all the things he could have said. He could have offered him something. An easier time of it. Prison benefits, TV, free phone calls. Anything.

Ben soldiered on, even more motivated than before. He took some of the rungs two at a time, but the frame behind him and his injured shins hindered any speedy ascent. A sweat had formed on his brow and he wiped it away with the back of his hand. Even when he pushed on to cover the final few rungs of that first ladder, the sweat had reached the palms of his hands, and each rung became harder and more treacherous. The small platform halfway up was his goal – a place where he was sure workers laden with heavy tools had reached before and lain on their backs rubbing their arms. But he knew he would not be afforded that luxury.

Finally, the platform was in reach, and although the transition from the ladder was awkward, he slid himself onto it, dried his hands on his trousers, and then peered through the door to the next ladder. It was almost identical to the first ladder. The same rungs, same steel frame, and it even covered the same distance. But without the thick tower walls to protect it from the elements, the steel was like ice.

"Jason, think about your niece, for God's sake," Freya called out, now joining in the effort. Ben hadn't heard what had been said during most of his climb, mostly due to the concentration required, but in part due to the thundering of his heartbeat in his ears. He stood, clutching the rungs, and felt his jelly-like legs barely able to hold his weight.

"I can't go back there," a new voice said, louder than Freya's or

Standing's. Closer and more desperate. "I can't do it. I'll finish it. I will."

"Jason, we need to find her. You're our only hope. You're her only hope. Can't you see that? We need your help," Freya called, and for once Ben heard the mother in her voice. He could imagine, in that tiny moment as he stood on the threshold of the rooftop, how she might have been with her ex-husband's child. How she might have loved him and cared for him. Her tone, though often hostile and sharp, was now caring, and in contrast to Standing's blasé and gruff comments, it was gentle. "Step away from the edge, Jason. Come down. I'll make sure you're looked after. My name is Detective Inspector Freya Bloom. Call me Freya. I'll see to it you're taken care of."

"Twelve years," King shouted back at her. "Twelve years I've been locked up. And for what?"

"Help us help you," Freya said. "If you fall, those twelve years will have been for nothing. Nothing, Jason."

Ben's hand, numb with cold, reached over the last rung of the ladder. Slowly, he pulled himself up those last few feet until he could swing one of his long legs onto the roof. Behind him were the treetops of the forest where Marie and Abigail had both last been seen. The roofs of Dunston were in the distance, a dark stripe between the white fields and a pale sky.

Before him, however, standing precariously on a low parapet wall on the far side of the tower, was Jason King. He was staring out at the fields beyond Nocton and further still to the undulating Lincolnshire Wolds on the horizon.

Standing to his full height, Ben felt the climb on his legs. They trembled with exertion, and to open and close his numb hands felt alien. Warming them against his body, Ben took a step towards King. The roof was just thirty feet across, and although Ben had imagined finding a series of pipes, it was free from any kind of obstruction, save for the remains of several abandoned bird's nests.

He took a step, hoping to close the distance before King saw him and did something stupid.

"Why don't you tell us what you want, Jason?" Freya called up to him. "Tell us what you want and we'll do everything we can to help."

Ben closed the gap, stopping just ten feet from King, working his fingers until he could be sure they wouldn't fail him.

"You lie. You always lie. This is my life. My life just wasting away."

"And Abigail's, Jason. Don't waste it," Freya added. "Tell us what you've done with Abigail. Tell us where she is."

"Tell us, Jason," Standing called, with far more aggression than he had used before.

"You're going to take me back, aren't you? You're going to take me back there."

"I can't make any promises," Freya said. "But we can make arrangements for you. We can make sure you're comfortable. But we need to know where Abigail is. If you don't help us, then how can we help you?"

"Abigail, Jason," Standing demanded. "Where is she? Now."

But King gave a little laugh. He raised his arms, embracing the cold wind in his face.

"Do you really want to know?" he called out, as Ben took another step. "I don't have her. I never have."

There was a pause as both Standing and Freya digested his response. Then Freya's voice cut through the wind.

"What about Marie Treverne, Jason? Tell me about her."

"No," Jason spat. "That's all you think I am, isn't it? Some kind of monster," he said, and Ben heard the tremble of emotion in his voice. "I'm not who you think I am. But the truth is that nobody will ever believe it. Not now."

"Where's Abigail, Jason?"

But King didn't reply. He simply shook his head once.

"Jason?"

His knees buckled under his weight and he leaned forward, letting gravity do its work.

CHAPTER FORTY-SEVEN

HAD BEN REACTED A SPLIT SECOND EARLIER, HE MIGHT HAVE been able to pull King back over the parapet wall. Yet had he reacted a split second later, he wouldn't have reached him at all and King would have fallen to his death. But as it was, through sheer tenacity, Ben had reached him and managed to grab onto his arm. King's fall was broken and he swung into the side of the building where his flailing feet found purchase on a narrow ledge just two inches wide. Ben's grip was all that prevented him from falling.

"Look at me, Jason," Ben said. "Just keep looking at me. Don't look down."

"I don't want to die," King cried out, with an almost instant change of heart. "Please. Please, don't let go."

Kneeling at the parapet wall, Ben held him fast. But there was no way he would be able to take King's weight should he slip.

"I need help," Ben called out, hoping his voice would reach them below. "Fast."

"Please. I didn't mean any harm. I'm not a bad person."

On the ground below, the uniforms had gathered. An ambulance would be on its way, and Ben was sure that the fire brigade would also have been called to make use of their access platforms.

But right now, all Ben needed was another pair of hands.

"Stay still, Jason. Keep looking at me. Everything is going to be okay."

The truth was that Ben had no idea if everything was going to be okay. His gloveless hand had been exposed to the brutal cold for too long, and the climb had consumed every bit of energy he had. For now, he was just keeping King balanced, keeping him flat against the wall, but a gust of wind could change that.

"Where is she, Jason?" he asked quietly. "Where's Abigail?"

"What?" the man replied, and he dared to look down, then panicked and pressed his face against the wall, puffing out air wildly with hyperventilation.

"Abigail?" Ben said, keeping his voice calm, as if they were just passing the time. "Tell me what you've done with her."

"I haven't done anything," King whined. "I haven't, I swear."

Gazing up from where his life was quite literally on an edge, Jason King locked stares with Ben. And in those wide, brown eyes, where Ben searched for the truth, he found only fear.

"I promise," he said, his voice barely audible.

"Tell me about Marie Treverne," Ben said.

"Who?"

"You know who, Jason. Marie Treverne. She went missing twelve years ago."

"I told them before. It wasn't me. I didn't do anything."

"I can let you go. I can let you fall, and nobody would know. There are more than a dozen people watching. A dozen witnesses that would all see you slip and fall to your death. They'll even say how I tried to save you. You'd be a memory."

"So why then?" King asked. "Why stop me?"

"Because I want Abigail. I want to bring her home. Your niece, Jason. Your bloody niece—"

"I can help," King said, suddenly as if an idea had just struck him. "I can help you find her."

"No. No, you tell me where she is."

"I don't know. I don't. But I can help."

"You were hiding in that building over there in the trees. Of course it was you. You couldn't help yourself, could you? You couldn't keep your filthy hands to yourself," Ben said. "We found her jacket among your things. You know the one? A bright red, waterproof jacket. The one she wore when she was running."

"I found it," King said.

"You disgust me–"

"I did. I found it, by the manhole. It was lying there."

"It was lying there when?"

"When..." King began, and he hit his head against the wall, clearly defying some kind of mental block.

"When, Jason? I'll let you go. I will. All I have to do is remove my hand and–"

"No. No, please. I'll tell you. The other morning. I saw him."

"Saw who?"

"I don't know. It was dark. Some bloke–"

"Oh, come on, Jason. You'll need to do better than that."

"Honest, I don't know. I slept in the building. Like you said. But I had to meet Terry."

"Terry?"

"Yeah. He was bringing me food and that."

"Terry McGowan was helping you evade the police?"

"No. Not really. I went there at first. Two weeks ago, when I got out. I went to his house. He said I couldn't stay. That I had tainted my sister's memory. I had to beg. I needed somewhere to stay. The weather. He showed me the building. Said nobody knows about it. Gave me two weeks. I told him I'd move on as soon as I could. Please. Please let me up."

"And then what?"

"I was going to find someplace away from here."

"Where?"

"I don't know. I didn't have a plan. All I know is that I'm innocent. I don't deserve this. I shouldn't be locked up. I didn't take Abigail, and I didn't take Marie Treverne." King's forehead was pressed against the wall. He pulled his head away and stared up at Ben, his eyes glowing with rage and terror. "I can never go back there. But if you don't believe me, then just let me go."

His stare was unwavering. In those cold eyes, Ben saw a broken man with nothing to live for.

Ben nodded, picturing his face beside Abigail's. Picturing the fear on her face. Then, without a moment's hesitation, he let him go.

Jason King seemed to float for a moment. His eyes widened and his mouth opened to scream as he began to fall away from the wall.

And then, from out of nowhere, a large hand reached over Ben and gripped onto King's wrist, then pulled him back into the wall.

King cried like a little boy as he pressed himself against the brickwork, and Gillespie stared down at Ben. He nodded a single question, unspoken yet as clear as the view to the Wolds on the horizon.

Ben leaned over and grabbed onto King's other wrist. With two men holding onto him, keeping his balance on the narrow ledge, King was far more stable. Yet, when he peered up at them both, his eyes pleading, his fear was even greater.

"It's not him," Ben said. "I was going to catch him."

"You sure about that, Ben?" Gillespie said. "The way I see it, we'd be doing the world a favour."

"Please. Please don't," King whined, and buried his face into the brickwork, muttering to himself.

It took a moment for Ben to consider the opportunity that was before him. It might be the only chance he would ever have to avenge Marie's death. He stole another look in the man's eyes.

A part of him wanted it to be him. A part of him wanted to send King to his death. Gillespie felt the same. He'd have no problem with it, of that Ben was sure.

But there *was* doubt.

"It wasn't him," was all Ben could say, and between them both, they hauled him up and over the parapet wall onto the solid, concrete roof.

CHAPTER FORTY-EIGHT

THE FIRE BRIGADE MADE LIGHT WORK OF BRINGING THE THREE men down from the tower roof, and Freya looked on with pride as two of her team led Jason King towards her and Standing. Ben shoved the prisoner towards Lincoln HQ's newest Detective Inspector and gave him a bitter look of distaste.

"There's your man, Steve," he said. "Do with him what you please."

Standing, magnanimous in victory, smiled back at Ben and offered him only a single statement despite what he had just been through. "I'll be sure to make sure DCI Granger hears of your efforts, DS Savage."

"No need. The credit is all yours. I want nothing to do with it."

"Very noble," Standing said, then turned to King. "Jason King, I'm arresting you on suspicion of murder. You do not have to say anything, but it may harm your defence if you do not mention when questioned something you later rely on in court. Anything you do say may be given as evidence. In other words, sunshine, you're nicked."

With a nod from Standing, two uniforms cuffed Jason King,

and as they dragged him away, King turned back to Ben, offering a last accusing stare.

"Put him straight in the transporter," Standing said as he followed, being joined by DCs Moray, Vaughan, and his new DS, who even now, Freya had not heard utter a single word.

"Alright?" Freya asked, her question aimed at both Ben and Gillespie.

"Aye, boss. You should see the views from up there. Blue skies on the horizon. I'd say things are looking up."

"What about you, Ben?" she asked.

He shrugged, the way Jess Henry might have.

"It's not him, is it?" Freya said, reading him like an open book.

He shook his head once.

"What did he say?"

"Nothing we didn't already know," Ben replied, as they all watched King being helped through the trees. "McGowan was helping him, bringing him food and a few bits."

"The hat," Freya said, and Ben nodded.

"That's why the lab found hair from them both."

"And Marie?"

He shook his head. "I wanted it to be him. Honestly, I really wanted it to be him. To have him there, on that ledge. The fact is that he's been locked up for twelve years. He couldn't have kept Marie alive."

"So you saved him."

"From death maybe, but not from Standing. That poor man has at least thirty-six hours of hell in front of him."

"Aye," Gillespie added. "Which gives us thirty-six hours to find the real perpetrator."

"No," Ben said, immediately and without doubt. "No, we leave it. It's Standing's case now. We've done what we can."

"Ben, you said you wanted to find Abigail," Freya said softly. "We still can. Granger will be over the moon with Standing. Standing will be busy with King. We can carry on."

But Ben shook his head.

"I've done Standing's job enough for one day."

"If you're sure?" Freya said, and without Gillespie seeing, she rubbed his arm to comfort him.

"There is one thing I'd like to do on the way back, if we could, that is?" Ben said.

"Sure. Where's Cruz?"

"I saw him on the phone to that wee lass," said Gillespie. "Grinning like a schoolboy, he was. I swear he's like a different bloke. When he eventually hits puberty, they'll make a fine couple."

Ben laughed, and it pleased Freya to see him smile.

But such a simple pleasure was cut short by Gillespie yelling across the field, "Cruz? Hey, Cruz?" A dozen uniforms and five or six firemen all looked up at the commotion. "Tell her you love her and let's move. The boss says if you aren't here at the car in two minutes, she'll tell everyone you wet yourself."

A few uniforms laughed, but Ben looked at Gillespie quizzically. "How did you find out?"

"About what?" Gillespie replied, looking back over his shoulder.

"About Cruz..." He stopped mid-sentence and closed his eyes.

"Ben, is there something we ought to know?" Freya asked.

"Know about what?" Gillespie said.

"About Cruz peeing his pants," Ben said.

"Cruz peed his pants?" Gillespie said, and the smile that was developing on his face was like he'd just found the winning numbers for next week's lottery. "I was just kidding. I made it up. Are you telling me he actually did it?"

"Leave it. I told him I wouldn't tell anyone."

"No way," Gillespie said.

"Honestly, Jim. The bloke's just got his first girlfriend. Give him a break, eh?" Ben said.

"He peed his pants, Ben."

"I know. But in fairness, I was in the process of strangling him to death."

"What?" Freya said, then shook the image away. "I don't want to know."

"Leave it, eh, Jim? He's okay."

"Aye, you're right. The little fella just started pulling his weight. We don't want the old Cruz back. Useless bugger."

They reached the car just as Cruz caught up with them, breathless.

"I had a word with uniform. They're going to stick around until the site's cleared," he said.

"Nice work, Cruz," Freya said. "Good initiative."

"Cheers, boss," he replied, chuffed with the praise.

"Got the names of the firemen too. You know? For the report."

"Nice," Ben said. "Is that an offer to type it up?"

"If you want," Cruz said, as he climbed into the back seat of Ben's car.

Exchanging an impressed look with Ben and Gillespie, Freya climbed in and the two men followed.

They waited for Ben to start the car, but he was distracted. Gillespie opened his mouth to make a comment, but silenced when Freya glared at him.

"You okay, Ben?" she said, as he peered through the window into the forest.

He didn't reply. Instead, he opened his door, climbed from the car, and walked into the trees.

"Stay here, you two," Freya said to the men in the back, and she followed Ben into the forest.

He hadn't walked far. Enough that the trees blocked the wind, and for a memory to stir, she guessed. She gave him a minute, then checking that nobody could see, she sidled up to him, linking her arm through his.

"You did what you could, Ben. Marie knows that," she said, leaving space for him to digest the words.

He didn't reply. But he smiled one of those half-smiles, more of an appreciation of sentiment than genuine happiness.

"Standing's on the job now," Freya said. "Perhaps a new set of eyes will help? As much as it pains me to say it. Right now, I'd give anything to bring Abigail back home. I have to remind myself that this isn't about my pride. It's about Abigail."

"Yeah," Ben said, his voice cracked and dry.

"We won't stop. You know that, right? Even if it means we work under Standing, we won't stop."

Ben nodded and cleared his throat.

"So?" she said. "You saved a man's life today. You're a hero. What's next? Do we go back to the station?"

"We find Abigail. Like you said, even if it means we work under Steve Standing, we find her," he said, giving her arm a consoling squeeze. "But there's something I want to do first. Something I *have* to do."

CHAPTER FORTY-NINE

THE HOUSE LOOKED PRETTIER NOW THE SNOW WAS MELTING, Freya thought. The flat-topped hedgerows that ran around the perimeter still wore a cap of white, as did the roof and even the old Sierra estate with the little Lincoln City Football Club sticker in the window.

But it was on the retreat, that was for sure, and that could only be a good thing as far as Freya was concerned.

"Are you sure you want to do this, Ben?" Freya asked, as he prepared to climb from the car. He stopped with his hand still clutching the door handle. The engine was still running, to keep the car warm more than anything, and his breath clouded in the fresh air.

"I have to," he explained, but offered nothing more and climbed out.

"Do you two want to stay here for a bit?" Freya asked, turning to glance at Gillespie and Cruz.

"Aye, boss. Take your time," Gillespie said, and he settled into the corner, making himself comfortable, while Cruz simply glanced up from his phone.

"Yep, we'll be fine."

By the time Freya caught up with Ben, he had already knocked on the front door.

"You can wait here as well if you want," he said.

"No chance," she replied, just as the door opened.

Freya had been expecting the old man, but it was the girl, and her face dropped into a horrified expression when she saw them both standing there.

A hopeful, "Yes?" was all she offered. She wore a woolly hat with a bobble that hung down by her ear. It was the type of hat that a snowboarder might wear – trendy in that scruffy, carefree style. Yet the bags beneath her eyes portrayed a girl who was far from carefree.

"Emily," Ben said.

"You've found him, haven't you?" The way she phrased it made it sound more like a question, with a rise in pitch near the end. But her expression was not one of hope.

"Can we come in?"

"We were just about to say a prayer," she said after a few moments of contemplation. "Perhaps you'd like to join us?"

"I would love that," Ben said, his expression softening.

Emily stepped to one side by way of an invitation, and Ben waved Freya in, ever the gentleman.

Marie's father was in the kitchen, sitting in the same chair as before, with his hands clasped around a mug of tea. He opened his mouth, as if trying to remember their names.

"Freya and Ben," she reminded him, and he nodded with a smile, then waited expectantly.

"Is there any news?" Emily said, as she entered the kitchen last and came to stand beside her father. She rested her hands on his shoulders, and he reached up to hold one and give it a gentle squeeze.

"I'm afraid so," Ben said, and he averted his eyes, finding a photo of Marie on the window ledge.

"Let me make you tea," Emily said, and busied herself with the kettle.

"We've arrested a man for the abduction of Abigail McGowan," Ben began. "I can't tell you his name. But I can say that he's being questioned now. We won't know anything until later."

"You questioned every red-blooded male in a two-mile radius twelve years ago. Look where that got us."

"The sad fact is, Emily, we may have found Marie, but I came here to tell you that right now, we don't know who took her or what she went through." He stared at them both, doing his best to look them in the eye and give them the respect they deserved. "I wish I had better news."

Emily's face twisted with a bitter hatred. Not for Ben, but for the facts, for losing her big sister, for whoever it was that had torn their lives apart. But before she could voice her opinion, her father spoke.

"It's better that way," he said, and seemed to chew on the inside of his cheek. "We've got her back. We can bury her. We can move on. Best not to dwell on matters of which you have no control."

He stood, and his chair scraped on the floor as he did.

"We are sorry, sir," Freya said. "We're still looking."

"And you'll be looking in another twelve years. I haven't got that long. I've got one daughter left and memories that nobody can take from me."

He pulled on his coat, and Emily moved to help him.

"I'm going to pay my respects. Join us if you will," he said, like a man who had come to terms with his loss.

Emily followed her father outside, and with a quick glance at Freya, Ben too left by the back door. By the time Freya had joined them, wrapping her coat around her, she found the old man crouching beside a flower bed collecting wildflowers.

Emily came to stand beside Ben and Freya, and then turned away to keep an eye on her ageing father.

"We created a memorial for Marie," she explained, and nodded toward the end of the garden where a simple cross had been fixed into the ground, with framed photos and the remains of previous flowers.

The new estate that had been built around the large property overlooked the garden, but Freya could imagine how it might have been before, with nothing but fields and trees to look out onto. Marie helped her father to his feet, where he formed a bunch from his pickings, as neat as if a florist had put them together. It was just a small bouquet, but pretty, despite some of his selection not even being in bloom.

"Marie's favourites," Emily explained, and Freya smiled in response.

They walked to the end of the garden, the melting snow now revealing a dedicated path to the hand-carved, wooden cross. Emily's father handed her the bouquet, then he folded his hands before him and bowed his head in prayer.

Ben and Freya followed suit.

"It's been twelve years, my dear," the old man began. "And soon we'll have somewhere to go and be with you. But we'll still come here. This is where you belong, and we're grateful to these kind people for finding you. We have to be grateful, Marie. No matter how bitter we feel. We have to try. There's another girl gone. Another family torn apart. I know what they must be going through. I know their pain. But I'm grateful for knowing where you are now. Help her. If you can. Help her find her way. I know you will."

Glancing to her side at Ben, Freya caught him looking away to wipe his eye. He inhaled long and hard, then, feeling her stare, he met it, eyes blazing. Reaching for his hand, she took it in her own.

"Would you like to?" Emily said, offering Ben the little bouquet.

He glanced at Freya, who nodded, and said, "Go on. She'll appreciate that."

And so he did. He knelt before the wooden cross, held the flowers across his opened palms, and studied them for a moment.

Then he sniffed at them, and cocked his head to one side.

"Do you want to say a few words?" Emily asked. "We don't mind if you do."

He laid the flowers on the ground and stood, taking a single step back. Then bowing his head, he folded his hands and spoke.

"Hi, Marie," he began, then gave the tiniest of laughs at the opening. But nobody minded. "I never stopped looking. And I never will." He straightened, then turned and shook the old man's hand. "Thank you," Ben said, nodding his sincerity. "Thank you so much."

"Anyone who was a friend of Marie's is a friend of mine," the old man replied, then leaned in to add a little humour. "Savage or not."

It was a perfectly timed line, delivered in a way that only the old man could have. But Ben was still perplexed by something.

"Tell me. Was that foxglove?"

Marie's Father nodded. "That's the farmer in you. There's also Camellia. But foxgloves were Marie's favourite. Always loved them, she did."

A wry smile crept onto Ben's face, which Freya found difficult to place. Was it humour? Or the simple pleasure of being with Marie's family?

They had made their excuses, said their goodbyes, and were heading back to the car when Freya noticed that Ben was no longer limping. In fact, he was walking faster than usual, and she had to lengthen her steps to keep up with him.

"Something on your mind, Ben?" she asked, as he pulled open the driver's door. He climbed in, and she did the same.

"Well, you two took your sweet time, eh?" Gillespie said, with an irritated glance at Cruz. "Another five minutes and you'd have had another murder on your hands. Romeo here says we should swing by the hospital to see Griffiths. I think he's missing his sweetheart."

"I didn't say that," Cruz said. "You're so full of it–"

"Foxglove," Ben said, cutting the childish argument short.

"What?" Gillespie said, leaning forward.

"Foxglove. It's a wildflower. Blooms in summer, but it's a perennial."

Glancing in Freya's direction, Gillespie pulled a confused face, suggesting that Ben had been working a little too hard.

"Doctor Bell," Freya said, falling in with what Ben was saying.

"Have you two lost your minds?" Gillespie said.

"Doctor Bell found foxglove in Marie's stomach. It's a poisonous plant. Deadly, in fact. It's what Marie Treverne used to..." He paused, cocking his head to one side again, as if some piece of information had just connected with another. "When digested in large quantities, it can induce a heart attack. The symptoms are horrific."

"I'm still not following," Gillespie said. "You're going to have to speak in English, if you don't mind."

"Smell my hands," Ben said, and he held his hands up to Gillespie's face.

"Ah Christ, man. That stinks of piss. Smells like Cruz's trousers."

"Eh? What?" Cruz said, and he found Ben's reflection in the rear-view mirror. "You said you wouldn't say anything. Ah man."

"Foxglove," Ben said again. "Smells like urine. It's a pretty flower, but it does stink. Especially large patches of it. It smells like a toilet."

Freya stared at him, feeling her jaw slacken as his theory hit her like a hammer. He stared back, smiled, then with one more glance at Marie's house, he put the car into reverse.

"Or a privy?" she asked.

Ben nodded. "Let's go and get Abigail McGowan."

CHAPTER FIFTY

It was early afternoon when Ben turned into the long driveway. Four doors opened in unison and Freya and her team climbed out, confident, angry, and with one name on their minds.

"Gutteridge," Ben called, as he slammed his hand against the front door.

"The van's here," Freya said. "He's home."

"Gutteridge, I know you're in there."

But no reply came.

"Cruz, Gillespie, round the back," Freya said, as she pulled her phone from her pocket. She dialled Chapman's desk phone and watched as Ben peered through the windows.

"DC Chapman," she said, answering the phone in her usual chirpy voice.

"Chapman, it's me," Freya began, and offered her no time for pleasantries. "I need a favour. Are you alone?"

"Well, no. DC Gold is here, and Anna's in the loo."

"Where's Standing?"

"In DCI Granger's office. He's brought King in. Walking around like he owns the bloody place."

"Let him have King. I need you to look something up for me. DVLA. Neil Gutteridge. What vehicles does he own?"

"Hold on," she said, and the sound of her fingers dancing across the keyboard came over the line.

"A twenty ten Ford Transit," Chapman began, and before she could relay the number plate, Freya read it out from the back of the van. "That's the one."

"Anything else?"

"A nineteen eighty-six Talbot Autotrail. Never heard of that. Should I look it up?"

"It's a campervan," Freya said. "Tell me it's a campervan."

"It is," came Chapman's reply. "Bloody awful looking thing."

"Is it taxed and insured?"

"Yep. Taxed until September."

"Gutteridge?" Ben shouted, kicking at the door to get his attention. "I know you're in there."

"I need one more thing," Freya said. "Get DC Gold to help if you need it."

"Go on. I'm ready."

"Find out if Neil Gutteridge and his wife ever registered a baby."

"A baby?"

"Please. I don't have time."

At that moment, Gillespie and Cruz came running from the side of the house. "Nothing," Gillespie said. "It's all locked up. No lights on. Nothing."

"Check the bed and breakfasts," Freya ordered, holding her phone to her chest and pointing at the two smaller outbuildings to the left of the house. They ran off, and Freya put the phone back to her ear. "Chapman?"

"Ma'am. I'm on the NHS database. I can see Neil and Gloria, but there's no mention of a baby."

"Get DC Gold to check them both. While she's doing that, I

want you to see if they've fostered, adopted, whatever. Check everything."

"I'll call you back in five minutes," Chapman said, and she cut the call.

Just as Freya pocketed her phone, she found Ben taking a step back, preparing to kick the door in.

"Ben?" shouted Freya, and he paused then turned to look at her. His attention was purely out of obligation. Her words, however, would be futile.

"We don't have a warrant, Ben. I can't let you do that."

"She's inside. I know she is."

"It's your job, Ben."

"All clear," Gillespie called from over by the bed and breakfasts.

"Go round the back," Ben instructed her. "You can say you didn't know I was going to do it."

"Ben, I can't."

"I'm going in, Freya. Job or no job." They shared a moment, and Ben's eyes told a story of misery and pain. "I said I'd find her. I promised her. I'm going to keep my promise."

She inhaled long and deep, the consequences seeming so small compared to a girl's life.

"Do it," Freya said, as Gillespie and Cruz returned.

"Do what?" Cruz asked innocently, just as Ben put the heel of his boot into the front door.

The door held fast.

"What are you doing?" Cruz said, fear in every tiny intonation of his voice.

Ben kicked again, to no avail. But his efforts were rewarded with some help. Gillespie stood beside him, prepared his footing.

"We don't have a warrant," Cruz said, as they both counted down from three.

"Three," Gillespie growled, his Glaswegian accent thick and strong.

"You sure you want to be a part of this, Jim?" Ben asked.

"Two," Gillespie replied.

"Then I'm in it too," Cruz added, and stood between the two much larger men, his arms around each of their waists.

"One," Ben cried.

The door crashed open, and all three men piled inside.

"You don't have to go in if you don't want to, Cruz. I understand if you don't want to be implicated," Freya said, as Ben and Gillespie moved in. "You do have a choice."

"Are we sure she's in there?" he asked.

Freya stared after Ben, who disappeared into the lounge.

"No," she said.

"Oh, sod it," Cruz said, and he ran in after them.

She watched with admiration, and the three men darted from room to room, calling out when they found a room to be clear, and a sinking feeling tightened a knot in Freya's stomach. Something was wrong. She wandered around the side of the house, to where she and Ben had been standing when they smelled what she had thought to be urine. The snow had mostly melted, exposing Gutteridge's crop of wildflowers. There were some small, red flowers, and purple ones. None of which she knew the names of. But there were also plants that bore no flowers at all. Small, green shoots with tiny leaves. She crouched, pulled one up from the soil, and inhaled. She pulled her head away in disgust and spat.

"Foxglove."

Her eyes were drawn to the tractor shed, where a similar array of wildflowers added colour to the foot of the otherwise dull and decrepit building. That was when she noticed the window in the side. It was divided into twelve smaller squares. But along the bottom row, a pane of glass had been smashed.

Checking around her, she took a few steps towards the two huge doors. And as she approached, she heard something. A rumbling from inside. Like an old generator.

Or the engine of an old 1986 Talbot campervan.

Her body stiffened at the realisation, and she was about to call for Ben when the rumbling deepened, growing loud and throaty. She barely had time to jump out of the way when the doors burst open, slammed into her backside, and knocked her into the hedge.

The campervan reversed in front of the house, skidding to a halt, and Freya just had time to look up from where she lay to see Neil Gutteridge fighting with the gear stick.

Ben came running from the house, followed by Gillespie. But they were too late. Gutteridge had found first gear and roared onto the driveway, leaving Freya with a view of the back of the camper, where above a broken taillight and through a grubby and tiny little window, a face stared at her.

"Abigail," she whispered in disbelief.

CHAPTER FIFTY-ONE

WITH NO TIME TO WAIT FOR CRUZ OR EVEN FOR FREYA TO collect herself, Ben and Gillespie climbed into the car. Ben lowered his window and paused long enough to call out to her.

"You okay?" he asked.

"Just go, I'll be fine," she replied, waving them on and collecting her phone from her pocket in a single move. She hit redial and waited for Chapman's voice. Cruz ran from the house. Late, as ever.

"Get in there and see what you can find," she said, pointing at the tractor shed. The call connected and Freya immediately began giving her appraisal of the situation. "Chapman. I need help. I need uniforms and fast. We've got her. We've bloody got her."

"Ma'am, I think you should probably come back to the station..."

Chapman's voice faded away, and Freya heard rasping as the handset was dragged across a face with at least two days' growth.

"Detective Inspector Bloom," DCI Granger said. "It's funny. I honestly thought I asked you to hand over any evidence to DI Standing."

"I did, guv. But we've had a development."

"I see. A development that coincided with DI Standing being otherwise engaged interviewing a man that has already been found not guilty for the abduction of Marie Treverne?"

"I didn't mean for it to work out this way, guv. Honestly. It was Ben who worked it out. We were..."

"Go on," Granger encouraged her.

"We paid a visit to the Trevernes. Ben knew her. He knew Marie. I shouldn't be telling you this, but–"

"But he knew her. I thought he was acting weird."

"Please, guv. He's okay. He just wanted to find Abigail."

"You should have told me, DI Bloom," Granger said. "You've put me in a tight spot."

"I know. I accept full responsibility."

"As I would hope."

"I'm sorry. It was a choice between helping Ben and doing what the rulebook says."

"And I would have done the same thing," Granger said.

"Boss?" Cruz said from behind her, and she turned to face him.

He held up an old, blue jacket, sniffed it, and pulled away.

"Should I hand Gutteridge over to Standing?" she said to Granger, as Cruz went on to discover more old clothing.

She gazed into the tractor shed, noting the heavy locks on the doors and a huge, dirty carpet that had been laid across the cold, concrete floor.

"Hand him over to DI Standing?" Granger said, and for a moment, Freya could have sworn he gave a little laugh. "Oh no, Freya. This one belongs to us. If you think Lincoln HQ are having this, you've got another thing coming. This, Freya, is what you might call something substantial."

"Guv," she said, biting her lip at the sound of his words.

"Bring him in, DI Bloom. I'll have DC Gold make the arrangements with the hospital. I'm sure there's somebody there who would like to see Abigail."

She sighed, and the weight on her shoulders seemed to dissipate.

"Thanks, guv."

"I think you'll find DC Chapman has found something interesting to tell you."

"Guv?"

"Ma'am?" Chapman said, after Granger had handed her back the phone. "I've got it. I've worked it out."

"I hope so, Chapman," Freya said. "For all our sakes."

And as Chapman recited the latest details she had gleaned, Freya eyed Neil Gutteridge's white Transit van on the driveway, and a plan hatched, wild and reckless.

Leaving Cruz to continue searching through what Freya was sure were Marie's old belongings, she took a walk over to the van. To her surprise, the keys were on the driver's seat. She opened the door, inserted the key, and turned it, and the engine fired up.

Cruz ran from the tractor shed when he heard her gunning the engine onto the driveway, and he looked completely bewildered in her side mirror as she drove away. His arms fell to his side when she turned left, hot on the trail of a 1986 Talbot campervan.

CHAPTER FIFTY-TWO

THE NARROW LANES IN BRANSTON BOOTHS BORE NO CENTRE white line, and on occasion, when drivers came upon another vehicle, etiquette stated that one would elect to make use of a passing point.

But there were no oncoming cars, and yet there was also no room on the lane for Ben to pass the campervan and force it to stop. They passed beneath a railway bridge and came to a crossroads Ben knew was notorious for road traffic accidents. But having pushed the campervan up to fifty miles per hour, Neil Gutteridge had no intention of stopping. Ben slowed, seeing the danger ahead, and nearly closed his eyes as the old camper drove straight over the crossroads towards Branston village.

There was no collision, and Ben had some ground to make up as a result.

"Bloody lunatic," Gillespie spat, and thankfully he didn't make a reference to the fact that he could have killed somebody. Ben was on the edge. He gripped the wheel tight and worked his way through the gears until he came up behind the camper again.

The road widened a little and Ben moved out to check for oncoming traffic. He swerved back when an old Fiesta came hurtling toward him, and then, seeing a gap, he dropped into third gear and went for it.

Gutteridge saw his intention and moved out to block him, but he hadn't seen what Ben had. Ahead of them, two liveried police cars blocked the end of the road.

The old camper braked, hard, and Ben overshot, skidding on the loose gravel to the side of the road. He checked his mirror and found Gutteridge was pulling a sharp three-point turn, using the entrance to a small park to manoeuvre.

"Turn around, Ben," Gillespie yelled, his hand on the door handle, ready to leap out.

The camper headed back the way they had come, a thick cloud of old diesel oil spewing out from its exhaust. Seeing the two police cars moving toward them, Ben reversed into the park entrance, found first gear, and followed the camper.

"Get Chapman on the phone. We need more units," he said to Gillespie.

"Aye, I'm on it," he replied, struggling to operate his phone at the speed Ben was driving. "We're going to need some medical assistance too by the looks of it."

Gillespie wasn't wrong. A white Transit was coming towards them. Ben moved out, flashing his lights to warn the driver, but if anything, it only seemed to make it worse. The driver moved to the centre of the road and began flashing its lights right back.

"Get out of the bloody way, you lunatic," Gillespie shouted, leaning out of the window, waving his arm. "Move."

But the driver of the Transit van wasn't budging. Gutteridge moved to the middle of the road too, and there was no way Ben could pass. Seeing what was happening, the driver of the lead police car behind them turned on their blues and twos. But even the wailing siren did little to convince the van driver he was in danger.

"Ease off, Ben," Gillespie warned. "This is going to be bad."

The closer the old camper and the van got, the faster the

distance seemed to close. Five hundred metres became three, then two, then, with no other way of stopping it, Ben braked, eyeing the driver behind who had already begun to slow.

All they could do was watch and pray one of the drivers in front saw sense.

"Ah Christ, Ben," Gillespie had just enough time to say before, at the last second, the camper swerved to one side. The wheels caught the grass verge and the whole vehicle bounced up into the air, ploughed through the hedge, and came to an immediate stop in the adjacent field.

"Go, go, go," Ben said, jumping from his car as the white Transit van screeched to a stop inches from Ben's car, leaving a trail of rubber on the tarmac. Ben wrenched open the passenger door and was about to scream at the driver when he found Freya, breathless and gripping the steering wheel for all it was worth. She stared dead ahead, then fell back against the seat. Gillespie pounded past Ben. He leaped up the grass verge and ran through the hole in the hedge.

"You bloody lunatic," Ben said, and slowly, she turned to face him. A smile crept over her face.

"You won't be mentioning my driving ability ever again, I presume?" she said, and Ben laughed. "Go," she told him, nodding towards the wreckage. "Go get your girl."

Ben followed Gillespie into the field. The front end of the camper had dug a channel in the soil where it had landed, but the momentum had pulled the vehicle onto its side.

Neil Gutteridge lay beside the camper in the mud and what remained of the snow. He groaned, and from what Ben could see, he had suffered a serious leg injury and wasn't going anywhere.

Gloria Gutteridge, however, had managed to avoid serious injury, and was in the field, backing away from Gillespie with a knife to her son's throat.

"Easy now," Gillespie said, his voice deep and calm. "Enough people have been hurt already."

The uniforms joined them in the field, and Ben pointed at Gutteridge on the ground. "He needs an ambulance. Call it in, then cuff him." He edged around the toppled camper, but Gloria saw him and she swung the boy around to cover Ben's approach, as if he was some sort of human shield. Both Ben and Gillespie edged forward in a two-pronged attack.

"Come on now, Gloria. You don't need to do this. You don't need to hurt him."

The boy was wide-eyed. Tears streamed down his face, but he didn't struggle. He spoke softly, albeit with a high-pitched whine.

"Please, Mummy. Please don't. You're hurting me."

"I'm not going to prison," she called out, ignoring her son's request. "I'll do it. If I have to, I'll do it."

"I've heard that already today," Ben said. "From the man accused of abducting Marie Treverne twelve years ago. You remember Jason King, don't you?"

Gloria's expression altered at the mention of the name of the man who had been in the papers, and had been blamed for the crime. But she said nothing. Her breathing sharpened. She wasn't a fit woman, but she edged back stealthily with the knife at the boy's throat. A single slip or stumble could slice his skin.

"I had to talk him off a ledge, Gloria. Can you imagine what that was like? Can you imagine if your life was so bad you could see no option but to end it all? How miserable he must have been?"

"Don't talk to me about misery," she replied. "You know nothing about what we've been through. But you wouldn't understand. You're a bloke. You wouldn't get it. What it's like not to have the means to do what God intended. It's torture, is what it is. Torture."

"I understand," a new voice said, strong and with remorse. Ben turned to find Freya stepping across the field, taking up a position between Gillespie and Ben. "I'm a woman. I've never given birth, and the one child I had in my care was taken from me, so tell me more about this torture, Gloria. Tell me how your suffering is so great that you ruined the lives of countless others to improve it. So you could have a child."

Ben glanced at Gillespie, who looked equally as confused.

"You know nothing," Gloria spat. "You don't care what God thinks. Told me yourself, you did–"

"I know nothing?" Freya said, and she broke ranks, stepping forward to close the gap, despite Gloria pulling the boy tighter. "I know everything, Gloria. I know how you tried to conceive but couldn't. And I know about the time in Lincoln."

"That was a long time ago."

"Even still," Freya said, and she looked up at Ben, realising that neither he nor Gillespie knew what she was talking about. "You took a baby, didn't you? Because you couldn't conceive, you stole somebody else's. I heard all about it. I heard how you waited in the supermarket for your opportunity, then walked out without a care in the world."

"I sinned, and I paid my penance," Gloria said. "I gave her back. I returned her."

"Only because you were caught. And it didn't stop there, did it? No. No, you tried adoption. You tried to foster a child. But who in their right mind would let you look after a baby after what you did?"

"I was desperate. You don't know what it's like."

"Oh yes, I do. And so do thousands of other women. Millions, probably," Freya said. "Tell me how you felt when Neil brought Marie Treverne home, Gloria."

The woman in the field stared back at Freya, then glanced back, searching for an escape route. She said nothing.

"Surely he must love you terribly, to do what he did. Twelve years ago. Just another day at work. Another day away from his tortured and depressed wife. If only there was a way he could help you. If only God would answer his prayers, so that the house he built might be filled with laughter and the sound of children's feet. And what do you think he thought when he peered into that manhole in that forest and found Marie Treverne down there?"

Freya stepped forward slowly. Holding her arms out to her sides, motioning for Ben and Gillespie to stay.

"Were you angry with him, Gloria? Bringing a beautiful young girl home? Did he have to explain why he did it? Or had you both planned it? See, I think you planned it. I think you had that tractor shed kitted out for the very purpose of keeping somebody locked away. Am I right, Gloria?"

The older lady shook her head in denial of the truth, and the boy's face was confused. He opened his mouth to speak, but his mother clamped it shut.

"Were you there, Gloria?" Freya continued, edging forward still. "Were you there when your husband raped that poor girl?"

"It wasn't rape," she spat.

"He forced himself on her. It may not have been for pleasure, but whatever the purpose, he raped her."

"It wasn't like that," Gloria insisted. "We made it nice."

"You made it nice for who?" Freya snapped, and her attention turned to the boy. "How long did it take? He's what, ten? Two years to get Marie pregnant. Two years of him..." She stopped, unable to even imagine what had taken place.

"God will provide," Gloria said righteously.

"And what about Jason King?" Freya said. "You knew he was hiding in the hospital. You both knew. That's why Neil conveniently forgot to give us the plans, isn't it? That's why you didn't want us in your house. Because you were packing. You were buying time, hoping we'd waste days with King. Meanwhile, you would have been taking Abigail somewhere. Where was it? Somewhere far away I bet."

"No. It wasn't like that."

"And what about King? Think about what he went through."

"Stop," Gloria said, the knife grazing the boy's skin. "Just stop. I'll do it. I'll bloody do it."

"Let him go, Gloria."

"No. He's mine. Nobody can take him away from me."

"But he's *not* yours, is he? Do you really want to have this conversation in front of him?"

"Yes. Yes, he needs to know how much I love him."

"You love him so much that you kept his mother locked up in a campervan in a shed for twelve years? Is that how much you love him? Let me guess. You wanted another child. You wanted another but Marie was at her wit's end. You dare speak of misery. I can't even begin to imagine how she must have felt all that time."

"She was fine. We gave her a good life. She had the camper and the shed. She was warm and we fed her."

"You took away her freedom."

"She took her own freedom."

"She killed herself. She reached out of the window and pulled up handfuls of foxglove. So what? You needed another girl? Was it really that simple for you? Was it not enough that you destroyed an entire family, that you sought to destroy another?"

"We treated her well."

"I know. You had your husband put her back where he found her. As if nothing had happened. As if she had been there all along. How very noble of you. I'm right, aren't I? Tell me, Gloria. I'm right, aren't I?"

The older woman nodded, and the resentment on her face faded to the beginnings of remorse. Freya was turning her.

"He knew about Abigail, didn't he? He knew she ran that route every day. He simply drove the camper to work that day, dumped Marie's body, and got you a new one. Was she a gift, Gloria? Is that how it worked? Was it a surprise, or was that planned too?"

"The boy needs a brother or sister. Ain't right for him to be alone."

"It isn't right? Oh, Gloria, there is so much that isn't right here," Freya said. "But I'll give you one chance. One single chance to please God, to please the jury, and to make things right for the boy."

There was a silence as Gloria stared at Freya, and Freya edged forward a little more.

"Let him go."

It was obvious even to the criminally insane that she had no means of escape. There would be no chance for her to salvage anything. She was cornered with nowhere to run.

"I love you, Daniel. You know that, right?" she said, placing her face beside his. "Everything I did, I did it for you. So you could have a life. Remember that. Pa and me, we love you very much."

"Drop the knife, Gloria," Freya said softly, closing the distance so that she stood over them. The blade had left a smear of blood on the boy's neck. It was a tiny scratch, but made with so little effort. "Look at his skin. Look at his eyes," Freya pleaded, staring at the boy, who was visibly trembling with fear. "Just look at what you've done to him."

She reached out, and Gloria didn't move. Freya held onto Gloria's hand, expecting the woman to turn on her. Better her than the boy.

But there was no resistance.

"What will happen to him?" the woman asked, and there was genuine concern in her voice.

"That's not for me to say. Maybe he'll go to Marie's father. Maybe the system will take him. He'll be looked after."

Her head bowed, Gloria held him tight. One last time. One last hug.

"Let go of the knife, Gloria. It's over."

It took a few seconds for the woman's shoulders to sag. Defeated, Gloria Gutteridge let her hand be pulled away from the boy. Freya tossed the knife behind her and took the boy's hand in her own. Then she glanced back for Ben and Gillespie to come forward.

"I'll give you this one chance to tell me where Abigail McGowan is, Gloria," Ben said quietly.

She peered up at him, squinting against the bright, pale sky behind him.

"Life will be much easier if you cooperate," Freya added. "I'll see to it."

Gloria shrugged, then glanced back at the upturned van.

"She's not in there. I thought she was. I saw a face in the window." Freya said, and she glanced at the boy. "But I was wrong."

"She's at the house."

"In the tractor shed?"

Gloria nodded slowly.

"We never hurt them, you know? We treated them well."

"No," Ben replied. "No, you just held Marie Treverne in captivity for twelve years until she took her own life."

"There's a space," Gloria began, and she looked from Ben to Freya. "In the tractor shed. Neil uses it to get under the camper. Like a pit. It's covered over, so you won't see it unless–"

"Unless you're looking for it?" Ben finished, and Gloria gave the slightest of nods, then buried her face in her hands.

"What have we done?" she said, horrified. Her breathing became loud and her huge chest rose and fell. "May the Lord have mercy on us."

"I don't think you'll get much mercy, Gloria," Freya said, and she turned away to leave her kneeling in the mud. She met Ben's eyes as he approached then stopped and touched his arm gently. "This one's yours, Ben," she said.

CHAPTER FIFTY-THREE

The paramedics loaded Neil Gutteridge with his ruined leg into the back of the ambulance while uniforms handcuffed his wife.

"Do you mind escorting her back to the station, Jim?" Ben asked. "Call Sergeant Priest on the way. Have him prepare a cell. I want to keep her under the radar until I get there, if you know what I mean?"

"Aye, Ben. No worries there. With any luck, Standing will be busy trying to get Jason King to talk."

"That should keep him busy," Ben said. "Thanks, Jim."

"Pleasure. You off to the house then, aye?"

"I'll call if we need you."

"Ah, you won't need me," Gillespie said, as he followed the uniforms and Gloria Gutteridge off the field. He turned and took a few steps backward, then called out to Ben, "Besides, I don't think I can stomach any more of Cruz and his whining. You keep him."

"Ready for this?" Freya asked. "Ordinarily I'd call for dogs to help."

"We won't need it," Ben said. "Besides, calling in a dog unit will definitely alert Standing. We'll have to use Cruz instead."

Using Ben's car, they left the Transit to be collected by a transporter, while Gillespie made safe the scene of the accident. Ben drove slowly. He stopped at the crossroads, remembering how the camper hadn't stopped, and how things could have ended very differently.

"How do you think it'll go down?" Ben asked.

"Abduction for them both. Maybe manslaughter. To be honest, there's probably a hundred crimes you could throw at them. None of them carry enough of a penalty."

The answer did little to satisfy Ben's hunger for them to suffer.

"Short of breaking the law ourselves, we've done all we can do," she said, clearly hoping to soften the blow. "No judge in England will let them get away with it."

"No. No, you're right," Ben muttered as he pulled the car into the Gutteridge's long driveway.

The tractor shed was dead ahead. The doors were open and the property was still. Ben parked the car and they climbed out, heading straight for the building. There was a pile of old clothes on the floor and the walls had been roughly boarded out. Apart from a space in the corner where an old mattress and an old carpet lay on the hard floor, it was empty.

"She said they kept her in the camper and parked it in here," Freya said, as Ben pulled the carpet away to reveal wooden boards covering an old mechanics pit.

"Except for special occasions," he replied. "When they kept her in here."

He dropped to a crouch and began pulling at the boards. He tossed them to one side with little concern for crime scene preservation. He was more concerned with the preservation of life. When three boards had been removed, he turned on the torch app on his phone and shone it inside. Freya bent to join him and together they came to a daunting conclusion.

"She's not here," Ben said, getting to his feet. "She's not here. They bloody lied."

"One second," Freya said.

"No, Freya. I'm calling Gillespie. He can bring Gloria back here and I'll drag her across the place on her knees until she tells me where Abigail is."

"Ben?" Freya said, having to raise her voice to get through to him. He stopped and stared at her, irritated by her apparent nonchalance. "Come with me."

"What?" Ben said, appalled at her lack of haste. "They must have taken her somewhere. The van maybe?"

But Freya was out of the door and marching across the driveway to the house. Ben ran to keep up with her and followed her into the hallway, a large space with a full two-storey ceiling. There were voices coming from the lounge, and slowly, Freya approached the door. She stopped at the doorway, listening, and she smiled at him, saying nothing.

The voice they heard was Cruz, rabbiting on about how he and Ben had chased someone through the forest in the dark. And how Ben had injured himself and Cruz had to pretty much carry him back to the cars, despite him being the biggest man Cruz had ever met. They peered through the doorway, intrigued. Cruz was sitting on a sofa at the far end of the room, relaxing with a cup of tea in his hand. Opposite him, on a couch that faced the other way, Ben could see the top of somebody's head. The tangled mess of unwashed hair needed no introduction.

"Boss," Cruz said, when Freya pushed open the door. "I figured I'd bring her in here. In the warm. You know?"

Ben was speechless.

"I found her under the carpet in a hole," he explained, then silenced, as he realised his explanation could wait until later. He stood and put his tea down, holding out his hand by way of an introduction. "This is Abigail. Abigail McGowan."

The tangled mess of hair didn't move. So, slowly, Ben and Freya moved toward them.

"I made her a tea," Cruz said. "She was thirsty and cold."

"You did good, Cruz," Freya said, offering him a smile and a nod. "You did good."

Abigail sat with her knees drawn up and her arms wrapped around them. Cruz had found her a blanket and the only part of her that could be seen was the top of her head down to her eyes.

Ben crouched before her.

"Are you hurt?" he asked, and she shook her head.

"Can you walk?" Freya asked, and she nodded.

"I think there's somebody who would like to see you," Ben said, then leaned in close the way an uncle might side with a niece or a nephew. "I think we should get out of here. What do you say?"

The girl nodded, and he helped her to her feet, keeping the blanket around her shoulders. He allowed Freya to take over, considering a feminine touch to be more appropriate. When they reached the car, he opened the back door for her, gesturing silently for Cruz to get in the front so Freya could be with her.

But Abigail stopped. She stared at the tractor shed, lost in thought.

"We caught them," Ben said softly. "They're in custody now. You never have to see them again."

But his words had little impact. A single tear ran from her eye, and from beneath the blanket, her hand rose up to wipe it away before Freya could find a tissue in her pocket.

"It's okay, Abigail," Ben said. "It's over. You're safe now. Come on. Let's get you out of here."

"There was someone else," she said, her voice taking them all by surprise. It was cracked and tired, but there was a strength to it.

"Where?" Ben said. "Do you mean they weren't alone?"

"No. Before me. There was someone else," she said, and she

let her blanket fall away to reveal a pair of old, faded jeans and a baggy Oasis t-shirt. "They said I should wear these. They said it was so they could remember somebody. Somebody special."

"She was special," Ben said fondly, making no attempt to wipe the tear that was forming in his eye.

"Did you know her?" Abigail asked, her voice flat and almost robotic. Perhaps it was through sheer exhaustion, or just that her senses had been numbed.

"I knew her very well," Ben said.

Abigail peered up at him, breaking her trance-like gaze at the tractor shed for the first time.

"What was her name?" she asked. "I'd like to remember her."

Glancing across at Freya, who wore a compassionate yet troubled expression, and Cruz, who looked just as awkward as he had when Larson had first started talking to him, Ben reached into his jacket. He withdrew his wallet, and from inside, he pulled out a photo. It was a photo that he had carried for twelve years yet had never once needed to look at. The image was cast into his memories for the rest of time.

He handed it to her, the photo of the pretty girl at a rock concert, whose light curls rested on the denim jacket she wore over a baggy Oasis t-shirt.

"Her name was Marie. Marie Treverne," Ben said, then paused, as if he was choking on the words that he wanted to say... no, needed to say. Abigail looked up at him with admiration and intrigue, and he said then, "Her name was Marie Treverne and I loved her more than anything in the world."

Clutching the photo, Abigail peered back at the tractor shed, then returned her attention to Ben.

"Will you tell me about her?"

"I hope so," he replied.

CHAPTER FIFTY-FOUR

EMILY TREVERNE HAD DONE A MARVELLOUS JOB. THE SCENE brought a tear to Ben's eye. Scant moonlight washed over the garden, providing vague outlines of trees and plants – shapes in the darkness. But it was the path of candles that lit the way to Marie's memorial and set in motion sparkles across the snow-covered ground.

It was as if there was no other world beyond the boundary of that property. It was as if nobody else existed. Just the moon, the flames, and the memories that each of them held. There must have been a dozen or more candles at the foot of the memorial. It shone like a beacon in the darkness. This was her night. Abigail's. It was only right that her memory should steal the moment. She had, after all, been deprived of creating new ones.

In Emily's hand was the largest bunch of foxgloves he had ever seen. It must have been her father's entire crop. Emily handed it to him, holding onto his hand as she did.

"Spread her love. Cast her memory far and wide," she said, then stepped back, waiting for him to lead the way.

Behind him, wrapped in her heavy, woollen coat, Freya linked her arm through Mr Treverne's. She nodded to Ben, as if she was reassuring him somehow, or telling him it was okay. Okay to what? To grieve? To remember?

Emily tossed a handful of the wildflower to one side, then threw more out, letting them slip through her fingers either side of the pathway. Ben followed suit, and Marie's father did too, so that, when the snow finally melted, the seeds of that wildflower would fall to the ground and the entire pathway that wound around the garden would be lined with foxglove. So that people would know. They would see the foxglove and they would remember. So that every time they peered from their window, they would see her. So that her memory would be carried on the wind to fly to the far corners of the world. Just as she might have done had she been given the chance.

The congregation of four stopped at the memorial, and each of them, though silent, were lost in thought. For Emily and her father, Ben imagined they were going over the same old memories they had been reliving for years; only this time, the needing was different. This time, the memories didn't just stop. This time, there was a conclusion, as devastating as that may be. They knew now. They understood. They had closure, and the peace was evident on their tired faces.

Freya was perhaps thinking of her own past. Maybe she had aligned the story to one of her own? Maybe there were people in her life that had yet to find a conclusion? Or maybe she was just savouring that sweet moment? That moment that justifies the hardship they endured in their day-to-day roles. The reason they dragged themselves from their beds every morning. To bring peace, however the sentiment is interpreted.

For Ben, the memories were clear. There was one moment in particular, he recalled, when they had lain in his father's fields and stared up at the moon. They had wondered what it was like up there and how it must feel to look back at the earth. But that had just been conversation. Those words had just been words. The substance had been the connection. They had lain side by side staring up at the moon, because Ben hadn't been able to look her in the eye. The moon had provided them that connection, and as bright as it was as they stood by her memorial, Ben's gaze didn't falter. He didn't look up to the moon to make that connection and had she been standing before him, he would have looked her in the eye. The words would have meaning too. Not just childish wonders of a faraway place, but the here and the now. He wouldn't back down. He wouldn't make that same mistake again.

"You're home now," he said, aloud and unashamed.

"You're with us," Emily added, and she gave Ben's hand a gentle squeeze.

"And may you never leave us again," Mr Treverne said, his voice louder and stronger than Ben had heard before. Perhaps his way of forcing his emotions to one side.

The three of them looked along the line, each of their gazes resting on Freya. It was her turn to add something, and for a moment, Ben thought she would freeze.

But she didn't. Freya always found something to say, and although she hadn't known Marie, although she barely knew the Treverne family at all, she owned the moment and brought the vigil to a conclusion in a way that only Freya could.

She began by scattering a handful of foxglove, then looked up and met Ben's stare.

"I know you stand among us," she said, her voice cracked and weak. "For I am in your shadow."

CHAPTER FIFTY-FIVE

THE STATION WAS EERILY QUIET WHEN FREYA AND BEN emerged from the fire escape stairwell and into the corridor. It was late, and most of the day shift would have gone home. In London, where Freya was from, the late shift was as busy, if not busier, than the day shift. But in rural Lincolnshire, she imagined the evening and early hours of the morning an ideal time to catch up on paperwork and reports.

"Hey listen," Ben said, as she placed her hand on the incident room door and prepared to shove it open.

She turned back to him, tired and in no mood for questions.

"What you said earlier, you know, at the Trevernes'."

"I couldn't think of anything to say. I didn't know her."

"No. No, it was great. It was lovely, in fact. But, you're not. In her shadow, I mean. You're not."

"That's nice to hear, Ben," she said, offering him the last of her smiles for that day. To leave it felt a little rude and uncaring. It was clear he wanted to talk about Marie, or at least he wasn't ready to close that particular chapter. "Will you go and see them from time to time?"

"I was hoping to," he replied. "I was thinking I might put

them in touch with the right person and introduce them to Daniel. I don't really know how it works, but surely he's better off with them than in some kind of institution."

From somewhere deep inside Freya, some part of her that reacted regardless of how tired she was, she found another smile. But more than that. She thought she knew the man well already, but there was a side of him on display that she imagined he rarely exposed.

"I imagine you're right. That's a lovely idea," she told him, and she pushed through into the incident room to a roar of cheers and applause, and the sleepy station came alive.

The whole team were there, most of them as dogged-looking as Freya felt. There was no popping of champagne bottles, but there were bottles of beer, and both Chapman and Gold were guarding a bottle of wine, each of them clutching a plastic cup.

It was DCI Granger who stepped over to them first, offering a large hand to shake. "Well done, Freya," he said, then turned to Ben. "Nice work. How are the legs?"

"Still holding me up," Ben replied, although Freya had an idea they were giving him more pain than he let on.

"Speech," Gillespie called out, and Granger, who would have usually glared at him for being so loud, smiled, then with a wave of his hand presented the floor to Freya.

She took her time, knowing that the success of any speech is to captivate the audience. And there was no better way of doing that than making them wait. She collected a plastic cup from a beaming Chapman, who then poured the wine, and it took every ounce of Freya's remaining strength not to examine the bottle. She was doubtful it would be a Chablis and was more inclined to believe the bottle would from the cheaper shelf. That was okay. It suited the company, many of whom she now referred to as friends.

"We got her back," she said finally, and she raised her cup to a raucous applause that faded when she raised her other hand. "If only speeches were that easy."

"Aye, you're not getting away with it that easy," Gillespie stated. "Come on. We've been waiting over an hour for this."

"In that case, I shall be brief," Freya said, regaining the floor. "I imagine you want to get back to your families. But I think it's worth mentioning that during the course of this investigation, I learned a few things about a few of you that I didn't know before. Things that only really come out during the hardest of times."

She glanced across at Ben, who stared at the floor then at the team, who'd had his back throughout. It was a far cry from the world she was from, where it was dog eat dog from the moment you stepped into the station to the moment you left.

"But we still have some work to do. Chapman, when you come in tomorrow, find out where the boy is. His name is Daniel. Find out how the Trevernes would go about taking him into their care. I think they'd like that. I think they've endured enough misery that they deserve it."

"Ma'am," Chapman replied, and as usual, she made a note in her pad.

"Sergeant Priest," Freya said, getting the attention of the man she deemed as the station's grandfather. He was solid, unfaltering, and the type of man she imagined to carry a few boiled sweets in his pocket. The gentle man took a sip of his beer and waited for Freya to speak. "How's Griffiths?"

"He's just fine. Thanks for asking, ma'am," he replied. "He'll be back with us on Monday. A slight concussion. Nothing major."

"Good. The man deserves something."

"Eh?" Gillespie said. "You mean like a medal or something? If that's the case, I should tell you about the time I got hit on the head–"

"I can only imagine you've been hit on the head on more than one occasion, Gillespie," Freya said.

"Aye. I have," he replied, missing the reference to his slightly off-the-wall mannerisms.

Freya turned her attention back to Priest and the injured constable.

"I was thinking more of an easy win. Something for him to get his teeth into," Freya said, and Priest cocked his head with interest.

"Tell him to look into Mr and Mrs Finch from Dunston."

"Right," Priest said, retrieving his notebook from his top pocket. He licked a finger and flicked his way to the next clean page, then waited with his pen poised.

"When we first looked for Abigail in the fields, her father told us the local farmer wouldn't appreciate us trampling over his crops. He said there had been reports of villagers pilfering his winter vegetables."

"You don't think it's them, do you?" Gold said. "They were lovely. She's the warden or something, isn't she?"

"Did you see the size of the hotpot she made? It was big enough for her to feed a small army. You'll also note that when they first arrived, they were dressed as if they had just come from the fields. It's just a hunch," Freya said, turning back to Priest. "But I'm usually right about these little things."

She gave him a wink and he smiled, grateful they were thinking of his team.

"I'll see to it he gets the job, ma'am," Priest said. "It's not exactly the Brinks-Mat robbery, but it'll get him back into the swing of things. Give him a boost, as it were."

"Thank you, Sergeant," Freya said, then raised her plastic cup. "To everybody else. That was a damn fine job, and I'm proud to be on your team. Now I'm going to go home, peel off these boots, and sleep for a thousand years."

Most of the team raised their drinks in response, and there were a few stifled cheers. But Gillespie had more to say.

"Is that it?" he said. "I was expecting something uplifting."

"What do you want her to say?" Ben asked. "They can take our lives, but they'll never take our freedom?"

"Aye, something like that," Gillespie said, as if he was actually offended by Freya cutting her speech to go home and relax. "I want to be inspired."

"Inspired or arrested?" Freya said, and the room hushed.

"Eh?" Gillespie said, sensing the electricity in the atmosphere. "Arrested?"

"Handling stolen goods," Freya said.

"You what?" Gillespie looked about the room for support, but everyone else appeared as perplexed as he was.

"You ate the hotpot," Freya said with a smile. "The rest of us had McDonalds."

Behind him, Gold, Chapman, and Cruz seemed to deflate when they realised it was a joke.

"I plead ignorance," Gillespie said, and he smiled.

"Then in that case, I'll drop the charges," Freya said. "Consider it conditional bail."

"What's the condition?" he asked.

"Two conditions. The first is that that this speech is over, and I can go home and sit in front of a fire."

Gillespie nodded. "And the second?"

"That when I tell you I don't want anything fried, what I actually mean is that I want the biggest, dirtiest burger and chips you can find me. Deal?"

"Aye, boss. That's a deal."

CHAPTER FIFTY-SIX

DURING THE PAST TWO DAYS, THE TEAM HAD WORKED HARD TO close the investigation down. Reports had been submitted, paperwork completed, and by all accounts, Jason King was being held in a secure facility while a decision was being made on his psychiatric needs. The decision was not for Freya to make, yet she found herself thinking of him as she nursed a cup of cocoa in one of Ben's armchairs, entranced by the dancing flames in his fireplace.

She heard the shower stop, and then heard Ben grunting and groaning as he towelled off upstairs and hobbled through to his bedroom. He was still in a fair amount of pain.

Imagining how her life might have been had she decided to stay in London, she considered her decision to have been the right one. The Lincolnshire evenings were silent and dark, unlike London's endless melee and incessant light. And she would never have sat beside a colleague's fireplace with a hot cocoa. There wasn't time to develop those relationships. There was always another investigation to pursue, more paperwork to ignore, and ladders to climb.

No. She had done the right thing. It was too late to turn back now, but a little reflection never hurt anybody. She had gone with her gut, and smiled at how it had been.

She sipped her cocoa then set it down on the arm, just as Ben entered the room wearing a pair of tracksuit bottoms and a t-shirt. He hobbled forward, his bare feet slapping against the floor before he dropped into the armchair beside her.

"How you doing?" he asked, sighing as he raised one of his feet to feel the fire's heat.

"I'm content," she said, and he gazed across at her.

"Content?"

"Yes, content. Why?"

"It's just a strange choice of words."

"What would you have me say? Ecstatic? Over the moon? Shattered?"

"I suppose, when you put it like that," he replied, clearly too tired to argue.

"How about you?"

He stared at the fire for a moment, as if he was thinking about his own choices of words. "Weirdly, no different to how I was a week ago, except for the two big holes in my shins."

"Are you still going on about them?"

"I'm going to have to see a doctor. They don't seem to be healing."

"Want me to take a look?" she asked. Then, without waiting for him to come up with an excuse, she ventured into the kitchen and found his first aid kit. A few moments later, she knelt before him as she had done a few nights before, then she gave his knee a playful slap. "Come on. Off."

"Off?"

"Yes. Off. You want them dressed, don't you?"

"Can't you just—"

She gave him of her well-practised *don't bother arguing with me* stares, and he gave her one his very well-rehearsed sighs before pulling his tracksuit bottoms down. He was wearing briefs again, which he covered as well as he could with his t-shirt.

Freya unzipped the first aid kit, found some antiseptic cream and two large bandages, then set to work. It took a minute or two for him to relax; the cool cream she applied invoked a pleasant sigh of relief, and she found herself rubbing it into the entire area, enjoying the feel of his supple calf muscles.

"What did you mean earlier?" he said eventually.

"When?" she asked, knowing full well where he was heading with the line of enquiry.

"At the vigil. You said you were in her shadow."

She stared up at him. He had his eyes closed, and she massaged his lower leg.

"Nothing really. She was the one though, wasn't she?"

"The one?"

"You know what I mean. The one. We all have them."

"Even you?"

"Even me."

He nodded. "I guess she must have been. There's been nobody like her since."

"Nobody?"

He shook his head.

"Not even Michaela?" she asked.

"Doesn't even come close," he replied.

"So if she came knocking right now, you wouldn't fall to pieces?"

"Are you asking me if I'm over Michaela?"

"In a roundabout way," she said, remembering that Gillespie had managed to do some damage repair on Ben's behalf. "You could still be in with a chance."

"If she came knocking, then maybe. But she'd have to make do with fish and chips and a stroll along the river."

"You're in no fit state to stroll anywhere," Freya mused, as she dropped his leg down and collected the other one in her hand, bending to study the wound.

It was precisely at that moment when somebody knocked on the window. Ben leaned forward and turned to the side to see a face pressed against the glass.

"Michaela?" he said. "What's she doing here?"

At the mention of the leggy blonde's name, Freya sat upright and smoothed a lock of wayward hair over her shoulder. She found Michaela at the window holding a bottle of wine as a peace offering. But it was the way her expression seemed to drop from a sheepish, apologetic look to sheer disgust and horror when she saw Freya's head pop up from between Ben's bare legs that really made Freya's night.

Nobody moved.

The bottle slipped from Michaela's hand and crashed to the ground; the sound of broken glass tinkling as it settled was the only noise.

"Do you think I can talk my way out of this one?" Ben asked quietly, smiling at Michaela who just stood there shaking her head.

"Can I be there when you try?" Freya replied.

And that was that. Michaela was gone, slipping into the darkness from wherever it was she had appeared.

Slowly, Freya turned to face Ben, very aware of what Michaela may or may not have construed from where she had been standing.

"Do you know what I think?" she said, as she raised his leg to finish the job she had started.

He didn't reply. He didn't even seem to care what Michaela thought.

"I think fish and chips is off the menu," she said.

"Beans on toast it is then," he replied.

The End

A single robin redbreast eyeballed her from where it was perched on a fence post. Beyond it, in one direction, the wild Lincolnshire Fens roamed for miles. Behind her, in the other direction, Lincoln Cathedral dominated the horizon. But in between those beautiful vistas was chaos.

Winter had drawn to a close. The first signs of spring were evident in the fields and on the verges. Yet the cold air lingered, and Poppy Gray bent double to catch her breath.

It wasn't the sound of footsteps that roused her, like she had been expecting. It was a whistle. The bird. Angered by her presence perhaps.

Or was it a warning?

It glared at her then whistled again. But it didn't move or flinch at Poppy's company.

Poppy stared back at the robin through bloodshot eyes, still wet from the tears she had spent. Her chest heaved from the exertion of running. She had no idea how far she had run, but she was sure she was safe now. Almost sure, at least. *Ninety-nine per cent certain*, her stepmother would have said. *As near as damn it positive*, her father might have voiced.

But there was the robin, defying her confidence.

She tried to piece the events together. The bend in the road. The screeching tyres. The little boy and those big, wide eyes.

And then that scream.

What a mess.

Should she turn back? It was all her fault. She should come clean. Yes, she should tell them all what happened. That would show them.

She knew the thoughts were futile. And when she heard the footsteps coming up the track, she knew she would never be given the chance to say what she had to say.

Preparing to run, Poppy pulled off her boots and looked down at her bare feet. She had two options – climb the gate and run through the field, or go further up the track. The field was open ground. She could be seen. And there was no clear way out. She would be trapped.

No. The path is best. Stay on the track. Find somewhere to hide. Stay there. Until it's dark. Until it's safe to go for help.

A figure rounded the corner while she debated, stopping to enjoy Poppy's quadary, equally breathless.

"There you are."

"Why are you doing this?" Poppy screamed, which only seemed to raise delight. "Please. I won't say a thing. Not to anyone. I promise."

They took two steps forward.

Blinded by tears and fright, Poppy ran, not daring to look back. She cast her boots into the bushes and sought the soft patches of spring grass for every step, though often the way was paved with sharp stones, and only her fear drove her forward, hoping, praying to find somewhere safe. A hole. A road. A house. Anything.

She ran until her legs were not her own and her feet were bloodied, broken, and bruised. She ran until her lungs could take no more and her vision succumbed to her tears.

It had been a bright, sunny morning. She remembered opening her curtains and taking in the view. One of those spring days where blue skies gave hope to the long depression of winter and the fresh air bit at her bare ankles. Fresh leaves clung to boughs, and long grass that had been flattened by winter now stood tall, erect with the warmth of the sun, concealing the deep ditch beyond.

She stumbled forward, expecting to find solid ground, but there was none. She reached out instinctively for a branch, but it snapped and she fell. A few moments passed. Time enough for her to question her injuries, and time enough for her to regret the life that still ran through her. To regret what she had done, what she had seen, what she knew.

Who she was.

A cool stream of water soaked her dress, but she cared little for the discomfort.

She rolled onto her back, pulling herself up into a seated position, and considered the fall fortuitous. Out of sight, but not out of mind. She could wait there. Beside the long grass and the trees, the sky above was all she needed. How long had it been since she had stared at it? How long had it been since she and her only friend had made shapes from the clouds? And how long had it been since she had felt the warmth of the sun on her bare skin?

She smiled, genuinely. The flow of tears stopped and dried, and for the first time, there was hope. True hope. Not the charade that her mind had convinced her with. True hope. Escape.

No more secrets. No more self-loathing.

A flutter of wings caught her eye. A familiar face stared at her from the tree above. He whistled then glanced around nervously.

She closed her eyes on her old friends – the robin and the sun – and slipped into a dream she had long since forgotten. But the dream was short-lived. A shadow passed over her. The heat on her face dropped by a degree or two. Enough to rouse her from her slumber. Enough for her to open her eyes and stare up. Enough for her to know escape meant death, and that death was imminent.

A silhouette stared down at her, the face masked by shadow. And above. Out of reach. Untouchable. Poppy's friend whistled once.

And she smiled.

"A robin redbreast in a cage puts all heaven in a rage," she said.

And the secrets she carried died with her.

ALSO BY JACK CARTWRIGHT

The DCI Cook Murder Mysteries

A Winter of Blood

A Secret to Die For

The Wild Fens Murder Mysteries

Secrets In Blood

One For Sorrow

In Cold Blood

Suffer In Silence

Dying To Tell

Never To Return

Lie Beside Me

Dance With Death

In Dead Water

One Deadly Night

Her Dying Mind

Into Death's Arms

Join my VIP reader group to be among the first to hear about new release dates, discounts, and get a free Wild Fens novella.

Visit www.jackcartwrightbooks.com for details.

COPYRIGHT

Copyright © 2022 by Jack Cartwright

All rights reserved.

The moral right of Jack Cartwright to be identified as the author of this work has been asserted by him in accordance with the Copyright, Designs and Patents act 1988.

All the characters in this book are fictitious, and any resemblance to actual persons living or dead is purely coincidental.

All rights reserved. No part of this publication may be reproduced, stored in a retrieval system or transmitted in any form or by any means, without the prior permission in writing of the publisher, nor to be otherwise circulated in any form of binding or cover other than that in which it is published without a similar condition, including this condition, being imposed on the subsequent purchaser.